"WE DON'T HAVE TO DO THIS, MARY GRACE," SLOAN WHISPERED

Mary rested her head against his chest, feeling the hard muscle beneath her. She knew she could say no. Deny him. But it would be denying herself, and she was so very tired of running from her feelings.

"No," she said softly. "I'm eager."

"For what, Sweet Mary? What is it you want from me?"

"I ache for you. I don't know what I want. I only know I need—"

He leaned over her and covered her mouth with his, cutting off her words.

CELEBRATE

101 Days of Romance with
HarperMonogram

FREE BOOK OFFER!

See back of book for details.

Bridge to Yesterday

◇STEPHANIE MITTMAN◇

HarperPaperbacks
A Division of HarperCollinsPublishers

This is a work of fiction. The characters, incidents, and dialogues are products of the author's imagination and are not to be construed as real. Any resemblance to actual events or persons, living or dead, is entirely coincidental.

HarperPaperbacks   *A Division of* HarperCollins*Publishers*
10 East 53rd Street, New York, N.Y. 10022

Cover illustration by Vittorio

First printing: June 1995

Printed in the United States of America

HarperPaperbacks, HarperMonogram, and colophon are trademarks of HarperCollins*Publishers*

❖ 10 9 8 7 6 5 4 3 2 1

This book is dedicated to my father, who,
despite a stiff leg like Sloan's, taught me
how to ride a bicycle, swim, and do anything
I put my mind to, and to my mother,
whose insatiable appetite for romance novels
spread to me and helped produce this book.
I miss them both and I hope they have
found each other somewhere else.

Of course, my thanks to my husband, Alan, who
is most certainly my hero, and my children, Arika
and Asa, for all the love, support, and snacks, and
their constant assertions that I was, in fact, a writer.

Thanks, also, to my agent, Laura Cifelli,
whose faith never wavered.

1

Mary Grace O'Reilly sped up Interstate 17 in Arizona in her rented Ford Mustang as though her own life depended on it. It was always that way when she was working. And she was always working. Hers wasn't what you could call a nine-to-five job. It was more of an obsession, even if she'd never admit it.

Still fuming from her lack of success in Los Angeles, she swerved around a slower-moving vehicle and honked at the driver as she passed. There seemed to be no one who understood the urgency of her mission.

When she'd approached the Los Angeles Police Department, they had insisted that without a court order, Benjamin Weaver's failure to be returned home couldn't warrant an APB. His abduction didn't interest anyone at the various television stations. Even the local paper opted not to report the story. It seemed that until the divorce and custody were settled, Benjamin Weaver was fair game. And although his mother, Marcia, was frantic, it seemed that everyone else had agreed to ignore the snatching. Everyone except Mary Grace, who refused to allow a four-year-old to become one more MIA in a domestic war.

Sun glinted off a blue sign that read "Food, Gas, and Phone. Next exit." A soft curse escaped her lips. She'd promised to call the office back in L.A. around eleven. She stole a quick glance at her watch: ten after twelve. Despite her assurances that she was perfectly capable of taking care of herself, the volunteers there would be worried about her. Pulling off the highway, she followed the signs to a ramshackle souvenir shop huddled by the side of the road. Its wooden porch needed only an old man with a Stetson hat pulled down low over his eyes and a cheroot sticking out from between clenched teeth to be confused with the back lot at Universal Studios. A soaring bird floated overhead, apparently waiting for the store to finish dying.

Inside it was dark and smelled faintly musty. It was over ninety degrees outside, and had to be at least eighty-five in the store. There was no sign of a phone. In fact, there was no sign of life, unless the mold growing in the corners of the old refrigerated case counted. Despite the labels promising "Ice Cold Coca-Cola" all over it, its shelves were stacked with dusty brochures. They had titles like *Sedona: Power Vortex of the Western World* and *Where the Navajo Legend Still Lives.*

"Can I help you?"

Mary Grace spun around at the sound of a man's voice.

"Ma'am?"

"Your case seems to be broken," Mary Grace said, gesturing toward the refrigerator. "Have you got anything cold?"

He gave the freezer a what-the-hell-is-that-doing-here look. "'Lectricity's out," he finally said. "Went out four, maybe five weeks ago."

"How about a phone, then?" she asked.

Like herself, he wore jeans and cowboy boots, but he also sported a cowboy hat, a knife on his belt, and a bandanna around his neck. No one had warned her that Arizona was still the Wild West.

"There," he said, jerking his head toward the darkest corner of the shop. "Think it still works."

It was a rotary phone. Mary Grace couldn't remember the last time she'd seen one of those. But it got her an operator, and the operator connected her to her office.

"Child Seek, Jan speaking. How can I help you?"

"It's me," Mary Grace said. "I'm in Arizona now, so you can stop worrying."

"Mary Grace? I've got Mrs. Weaver on the other phone. Hold on, and I'll tell her you've got everything under control."

"Just patch her through, Jan. I'll tell her myself." She lifted the hair off the back of her neck. The little phone booth was hot as hell, and she thought something might have crawled into her shirt. She prayed it was just sweat.

"Mary Grace," Jan cautioned, "I can tell her. You have enough to take care of without Marcia Weaver crying long distance. I can handle it."

"Thanks, Jan, but she'll feel better if she talks to me."

"Oh, *she'll* feel better. It's *you* I'm worried about."

There was a brief moment of silence, and then Marcia Weaver's voice crackled over the line. "Miss O'Reilly? Are you there?"

"Yes, Mrs. Weaver. Can you hear me all right?"

"Oh! Thank God you're there. I spoke to Jim's supervisor. I pretended I was the bank and needed more information for his loan. It's not enough to be the mother of his child. He said Jim was taking off a few days. When I pressed him he said he thought he might be calling in from the road. The road, Miss O'Reilly."

"I knew it. I told you he'd drive, didn't I?" Mary Grace asked. Unless they had access to a private plane, they never flew. It was too easy to trace.

Mrs. Weaver went on about her soon-to-be ex-husband and how taking Benjamin out of the state before the custody hearing was just like him. Then her voice became choked with tears. "You *will* find Benjamin, won't you?"

"Yes," Mary Grace answered. "I will find him."

"And you'll bring him back, right?" Mrs. Weaver was openly sobbing now, and Mary Grace blinked her own tears away.

"I'll find him," she repeated. If she couldn't bring Benjamin back, she'd stay on Jim Weaver's tail until the lawyers could get some kind of court order to get the boy returned. The important thing was to make sure that his father didn't just take Benjamin and disappear off the face of the earth.

"Are you all by yourself?" Mary Grace asked as the soft sobbing continued. "I could ask someone from the office to keep you company while you wait."

A man's voice came over the line. "Miss O'Reilly?"

"Who is this?"

"It's Sid Lerner. Marcia's father."

"Yes, Mr. Lerner. I'm two hours north of Phoenix, now."

"Please find him, Miss O'Reilly. You don't know what it's like to lose a child. I hope you never know such pain and heartache. I pray for you. . . ."

Her own tears began to fall.

"I'll find him. I promise." She disconnected the call with her finger and held the receiver against her chest for a few moments. She hated Jim Weaver and all the other fathers. Every stupid last one of them, putting what they wanted in front of what they had to know was best for their kids.

When she emerged from the phone booth, the storekeeper was waiting for her. He looked her over and handed her a cold bottle of Coke. "Keeps cool in the cellar," he said.

She smiled her thanks. "Do many people come out this way? I'm looking for a little boy and his dad."

"See plenty of little boys and their pas. He yours?" He was staring at her blouse. She looked down and saw the wet spots her tears had left on the faded blue chambray. For a moment she thought of playing on his sympathies. But her conscience wouldn't let her do it, no matter how much she would have liked to claim any of the children she sought as her own. She wiped her cheeks.

She pulled out a picture of Benjamin and showed it to the man. "I'm trying to find him for his mama, who is crazy with worry over him. If you've seen him, it could help a lot."

The man studied the picture. In it, a boy of four or so was nearly strangling a fluffy dog in a loving embrace. The man bit at the inside of his cheek. "He's with his pa, you say?"

Mary Grace nodded and reached for the photo. The man seemed reluctant to let it go. "Anything might help."

He shifted his weight, rubbed his chin, and wiped his hand on his jeans. "Day before yesterday," he said, "couple of guys came in here. Hunters, maybe. I remember a rifle rack in the cab of their pickup. Said they were waitin' on a man with a kid. Showed me his picture. Asked if I'd seen him. Could have been this one." He shrugged and handed her back the picture of Benjamin, the boy's brown eyes smiling out at them.

"Do you know where they were headed?"

"Only one place hunters would be headed around here," he said, going around the counter to the cash register and ringing up Mary Grace's Coke. "You got a map? Oak Creek Canyon's kinda tricky."

After half an hour of recommending first one way, then another, Mary Grace left with a pencil sketch of the area. With a wave, she climbed into the car once again and pulled back on the road.

An hour and twenty degrees later, Mary Grace finally pulled the car to the side of the road. She'd driven straight through Sedona, its streets lined with tourist shops that tried in vain to hide the view, and then left civilization for the mountains once again. There she lumbered behind pink jeeps full of tourists marveling at the spectacle of Oak Creek Canyon. She too had marveled, until she realized she was hopelessly lost. It had been almost an hour since she'd seen the last pink jeep. Since then, she hadn't seen a living soul.

She grabbed the pencil-sketch map and walked to the road's edge. Below her lay a canyon crisscrossed by half a dozen roads. By turning the map she saw the route splayed out beneath her. Amazingly, she was almost there. Unfortunately, though, she was about two hundred feet above where she was supposed to be, with no visible means of getting to the roads she sought. Still, down there somewhere were two men waiting for Benjamin to show up, and she fully intended to be there when he and his father did.

In the car she shoved her bush of curls up onto her head, not caring that she must look like a red mop on its end, and fastened the hair off her sticky neck. Then she put the car in reverse and slowly backed onto the roadway, looking for a way down to the canyon floor. When she finally saw a cutoff sloping downward, she turned off the paved road and followed it. After about half a mile, it was clear that the car could go no farther. She got out to take a look. About thirty yards on, the path ended abruptly at a narrow natural stone bridge that jutted out over the canyon, the result of thousands, maybe millions, of years of rushing water carving an archway that led nowhere.

Wondering what she should do now, she made her way toward the bridge to take a peek at where she was. As she picked her way through the scrub, she slipped and cursed her new cowboy boots. Having heard from the girls at the office about scorpions and snakes, she'd ruled out her Nike's and gone with the boots. But how ever did the cowboys get away from the bad guys in slick-soled shoes that didn't give at the ankles?

One foot on the stone bridge, she looked gingerly over the edge. Beneath her, several hundred feet at least, lay a dried up riverbed. Stones and boulders, every shade of red and orange and copper known to God or man, lay piled on top of one another. The river had no doubt once stretched for miles. For as far as she could see the scenery didn't change. So this was what they meant when they talked about mystical Sedona. Despite being a skeptic at heart, she could feel the energy around her.

People who were into these metaphysical things claimed the area had some kind of electromagnetic field, like the Bermuda Triangle or something. Even the man who had given her the directions at the little store had carried on about psychic energy fields and spiritual vibrations. He'd claimed his brother had seen the face of an Indian in the rocks telling him to leave and never return. Too bad some of the store owners in Sedona hadn't had the same vision. Mary Grace thought it was a sin to be selling Vortex T-shirts and thirty-one flavors of ice cream in the midst of the most glorious show nature had to offer.

A stone loosened beneath her foot, and she jumped back away from the edge. It fell, turning over and over, and she waited for the clink as it hit the rocks below. When it didn't come, she bent slightly to look over the edge. The ledge beneath her shifted, and her arms flew out like a clown on a diving board who had changed his mind at the last minute. She tried to turn and thrust herself toward the safer ground of the precipice, but her body refused to cooperate. She jerked in a wild dance of arms and legs trying to propel herself to safety, but not getting any firmer footing. And then it was too late.

Her scream echoed against the canyon walls, a wailing that just went on and on, bouncing from one boulder to the next, overlapping one cry upon another as she drifted in free fall down into the canyon. She gasped for a breath but none came, as though suddenly she was sucked into a vacuum. Her descent slowed until she felt weightless, drifting like some discarded letter in a gentle breeze. And yet there was no breeze, no air at all, not even to breathe. No sound, either. As in some nightmare, her mouth was open, but nothing came out. And nothing moved, except Mary Grace. She fell in slow motion, like some special effect in a movie. Only it wasn't a movie, and she prepared herself to die, waiting almost impatiently for her life to flash suddenly before her so she could regret her mistakes and repent before she crashed to her death on the rocks below.

And then the air filled her lungs and she shrieked again, just as her body hit the water with a tremendous splash. She sank through it until her arm hit gently against the bottom and she rose, gasping for air, to the surface.

*　　*　　*

Sloan Westin lay flat on his belly, blending into the rocks on which he lay, watching the river. He knew the Tate boys were somewhere on the far side, along with Emily and the baby, all holed up in that shack, comfortable and secure in the belief that he was dead.

He hadn't taken his eyes from the scene for a moment. He couldn't take the chance of missing the direction from which one of the boys might come. How else was he going to find a hideout that half the lawmen in the Arizona Territory and twenty fresh Pinkertons hadn't yet uncovered?

So when the shout pierced the calm afternoon, it was like a real bolt from the blue. No one had come from either side of the river, and suddenly here was someone bobbing like a cork at the surface, sputtering and dragging in great breaths. And the splash! Like he'd jumped right off the edge of the canyon. Or fallen.

He had no way of knowing whether the kid had meant to jump into the river, but from the way he was clawing at the rocks, it was clear he was sorry to have found himself in it. Sloan considered helping, but weighed against that impulse a bum leg, the steepness of the mountainside, and the time it would take to get down there, not to mention the risk of being discovered before he was ready to make his move. He decided to stay where he was.

The California sorrel he had tied to a lone mesquite tree shook her head, rustling the leaves. It sounded like the wind, and Sloan was sure no one would pay the noise any mind, especially with the kid shouting as he fell into the water. Sloan stayed where he was and watched. He had no intention of showing his hand until it was too late for the Tates to do anything about it.

The boy, whose red hair stood out from his head like a well-used oil-lamp wick, had managed to pull himself onto a flat rock just beside the river. The fool had on his boots, so he was either planning on taking the "big jump" or had merely slipped and was lucky to be alive. But the boots surely weren't making things easy for him now, and Sloan watched with detached amusement as the boy twisted and turned, trying to keep his balance on the rock while he got the wet boots off his feet.

Even from a distance Sloan could see him shivering, running his hands up and down his arms, wringing his shirttails, and then going back to the task of yanking off his boots. It took great self-control for Sloan not to let out a whoop when the lad finally succeeded in getting one boot off and throwing it on the river bank. The kid used his free foot to help get the second boot off with more ease, and it followed the first to the shore.

Stooping to rest one hand on the rocks, the boy then eased his way toward the safety of the solid shore. Sloan ducked his head quickly when the youth shaded his eyes and looked up to the cliffs.

"Is anybody there?" a high-pitched voice yelled. Sloan could hear the tears in it and wondered just how young the stranger was. Suddenly he was glad the boy had made it to the safety of the shore. The voice was quavering with the cold, and Sloan wanted to tell him to get out of his wet clothes, but he didn't dare give himself away.

Luckily, the boy was smart enough to think of stripping on his own. When his cries brought no answer, he began to unbutton his shirt. His back was to Sloan, and as he removed the soaked shirt, Sloan caught a glimpse of strapping across the boy's back. Wondering just what it was the boy had strapped under his clothes, Sloan raised his head slightly, knowing his buckskin-colored Stetson blended in with the rocks, as did everything else he had chosen to wear, ride, and bring. The boy was peeling off his blue jeans, probably store-bought Levis from the way the sun glistened off the rivets. Beneath the jeans, instead of the usual drawers, was some kind of small dark cloth that just barely covered the boy's ass.

Again the boy called out, asking if anyone was out there, and then he reached back and unfastened the strapping that wound around his back and shoulders. He laid each of the garments out on the rocks to dry, and then sat down himself. Reaching up into the mass of red hair, he pulled out some pins and let loose the curls.

A curious feeling began to rise in Sloan's stomach, and he slowly turned to make sure there was no one coming up behind him. That gut knotting always meant something was amiss, but until the boy stretched himself out on the rocks to dry, and Sloan looked down to see two creamy white breasts with deep rose nipples attached to what he had thought was a young man's chest, he didn't know what was wrong.

She spread her hair out around her head like a halo, and except for the tiniest triangle of cloth, which appeared to be attached to a ribbon and which covered only her most private of places, she lay in the sun, naked as the day God made her. She lay there for the better part of what was left of the afternoon, sleeping on and off, sitting up and checking on her clothing every now and then, always looking around, and not dressing again until nearly dark. Sloan knew just how long she lay there buck naked because he didn't take his eyes off her once during the course of the whole afternoon. Of course, his mind was on the Tates, no matter where his eyes might happen to roam.

2

She'd gotten back into the still damp clothes as though that would solve everything. Well, at least she was alive. After falling hundreds of feet, that was no small thing. But where the river had come from was anyone's guess. She was sure there had been only rocks when she'd looked down from the bridge.

And what was she supposed to do now?

Nothing like a brush with death to throw a crimp in your day, Mary Grace. Your car is several hundred feet above you, your map is in the car, you're somewhere in no-man's-land, and it's getting dark.

Her boots rubbed against her feet through her very soggy socks, and she knew she'd be facing blisters long before she found a bed to tuck her boots beneath. Her damp jeans chafed her inner thighs and felt cold and clammy as the sun played peek-a-boo with the few trees that lined the ridge above her.

On the map there had been two roads that converged like a squat *X*, and the house she was looking for was somewhere up the left fork. She couldn't see anything that even resembled a road now that she was down on the floor of the canyon. Had she not been a grown-up, had she not learned to be brave and resourceful and strong, she might have given in to the tears that threatened to flood her vision. Instead she sniffed loudly and wiped her nose on her sleeve.

Feeling not a whit better but refusing to give in, she squared her shoulders and headed off in what she hoped was the right direction. Soon the stars would be out, and she could use them to guide her.

How could it have gotten so cold when it had been over a hundred just a few hours ago? It was just like everyone always said about the desert. As soon as the sun went down, all the heat disappeared. When she'd stopped the car she'd been sweltering, and now she couldn't stop shivering.

The world had never seemed as quiet as it did while she walked toward nowhere in the darkness. Only her steps, echoing against the rocks, kept her company. Each time she stopped, there was only the wind. So far from civilization, she couldn't even hear the sounds of a highway or the roar of a plane. And if the silence was frightening, the darkness was terrifying. When night fell over the canyon, it didn't do it gradually. One moment she had been overwhelmed by the beauty of the mountains against the pinks and purples of the sunset sky, and the next there was nothing in front of her, nothing behind her, a million stars above her, and the creeping fear that at any moment there could be nothing below her. The thought of falling off the earth twice in one day stopped her in her tracks.

Fine, she thought, trying not to give in to her fears. Benjamin would still be there in the morning and she could find him then. The best thing was simply to sit down and wait it out until dawn. More with her hands than her eyes, she made out the shape of a small boulder and leaned against it. As she sank slowly to the ground, her stiffened jeans cut into her inner thighs and against her calves. Man, it was cold. *How cold is it?* she joked with herself. *It's so cold that . . .*

Whatever it was, it scurried over her right leg and began burrowing under her left. She held her breath and stayed perfectly still, reciting her prayers without even moving her lips. She could barely detect a movement beneath her left thigh. Would lifting it let the trespasser by, or invite him to taste her soft flesh through her tough jeans?

Patience is a virtue, Mary Grace. Be virtuous, she told herself, aware that what might be a scorpion was slowly working his way out from under her leg. A moment more, two at most. Then she was up like a flash, stamping and jumping and shouting in the dark as though the scorpion had actually hit his mark.

Well, some people could sit in the middle of the desert and wait for the sun to rise, Mary Grace supposed, but she wasn't one of them. She groped in the darkness, heading in what she prayed was the right direction.

From the blisters on her feet she guessed she'd been walking a couple of hours when she finally saw the smoke. It was like a white cloud against the dark sky, and it took her nose to tell her what her eyes were seeing. Civilization! She ran toward the sooty haze, her feet burning as her blisters rubbed against her wet socks and stiff boots, amazed by how much farther it was than it appeared. Who'd have thought that you could smell smoke miles away?

Still, she kept going, her bones aching, her body cold but her feet on fire, until she saw the cabin. Lights blazed in the window, a man's voice crooned a song that sounded like a lullaby, and the smell of roasted chicken filled the air. But she couldn't go up to the door. Not yet. Not until she could stop the tears and pull herself together. It took a long time.

Finally a man came out onto the porch, followed by a second, much shorter man and a mangy dog who appeared to have only one ear. Were these the men waiting for Benjamin? Could her luck be that good? And they'd been singing a lullaby. Was Benjamin already here? She cleared her throat and the two men fell to the porch floor. The dog bared its fangs and growled. In the dim light that came through the windows, she could see that the two men were holding guns, and that they were pointing them in her direction.

"Who's out there?" one of the men yelled into the darkness.

She wasn't sure how to answer. Her name wouldn't mean anything to them, and identifying herself as a member of Child Seek might only anger them and end any hope she had of tricking them into giving themselves away.

"I am," she answered in a rather meek sounding voice. She cleared her throat again. "I mean," she said more strongly, "I'm sorry to bother you, but I've lost my way and I . . ."

"Come into the light where we can see you," ordered the man who had spoken before.

"And don't try anything funny," the shorter one added. He looked younger than the man who had called out to her, maybe still in his teens, and his curly blond hair glowed in the porch light like a halo around his head.

"No 'Heeeeere's Johnny?'" she asked, trying to be facetious as she stepped into the clearing in front of the house. "No ten top ways to know you're lost?" On closer inspection it was clear that the men were holding rifles. It was just as the man at the store had said, two men with hunting rifles. Only he'd forgotten to mention Fang, who was rigid with suspicion.

She felt a nudge from behind her and screamed out, sure that one of the dog's siblings had managed to creep up on her.

"Skitterish, ain't ya?" a man said, and she turned to find a third man, this one holding a rifle just inches from her middle.

"Oh my God!" Mary Grace said. "You scared me to death. Where the hell did you come from?"

The man grinned at her. In the darkness he looked so sinister, the glow from the windows glistening in his eyes, reflecting off a jagged scar on his cheek, that for a moment she felt trapped in a made-for-TV movie. She just hoped she had Victoria Principal's role. Victoria always managed to survive attacks by crazed lunatics in the woods.

"Hey, relax," she told him, drawing on a bravado she didn't feel. "Put that thing down, OK? Look, if you guys want to be left alone, that's perfectly all right with me. But could I maybe just stay on your porch tonight? I'm really not too cool with all this desert stuff and I . . ."

A cough came from within the house, a weak, sickly sound, and the men seemed to forget all about her. The young man rose, put his gun down against the door frame, and moved to go into the house, shaking his head. "Stay here, Dukeboy," he told the dog, who returned his attention to Mary Grace. The other got up, first to his knees and then to his feet, and leaned against the railing.

The man with the scar prodded her gently from behind and gestured with his head for her to go up toward the porch, where the dog and a man with two gold teeth stood waiting for her. Both of them were drooling as they watched her mount the steps. It was deadly silent. And then she heard a woman's voice. It was faint, interrupted by coughs and wheezes, but it was definitely a woman's voice, and the men strained to hear it.

The youth returned, something on his boots jangling with every step he took, making him sound like some janitor with too many keys. Spurs, maybe? No one wore spurs anymore, did they? He whispered something to the man who still held the rifle on her. He grimaced, his scar pulsing in his cheek, but nodded and put the rifle down.

"She wants to see ya," the young one said. He held open the door, and Mary Grace shrugged and went in, grateful Dukeboy was left on the porch.

The cabin was cozy, the light from an oil lamp casting a yellow glow on the small room. It was cluttered with the debris of three men living without a woman's care. Plates were scattered, their dried contents stuck to them and covered with dust or soot. Someone had taken the care to put curtains on the windows and doilies on the couch, but now they hung at angles and threatened to slip to the dirty floor at any moment. Mary Grace fought the urge to straighten something as she took in the room. A fire burned softly in the fireplace, its hiss almost a whisper as if out of respect for the sick woman in the next room.

The bearded man with the gold teeth stood impatiently waiting for Mary Grace to follow him, obviously displeased with her examination of the house. Her eyes lit on yet another rifle, this one leaning up near the doorway by which the man stood. He followed the line of her eyes and frowned. Raising the rifle, he jacked it open and removed two bullets, or shells, or whatever it was they put in rifles. It amused Mary Grace that he thought she would try to steal the rifle and use it on them. She barely knew which end to point. When he returned the rifle to its place by the door it was with such a thud that the noise echoed in the room.

"You ready now?" he asked her as he opened the door and signaled for her to follow.

The bedroom was darker than the main room had been. Darker, and cooler. It took a moment for Mary Grace's eyes to adjust, and while they did, she hugged herself for warmth. She'd given up any hope that her socks would ever dry, and was just looking forward to taking off her boots and rubbing some circulation back into her feet. Maybe they would let her stand in front of the fire for a while before sending her back out into the night. *If* they sent her back into the night. She felt a shudder in her chest. The cold? Or fear?

In the center of a small bed lay a tiny woman, her body barely noticeable under the heavy quilt that stretched across her. She had long blond hair, and it flowed around her like a princess in a storybook. Her face was flushed, even more so in the flickering light of the oil lamp near her bedside. Her eyes were closed, but Mary Grace had no doubt that when she opened them they would be china blue.

"Emily, honey," the man said gently, and she opened her eyes. Mary Grace had been right. "This here's the lady you was askin' on."

Mary Grace watched Emily swallow. It was obviously a great effort. "Who are you?" she asked. Her voice was so soft Mary Grace could barely hear her.

She crept closer to the bed, where Emily could get a good look at her. Maybe Emily could tell the men to let her take Benjamin and leave.

"My name is Mary Grace O'Reilly," she told the woman honestly. "I've come to take the boy."

Emily smiled at her wanly. She closed her eyes and crossed herself. "Thank you," she whispered toward the ceiling. "I've been praying you would come. They love him, but what do men know about taking care of a baby?"

"We've been doin' everything you told us," the man with the gold teeth said, suddenly less fearsome in the sick woman's presence.

She nodded. "You and Harlin been real good, Wilson," Emily said, "considerin'. But a baby needs a mama, and I ain't gonna be here much longer to see to him."

Mary Grace looked around. No one disagreed with her. None of this made sense. Emily wasn't Benjamin's mother, so why had the men brought Benny here? Surely they couldn't expect Emily to take care of someone else's child in her condition.

"Has she seen a doctor?" Mary Grace asked. "What's wrong with her, anyway?"

"Doctor says there ain't nothin' he can do," the young blond man named Harlin started to explain, but Wilson interrupted him.

"Shut up," he said, and Harlin scowled but kept quiet. "Doctor's been here. Twice," the man said. He stared at the foot of the bed, never making eye contact with the woman in it.

"Look," Mary Grace began, "I don't know what's the matter with her, but it looks to me like your wife needs a doctor pretty badly. Why don't you just take her to a hospital?"

"A hospital?" Wilson laughed. "Nearest hospital's in Jerome. Emily'd never make the trip to the wagon in the barn, never mind all the way clear to Jerome."

"Couldn't you have her airlifted? At least call the

doctor again and maybe he can prescribe something over the telephone."

Harlin stared at her as if she had suggested they take Emily to the Mayo Clinic on a bicycle. Wilson just snorted.

"Come from the big city, don'tcha?"

Mary Grace spun around. It was the third of the men speaking. She hadn't even heard him following them, but then the short one's spurs jangled so loudly it was hard to hear anything else when he was on the move. It was the second time this man had sneaked up behind her, and the shivers that ran up her spine weren't from the cold night air.

He spoke again. "Ain't got a telephone way out here." He had an ugly scar running down his cheek, and he turned so that it shone in what little lamplight there was.

"Ain't got nothin' out here," Emily said, her eyes on Mary Grace. "Nothin' but sickness and death. Wilson, get me some water, will ya?"

Wilson came over to the bedside and poured some water from a pitcher. Gently he lifted Emily's head and placed the glass to her lips.

"Your wife looks pretty sick," Mary Grace said. "Doesn't a neighbor have a phone?"

"Ain't my wife," Wilson said, the gold teeth catching the oil lamp glow and shooting sparks into the darkness.

"And we ain't got no neighbors," Harlin said, a smirk touching the corners of his mouth.

"Is she *your* wife?" Mary Grace asked the third man, the one whose name she still didn't know. He seemed the calmest of the three, but in that calm lurked a restlessness that made her more frightened of him than she was of the other two.

"No," he answered, leaning on the door frame as though he hadn't a care in the world. His eyes ran over the sick woman's form, exposing the good side of his face, almost handsome in the dim light. Mary Grace felt his gaze turn to her, but when she looked at his eyes, they were focused on the far wall, as if the shadows held some fascination for him.

"Well, whosever wife she is, she seems pretty damn sick," Mary Grace said.

"You got some mouth on you, girl," the man answered. "Where'd you come from, anyway?"

"Yeah," Harlin seconded. "How'd you find this place, huh? How'd she find us, Mason?"

Emily reached out and placed a limp hand into Mary Grace's own. It was warm to the touch, and Mary Grace put the back of her free hand against Emily's brow. Not surprisingly, the woman was burning hot.

"I fell from the sky, actually," Mary Grace answered, a note of exasperation in her voice. She thought about her answer. It was true, almost. "What difference does it make? We've got to do something about . . . this woman. Whose wife is she, anyway?"

"Her husband's dead," the third man said, pushing off from the wall and coming into the room. "Died right after . . . well, you might say he died on his wedding night." The three men laughed, and Mary Grace looked down at Emily, questioningly.

"You really did come from the sky, didn't you?" she asked, ignoring the men. It took a lot out of her to say the words. Wilson put the glass of water to her lips again and raised her head slightly to help her drink it. He looked up at Mary Grace, pleading silently for her to agree with Emily. The dog howled outside, a lonely, haunting call that ran down Mary Grace's back.

She smiled down at the woman, who couldn't have been more than twenty or so. "Yes," she admitted, "I did."

"And you were sent to take care of my baby?" Emily asked, her breathing labored and her hand slipping from Mary Grace's own.

"I was sent to . . ." Mary Grace looked around the room. Harlin had tears in his eyes, and the one they called Wilson was staring at a crack in the ceiling. The third one, Mason, turned and walked quietly out of the room.

"I . . . I . . . ," Mary Grace stammered, but was interrupted when the man returned, carrying a sleepy child who rubbed at his eyes with a closed fist. He couldn't have been more than five or six months old.

Emily began to cough uncontrollably, but the baby, unaware that his mother was dying, still reached out for her, and Mary Grace's arms went up of their own accord as she came forward and took the baby from the man's hands. She stood with him in the doorway, patting his back and feeling his heavy head bang against her chest as he tried to fight sleep unsuccessfully.

It wasn't Benjamin, that was certain.

"The good Lord sent you to watch my baby, didn't he?" Emily begged, between coughs. "And you boys know that the Lord'll punish you just as sure as he's punishin' me if you hurt one hair on this angel's head. That's why you're here, Mary Grace O'Reilly, ain't it? God sent you just for this here boy. . . ."

Mary Grace thought about it as she kissed the top of the baby's head and smelled the warm sweet smell of his sleeping body. He found his thumb in his sleep and began to suck on it. That and the sputtering of the oil lamp were the only sounds in the room. Who knew better about punishment from the Lord?

"Yes," she said, as much to herself as to the woman lying near death in the tiny bed in the crowded room.

She tried to ignore the fact that the man who had brought the baby into the room now stood pointing a rifle at her head. After all, if he really meant to shoot her, he'd take away the baby first.

"Take Horace and put him back in his bed," he told Harlin. "And then show the lady where she can sleep."

"Guess that'd be under Wilson," Harlin said with a smirk, but his smile quickly faded at Mason's scowl.

"Nobody's gonna be mountin' nobody," he said with finality. "And somebody feed Dukeboy. That damn dog's howlin' is makin' me crazy."

He gestured with his head for Mary Grace to follow him and pointed his nose at a door across the hall. She pushed open the door, smiled in thanks, and shoved it closed behind her. Then she pried off her boots, peeled off her damp socks, and crawled into the strange bed, her heart hammering and her head swimming. It smelled as if wild animals had used the bed for mating, but it was soft, and warm, and she was so very tired.

She wondered whether anyone had noticed yet that she had fallen off the face of the earth. No doubt Benjamin's mother and grandfather were frantic by now, and that meant they'd have called Jan at the agency. For a moment, she wished she were an important person. Right about now she could use some pull to merit an APB.

Please, she whispered in the darkness, *let someone be looking for me.*

Daybreak brought a surprise Sloan Westin hadn't been expecting. He'd seen to his needs and his meal long before sunup and had been waiting on the ridge only a short time when he spotted Wilson Tate's horse bearing two riders down to the river's edge. Wilson reached behind him and lowered the redheaded woman Sloan had observed the previous day.

She was no longer wearing her Levi's but instead had on the same kind of long skirt and Mexican-looking blouse Emily Tate often wore. Wilson handed her down a soft sack and said something to her. Sloan strained, but he couldn't hear a blasted word. He watched Wilson gesture in the direction of some rocks and saw the woman shield her eyes from the sun as she followed his finger. She looked at the bracelet on her wrist and nodded. Then she stood watching as Wilson eased his horse toward the rocks he had pointed to and rode slowly away. She stood with the bundle on the ground next to her for a moment or two, as though she wasn't sure what to do, and then picked it up in her arms and headed for the river bank.

God! She probably couldn't teach a hen to cluck, he thought as he watched her approach the river, shoes still on, skirt dragging on the ground, brainless as the baby whose diapers she was no doubt about to wash. He clucked his tongue and fought the urge to spit out some words that came quickly to mind. Foolish dolt of a woman. But what did he expect from someone who'd get mixed up with the Tate gang? He rubbed at his leg, sore from staying in one position so long, and included himself in the category.

A few feet from the river the woman sat down on a small rock and removed her shoes. She had ditched the boots and was wearing soft leather ones. From his vantage point they looked like Apache moccasins, but he couldn't be sure. He'd learned from the Havasupai tribe that the Tates had some sort of arrangement with the Tonto Apache, trading them stolen rifles for various goods and services. He'd heard, too, that the Apaches had offered them their women. But this was no Apache whose very white legs were now exposed as she tucked the front of her skirt up into her waistband and waded into the water with the bundle of dirty clothes.

He hadn't seen a white woman's legs, excluding the show this one had given him when she'd first fallen into the water, in over a year. Fourteen months, if he'd wanted to be exact. And the way things stood now, he wasn't too sure he'd ever be between a pair of them again. He could still perform, all right. He'd checked that out with a willing Hopi woman who had pleasured him right in the wickiup of the chief's own son. But the bullets that had riddled his body had left his right leg nearly useless, and he knew that between the scars and the awkwardness he was some sorry excuse for a man. Certainly no woman's fantasy anymore.

He thought about the women who used to throw themselves at him after a winning ride at the rodeo in Prescott, or the ones who chased after him when he came into town for a good time. Boys were always complaining that there weren't enough women in the Arizona Territory, but there were always plenty for him, waiting for him after a roundup, offering him home-cooked meals, wanting to wash his clothes. . . .

She squealed as she went down, and Sloan stifled a laugh. A fly on a horse's ass had enough sense to seek high ground when crossing a river, but not this woman. The back hem of her skirt had gotten so wet that the weight of it had finally pulled her down. She sat in the river, her bottom half soaked, trying to right herself before the current got a hold of her.

Wilson, who was apparently bathing farther upstream, came toward her in his wet long johns, slipping and sliding on the rocky bottom, cursing at the top of his lungs. By the time he got to the woman, she had begun to drift along with the water flow, and the river was littered with floating bits of dirty cloth that Wilson grabbed for as he chased her into the current.

"For God's sake!" he shouted after her. "Grab on to something!"

"I'm all right," she yelled back at him, making her way to an outcropping of rocks. "Get my jeans!"

"Yer what?" he shouted as he caught up with her, overalls in hand, and dragged her roughly from the water. She was thoroughly drenched, and even from two hundred feet above them, Sloan could make out two dark nipples through the sodden fabric. Or maybe he just imagined it—he wasn't sure.

He thought maybe he'd be treated to a show, as the two stood there staring at one another, the water dripping from their clothes, but Wilson just whistled and his horse came running from where he had left him farther upstream. Pulling the blanket roll from his saddle, Wilson handed it to the woman and took the horse's reins. He walked back in the direction from which he and the horse had come, never looking over his shoulder.

Probably not Wilson's woman, Sloan figured. And surely someone this inept couldn't belong to Mason. Harlin? Jeez . . . she was perfect for Harlin. Two imbeciles. Weren't there laws about mating morons? The thought slipped his mind when the woman eased out of her clothes for the second day in a row. She wrapped the blanket around herself and then tried to retrieve the clothing that had caught on the rocks.

"Wilson," she shouted. "Can you hear me?"

"What now?" he yelled in response.

"Just stay where you are until I call you, OK?"

No answer.

"OK?"

From where Sloan was, he could see Wilson hiding behind the rocks, not twenty feet from where the woman stood waiting for an answer. Wilson's face was pressed up against the rock, and Sloan guessed he had a perfect view of her through a crack, but she was unable to see him.

"What's wrong?" Wilson yelled back, but somehow his voice wasn't all that strong.

"Just stay there, all right?"

"All right," he agreed, and Sloan shook his head. Dirty bastard, he thought as he watched her drop the blanket and run bare-assed to the river, snatching the cloths as quickly as she could. A scrap of pale blue lay on a rock at the far side of the river and she waded in to get it. Midstream she leaned her head back and soaked her hair. Her face was pointed toward the sun, a smile on her lips, and Sloan hoped she'd open her eyes. He could almost get a good look at her. He wished he'd bought those binoculars he'd seen as he passed through Jerome, but he hadn't wanted to attract any attention. He'd only been there for a few hours, just to pick up some supplies, and no one had recognized him with his new beard and longer hair. It wouldn't have done to flash a lot of money around, even in a town like Jerome.

"Get your stuff and let's go," a voice said, and Sloan saw Wilson standing at the water's edge, waiting for the woman to get out. The sun glinted off his gold teeth as he stood with his arms crossed, waiting impatiently. If this was Harlin's woman, or worse, Mason's, he was about to get into a heap of trouble.

The woman swam to the cloth, snatched it off the rock, and slipped it around herself in the water. It was the shirt he'd seen her take off the day before. How long was it? Sloan tried to remember. Would it cover everything? She'd left the blanket too far from the water to just grab for it.

"Turn around, Wilson," she said, and her voice carried up to Sloan's hiding place. It was a musical voice, filled with laughter, as though she thought her predicament was funny. "Come on, Wilson. I'm not getting out until you turn around."

Wilson didn't say anything. Sloan couldn't tell if he shrugged.

"Please," she asked then, more quietly, the playfulness gone from her voice.

From the ridge, Sloan saw the rider seconds before Wilson heard the horse. Wilson spun around, reaching instinctively for a gun which wasn't at his hip.

A low voice rumbled, unintelligible to Sloan, but easily recognizable. It was Mason. Wilson's hands went down, and he whistled for his horse.

Mason swung out of the saddle and came to the water's edge, picking up the blanket on his way. He held it out, his eyes averted, and the woman grabbed it and wrapped it around her. She then gathered the diapers and other clothing that had survived her attempts at washing and silently donned her shoes. Wilson mounted his horse and headed in her direction, but Mason smacked the horse's flank and with a lurch sent Wilson heading home.

Sloan watched the conversation between Mason and the woman, he cupping her face to look in her eyes, she staring back at him. Apparently satisfied, Mason mounted his horse and contemplated his charge. Then he scooped her up and sat her across his lap, letting her adjust the blanket that covered her, and headed slowly in the direction he had come.

Sloan waited until the three were long gone. Then he rose slowly, awkwardly, using his good leg and his arms to right himself, and surveyed the area. Now that he knew where the Tates and their women bathed, it was only a matter of time.

3

Harlin was waiting on the porch with the baby when they returned from the river. He looked strangely at Mary Grace's attire but made no comment about it.

"She's worse," he said to Mason.

Mary Grace slid from the horse, and Harlin caught and steadied her as though she were a piece of baggage he was unloading. Mason handed her the soggy bag of laundry and pointed to a clothesline around the side of the house. She wanted to take the baby with her, but between the wet laundry bag and the blanket which hid her naked behind, her hands were fully occupied.

The last time she had hung wet laundry on the line had been the week before she had left Roscoe, New York, and her family, forever. She'd hung diapers then, too. Her mother was perpetually pregnant or with a baby on her hip. *My duty,* her mother had called it. *God's will,* was what her father said. *Babies,* Mary Grace thought. *What had God to do with it all?*

The laundry hung, Mary Grace passed a watchful Dukeboy and went into the house. She went straight to

Emily's room to ask her if she could borrow another skirt and blouse, just until the other set dried. When she entered, the three men were kneeling by the bed, their hands clasped in prayer. The sight shocked her. Somehow she had convinced herself overnight that Emily Tate couldn't be as sick as she seemed or someone would have gotten her to a doctor before now.

Mason looked up as she stood in the doorway. She covered her mouth with her hands, and Mason shook his head and stood up. His steps were heavy as he left the room and motioned for her to follow.

"Is she . . . ?" Mary Grace started.

He shook his head. "She's sleepin', again. Does that more than anything else. That and nurse the kid. Been six months, now. Never really recovered from having Horace."

What an awful name for a baby, Mary Grace mused. It was a petty thought to have at such a terrible time, but she couldn't help herself.

"Named him after her father. Hers and Harlin's."

"Then Harlin is her brother," Mary Grace deduced.

"Harlin, Wilson, me. We're all her brothers. Only Wilson and me, we had a different daddy. But we all had the same mama. She died after givin' birth to Harlin, sick all through, just like Emily."

"Emily was sick when she was pregnant?" Mary Grace asked, trying to follow the conversation.

Mason nodded.

"And she stayed here with you? Her husband was already dead?"

Mason nodded again, thoughtfully. "That mighta been a mistake," he said. "More I think on it."

"A mistake?"

"Mason," Harlin yelled. "Come quick! She's breathin' funny, Mason. Hurry!"

Mason scrambled up from the couch where he and Mary Grace had been sitting. Shivering from the cold, she wrapped the blanket tighter around her, and shuffled behind him at a distance.

She stopped once again at the doorway. Emily's eyes were wide open and she looked frantic. "Mary Grace! Get Mary Grace! Where is she? Is she dead, too?"

"I'm here," Mary Grace said quietly, stepping forward. "I'm right here. Lie back, now." She turned to Mason, aware now that he was the one in charge. "You have to get her to a hospital, or she's going to die. She's dehydrated and they can get fluids into her."

"She won't drink anything no more," Harlin said, showing how the water just trickled down her chin when he raised the glass to her lips.

"They'll use an I.V.," Mary Grace said.

"An I.V.?"

She remembered the bloody rags in the bundle of wash. "Has she been bleeding since the baby was born?"

No one answered her. She took that as a yes.

"Why haven't you done something before this?" she begged them. "How could you let her get so sick?"

"You heard her yourself," Mason said as he took his sister's hand in his own. "God's punishing her for the life she led. It's His will. It's too bad, though, about the baby."

Mary Grace could hear her own father's voice, reciting those very same words. It was the zealot's explanation for suffering and death and a way for them to escape the responsibility for doing anything to help.

"Mama!" Emily yelled, obviously delirious now. "Mama!"

The men backed away from their sister's bed, and Mary Grace came forward, sitting on the edge of the mattress and taking Emily in her arms.

"I'm here," she crooned. "I'm here. Everything's going to be all right."

"He's dead!" Emily said. "They killed him! I didn't think they'd kill him. Now what will I do? God'll never forgive what I done, now that he's dead."

"No, no, Emily. He's all right. Everything is all right."

Emily pulled away from Mary Grace's arms to look into her face. Her eyes were clear and bright, and they connected with Mary Grace's. She seemed completely lucid again. "Do you swear?"

Mary Grace didn't hesitate. "I swear."

"I believe you," Emily said, and Mary Grace felt the girl's body go slack against her.

"Emily?" she whispered. There was no response. Tears welled in her throat, behind her eyes, in her cheeks. Her arms grew rigid, and Wilson eased Emily out of them and down onto the bed. Mary Grace's blanket slipped and went unnoticed, exposing her legs, her wet shirt split on her flat stomach.

A shuddering breath rocked Emily's chest, startling them all, and Mason leaned down and lifted the edge of the blanket and covered Mary Grace's lap with it.

"I thought she was gone," Harlin said in the quiet of the room.

Mary Grace nodded. "She just . . . she just . . ." And then she started to cry, big wracking sobs that shook her body and nearly knocked her off the bed. Mason steadied her, and she grabbed him, pressing her cheek against his thigh and letting him stroke her hair.

He smelled of horses and worse, but he was alive and real, and she clung to him shamelessly until she felt a light tug at her arm. She turned slowly to find Emily's eyes open, her tongue wetting her dry lips.

"The baby's crying," she said, with great effort. Even

though she was dying, her first thoughts were of her child. *Once a mother,* Mary Grace thought, and let the rest of the saying go as she heard the baby's wail. Mason motioned to Harlin, who left and came back with the child, handing him to Mary Grace. He quieted immediately.

"He's a beautiful baby," Mary Grace said to Emily, patting the baby's head. "I think he favors his uncles with this dark hair."

She shook her head very slightly. "Looks just like his pa. Glad to have been a part of that. His pa was a handsome son of a bitch."

Mary Grace couldn't help being a little shocked. She kept thinking Emily was some fairy princess, lying in state, her blond hair flowing around her. And then reality would intrude.

"The man coulda charmed the habit off a nun. Course I wasn't no nun. Still ain't right to kill a man over a roll or two in the hay, no sir. 'Specially not a man what loved ya."

The baby wriggled in Mary Grace's arms, reaching for his mama, who put out her hand and let the baby wrap his fist around one of her fingers.

"You're as doomed as your mama," she said to the boy. "God help you if you turn out like your mama's kin. The devil take you if you turn out like your pa."

She struggled to sit up a little, just enough to reach the boy's hand with her lips. She kissed the hand gently and fell back onto the pillow.

"I think I'd like to sleep a little now," she said and closed her eyes.

Mason took the baby, balanced him against his shoulder while he opened a drawer, and pulled out some clothing for Mary Grace. He handed her a small pile and motioned for her to leave the room.

On her way out she heard him whisper to Emily. "He didn't get no worse than he deserved. Nobody does."

Mary Grace hugged the clothes to her body and hurried to the room they had let her sleep in the night before.

He had made his way down the side of the mountain, the surefooted horse he had purchased from the Havasupai accustomed to going down winding trails on the sides of canyons. He had considered his options carefully and decided he wouldn't so much as spit until he knew which way the wind was blowing.

Maybe Emily had already found herself someone else. She'd be one less problem to reckon with if she wasn't looking to hog-tie him with the bands of matrimony. The other woman wasn't worth his worry, being too feeble to smell a fire if she was locked in a furnace. No, what he needed to know was how many men there were: three, or a fourth belonging to Emily; where they were keeping the baby; and the lay of the land.

He'd found himself a fine hiding spot, maybe a couple hundred feet or so from their cabin, and settled himself in for the day, savoring the feeling of being the hunter and not the prey. Maybe he'd get lucky and that redheaded stick of a woman would come out and strut her stuff again. She sure did have a problem keeping her clothes on.

But it was Wilson, not the woman, who came out of the house as he watched. The big man with the dark beard and the two gold teeth went straight for the shed and emerged with a shovel, a brown dog on his heels. When he returned to the porch, Mason was just coming outside. The dog's tail began wagging at the sight of him, but Mason didn't appear to be in the mood for playing. He was wearing his church clothes, and Sloan felt a twitching up his arms. It looked to him like maybe there was one less son of a bitch he'd have to worry about as Wilson nodded, took the shovel, and climbed the ridge. At the summit he plunged the shovel into the earth over and over again until the purpose became unmistakable.

A ripple of disappointment went through him. Harlin hadn't been down by the river yesterday, and now it looked like they might be getting ready to bury him. Sloan Westin had his heart set on putting an end to Harlin Tate with his own hands. He had decided even a bullet was too good for him, and had lain awake nights among the Havasupai at the bottom of the Grand Canyon devising for Harlin Tate deaths too horrible to confess aloud.

Wilson struggled to dig the grave in the hot sun. He mopped his brow, took off his shirt, and continued to dig as if nothing else was going on in the world. He looked like a simple country farmer who might be burying his wife out there on the ridge, and not the scum of the earth Sloan Westin knew him to be.

The redheaded woman came out of the house, dressed up in a dark printed wrapper that set his teeth on edge. He remembered the wrapper real well. Remembered how proud of it Emily had been. Remembered her warning him to be careful with it as he unfastened the buttons that ran down the back. Remembered clutching the hem of it after he had fallen to the ground. Remembered her yanking it from his grip and running, running. And then he couldn't remember anything. Nothing about how he'd wound up at the bottom of the canyon, strangers tending to him . . . smoke and magic words . . . feathers and potions. . . .

The woman was on the ridge, talking to Wilson. The baby was crying inside the house, and the woman raised her head as if to hear better. She said a few more words to Wilson and then came running down to the house, tripping on the hem of the dress and nearly falling. Probably Harlin's woman, and too grief stricken to think about lifting her hem. Or just too feeble. He didn't know which.

Wilson returned to the house and washed with water from a bucket on the porch. When he was done he entered the house, and the redheaded woman came out and sat on the porch with the baby in her arms. She hugged the child tightly to her chest and kissed the top of his head over and over again. If only Sloan had bought those binoculars in Jerome. He couldn't make out a feature on the kid's face. Couldn't see if he had dimples like his grandma, big hands like his pa and his grandpa before him. Couldn't see nothing from so far away. Damn, and damn again! He'd sure like to get a better look at that child.

"Open the door, Miss O'Reilly," someone called from inside, and she rose and pushed the door inward into the house.

Mason came out backward, struggling with the end of a makeshift coffin, nearly falling down the two steps that separated the porch from the ground. Wilson held up the middle, as best he could, from one side. Around his legs, the mangy dog danced and nipped at his heels, almost tripping him up, until finally Wilson delivered a swift kick to the dog's soft underbelly. At the far end of the coffin, his face clearly visible to Sloan, was Harlin Tate, a blond halo surrounding that little boy face of his.

Well, at least it wasn't Harlin making the trip to meet his maker. Sloan could still look forward to the pleasure of doing unto others as had been done to him.

He waited for Emily to emerge, one eye on the procession, the other on the door. She didn't come. Had she run off again, this time abandoning the baby?

The funeral was a quick affair. The woman, carrying the baby, who Sloan noticed didn't cry once throughout the whole service, returned to the house with Harlin and Mason. Wilson stayed up on the hill, fashioning a marker of sorts and banging it into the ground.

Sloan waited until nightfall to make his way up to the hill. In the dark he tried to make out the words on the wooden cross stuck at a slight angle by the head of the grave. Finally, he lit a match, blocking the light with his body so that he couldn't be seen from the house.

REST IN PEACE
EMILY TATE
BELOVED DAUGHTER, SISTER, AND MOTHER
'75–'94

There were coyotes in the distance. The moon came out from behind a cloud, illuminating the marker as if that was its sole purpose for hanging in the sky. From the house he could hear a woman singing softly to a baby and the sounds of men arguing. The back door slammed, and he could hear the jangling of Harlin's spurs.

"Shit," Sloan said as he took one last look at the grave and hurried off the hill toward where his horse stood silently waiting.

So Emily Tate was dead, God rest her soul. With a family like hers, she was probably better off. Beloved daughter. It had never occurred to him that boys like the Tates had folks of their own. Folks who might be grieving somewhere for Emily. It made him wonder about his own folks.

By now they must have given him up for dead.

4

Three heavyset men carried crates and barrels from room to room at the Bar W Ranch. Anna Westin directed the men from her chair, too weak and disinterested to care which of their belongings went back east with them and which were sold or given to those less fortunate than they. She had already told Ben which things mattered to her, and she wished he would take care of the rest himself and leave her to mourn her son in peace.

"Ma'am?" Sunny, the foreman of the ranch and one of Sloan's favorites, approached her. In his hand he held a gold pocket watch. He held it out to her and shrugged. "Found this in his bottom drawer, Miss Anna. Be a shame to lose it now, after all these years."

She nodded, but nothing could make her hand reach out and take the watch from her husband's foreman. It sat in the man's work roughened palm just the way it had sat when Ben's father had given it to him, and when Ben had held it out to Sloan on his sixteenth birthday.

"Well, son," he had said. "Guess this is yours, now."

She could picture so clearly the smile coming to her son's face, the dimples which were her own creasing his cheeks as he reached out for the prized keepsake.

"Not so fast," Ben said. "This is only yours in trust, son. You know what that means?"

Sloan nodded solemnly, but Ben explained anyway. Ben was always doing that. Needed to spell everything out, dot every i, cross every t. That was why he couldn't accept Sloan's death. No body. Only a lot of rumors, he said. But in her heart Anna had no doubts. There had been no word from her precious son in over a year.

And he wasn't without enemies. His easy way with women had him climbing out more bedroom windows than Anna liked to admit. Husbands and fathers and brothers all over the territory suspected him of messing with their women.

"Miss Anna?" Sunny still stood in front of her, his arm still outstretched, the watch still in his hand.

"Put it away. Give it away. You keep it," she said, her voice an emotionless drone.

"I'll hold it for him, ma'am, if you don't mind. He'd be mighty angry if he was to come home and find it gone."

She shrugged. "Sunny," she said gently, closing her eyes and resting her head back, "he ain't coming home. And if he did, he'd find us gone, lock, stock, and barrel."

"Don't you think that might be a mistake? Won't you listen to Ben and wait a while longer?"

"This wild land took everything that ever mattered to me," she said. "Took my youth, my health, my babies, one after another. Then it took Sloan, the only one I got to see grow up. Ben wants to stay? Let him. I'm gonna be on the train to St. Louis come Friday, and there ain't nothing short of a miracle gonna stop me."

The argument had exhausted her. No doubt she was dying, and Ben simply wouldn't tell her. He was trying to protect her, as always. But he'd never been able to stop all the deaths and the pain, and he wouldn't be able to hold on to her now. Doc Geiger didn't know what he was talking about, saying it was all in her mind.

She must be dying. Why else would Ben agree to leave the ranch, the land, the horses? He claimed it was because he'd no heir, as if it had been for Sloan's sake all along that he had built from nothing one of the best breeding ranches in the west. Maybe so, but it had taken their son's death for her husband to realize how much he had loved the boy.

Maybe he wouldn't be dead, she thought, if Ben had cared enough to keep him on the right path while he was alive.

A baby without a mother. Mary Grace let her imagination soar as she held the Tates' nephew in her arms. If only this were her baby. But she knew better than to indulge herself in the world of "if onlies." She had spent a long time in that world, and it had tortured her in the end.

And now she had foolishly agreed to watch the baby while her hosts ran what they called an important errand. What else could she do? The men had just lost their sister, and there was no one else to take care of the child. She couldn't bring herself to think of him as Horace. A baby as handsome as he was ought to have a better name. Like Paddy. Patrick Sean O'Reilly. It had a nice ring to it.

Her imagination was getting the best of her again, and she chided herself. People didn't get second chances in this world, and she knew it. Knew it better than anyone, maybe. If she couldn't change the past, she was determined to learn from it at least. The baby in her arms clutched a fistful of her hair and pushed it into his mouth.

"No," she said gently, pulling the hair out from

between his chubby fingers and kissing his fist in payment. The baby turned his head in toward her breast, nuzzling her and smacking his lips as he looked for nourishment.

"No," she said again, but this time tears choked her voice. She knew she had to leave before this baby found the place in her heart she had closed and locked years before. As soon as his uncles returned, she would have to be on her way.

Her hope was that they would return with Benjamin. In their grief she was sure she could make them understand that Benjamin belonged with his mother. Every child had that right.

She wiped a stray tear with the back of her hand and sniffed back the rest that threatened. She was ready to kill Benjamin's father with her own bare hands for putting her in this position to begin with. How could he have arranged to take his son to the most backward place on the face of the earth? Even Appalachia had TVs now, she thought.

Did they still bury people outside of cemeteries anywhere but here? It reminded her of the time she had trailed Jessica Chandler's kidnappers into the Ozark Mountains. But there she'd been close enough to her car to alert the authorities. She remembered looking down the barrel of a rifle and being told to "git." The authorities had credited her with saving Jessica's life. Jessica was too young for it to have any lasting effect on her, but Mary Grace would never forget the cabin she had found the baby in—dank, dirty, without electricity or running water.

And behind the house, the old family graveyard had stood, a laundry line hanging above it, a testament to the idea that life goes on. Not here, she thought as she busied herself in the kitchen getting something for the baby to eat. Here, someone died. And whether the men brought Benjamin back or not, she was leaving the moment they returned. The baby smiled at her and the mashed potato she was feeding him oozed out of his mouth.

"And I'll send the authorities back for you," she assured him. "This is no way for a baby to live." She looked down at the skirt and blouse she had on. How Emily had managed to stand her brothers' ridiculous old-fashioned ideas was beyond Mary Grace. Mason had asked her nicely not to wear the jeans she had come in around his brothers, and she'd complied, but what she could manage for a couple of days was a whole lot different than what she could tolerate as a way of life.

The men didn't even have a car, as far as she could tell. They'd ridden off to town like cowboys, and when she'd asked to accompany them, they'd promised to take her to town as soon as they returned from their important errand. There, they assured her, she could telephone her office. And so she waited. And waited.

She and the baby were both asleep when the men rode up. She didn't hear them come in until their voices filled the house and the baby began to cry. For a moment she thought she was dreaming, like all the other nights when she had heard a baby crying out for her and had awakened in her empty room alone. This time the baby's cry continued in the darkness, and she reached over and pulled him from his cradle.

"He said he wasn't gonna kill no more women," Wilson shouted. "He swore it, Mason."

"Keep your voice down," Mason reminded him. "I don't want Miss O'Reilly hearin' any of this."

"I didn't mean to kill her, Mason, honest. The gun just went off. . . ."

"Again? The man can hit a tin can from two hundred

feet away, but he can't keep his gun from goin' off by accident? Mason, he—"

The room silenced when they noticed Mary Grace and the baby. She stood in the doorway, her heart pounding, not believing what she had heard.

"Go back to your room," Mason said. He stared at her, waiting for her to do as she was told.

"Who are you?" she finally asked, clutching the baby tightly as though one of them might try to take him away.

"You ever hear of the Tate Gang?" Harlin asked, the stupid smile she had seen so many times lighting his face.

"Who?"

"Shut up, Harlin," Wilson said. He opened his rifle, and her breath caught in her throat. He began stuffing a rag down one of the barrels.

"Will not," Harlin said. "I'm proud of who I am."

"Go back to your room," Mason repeated, this time more ominously.

"I can't," Mary Grace said, her voice smaller than she would have liked. She sat down with the baby asleep in her arms. Maybe she had misunderstood. Maybe her ears were full of sleep, her mind still full of dreams. "You'd better tell me everything."

"You ever hear of Jesse James?" Harlin asked, but before she could answer, Mason was on his feet and in front of her.

"I said go back to your room," he ordered between clenched teeth. This time he put one hand under her elbow and lifted her out of her seat. "It's best if you get some rest, and then we can discuss this all in the morning," he said, ushering her to her door without her consent.

"Harlin's crazy, isn't he?" Mary Grace said. She couldn't pull her eyes from the scar that ran down Mason's cheek. It pulsed under her scrutiny.

Mason shrugged. "Yeah, I guess that's it," he said, waiting for her to enter her room. "But you ain't got nothin' to worry about." Then he shut the door behind her.

Mary Grace laid the baby in the cradle and paced the room nervously, finally sitting on the rag rug beside the door with her ear near the floor, hoping to hear anything else the brothers might reveal.

She had some trouble understanding Mason's words, his deep voice rattling the floorboards beneath her.

"Great, Harlin. Just great. Now Miss O'Reilly's gonna want to leave."

Harlin must have shrugged, or said "So what," because again it was Mason's voice that Mary Grace heard.

"So who's gonna stay home with Horace when we need to go out? Or were you plannin' to take him? Strap him to your back and jump on the train, you idiot!"

She could hear the boom of Wilson's voice but couldn't make out the words over Harlin's footsteps and the jangling of his spurs.

"She couldn't find her way back here if we drew her a map," Mason argued.

So they'd gotten to the heart of the matter. She knew where they were. And if she left, she could lead the authorities back.

Now, were they just trying to scare her with all this bad-guy talk so that she'd leave and forget about Benjamin? Or had Harlin really killed someone?

She heard footsteps and quickly dove for her bed. They stopped outside her door, and she heard the door knob being turned. Through slits in her eyes she saw Mason Tate's silhouette fill the doorway.

"Miss O'Reilly?" he whispered.

She didn't answer.

"I hope you ain't plannin' on goin' anywheres," he said quietly, watching for a reaction. She gave him none, and he quietly shut the door, leaving her alone in the darkness. Mary Grace crawled further under the blankets. Suddenly she was very, very cold.

"I guess you're a mite uncomfortable," the man behind her said, and Mary Grace craned her neck around to glare at him. The saddle's pommel was drilling a hole in her hip, and each step the horse took caused her agony. She still couldn't figure out quite how it had happened. One moment she was down by the river, putting the basket of wash down and reaching in to pick up the baby, ready to make a run for it before Horace's uncles realized she was gone. And the next she was tied up like a sack of potatoes and thrown over the neck of a horse the size of a B-52.

"Look," the man said, and it was clearly an explanation, not an apology. "I wasn't plannin' on takin' you with me."

She grunted. It was the best she could manage under the circumstances.

"The idea was for me to grab the kid, but when you opened your pretty little mouth and started screamin', I saw I really didn't have no choice."

He shook his head and then shrugged, shooing a fly away from Mary Grace's face at the same time. At the mention of the baby, she was all attention. So it was her little Patrick the man was after, and not her. Well, it was a good thing she'd screamed, then. And she wasn't sorry about the biting and clawing, either. She would never give up that sweet child without a fight. If she was willing to steal him away from his blood relatives, she wasn't about to turn him over to some Roy Rogers wannabe.

"Leastwise, I got the baby," he said, and Mary Grace wriggled herself around to stare at him through narrowed eyes. A dirty blond beard covered most of his face, but through it she could see a row of shiny white teeth. He was smiling, the idiot, as though he didn't have a care in the world.

"So you belong to one of those Tate boys, do you? Or just watching the baby? Not that it matters to me, mind ya. I'm just curious." He talked in a voice just above a whisper, a soft voice that would calm a child or an animal but which was driving Mary Grace crazy. How could he be having a normal conversation at a time like this? The man had to be insane.

He went on amiably, as if it were the most normal of situations. "Mason, I think he's the most nearly human, though that might be stretching it a bit. And he didn't seem all that cozy with you at the river yesterday. Harlin, now, he's just crazy. Been crazy since . . . well, since always, near as I can recall. But I don't know that he's crazy enough to let you go down by the river alone with Wilson. Which brings us to Wilson, who's just plain mean. Meaner than a grizzly."

It was hard for Mary Grace to get a really good look at the man riding behind her. It was hard for her to get a good look at anything but the horse's underbelly, a fancy rifle with a hunting dog carved in silver near the trigger, and the parched road as it passed beneath them, filling her nostrils with dust. No place in the world was as dry as Arizona, and when she finally got Benjamin and returned home she was going to spend a week in a cool tub with one tall drink after another. After what she was being put through, she'd have earned it, she thought.

Twisting around, she tried to get more than just a glimpse of her abductor. He was bigger than the horse, if that were possible. Maybe it was just the angle that made him appear so large and fearsome. Or maybe it was the stark contrast of the smallness of the child pressed against his chest in the makeshift sling. The man was staring at his hand again, opening it and then clenching it into a fist as though he were testing it. For heaven's sake, she thought. It was just a small bite. It wasn't as though she were rabid. She hoped it hurt him as much as this ride was hurting her.

"I guess you could hold your own with old Wilson, after all." He laughed, putting his hand in his mouth and sucking on it. *Good,* she thought. *I hope it hurts like hell.*

At least with his hand in his mouth he was quiet for a while. Only the horse's feet made any noise as they rode on, higher and higher, the animal more mountain goat than horse. The baby was sleeping against the man's chest, and Mary Grace O'Reilly was waiting to see what would happen next.

The rocking motion of the horse was lulling her into a dazed trance when the man spoke again, startling her.

"You got a name?" he asked. The effort of turning to look at what kind of idiot would ask a question like that seemed too great. She stayed where she was.

"Want me to guess? I'd bet from that red hair and that pretty little way you had of screaming at me that it's Colleen. I think that means pretty girl in Irish, don't it? Yup, Colleen is my guess."

He paused for some reaction from her, but she gave him none. What way of screaming? She'd hardly gotten a word out before he'd clamped his hand over her mouth and shut her up. And she didn't care how many of her relatives had said it. She didn't sound anything like her mother when she was angry.

"No? Not Colleen? Then how 'bout Mary something? Mary Margaret? Mary Ann? Mary Francis? You Irish always have more than one name."

She grimaced, as much from the pain as from listening

to the stranger who straddled the horse behind her. Her skin tingled where the firmness of his thighs rubbed against her side, despite the layers of clothing she wore. The gentle resting of his rein hand against her buttocks was an added indignity. If it weren't for his incessant chatter distracting her, she thought she might have gone mad.

"Well, if it ain't Mary something, it's something Mary, right? Close enough. So, Mary love, which Tate is it?"

She wrenched herself sideways and probably would have fallen right off the horse if he hadn't pulled her firmly against him. She had a choice: the saddle pommel, or the inside of his thighs and what lay between them. Talk about being caught between a rock and a hard place. If she hadn't been so frightened about what their captor had in mind for her and the baby, she might have found the thought amusing.

"Whoa there," he ordered, and she was unsure whether he was directing his command to his horse or to her. He secured her squirming form, tucking the skirt she had borrowed from Emily beneath his leg to hold her in place.

"Don't like talking about the Tates, then?" he asked, and gave the horse a kick. "Damn slow going with all this weight." Well, she certainly hadn't asked to come along. The first ripples of anger began building within her, replacing the fear and giving her strength.

"Can't say as I blame you. I loved a Tate myself once, and all it got me was a bum leg."

He paused a moment, and Mary Grace treasured the silence. She had noticed his leg was stuck out at an odd angle for a rider. She had a good view of it, thrown over the saddle the way she was. It was ramrod straight, as though he were a Christmas nutcracker with no knee, at all.

"A bum leg and my son," he added.

Mary Grace stiffened. So that was it. He was the father Emily and her brothers had talked about. The *dead* father. Then presumably he at least meant the baby no harm. As for her, well, that remained to be seen.

She was pressed up against the saddle horn, finding it impossible to relax her body enough to ease her aching hip off the protrusion. Her captor's hands moved her like a rag doll once again, making her only slightly less uncomfortable. How long had they been riding? The sun hadn't moved more than a millimeter in the sky. It was still morning. It felt like she'd been in this position for hours. Days. Forever.

The baby stirred, probably aroused by the change in position. She felt the horse come to a halt, despite the fact that the man had not directed it to. She refused to look behind her.

"Damn," he muttered, shifting in the saddle. "I don't know what I musta been thinkin'. Guess I can't put this off forever, can I, Mary love? Or should I call you 'something Mary'? Sweet Mary? How would that be?"

He put his hand on Mary Grace's bottom, squeezing gently. She stiffened with fear.

"I'm real sorry to do this," he admitted, and she held her breath. "Especially not even knowing your name, or nothin', but I'm afraid I've got no choice. I don't suppose waiting would make it any easier."

He ran his hand slowly down her hip and followed the line of her thigh. This was ridiculous. He couldn't. Not with a baby strapped to his chest, on a horse, out in the open. . . . He reached her ankle and pulled up slightly on her skirts. Oh, dear God! He intended to! The bravado which had stood her in such good stead over the last week broke as the cool air tickled her skin and sent shivers up her legs. *Hail Mary, full of Grace,* she prayed. *I know it's been a long time.* She could feel his warm hand on her bare leg and her breath caught in her throat. *No. No. No!*

His hand inched higher, burning a path upward until it stopped suddenly and she heard the fabric ripping beneath his hands. All those years at St. Andrew's School and the words wouldn't come to her. Nothing came to her except the memory of nights in the dark and groping hands. *Hail Mary, full of Grace . . . Hail Mary . . . Oh dear God!*

She twisted around and stared at him in horror, tears threatening in her eyes. The son of a bitch looked at her and shook his head pityingly. She couldn't believe it. Quickly she turned away, looked back at the ground, not wanting to give him the satisfaction of seeing her cry. She could feel him still fumbling behind her and pictured what he was doing. Just like the last time, she had to imagine and suppose in the dark. Yes, her knowledge of men and women was limited, but he'd have to get her off the horse, put down the baby. . . .

She was trembling all over. Even the horse was aware of it as he stomped his feet impatiently. Well, he'd have to untie her to get at her, and then she could defend herself. She could run. She felt incredibly stupid and vulnerable. Where could she run? With what could she defend herself? The man and his horse were in their element, obviously. And she was at their mercy.

"Now there, Sweet Mary, it's just a petticoat. Nothing to cry over. I'd offer to buy you another, but I'm sure we won't be together all that long. Besides, seems to me it isn't even yours, is it? Didn't wait long before layin' claim to everything she had, did ya?"

A soiled diaper fell to the ground with a thud, its ammonia fumes rising up toward her and making her gag. Relief warmed her body and she sagged against the horse, surprised to find that she had been as rigid as a corpse.

"Lucky thing we brought along Sweet Mary, huh son? Sweet Mary and her supply of these rags. Looks like providence and your mama's gonna provide just fine for you."

The baby, oblivious to all but his own comforts, made the usual baby noises. His gurgling reassured Mary Grace that the experience hadn't harmed him any, so far. For a fleeting moment, it occurred to her to warn their captor what would inevitably happen now that the crisp April air was hitting the baby's little acorn. But a string of curses told her it was too late, even if she'd been willing to alert him. Or able.

"Shit!" the man yelled out, trying to aim the child away from him, spraying her still bared leg in the process, dampening her satisfaction only slightly.

"What are you doing, you little . . ."

Mary Grace felt the shaking before she could recognize its origin. The horse pranced nervously beneath them, and the baby stopped the jabbering he had begun.

Dear God, if he hurts that child, I'll rip his putrid eyes out of their sockets and shove them down his bloody throat! And then she heard it, quiet at first, and growing louder till it filled the valley around them. He was actually laughing, a belly laugh that shook against her, nudging her sore side against the saddle horn.

"Well, I've gone and produced a goddamn water fountain, haven't I? Don't feel bad, kid. Same thing happens to your old man when the cold air hits his privates, too. Good to know we've got something in common, already."

Then Mary Grace felt the baby resting on her back, and grimaced. Nice of him to think of her as a piece of furniture. So she was to provide the diapers and the changing table both, apparently.

"OK, son. I admit I don't have no notion how to put this on you proper, so this'll have to do. Try to go back to sleep and I'll wake you up when there's somethin' for you to eat."

Miraculously, the baby complied, and they rode on for a while in silence, Mary Grace trying to think despite the overwhelming nausea that being carried in this position produced. What she wouldn't give to sit upright for five minutes!

"Sweet Mary? You asleep?" The voice was quiet, nearly tender.

She pretended she was in hopes that he would stop his talking, but he shook her gently, instead.

"Miss? I figure I can let you go as soon as we get near that clump of trees. We're well out of the canyon and I can make better speed now without your extra weight. If you start heading back now, you can reach the place where I found you before dark. I figure whichever one of the Tates it is you're attached to will be out looking for you and you won't have to go all that far on foot. I really am powerful sorry to have had to drag you along like this, but I can't see as how you left me much choice."

Now he was going to leave them here? What was the point of that? Unless he meant to leave just her and take the child. Well, if that was what he meant, he'd have to think again, wouldn't he? She was not about to let him go off with her baby. Not little Paddy.

"Now, you can make this hard, or easy," he told her as they neared the bushes. "I'm gonna put you down and untie your hands. I figure you can do the rest."

He lowered her off the horse and tried to set her on her feet, all without getting out of the saddle. She fell in a heap like a rag doll, the dust of the road rising around her in a puff. She scrambled about trying to right herself, aware of how close the horse's hooves stood ready to stomp her beneath them.

"Damn," the cowboy spat out, getting awkwardly down from his mount. "Sorry. I should have figured you couldn't stand like that."

He rolled her onto her stomach and loosened the ropes on her wrists. Before he could even back out of her way, she'd pulled the gag from her mouth, and after spitting out several hours' worth of road dust and wiping her lips quickly with the dirty handkerchief, she began sputtering at him.

"Of all the stupid, idiotic things to do. What in the hell did you think you could accomplish by . . ."

At her shouts the baby began to cry. The man looked at him, mildly surprised, and then turned on Mary Grace. "Now look what your yelling's done. Didn't you learn nothing from the last time you shouted out?"

"And did it occur to you he might be crying because you've stolen him away from his family, stuck him on a goddamn elephant, and haven't fed him all day? It's not my yelling, it's hunger, you idiot! Haven't you got a canteen of water?"

"Course I got a canteen," he hollered back, but made no move to get it.

"Give me the baby and get it," she instructed and laughed at his hesitation. Pointing to her still-bound feet she asked him, "And does it look like I'm going anywhere?"

He clumsily leaned over until his hands could support a good portion of his weight and pushed himself up onto his good leg. He seemed embarrassed by his efforts.

"What happened to your leg?"

"Shot," he answered without elaborating. There was a strained silence, which Mary Grace finally broke.

"And we'll need another strip of my slip. Unless you brought a bottle and a nipple for the baby?" She stared at him, and he shrugged slightly.

"Your slip?"

"Yes, my slip. Did you use all you ripped off?"

"Oh, you mean your petticoat. 'Fraid he used it all, and then some," he said, pointing first toward the baby and then to the big wet stain on his shirt.

"Well, we'll have to rip a little more." Her hands were full of the baby, so she waited for him to help her.

When he brought her the canteen, she juggled the infant so that she could reach the petticoat herself. Then she waited for him to settle himself down, noting again the embarrassment he showed with regard to his leg. She made no mention of it but simply handed him the edge of Emily's frilly slip and allowed him to rip it.

"Make sure this part is clean," she warned him. "I need just a strip."

He looked at her oddly but did what he was told. Then she soaked the rag with the water and let the baby suck on it, which quieted him immediately. While the baby drank, the man unbound her feet.

"You want to tell me what the hell is going on?" Mary Grace demanded. Untrussed, on solid ground, with the baby in her arms, she felt much less frightened of the man, who couldn't pry his gaze from the child she held. "If I'm not mistaken about them, I think this baby's uncles are murderers, and they aren't going to take too kindly to what you just did. We have to go to the police and tell them what I heard. I'm sure they'll give you some kind of protection, and I can get the baby to child welfare and they'll find a good home. . . ."

He interrupted her. "Nobody's findin' a home for what's mine."

"You really are his father? They said his father was

dead," Mary Grace said. She held the baby tighter to her, flexing her feet to get the circulation back.

"Why else would I have taken him, you little fool? I'm his pa, and he's stayin' with me. Let the Tates try to take him away. I'll be ready." She noticed then that he had brought the rifle with him to where they sat, and that he had another gun strapped to his hip.

"This is ridiculous," she argued, placing the rag against the baby's lips to remind him why it was there, and wrapping her skirts around him to keep him warm. "If the baby's yours, why didn't you just sue for custody? You could have gotten a court order, now that Emily's . . ." She stopped midsentence. Did he know about Emily? Did he know his wife was dead?

". . . dead. So who's gonna say I'm the daddy? Just my word. Besides, we're talkin' about the Tates. The law don't mean nothin' to them."

Mary Grace's shoulders sagged. Her side ached and so did her head. She was bone tired and confused. "Look. We've got Horace. Let's just go to a hotel, wash up, get some food and some sleep, and we'll go to the police in the morning."

"Horace? They named him Horace? Just shows they ain't got a lovin' or sensible bone in their bodies. His name's Ben, after my father."

Ben? Could wires have gotten crossed somehow? Had she been pursuing some other child named Benjamin? "Benjamin?" she said, blinking quickly as though that would somehow make things clear. "This is Benjamin? You mean to tell me I've been chasing the fucking wrong child?"

Sloan looked at the woman holding his son. He couldn't really blame her for being upset. He hadn't exactly treated her with the courtesy due a woman. Of course, judging from the mouth on her, the way her

hair was left like she'd just got out of some man's bed,
and the fact that it wasn't just some man but one of the
Tates, she really didn't deserve to be treated like a lady.
Still, some kind of shock seemed to be setting in. Tears
were rolling down her face, but she was laughing.

"You mean to tell me," she said, nearly gasping for
breath, "that I fell off a goddamn cliff, nearly drowned
in a river, walked across the desert in the middle of the
night, had rifles aimed at me, watched a woman die in
my arms . . ."

She paused, and Sloan lowered his eyes out of
respect for the mother of his son. When he looked up,
she continued.

". . . tried to run away with a baby, got kidnapped,
and spent a day across the front of a horse, and all for
the wrong child?"

"The wrong child?" Sloan asked. He had no idea
what she was talking about.

"I'm looking for Benjamin Weaver. Blond kid, four
and a half years old. Somehow my sources must have
gotten screwed up."

"Screwed up?"

"Do you repeat what everyone says, or is it just me?"

"Repeat you? I'm just tryin' to understand you. I
reckon the ride jiggled all your brains loose." He looked
at the mess she presented, her hair flying every which
way, her cheeks flushed, her blouse off one shoulder.
"Reckon that wasn't all that got jiggled."

She looked down and straightened her clothes,
embarrassment painting her cheeks pinker still. "Look,
Mister. This is your son? Fine. Let's take him to the
authorities, and you can clear up everything with them.
You can drive me back to my car and I'll go back to
looking for Benjamin, *my* Benjamin, if there's still a
trail to follow."

The baby caught a lock of the woman's hair and put it in his mouth. She didn't appear to notice, so Sloan leaned over and took it away. Up close the woman was covered with freckles. For a moment he wondered if they covered every inch of her. The freckles were one thing he hadn't seen from the distance.

"You ever talk sense?" Sloan asked her. "'Cause your talk's harder to follow than a flea on a zebra dun."

"I'm hard to follow? Am I the one who came riding up on a horse, grabbing an innocent woman and dragging her across the goddamn desert?"

"Innocent?" he asked. She blushed and looked away, shifting the baby in her arms and wetting the rag again, then returning it to the child to suck on. He wondered what he would have done about giving the baby water without her. He'd have thought of something. He always did. "You've an interesting way of putting things, Sweet Mary. And I like the accent, too."

"I've no trace . . . I haven't any trace of my mother's brogue. End of discussion on that." She crossed her arms over her chest.

Damned if she wasn't red from her toes on up to her hair. What an angry little cat he'd found, even if all her claws were hidden by her softness. He leaned back and let her anger burn out, only to be replaced by confusion.

"OK. I can see how you thought going through the courts would be an exercise in futility. But can you tell me why we had to spend the whole damn day on a horse? I realize that the Tate place is pretty inaccessible, but . . ."

She rubbed at her hip again. She'd have a beaut of a black-and-blue mark there in the morning, he was sure. His own leg ached from the ride, and he lay nearly prone, placing his weight on his elbow while he studied her. He still didn't know her name. It was just as well. The last time he'd been with a Tate woman had been enough for a lifetime.

"Ben is mine. You can go on and head out. All you got to worry about are snakes. Walk heavy and they'll hear you coming and get outta your way. You'll be fine, and the boys'll find you sooner than I'd like to think."

She looked at him in disbelief, shaking her head as if she hadn't heard him right, and so he repeated himself.

"You're free to go. So now, go on." She didn't move, so finally he did. He felt her eyes on him as he rolled over like some two-year-old on all fours and eased himself up with his arms, his body bent at the waist to accommodate his stiff right leg.

"You gonna tell them which way I'm headed?" he asked her.

"No."

"They gonna do anything to you for what happened?" he worried.

"No."

"Well, you best get goin' before it gets much later. I wouldn't like to think of you out after dark."

"I'm not going anywhere," she informed him, placing a kiss on the baby's head. "And neither is this baby. You can get on that stupid horse of yours and find a car and come back for us. This baby needs to eat and have a bath and go to bed. In fact, so does this woman. There must be a main road here somewhere where you can flag down a car."

"Flag down a cart?" *What in hell was she talking about now?*

"Not a cart. A car," she corrected. "You know, four wheels, a motor. You turn the key, magic! It goes. We take it to a town. We use the phone. I call my office in L.A. I jump on a plane, fly home. . . ."

He guessed his mouth must have dropped open, because she stopped talking. Maybe she had finally run out of things to say.

"Lady," he asked, "anybody ever know what it is you're jawing about?" The leg bothered him so much he tried using the rifle as a cane to help support him. It was too short, and he cursed the barrenness of the desert. A saguaro cactus didn't make a great leaning post.

"Everyone outside of the state of Arizona understands me," she said, rising easily from the ground, even with the baby in her arms. "But in Arizona . . . riding horses and living without electricity and plumbing . . . when are you people going to come into the twentieth century, anyway?"

"The twentieth century!" He laughed. "When it gets here!"

"Not the twenty-first, you idiot," she yelled at him. "The twentieth! You know 1994, 1995." She rolled her eyes as though he were the one who was confused.

"I know what the twentieth century is," he shot back. "And I'm afraid we're all just goin' to have to wait for it to get here. But not in the middle of the desert. It's gonna get cold and I want to get to shelter before dark. If the Tates are following me, I want half the territory between us by morning."

He went to take the baby from her arms, and she swayed, a dazed look on her face. She gave the baby up without a fight and stood staring at the sky as if she expected to see something there. She was as white as a stiff, and Sloan grabbed her arm to steady her. She didn't notice.

"You all right?" he asked. She was shaking, and her color went from white to green.

"What year do *you* think it is?" she asked him. She didn't look his way. She was searching the horizon for something, but he had no idea what it might be. The Tates? He listened but heard nothing.

"I don't think, Sweet Mary, I know. It's April of 1894. I believe it's Tuesday the third, but I was on that ridge a long time. It could be Wednesday, the fourth."

She turned her head to him slowly. If he'd ever seen eyes that sad, he couldn't remember them. She spoke to him like she was in some sort of dream, or one of those trances at a magic show.

"There aren't any power lines. No wires. Not one plane since I got here."

Sloan's horse nickered and shook his head.

"Listen to me," he said, grabbing the woman and trying to get her attention. "Someone's coming. No doubt the Tates. I'm gonna have to take off with Ben. You just wait here and they'll find you. It'll be fine. Just give me the rest of your petticoat, in case, and then I'm leaving." She made no move to obey him.

"Sweet Mary, I said give me your petticoat. Now let's go."

"It's 1894?" she asked. He nodded. He didn't have much time.

"I gotta go," he said, deciding he'd just have to do without the petticoat. He took one last look at the woman. She was shaking her head, looking frantically around. Suddenly she turned away from him, and he could hear her heaving. He felt the bile rise in his own throat at the sound and stood by helplessly until she finished.

"Here," he said, handing her the canteen. "Rinse your mouth."

The woman took the canteen, but her hand shook so badly that Sloan had to help guide the container to her mouth. She drank and then spat.

"Now, I really gotta go, Sweet Mary. Just tell Mason the truth. It'll be all right."

She grabbed onto his sleeve, and he turned to her, cursing his stupidity for ever bringing her along. He should have just tied her up and left her there. He'd have gone twice as fast without her on the horse with him, and he wouldn't be standing here now, knowing the Tates were on the way, and unable to leave her on her own.

"The truth?" she said. "The truth is that it can't be 1894. That's a hundred years ago. I can't be here. I have a job, an apartment, a car with a phone in it. It can't be 1894. It can't."

Sloan thought about the first time he had seen the woman. He'd been watching the river carefully and suddenly she was there, out of nowhere. A nagging suspicion crept slowly up his spine. Impossible. A year with the Havasupai and he was believing in their legends. She simply had to be confused. She couldn't be from 1994. That was ridiculous.

He felt the woman's forehead. She didn't have a fever, wasn't delirious. The baby was fidgeting, no doubt hungry, and he knew he had to get a move on.

"I've got to leave you, now, Sweet Mary. I've got to go." Still she held on to his shirt. He tried to take a step toward his horse, and she took one, too.

"You can't come along, Sweet Mary, and I ain't got time . . ."

"Then are you going to waste it arguing?" she asked as if she'd suddenly come to her senses.

"No," he said. "You can't come." He set her away from him, but when he got to the horse, she was there.

"They're murderers. Are you really going to leave me to murderers? And you need me, anyway. You don't know the first thing about taking care of a baby."

She put her foot gently on the instep of his good leg. It threw him off balance and he leaned against her for a moment. For all her thinness, she was softer than he'd expected. She snatched the baby out of the sling and hugged him to her body.

"You need me," she repeated, reaching out and pushing him softly. He nearly fell, but caught himself against the horse, who shied away. If she hadn't got off his foot and grabbed his arm, he'd have fallen, and she knew it. What a sorry excuse for a man he'd turned out to be. Before Emily Tate there weren't ten men in the whole damn territory that would have dared push him, let alone a woman. Now some little wisp of a thing could knock him off his feet. But need her?

"Damn you! Don't you know better than to anger a gimp?" He pulled away from her and grabbed the horse's reins.

"And I'll be riding upright this time," she informed him with that slight Irish lilt to her voice. She left her hand on his arm; with the other, she cradled his child.

He debated the idea in his head for just a moment, and then he put his left foot into the stirrup and hauled his stiff right leg around with a low curse.

"Hand me up the kid." She moved closer to the horse but then hesitated. She held his son protectively, as if she could shield him from the elements with her arms, alone.

"You can't get up here with the babe in your arms, now can you?" He raised his eyebrows.

"And if I hand little Paddy up to you, what's to say you won't just ride off with him in your arms and leave me here?"

"Little Paddy? I thought you said his name was Horace," Sloan responded, thoroughly confused.

"I couldn't stand it, either," she admitted, a girlish giggle escaping with the admission.

"Well, if you don't hurry up onto this horse, all three

of our names'll be followed by 'Rest in Peace,' honey. Let's go."

The sound of horses' hooves echoed against the mountains surrounding them. Sloan reached down, grabbed the baby, and tucked him back against his chest. The woman stared intently at him, daring him to go back on his word.

Reluctantly, his hand went down and clasped hers. In one easy stroke she was seated behind him.

"You weren't kidding, were you?" she asked. "About it being 1894?"

He shook his head. The land bridge had been right near where he had lain in wait. What was it the Indians called it? The Bridge to Somewhere Else?

"It's 1894, Sweet Mary," he said.

"My name is Mary Grace O'Reilly," she corrected. He liked Sweet Mary better.

"Sloan Westin," he replied, as if they were introducing themselves at some church social.

The clatter of hooves grew louder still.

"If we can hear them . . ." Mary Grace warned in Sloan's ear.

"Shit," he replied.

"Will you be able to keep him quiet?" Sloan whispered in the darkness.

Mary Grace nodded, then realized he couldn't see her, and made a tiny affirmative noise. Fear sent goosebumps up and down her arms, and if she hadn't had the baby to cling to, she might have hugged herself until she broke in two.

She felt Sloan's arm go around her, guiding her against his warmth. "You're shivering." He ran his hand up and down her arm, trying to warm her. "Put your hand in here," he said, taking one of her hands and putting it inside his shirt.

Tentatively, she unclenched her fist and rested the palm of her cold hand against the coarse hair of Sloan's chest. The heat of his body warmed her hand's chill.

They could see nothing in the darkness of the tiny room, hidden in the bowels of the Indian ruins, all dry and cold and so very empty. Mary Grace had followed Sloan down the ladder at the last moment, not wanting to be hidden in the dark kiva any longer than necessary. Hundreds of years ago this had been an Indian sacred place, used for ceremonies.

Mary Grace could swear that the spirits still inhabited the room as she huddled on the floor listening for human sounds. She heard instead the scurrying of some small animal and flinched instinctively. Sloan patted her arm gently, pulling her still closer against him.

"God, you're stiff, woman," he said. "I'm just offering you the warmth of my body."

He reached across her to scoop her into him, and she felt his hand touch her naked legs. At the contact, she jumped away like a frightened jackrabbit, banging her head against the hard stones behind her and gasping loudly.

"No wonder you're cold! What the hell are you doin' with your damn skirts up?" he asked, tugging at them to no avail and tracing them until he could tell that they were wrapped snugly around his son.

"Don't you know how to talk?" he said through gritted teeth, barely controlling his temper. "He's my son and I can see to his needs." He took his arm off her shoulder. Even in the dark she could tell he was removing his shirt. He tried to pry the baby from her arms, but she refused to let go. The baby was nearly asleep. Jostling him now could make him cry. Besides, she needed to keep him pressed tightly against her to keep her pounding heart from breaking through her chest. With a sigh, he put his shirt over her legs and leaned back against the cold stones.

"Thank—" Mary Grace began, but Sloan quickly put his hand over her mouth. It tasted fairly salty as she quickly closed her lips and nodded that she understood. He moved his arm around her and pulled her tightly to him. His body felt remarkably warm despite the coolness of their hiding place. His other hand moved at his side. She heard the gun slip quietly out of his holster, metal against leather, as if it had made that trip a thousand times before.

Boots on rock and adobe floors made a hard, cold sound that echoed off the stones around them. In the room above them, a piece of furniture scraped against the floor, and footsteps stopped above their heads. Mary Grace inhaled sharply. Sloan smelled of sweat, the baby's pee, and something undefinable. It was a sharp, pungent scent not all that unpleasant. Mary Grace burrowed deeper against him, and his arm tightened around her protectively. The tension in his body was overwhelming, and Mary Grace knew from the feel of his taut left leg beside her that if he'd had two good legs he'd have been up on them. Now, it was suddenly too late.

"Harlin, what the hell ya doin'?" Wilson Tate hollered, the words reverberating in the clay cavern in which Mary Grace and Sloan hid.

"Look here," he answered, and they heard a second set of boots cross over their heads. Once before she had huddled in the dark with a man's arms around her, waiting for voices to pass them by and leave them alone again. This man sat as rigidly as the other one had. This one's hand had covered her mouth, touched her leg, just as the other one's had. She took shallow little gulps of air, fighting the rising panic within her. In her head, voices rang out from beyond a closed door: *Have you seen Father Dougan? Is anyone in there?*

"I found me a lady's whatchamacallit, Wilson. Think it's whatshername's?" The voice belonged to Harlin.

"All that stuff looks the same to me. The only difference is the woman in it."

"Look, Wilson, it's ripped. Do you suppose Mason's right and it coulda been Westin, and he got up into her panties? 'Spose they did it right here on this floor?" He stamped, and Mary Grace felt dizzy and sick to her stomach. Sloan sat rigidly against her. "Mason'll sure be mad if she's gettin' poked."

"Well, if it is Westin what's got her, I'd be surprised if he could do much with her. But if he's still alive, he mighta been willin' to poke anybody what wants what's left of 'em. I'd guess between her looks and his remains, it wouldn'ta been much to see."

"You suppose she's got them freckles even where the sun don't shine?" Harlin asked.

The baby stretched in Mary Grace's arms and made a sucking sound. Sloan tensed, and she felt his hand move by his side. Was that the click of the hammer being pulled back? The baby smacked his lips again, and she pushed her knuckle against his lips. Accepting the substitute, he rubbed his sore gums against her finger noisily. It was the best Mary Grace could do. She just had to hope the Tates couldn't hear through the adobe floor.

Another set of footsteps joined the others. Mason Tate's voice filled the ancient ruins and echoed in the musty cellar around the hidden threesome.

"From the looks of it outside, they was here. I'd guess Sloan Westin isn't takin' off his boots behind no pearly gates, Harlin. I found this," he said, and Mary Grace wondered what he was showing his brothers.

"S. W. And that's her hair, all right," Wilson agreed. She could feel Sloan nodding in the dark.

"And look here," Harlin said, apparently showing him the petticoat. "And it's ripped, too."

"And Emily not cold in her grave. I thought you gelded him, at least, Harlin. Ain't that what you said?"

"I guess I shoulda aimed better when I run 'im off. If Emily hadn'ta been screamin' so 'bout how sorry she was, I'da been sure to get 'im in the balls. Still, I musta done him good. Ain't nobody caught 'im with their woman since I found him between Emily's legs. . . ."

Mary Grace could feel the heat rising from Sloan's body, despite the fact that she leaned away from him. His body was taut, the breathing controlled. She shivered, but he was lost in the moment, his body rigid in the face of danger.

"What are we gonna do now?" Harlin asked.

"We're gonna go rescue Horace and Miss O'Reilly," Mason answered calmly. "Then we're gonna cut off what's left of Sloan Westin's privates and feed them to Dukeboy."

"Yeah!" shouted Harlin, his voice covering the sound of Mary Grace's retching. "Let's get 'em."

They waited for the clatter of horses' hooves before Sloan threw back the trapdoor. Light and fresh air streamed into the kiva, and Mary Grace gulped in big breaths of it. Upstairs, Sloan cleaned out a cup with a whisk of the forgotten petticoat and filled it with water. He handed it to Mary Grace, who took it gratefully with both hands.

"Drink it slowly," he warned her. "I don't know where the next drop'll be comin' from."

5

Sloan was surprised at how easy it was to convince Mary Grace that the safest place for them to spend the night was in the Sinagua Indian ruins. After all, the Tates had already been there and moved on. The poor girl must have been too tired and confused to argue. But not too tired to mash up the green squash he had been fortunate enough to find and to feed it to his very hungry son.

Boy, that little fellow could eat! The squash disappeared faster than a rabbit at a coyote convention. And the water rag didn't seem to be satisfying his thirst. He kept turning his head in Sweet Mary's arms and trying to find a teat worth draining.

"There's nothing for you there, Paddy," she said. "I'm not your mama." To Sloan it wasn't clear who she was reminding, the baby, herself, or him.

"Ben," he corrected. "After my father. Which is just where he's going once we get outta this mess."

"You're taking the baby to see your parents?" Mary

Grace asked. She was sitting with her legs spread wide, stretching the skirt like a hammock for the baby to lie on while she changed his diaper. The cold of the floor must have been freezing her little ass off, he thought, judging from how cold she'd been down in the kiva, but she'd found a way to keep his son's bottom from touching the floor.

"Gonna give Ben to my mama to take care of while I go back and thank the Tate boys properly for what they done to me," he said. She'd had the fresh cloth ready, and before the cold air even hit it, the diaper was over his little pecker and she was pinning it in place.

"And then you'll go back for the baby?" she asked around the pin in her mouth.

He leaned over and added a slender stick to the small fire they had allowed themselves.

"You know we really should get those diaper pins with the little plastic part that prevent them from . . ." she stopped and looked up at him. "Never mind. They probably don't exist yet."

Did she really expect him to believe that she was from the future somewheres? The thought that it might be possible fascinated him. It was about the only thing the Indians could agree on—Oak Creek Canyon. It wasn't just the Havasupai, but the Yavapai and even the Apache and Navajo, too, who called the canyon the home of the Great Spirit. The shamans had told him it was where they went to pray to their ancestors and said that men could realize their true dreams and ambitions there. The Indians themselves would never live in the canyon. It would be like living in a church.

"Ow!" The pin she'd been fiddling with stabbed her, and blood puddled on her fingertip. She stared at it. "Well, then, I guess it's not just a dream."

He came over and bent his good knee, stretching his

stiff leg out next to him, and took her hand in his. He tilted it until the firelight glistened off the perfect scarlet dot. It was just a little pinprick, and he popped her finger in his mouth and sucked on it for a second. Even in the dim light, he could see a blush creep up her cheeks. He let go of her hand, and she pulled it back quickly and finished seeing to the child.

He'd sure pegged her wrong when he'd figured she was one of the Tates' women. It was obvious she wasn't any too comfortable around men. Leastwise, any contact with him seemed to make her uncomfortable. Oh, she was fine mouthing off to him the way she did, and she could hold her own with the pain of riding and sleeping on the floor and lugging around his boy, but when it came to the simplest of touches, she seemed to go to pieces. She was trying to hide the fact, but those cheeks of hers gave her away every time. Well, she had nothing to fear from him. And she could thank Harlin Tate for that.

"I didn't mean to be too forward," he said, standing upright again and trying to look anyplace but at the rise and fall of her breasts as she tended his child.

The firelight played on her hair as if little lightning bugs were dancing around her face. She waved his apology away with her hand.

"And while I'm at apologizin', I might as well ask your pardon for the things I said about you and the Tate boys. I guess I just thought, with you being in the house with them, and takin' your clothes off all the time . . ."

Her head spun around and her eyes opened wider than a snake's jaw. In the darkness they looked all black, not the soft green he had seen earlier. Everything about her was soft, from the wispy red hair that seemed to float around her face and down her back, to the moccasins on her small feet.

"Taking my clothes off?" She pretended to be looking

for something to wrap the baby in, as though they were in a regular home and all she had to do was reach out and grab a clean vest for him. She'd insisted Sloan take his shirt back after they'd emerged from the underground room, but now he unbuttoned the cuffs once again.

"So you still say you're from the future?" he asked, fishing around for a change of topic. *I saw you at the river, naked as the day God made you.*

She nodded. "I fell off a cliff. I thought I was going to die, but I landed in a river, instead." *You saw, didn't you? You saw everything.*

The firelight caught the bracelet she was wearing, and he tried to get a closer look without taking her hand again. Damned if it didn't look like a miniature timepiece strapped to her arm.

"What is that?" he asked, gesturing toward her wrist.

"My watch? Surely you have watches. Even Scrooge checked his watch, and Dickens is a lot older than the 1890s."

He couldn't help picturing his father's pocket watch. A knot formed inside his chest at the memory. "Course we got watches. I just ain't never seen one tied to someone's arm before."

"Oh." She looked surprised. "Wristwatches. This one is nothing. One of the guys in my office has one with a calculator in it."

He didn't want to ask her what that was. He hated feeling like a fool around her when, after all, she was the one who was strange.

"I fell off a cliff once," he said, returning the topic to her fall while he shrugged out of his shirt and handed it to her to wrap around the baby. "It was still 1888 when I landed in the creek."

"Well, it was 1994 when I drove up to that ridge,

and if you're not just messing with my head . . ." She paused, her eyes fixed on the wall behind him as if she couldn't stand to look at his naked chest. He'd thought the two wounds on his chest had healed pretty well, but she wouldn't even let her eyes wander to his body. She searched the wall, the floor, the fire, his face. Anywhere but the chest that was within her reach. He didn't want to think of how she'd feel about the rest of his scars, the ones that were even lower. Not that a woman like her was likely to see them.

"1994, huh?" he said. His annoyance showed in his voice, and he made no attempt to hide it. "Well, in 1994 do they sleep sitting up?" She was leaning against the wall, her feet still spread, Ben asleep on her skirt, and she shrugged as if she had no choice.

"He'll be cold on the floor," she explained, as if he hadn't figured that out.

"I told you before—I'm his papa. I'll see to him." He eased his way down to the floor, not far from the fire, and reached his hands out. "Give him to me. He can sleep on my chest, and we'll both stay warm."

And me? How will I stay warm? She picked the baby up gently without awakening him and scooted over to Sloan. One arm acted as a pillow for his head, the other reached out to take the baby and steady him on his broad chest. The firelight caught two ragged circles on his lower right side, down near the end of his rib cage. The bottom half of one of the circles disappeared into the waistband of his pants. He took the baby and placed him over the scars. Embarrassed, she turned away.

"Don't sleep too far from the fire," Sloan warned her. His voice was sharp, and she couldn't account for the sudden change in him. "It's gonna be a cold night."

On the opposite side of the small fire, she settled

down and tried to make herself comfortable. The floor was hard and cold. Every muscle in her body ached, and she shifted from one side to the other until she found a position that didn't rest on one of her many bruises.

Except for the crackling of the fire, the adobe fell silent. And yet, the quieter it became inside, the more aware Mary Grace became of the noises outside. Was it an owl's cry she heard in the distance, or an Indian sending a signal? Was that a coyote? She heard a screech. Another.

She raised herself on her elbow to see if Sloan was awake. "Mountain lion," he said simply. "Go back to sleep." But she saw that he had moved his rifle to within his reach.

"It's a pretty fancy rifle, isn't it?" she asked, trying to fill the quiet with the sound of her own voice.

"A gift. It seems to like me. Lost it twice now, and each time it finds its way back to me."

She lay back in silence. Perhaps the man, like the mountains, had some kind of magnetic force. On the inside of her eyelids she could see him, the Pied Piper of Oak Creek Canyon, his rifle following him, and behind that, his baby, and behind that, Mary Grace O'Reilly.

"But won't the Tates just follow the horse's tracks right back to us?" Mary Grace asked when she returned from relieving herself and saw the stallion waiting on the mesa for them. Before he answered, Sloan handed her a cup of something warm. He had managed to find some clay pots and had heated water in them. To the water he had added pigweed leaves, which made quite a palatable tea.

"Climber prefers the rocks to the desert. Either way, his trail should be impossible to follow." He pointed to the horizon. "You see those clouds? Whole damn trail ought to be washed out before noon."

"So we wait here?" Mary Grace asked, taking the baby back from his daddy and straddling her hip with him. She was surprised to find him dry. She smiled at Sloan, but his attention was fixed on the sky, an ominous green color that made the stillness around them even more unnerving. Far to the west she could see black clouds that boiled on the horizon, rising up and reaching, reaching. Clearly it wasn't safe to leave the shelter of the adobe ruins.

"Can't stay here," he replied, placing his fingers in his mouth and whistling across the flat land to the west. The horse raised his head and turned toward them. Sloan whistled again, and the horse came running.

"They all really do that!" Mary Grace marveled at Sloan's stallion just as she had been surprised by Wilson's. "I really thought that they did that just in movies and on TV."

Sloan looked at her oddly, and she realized what she'd said. She shook her head. There was so much she could tell him about, so much of more importance than *Bonanza*. He shrugged off her comment and turned his attention to Climber, stroking the horse's nose, patting its neck. He reached into his saddlebags and moved things until he found what it was he was looking for.

"Shoulda taken this out last night before I let the damn horse go," he said. "Don't know what I was thinking of." He pulled out a poncho-like garment and handed it to her. Then he removed the sling he had carried the baby in the day before, and put it over Mary Grace's head. But he put it on backward, the knot between her breasts, and then took the baby from her arms. He had a way of touching her, at once intimate and yet impersonal, that unnerved her. He touched her the way a man touches a woman, gently, his hands aware of her breasts, her hips, the smallness of her compared to the size of him. And yet she felt she could have been any woman, an anonymous someone of the female gender. Oddly, she was disappointed. It wasn't like her to want to be noticed by a man, and it left her confused.

He tucked the baby into the fabric strap against her back. "He's got to go on your back, or he'll get crushed between us. When we get onto the horse, put the poncho over yourself and Ben. It'll keep you dry."

The sky was darkening perceptibly. Mary Grace thought she could see the rain in the distance, a heavy wall that moved closer and closer toward where they stood.

"But why don't we just stay here?" she asked, watching him swing up easily into the saddle. On the horse he was as at home as any man with two good legs.

"If Mason has a brain in his head, they'll come back here when they see the storm coming. If not for their own shelter, then because they know we know about this place and they'll figure we'll come back." He settled her behind him and tried to help her get the cloth over her head as best he could. He felt her fumbling behind him and turned to see what she was doing. She had bunched the poncho up in front of her and was trying to widen the neck hole.

"Just put it over yourself. Ben'll be OK under it," he insisted.

"Are you sure we should go?" she asked him again. "There's no sign of the Tates."

"You don't seem to be understanding me, Sweet Mary. The Tates are out there, and they're hoping to kill me. I don't know what exactly they have in mind for you."

She'd seen the look in Mason Tate's eyes when he

thought she wasn't looking, sizing her up as though he was checking the fit. To his credit, he hadn't touched her, but she wasn't looking forward to ever seeing him again. And if they found her, it wouldn't just be Mason, but Wilson, too.

She swallowed hard. No man was ever going to have his way with her again. No amount of sweet talk, no promises, no threats would make her do anything she didn't want to. Not again.

"Let's go," she said, trying to shake off the memories. "Before we drown in the rain."

He didn't answer her. He just kicked the horse and moved out slowly.

"Do you have a knife?" she asked once they were on the way. She'd tried just pulling at the neck of the poncho but hadn't widened the opening at all. In the distance the rain moved like a sheet in their direction, and the horse began to prance beneath them.

Remarkably, Sloan didn't ask her why she needed a knife. He simply pulled one out and gave it to her. Nothing he said could have convinced her they were in as much danger as that inattentive gesture.

She slit the neckhole and widened it with a tug. "There!" she said after a minute and handed the knife back to him. By now, fat drops of rain had begun to hit them with a vengeance. They were few and far between. One hit her shoulder, then a few moments later another smacked her on the forehead. Fierce, angry drops, that threatened a deluge when that dark cloud finally reached them. "Take off your hat," she said against his ear, and he twitched at the sound of her words as though he had altogether forgotten she was there.

Her breath was hot on his neck. One arm encircled his waist while the other fidgeted behind him. "What?" Sloan asked.

"Don't argue. Take off your hat."

He did and she slipped the poncho over his head, so that the three of them were all under it together.

"I don't mind the rain," he said, replacing his hat on his head, and feeling both her arms come around him and grab onto the cloth of his shirt, a fistful in either hand.

"Tough," she replied, adjusting herself behind him.

He could feel her trying to keep her distance, centering her weight on her buttocks instead of her thighs, hoping her chest wasn't coming in contact with his back. He knew this because all he could feel, instead of her weight against him, instead of the softness of her breasts against his muscles, were her nipples, hard from the cold, rubbing against his back through his wet shirt and driving him mad.

As Climber lumbered down the canyon wall, Sloan leaned back into Mary Grace, forcing her into the cantle of the saddle. But the baby was on her back, and Sloan could tell she was afraid of crushing him.

"Fold your arms behind you, in the small of your back, under Ben's bottom," Sloan directed her over his shoulder. "Lean on your palms."

It was cold around his middle when she took her arms away, and he tried to keep himself upright while she shifted in the saddle. When she was ready, he leaned into her gently, and rocked against the soft pillows of her breasts, first one and then the other, while the horse trudged down the mountain.

If he'd wondered whether his desire would ever come back, he had his answer. But desire didn't equal ability, and he had yet to figure out the mechanics of mounting a woman with a stiff leg, much less letting her see what Harlin Tate had managed to do.

He knew her hands had to ache from holding both

her own and his weight off the baby's legs. The rain was coming down steadily now, and his hat kept hitting her somewhere and reseating itself on his head with every step the horse took.

Out of nowhere, without any warning, she suddenly screamed. "No!" she shouted. "Please, no!"

Sloan jumped forward, the saddle horn nearly gelding him, the poncho strangling him and pulling him back, the horse stumbling with the shifting weight and then righting itself.

"Are you all right?"

There was only a choked sobbing near his ear. He couldn't see her behind him, couldn't swing off the horse without putting her off first. He reached behind him and pulled her up against his body. The horse was on solid ground now. There was no more need to lean back.

"Better?"

He felt a slight nod against his shoulder. He let the horse have some head, and they moved away from the mountain toward an outcropping of boulders that under any other conditions could have afforded them some shelter. But being in the valley during the rain could mean disaster. Flash floods were common, and Sloan couldn't count the number of men who'd bet their load of copper or silver against the fates and lost.

"You OK?" He wished she'd answer him. Her cry hadn't sounded like mere discomfort. It had sounded like something else—like panic.

All the noise and movement seemed to irritate the baby, who let his misery be known with a wail. That seemed to bring Mary Grace to her senses. Sloan could feel her stiffen behind him as if she'd come awake from a dream.

"Was I hurtin' you?" he asked, feeling her wipe at her face behind him. "Was I too heavy on you?"

"I'm OK," she said. There was an edge to her voice as if she were angry at him.

"But you—" he began.

She cut him off. "I'm all right."

But clearly she wasn't. And damn, in this position, he couldn't look her in the eyes and see what was wrong. Just like the other women he'd known, this one was playing games with him, saying one thing, meaning another. How the hell was he supposed to guess what was setting her off? And now the rain was coming down in earnest. He could hardly see the trail.

"The remainder is all uphill," he said, glad to be resting his weight on his own butt once again. "If you want, you can rest against me."

"What?" she shouted at him over the baby's high-pitched wail.

Sloan didn't repeat himself. In the distance he could just make out something moving on the top of the ridge. Two somethings. Three.

He eased the horse behind the rocks, a soft curse escaping his lips. There wasn't time now to ride the horse to the high ground on the other side of the canyon. Already the stallion's feet were sinking into the mud from the weight of his burden, making smacking sounds as he raised them out of the muck.

The three shadows were motionless on the mountainside.

"Quiet him," Sloan ordered, shrugging out of the poncho and lowering Mary Grace into the mire beneath them. He set her down as gently as he could. Still, her feet sank into the wet earth, and she fell to her knees. God, if she couldn't manage it on two good legs . . .

He threw his right leg over the horse's loins and pulled his left foot out of the stirrup. His right hand held the rifle as he lowered himself into the mud. He turned and faced Mary Grace, who was struggling with the rain gear while the baby cried loudly. Both the woman and the child were oblivious to the danger they were in.

Sloan managed to keep his balance somehow and get to them. He pulled the poncho off Mary Grace with one sweep and grabbed the baby up out of the pouch on her back.

"You've got to quiet him," he told her, resting his hand lightly over the baby's mouth, his lips near Mary Grace's ear. They were hidden from view, but the canyons did funny things to sound, magnifying it, bouncing it off walls, repeating it.

"What is it? What's wrong?" she asked, barely above a whisper. "Are they here?"

He nodded tersely and spread the poncho over her head like a tent, leaving her and the child beneath it. Then he busied himself with the horse, making sure that it, too, was hidden by the rocks.

When he returned, the child was quiet. He leaned down, one hand steadying himself on the rocks, and picked up the edge of the blanket. Beneath it Mary Grace had bared her breast, no doubt in desperation, and Ben was sucking on her nipple, trying hopelessly to get the sweet nectar he was used to. Sloan stood fascinated for a moment, watching the baby smack his fist against Mary Grace's chest in frustration.

"Ah, Sweet Mary," he said as she winced in pain. Her eyes shone with tears, but she let the baby continue biting on her, trying to hide herself from Sloan, trying to keep herself upright against the boulder, trying to survive. Silently he handed her a dried peach he'd found in his saddlebags and gestured for her to give it to the baby. She held on to the edge firmly and put it between the baby's gums, covering herself at the same time by lowering her shoulder and pushing the blouse up with the baby's body.

"There's a cave," he told her in hushed tones. "Do you think you can follow me?" Tears ran down her cheeks as she nodded and pushed herself away from the rocks.

He turned to lead her, but the mud had a hold of his bad leg, and he couldn't lift it to swing it in front of him. It was like being in quicksand. For a brief moment Sloan thought he would have to crawl on his belly in the mud to get anywhere. He stood stuck in the mire until beneath his armpit he felt Mary Grace's strong shoulder, pushing up against him, encouraging him to lean on her. Pressing down on her until she nearly crumbled under his weight, he freed his foot and stumbled forward.

Together they limped to the cave, a small triangular opening in the rocks that sheltered them but did little else. Sloan eased Mary Grace down to the stone floor and slid down next to her. He took the baby, and before she could cross her arms against her chest he saw a pale red spot on her blouse. She was hugging herself in pain, silent tears running down her face. He told himself he'd only asked her to quiet the kid, not give him a pound of flesh, but it didn't help. Damn stupid woman, letting herself be in pain on his account. Who asked her, anyway?

Her bottom lip disappeared into her mouth, and still she tried to smile at him. He didn't know what to say. And so he busied himself with the baby, refusing to let him leave his arms and return to Mary Grace's. At least he could do that much. No doubt she'd never want to hold Ben again. To his surprise, she bent her head toward the baby and kissed his flailing fist. But her arms stayed glued to her chest, and her knuckle was clamped between her teeth.

How long could they stay in the cave, he wondered. The rain had lessened some, but the streams were no doubt bursting by now, and a flood could come even after the rain had stopped. Were the Tates still out there on the ridge, watching? For himself, he had no preference between drowning and being shot to death, although having already virtually suffered the latter he leaned slightly toward the former. But the Tates would never hurt their nephew, and he could make it appear that Mary Grace was an unwilling hostage.

Mary Grace. She was unlike any woman he knew. Except maybe his ma. His pa used to tell him stories about how the two of them had come west from St. Louis with a wagon full of hope and little else. A flood had ruined most of their provisions, and they were reduced to scavenging to survive. Never a complaint, his father had said of his mother.

He looked over at the woman with the red hair and freckles who had fallen into his life. Her eyes were closed, and her head rested against the cave wall. Where had she come from, really? And what would happen to her when this was all over? And worse, why did he care? Why did he want to know that she would come out of it all right? She was nothing to him. No woman was. Except his ma, but that was different.

Then he heard the distant rumbling. It was the water coming, rushing for them. There wasn't even time to explain anything to Sweet Mary. He managed to get on his feet and then picked up the baby from the muddy floor.

"Get up!" His voice was loud and gruff, echoing off the walls of the cave. She opened her eyes with a start, blinking at him as if to see him more clearly. He hadn't realized she'd fallen asleep. "Do what I say," he said in a softer voice, giving her his hand to help her up. When she was on her feet, he handed Ben to her.

"I'll go out first. If they're out there, you'll hear the shots. Scream your bloody head off so they don't hit you or the baby. You understand?" He turned and looked at her. She was white with fear.

"Don't go out there," she begged him. "We'll be safe in here."

But the sound of the water grew louder still, so loud even she had to hear it and know what it meant. Gently he placed a kiss on the top of the baby's head, and touched Mary Grace's soft cheek. Then he was gone, the baby reaching for him long after he had vanished from their sight.

She listened for the sound of shots but heard nothing above the roaring of the water. Unexpectedly, a hand appeared at the top of the cave opening, hanging down like a dead man's, over her head.

A hand, then an arm. It was Sloan's. She screamed, and he waved to quiet her. He wasn't dead, then. He beckoned her with one finger, and she inched out of the cave and turned to look at him. His mouth was moving, but his words were swept away by the wall of water rushing toward her.

She yanked the baby from the sling and stood as tall as she could, holding him high above her head. She sank into the mud, found firmer footing, tried again. And again, and yet again, until she felt the little boy lifted from her fingertips.

"I've got him," Sloan shouted, and then his hand was down again, reaching for her. She hung in the air as he strained to lift her onto the rocky plateau, her feet inches above the rapidly rising stream.

Her back hit the rock first, smashing against it before he could manage to ease her up onto her bottom. The pain shot through her, and she'd have fallen from his hands if he hadn't tightened his grip and hauled her up without any help from her. Once out of the river's way, she leaned back on the rock, trying to catch her breath.

"Don't get too comfortable," he told her when he had settled the baby against his chest. "This isn't high enough." There was no walking on the slippery rocks. Sloan crawled, his right leg out to his side, looking for a way to the next plateau.

Mary Grace strained to stand, but her muddy skirt was so heavy she could barely get to her feet. She tried to rip the skirt, but the fabric refused to give.

"Come on," Sloan shouted. Somehow he'd made it higher and was once again reaching down to pull her up. She slipped out of the soaked muslin skirt and scurried toward him, dragging the skirt behind her. She threw the skirt up next to him and then put up her hand. This time he lifted her right past the edge of the cliff and set her down gently.

"You're much lighter that way," he remarked, his eyes averted from her long, pale, freckled legs that disappeared beneath the edge of her blouse.

She looked up toward the ridge where the three riders had been. It was empty now, the rain so hard and dense that the mountain seemed connected to the sky.

Ben was fascinated by the rain and the flood. Or maybe he was just so cold, like Mary Grace, that he couldn't even cry. So all three of them watched the moving wall of water pass beneath them, filling the cave, washing out the path they traveled. Debris floated in the instant river beneath them, which swelled and swelled to accommodate the trees, rocks, and animals it carried along. A full-grown deer floated by, its antlers smashing into the rocks, its wide-open eyes frozen in fear. Mary Grace hugged the child closer to her chest.

"It's all right," she assured him. "It's all right." The

baby's eyes were on her; hers were on Sloan. His searched the river that surged beneath them. Walls of dirty rushing water smashed heavy boulders against their little outcropping like hardened dirt rocks against a fence post. He huddled his little son and Mary Grace against him, trying to shield them with his body, not even noticing when the rain let up and the noise of the water began to lessen.

"I think it's over," Mary Grace said finally, withdrawing from his shelter and lifting her head.

A ray of sunlight struck the pile of rocks on which they'd weathered the storm. Sloan straightened his body, trying to unkink his arms and leg, arching his back, rubbing his right leg to restore the feeling.

"I know this is a helluva time to ask," Mary Grace said once the danger seemed passed. Her teeth were chattering, and her skin had taken on a distinctly bluish tint. "But you do have a plan, don't you? I mean, beyond just loving your son and wanting him back?"

Sloan threw back his head and laughed. For nearly a year he had lain on his back in the wickiup of the chief's son on the Havasupai reservation making plans. Of course, he hadn't known about Ben then. He had simply been obsessed with how to kill Harlin Tate. Just shooting Mason and Wilson would do. And Emily, well, he had planned to make her pay, as well. But his life had centered around Harlin. And once he had made Harlin pay, he would get his life back.

"Ben didn't enter the plan at all," he admitted. "He was sort of a bonus, if you could call him that. Taking him away from Harlin was just one more step in getting my old life back. The plan was to make Harlin Tate pay. And pay. And pay." He searched the area beneath them, looking for the horse. There was no sign of Climber anywhere.

"But then when you found out about the baby," Mary Grace continued. "Then things changed, right?"

"Right. I had to take what was mine. You sure were a snag in the wire roll," he said, patting the downy black hair on the baby's head.

"And now that you have your son . . ."

"Gonna bring him home to my mama and come back for Harlin. You see, I had a certain way of life, let's say, and Harlin Tate took that away from me. Now I may not be the man I was, but I'm still a man, and until I make Harlin pay for what he done to me, I ain't gonna be able to look at myself in the mirror without wantin' to spit."

"Excuse me?" Mary Grace said. Her eyes were wide with disbelief, and there was no mistaking the anger in her voice. "We're on top of some boulder, in the middle of nowhere, your son and I are freezing to death, we have nothing to eat, no horse, as far as I can see, and all you want to talk about is revenge? And on top of that, you probably think you're Superdad for going after this child. Isn't it just like a man to think he's a father just because he slept with a woman?"

"Last I heard, that's all it takes," he said, trying to figure out just what had this woman so riled she could have eaten his liver for lunch, raw. Was it his fault that it had rained? She'd have drowned without him. And this was how she showed her gratitude? If he hadn't lifted her up . . . He interrupted his own thought. Before he'd lifted her, she'd handed up his son. Of course, she couldn't have climbed with him any better than he could have. When he raised his eyes to her, he found her staring back at him.

"You don't love this child, do you? You just want to do the macho thing, even if it risks all our lives. Is that it?"

"If you'll bother thinkin' back, Miss O'Reilly, it was you that insisted on staying with my boy and me. It ain't my fault you ain't cozied up with old Mason Tate's fat to keep ya warm, now, is it?" He looked at the woman sitting next to him on the rock, holding his son, and wondered what it was about her that left him saying things he didn't even mean. There they were, soaked through to the skin, and it worried him some that the baby had stopped fussing.

"Is he OK?" he asked.

"He's still breathing, if that's what you're asking. It all depends on what you mean by OK." She shifted the baby, and he saw the red stain on her blouse had elongated with the rain, stretching down several inches from the tip of her breast. He saw her grimace as the baby snuggled closer and knew he was putting them through a lot. But as he'd said, he hadn't invited her, and how was he supposed to know what a kid needed? With the Tates close enough to track them by the baby's scent, he had more to worry about than a woman's bruised feelings.

"Is he sick?" Sloan asked.

She felt the child's forehead. "Not yet," she said. "He's sleeping. This has been quite a day for a six-month-old."

"He's only four months," Sloan corrected.

"Four?"

"I'm not likely to forget when I met Harlin Tate, to the minute, nor when I . . . was with his sister."

"But," Mary Grace began, then realized there was no point in arguing with him. After all, who would know better? Her or the baby's father? "I repeat, you do have a plan, don't you?"

"I told you. I want my life back. I want to be the man I was, a hard ridin', whorin', son of a bitch cowboy that never asked nothin' from nobody and never took shit from nobody, neither."

"Well, you've got the son of a bitch part down," Mary Grace said. "Will killing Harlin get you the rest of it? I think not."

She sounded like some schoolmarm. "Oh, you think not," he said imitating her. "Well, you don't know what it's like, giving up the life you had. I was a broncobuster on my father's ranch. You know what that is? I rode the wildest horses there are until I rode all the wild out of 'em. The rodeo in Prescott? I used to win it with my eyes closed. I could take down a seven-hundred-pound steer easy as a two-day-old calf. Got me more silver belt buckles as prizes than there are days in the week to wear 'em. I won't even go into the women part, you bein' a lady and all. But you wouldn't understand. I want my life back."

He took off his shirt and wrapped it over her legs. At least that way he could keep his eyes from tracing the path up her legs to the point where they joined. The point where her red hair would be deeper, where he could lose himself the way he always had before. His gut twisted. Remembering was doing his insides no good at all.

She took the shirt off her legs and wrapped it around the baby, then shifted her body around so that her legs were no longer visible to him. When she turned to look at him, her eyes were full of tears.

"*I* don't understand what it's like to want your life back? *I* don't understand?" she said, her voice rising to a fever pitch. "I'm the one who lost her life here somewhere. You've got a bum leg. Well, poor you. I've lost my goddamn life! I don't know a soul alive today, and no one knows me. If I fell off this stupid rock and died, no one would know, or care. Don't talk to me about wanting your life back, you selfish, self-centered, vengeful lunatic. Your son and I just might die because of your stupid vendetta, but do you care? No. You're worried about honor and garbage like that. . . ."

The sun was peeking out from behind the clouds, warming the day quickly. Sloan's chest was dry, and if they spread the clothes out, it wouldn't take long for them to dry, either. He pictured her the way he saw her that first day, sunning on the rocks. Way down in his groin he felt the stirring of something warm, and he knew it wasn't just the sun through his Levi's. He could suggest they take their clothes off and let them dry.

He lifted his head to look at Mary Grace, who had turned away after shouting at him. Her back was shaking, and he had no way of knowing if she, like the baby, was crying or simply shivering in her wet clothes.

"You're wrong about one thing," he said quietly. She seemed to hold her breath.

"Someone would care if you died."

She didn't ask whether he meant himself or Ben, and so he didn't have to say. He wondered about the people who did care about her. He wondered, too, if he should count himself among them.

6

"Mr. Westin?" Mary Grace said quietly in his ear when the baby had finally succumbed to the rocking motion of the horse and fallen asleep.

He sighed. "Sloan. Hey you. Cowboy. Anything but Mr. Westin. Huh, Sweet Mary? Can you manage that?"

"I . . . are we going to die, anyway? Because if we are, I'd just as soon get it over with. There isn't a part of me that doesn't hurt. My face is so sunburned I don't think I could smile if there was something to smile about, and my throat is so dry I can hardly swallow."

"Just hold on till nightfall. OK, Sweet Mary? Just hold on till then, all right?"

She tried to answer, but it took too much effort, so she just nodded and leaned her head against his back. He took the canteen from her, took a small swig, and put the strap back over his saddle horn. He'd promised to fix everything, but words and plans weren't enough to keep his son fed and dry. Nor the woman, neither.

"Sweet Mary?" he said softly, but she didn't respond.

He could feel her weight against him. "Mary Grace?" Still nothing. "Sleep well, then," he told her and gave Climber an inspirational sermon in the flanks with his spurs. The horse lifted his head as if to ask what more his master could want, and Sloan clucked at him out of the side of his mouth.

"Get on with ya, then," he told the tired stallion. "You'll be swimmin' at the end of the trail."

The damn horse was getting slower with every step, and Sloan began to face the possibility that the Tates might win what would be his last showdown. Wasn't it a damn shame that the one that really mattered, the one that could cost Ben and Sweet Mary their futures, would be the one he couldn't pull off? He'd talked, conned, or fought his way out of a hundred tough spots before ever meeting Emily Tate and her crazy brothers.

The baby began stirring. Sloan heard the now familiar gurgles and coos as Ben tried to rouse Mary Grace, still sleeping against his back. How long could he keep the horse going before Ben began to raise his voice and give his uncles a reason to head in their direction? Not long, as the baby finally began to cry, and Sloan had to give in and give them all a rest. He lowered Mary Grace and the baby to the ground and dismounted after them. Putting some water in his hat, he gave the horse a lick's worth, and then turned to look at his charges.

Mary Grace's face was bright with color, putting to shame the flowers on the saguaro. Her lips were white and dry, and they cracked when she tried to smile at him. Lord, how had he gotten himself into such a mess? Ought to teach him where not to drop his drawers. Only the lesson was a useless one, now.

The baby was shrieking in Mary Grace's arms, and she was having a difficult time just holding on to him as he arched his back and stiffened his legs against her belly.

With every muscle apparently aching, she lowered herself to the ground and placed the baby once again on her skirt, hammock fashion, only this time she put him on his tummy. She undid his diaper and exposed his sore bottom to the air. He cried out in pain, and Mary Grace shook her head and cursed softly. He'd never heard a woman of breeding cuss before, and he tried to hide his shock.

"He's got a pretty good case of diaper rash," she said, looking up at him. "We've got to find something to put on this sore little bottom."

It wasn't bad enough, those soft green eyes pleading with him to solve all their problems. The baby had to lift his dark little head and stare at Sloan with those enormous blue eyes, too.

"Maybe you could cut one of these cactus leaves," Mary Grace suggested. "You know, aloe is really good for rashes and burns." She reached out toward a yucca plant, but Sloan's voice stopped her.

"That ain't aloe, or whatever you called it. It's yucca. And yucca's gonna make a bad thing a lot worse. Like pourin' whiskey on a campfire to put it out." She was shielding the baby's naked bottom from the sun with her hands. He wondered if all women were that protective of their babies. Then he reminded himself that it wasn't her baby, but his.

He whistled to the horse, who came obediently and stood blocking the sun from streaming down on both the woman and the child. Then he looked around him, surveying the landscape. Not twenty feet away, a stand of prickly pear cactus spread its flat pads out and up from the desert floor. It wasn't the best medicine, but it would do.

He slipped his knife out of its sheath and hacked a pad off the prickly plant. With the blade he stabbed it and lifted it from the ground. Its insides oozed where it was cut, and he hurried back to the baby and Mary Grace, his free hand catching the drippings as he went. As it dripped gently on the baby's bare behind, like manna from heaven, he watched Mary Grace spread it gently, using just one finger, touching the child as little as she could. The baby stopped his fussing almost immediately, and when Mary Grace looked up at him, Sloan used the precious liquid he had caught in his hand to coat her sunburned face and lips, careful not to get any in her eyes. Then he removed his hat and placed it on her head. It fell over her forehead, momentarily blinding her, and he couldn't help but laugh.

"Not much of a head on your shoulders, huh?" he said.

"Don't make a joke out of it," she said quietly, pushing the brim back so that she could see his face. "It's nice of you to give me it."

"Gettin' too small on me," he said, ruffling his hair. "What with all this."

She looked at him skeptically. Why did he feel like she could read him as easy as some dime novel?

"OK," he admitted reluctantly. "It's nice of you to take care of my son. You make a good mother there, Sweet Mary."

She stiffened, and the smile left her face. Now what had he said that made her mad? He wasn't suggesting anything.

"Not that I'm lookin' for a mama for him," he corrected. "I've got one all lined up." As soon as he could, this child was going to be at the Bar W Ranch, with his grandmama's arms around him, sinking his teeth into something worth eating. Did he have teeth yet? He thought about the job the baby had done on Sweet Mary's breast.

But in his mind he saw not the baby at her breast, but himself. He imagined gently brushing his lips against the soreness, kissing away the hurt. God, he was horny all of a sudden. Nearly a year and a half without a woman could do that to a man. But why now? Why not when he was in Jerome and could have bought a dozen women to satisfy him? Why now?

So his plans hadn't changed, Mary Grace thought. Just drop Ben off and get back to killing the Tates. And no place for her in his plans. Well, she'd known better than to start loving this baby. She always knew better. That's why she always turned the children over as soon as she found them. That way there was no chance to get attached. She prided herself on her ability to stay detached. She was not going to let herself down now.

"Do you have anything I could feed him?" she asked.

The knife with the prickly pear pad was still in his hand. "You might want to put this on your . . . well, if anything's sore . . . I mean . . . I appreciate what you did for Ben . . . Well, for all of us . . . I'm sorry he . . ."

He eased the plant off his knife and warned her about the thorns. "I'll find something to eat," he said and turned his back on her before he could catch her smile. For such a man of the world he surely got tongue-tied about her breast. "Then we gotta get going. So get your business done and stretch your legs before I get back."

Mary Grace looked down at her blouse. The rain had so diluted the blood on her shirt that there was barely a tinge of pink left on the thin fabric to remind her of the incredible feeling of a baby nuzzling at her breast. Before it had begun to hurt, it was the sweetest feeling she had ever known. It was as if she and the baby had been one, bound together by the clasp of his lips and the trust he had that she would satisfy his most basic needs.

Of course, she hadn't been able to, hadn't been any use to him at all. There was nothing inside her body to nourish a baby, or anyone else, for that matter. Gingerly, careful not to prick herself on the spines, she touched the oozing plant Sloan had left for her and then lowered the neckline of her blouse. Her nipple was red, the tip crusted in dark dried blood. Her finger hesitated just inches from her body. But instead of coating her nipple, she rubbed the soothing ointment on her throat and covered herself up once again. It was worth the pain to be reminded of how it felt to be a mother, even if only for a few desperate minutes of her life.

A mother. To think that once she had wanted to become a nun and never have children of her own. Of course, she'd been very young. Young and gullible. Now they'd call it vulnerable, for the sake of tact. What a different life she might have had. Spared so much pain.

She could hear Sloan Westin making his way back to her, his boots clunking on the hard ground. Under all that dirt and all that anger, what kind of man was he? Whatever kind it was, it made her feel like a different kind of woman. He seemed to ignore all the subtle signals every other man had been able to see. The unspoken warnings to leave her alone. The clear desire to be left untouched. He paid no attention to any of them.

She rubbed her arms, feeling chilly even in the strong southwestern sun. Maybe he was ignoring the signals. Or maybe, just maybe, she wasn't sending them, at all. She'd better be careful. The Tates weren't the only ones who posed a danger.

"Here," he said, as he prepared the cactus fruit he had found. She looked miserable, and she jumped away from him like he was holding out a hot poker, not merely a bit of food. "Let's get to eatin' some of this here fruit. It's sweeter than honey off a pretty girl's lips."

He knew her gut wasn't working so well from the time she kept taking to do her business. He also knew women well enough to know it was something they wouldn't want to talk about with a man, least of all a man they hardly knew. She shook her head when he offered her a slice of the pear.

"It's good for ya, Sweet Mary," he said, trying not to seem what a woman might call indelicate. "Come on, honey, eat some."

Ben reached out his pudgy hand and tried to grab at the fruit. Damned if that little one didn't know a good thing even if the stubborn woman holding him hadn't the sense to know what fruit would do for her. A smile curled his lips as an idea hit him.

"Well, I don't know, li'l one. I give you this here fruit, and me and Sweet Mary here will be scrambling for a clean diaper before we're back in the saddle." He looked at Mary Grace and watched for signs that she had taken his meaning.

With her face an even brighter crimson than the sun had painted it, she reached out and took the juicy morsel off the end of his blade. She was still just holding it while he readied another piece for the baby.

"Watch the pits," he warned her. Then he cut another slice, this one smaller, checked it for pits first, and handed it to Ben, who greedily stuffed it in his mouth and smiled. Pink juice trickled down his chin and onto his shirt while he made smacking noises with his tongue and waved his arms in the air.

With a great deal of amusement, Sloan watched Mary Grace try to keep the baby from dripping on her blouse, which was already stained with dirt, mud, and her own blood. The thought sobered him, but only for a moment as Ben got the notion it was some sort of game Mary Grace was playing. Laughing and spitting until it became pointless for her to try to escape him, the baby decorated her shirt artlessly with his lunch.

"What does it taste like?" she asked warily, examining the dripping fruit in her hand.

What difference did it make, he wondered irritably. *Put the damn thing in your mouth and let it do its business so you can do yours.* "It's sweet, like fruit."

She continued to look at it suspiciously.

"Hell, woman, I didn't bring you all the way out into the middle of the desert to kill you. If I'd a wanted to do that, I coulda done it back in Oak Creek Canyon and saved myself a lot of trouble." He took the piece she had been holding and popped it in his mouth as if to prove it wouldn't hurt her. Hell, Ben was lapping it up, wasn't he? He cut another slice. After checking it for pits, he gave it to the baby, who obviously was enjoying this gift from the desert.

He offered another piece to Mary Grace. She took it and this time bit off just the very end. Surprise registered on her face, and she smiled broadly at him. Her lips cracked, but it didn't diminish her indisputable joy.

"It's good! No, really! Kind of like a cross between a strawberry and a tomato. I'll have another," she said, putting out her hand for more. He handed her another piece and took another for himself. She wolfed it down faster than a woman changes her mind, and asked for another. But before he could give her one, Ben began to squirm, and the look on his face told them that he wasn't going to wait until the fruit made it through his system.

Diapers were a precious commodity, what with Ben's rash, no water to wash them in, and no remaining petticoat. Whenever they could, they left his bottom naked.

Sloan held the baby by his underarms and kept him at arms length, while the baby attempted to do his business. Mary Grace grabbed the child's legs and held them out so that he would soil himself as little as possible, and shortly the deed was done.

"What's macho?" Sloan asked as Mary Grace tried to clean the baby's bottom with the corner of an already soiled diaper and reapply the ointment from the prickly pear pad.

When she looked up, she seemed confused. "Macho?"

"Now who's repeating?" he asked, comfortable with the upper hand.

"Why do you want to know about macho?"

"You said that's what I was doing. On the rocks, in the rain? Remember? You said something about how I was doing macho."

"Being macho," she corrected. "Or doing the macho thing." While she spoke, he pulled a soft leaf off a mesquite tree and swabbed the baby's still dirty bottom with it.

"Don't worry about it," she said, smiling up at him. "It doesn't apply." It was clear she wasn't going to tell him, but the warmth of her smile told him two things. First, that it didn't matter anymore. Second, that it sure hadn't been a compliment.

He mounted up, and once the baby was secure against his chest, fascinated by his silver buttons, Sloan reached down for Mary Grace.

"Are we headed somewhere?" she asked. "Or are we going to be like the ancient Jews and just wander in the desert for hundreds of years?"

Sloan grasped Mary Grace's hand and pulled her up behind him. "How would you like a nice leisurely bath, Sweet Mary?" he asked. "With warm water, and soap for your hair?"

"Are we almost to your parents' ranch, then?" she asked. He didn't know if she was glad at the idea or not. There was a wistfulness in her voice, he thought. But that made no more sense than trying to shear sheep in the snow. Who'd want to be stuck out here in the desert? Especially with him and his son.

She was riding closer to him than she had been, her arm rubbing Ben's back. As she patted his son, her elbow ran up and down his inner arm like a rattler's tail twitching. He stilled her before any more crazy ideas came into his head. If there was one thing he was sure of, it was that Mary Grace O'Reilly was just as anxious to be free of him as he was to be free of her. "No, but there's a place I know . . ." He sat up, suddenly all ears. "Ssh." He felt her arms tighten around him. Slowly he twisted in his saddle and searched the flat land around them. Not a place to hide. But, as far as he could see, not a thing to hide from.

"It's all right," he told her, his eyes finding the source of the noise. "Look over there."

A herd of pronghorn antelope played in the distance, looking somewhat like popping corn as they jumped over each other. Mary Grace sighed behind him, her breathing warm against his back as she took in the sight.

"Show Paddy," she told him. "Can he see them?"

Sloan looked down at the baby against his chest. He was comfortable, not crying, fiddling with Sloan's buttons and gurgling to himself.

"He sees them," Sloan lied.

"His first antelope!" she cried. "You should write this down. You know, keep a record." Her voice faded out.

"Don't worry," he said. "I won't forget."

She nodded behind him, her head against his back, and he felt a momentary wetness. Women! They cried at anything!

7

Ben Westin's stallion knew the way back to the Bar W Ranch without his guidance. He let the horse set the pace, an easy trot that would get him home before dark, but no sooner. He wasn't looking forward to facing Anna. He had no news for her on Sloan's whereabouts, though he knew in his heart his son was alive.

It was the strangest thing. He and Sloan had never been very close. In fact, the closeness in the family had been between Anna and the boy, leaving him out in the cold for all the boy's growing-up years. Yet since Sloan's disappearance, Ben had felt a tugging at his soul so strong that it had made him search every corner of the territory for his son.

It so unsettled him that he'd finally given in to Anna's wishes to go back east. Anything to get away from the constant calling of a voice that wasn't there. And the fact that Anna couldn't hear it, didn't leap from their bed at night and run to the window to see an empty meadow stretched out in the moonlight, only made matters worse for both of them.

"What?" she would ask as he bolted toward the doorway. "What do you hear?"

"Nothing," he would respond, while his ears still rang with the sound of his son calling out to him.

The ranch was in sight, the corral empty, someone smoking a cheroot on the porch. Anna didn't permit smoking within the confines of the house. She claimed the odor stayed in the curtains and furniture, but Ben believed that she simply wanted him out of her house. He never objected. Of late he found himself smoking more, perhaps just to get away from her.

The man on the porch raised his hand in greeting. Sunny. Only one of so many things Ben would miss when they left Arizona. But Sunny had to stay behind. What if Sloan should make it back? Someone had to be there for his son. Someone who believed he would be coming back.

"Long trip?" Sunny asked, grabbing the horse's reins and throwing them over the railing for Ben. His eyes begged for news, but he knew, after so many trips and so many disappointments, that it was better not to ask.

"No longer than all the others," Ben sighed. "And no shorter, either."

"Sorry." Sunny offered him a cheroot, which he declined.

"How is she?" he asked, inclining his head toward the house.

"Sure she's dyin'," Sunny said, his eyes rolling. "Doc came out yesterday. Told her to get some sun, go into town, but she ain't been outta that chair 'cept to go to bed."

"She eating?"

Sunny nodded. "You didn't hear nothin' that might change her mind about going to St. Louis? Nothin' that might give her a little hope?"

Ben shook his head. "Checked with the ladies in the cribs, this time, like you suggested. There ain't a paid-for woman in the territory I didn't ask, and while they all knew him, not one of them has seen him in over a year."

"Heard the Tate girl, Emily, got herself planted," Sunny said, glancing out over the field, unable to look Ben in the eye.

"I still don't believe all that, Sunny," Ben said, shaking his head. "My son was too smart to get mixed up with the Tate boys. It can't be the way they said."

"He threw away his life over some woman," Anna Westin said as she came slowly onto the porch. God, she'd aged in the last year. "That's your fault, Ben Westin, and I'll never forgive you."

Ben rolled his eyes at Sunny and grimaced. Here it came again. How he'd never taught his son to respect women, how he'd taken him to the cribs when he was barely old enough to be out of his own.

"Sloan's a good-looking boy. He can't help it if women just naturally take to him. So he maybe sampled more than his share, Anna," Ben began.

"And it cost him his life," she yelled. "His life!"

"He ain't dead, Anna," he said quietly.

"What?"

"I said he ain't dead."

"Did you find something?" she asked, her hand on his arm. She turned her face toward his, and he could see for a moment the woman he married so long ago, her eyes glistening with tears, her lip quivering slightly, the tip of her tongue caught between her teeth, and those deep dimples she shared with Sloan.

He nodded. "It's too soon to be sure," he said. She could take it however she wanted. It didn't matter to him. Not much did, anymore.

*   *   *

Mary Grace had no feeling left in her legs. They had gone through discomfort, then pain, and now they had slipped into the numb state she currently found herself in. She felt nothing below her waist anymore, not the need to relieve herself, not the soreness of her bottom, not even the intimacy of Sloan Westin's seat pressed against her most private of places.

Her arms weren't much better. The only thing that had kept them from going to sleep was that she could, every now and then, let go of Sloan and shake the feeling back into them. But since the baby had fallen back to sleep, she'd been afraid to move and disturb him.

So, when Sloan finally stopped the horse, she wasn't sure she could trust her legs to hold her up.

"Where are we?" she asked, stalling while she tried straightening her legs and bending them again, testing whether they would support her when Sloan lowered her to the ground. They were surrounded, for the first time since they had met, by cacti. While the exposure on the open desert frightened her, here among the strangely shaped trees, behind any one of which the Tates could be lurking, she was even more afraid.

"Welcome to the Joshua-tree forest," Sloan said, gesturing with his hand at the contorted plants around them. He breathed in deeply himself. "Take a whiff."

Perfume filled the air around them. Mary Grace inhaled and shut her eyes to savor the pleasant aroma.

"Sweet. Like you," he said, shifting to lower her off the horse and place her gently on the ground.

Mary Grace had no illusions about her condition as she leaned against the horse to keep her balance. "I wish I smelled so sweet," she said to the horse's rear. Miraculously, she managed to keep her footing. She looked down at her feet as if to make sure they were touching the ground and cried out. There, at her feet, were the remains of a dead snake. She knew it was dead. She could see the luster gone out of its pebbly black and orange skin.

Sloan's gun was out of his holster, and he was looking for a place to aim it. "What?" he asked her. "What is it?"

She pointed, and he squinted his eyes to make out the snake in the dark.

"Ain't nothin' but a dead old coral snake," he told her. "I'd hate to hear you if you saw a live one!"

"Oh God! If there's a dead one there could be a live one, couldn't there?" She moved closer to Sloan and the horse.

"They ain't nothin' to worry about," he told her in a voice so calm it was almost unnatural. "You hear me, Sweet Mary? You ain't got nothin' to worry about. A coral snake can't hurt you."

She shook her head at her own ignorance. What a silly fool she was becoming, scared of her own shadow. She reached up to take the baby from Sloan, but before he put Ben in her arms she stumbled and wound up on her hands and knees.

"Jeez," Sloan said, moving the horse slightly so that he had room to swing off. "You all right?" he asked, leaning to help her up.

"Don't you get tired of asking that?" she said, straightening up with as much dignity as she could muster. "Aren't you just sick of taking care of me? It's like having two babies along with you."

He grabbed at her arm, but she pulled away and headed off into the bushes, stamping to warn any creatures that might think of her sore bottom as a tasty meal.

"Take your time," he yelled after her, and she could hear him moving around through the brush. What she wouldn't give for the privacy of a little bathroom now. She'd sell her soul for a piece of toilet paper. Her stomach ached, no doubt objecting to the new foods it was getting. Apparently, cactus pear didn't have quite the same effect on her as it did on little Patrick. *Ben, Mary Grace. The baby's name is Ben. Sloan's baby. Sloan's baby's name is Ben. That wasn't so hard to remember, was it?*

And they weren't a family, the three of them, no matter how good it felt to pretend. At this point in her life, she thought she knew better than to play that dangerous game. Men weren't built that way. They didn't have that need for family, that desire to take care of their own. Even the men who kidnapped their children were doing it to hurt their wives. They certainly weren't doing it because they loved their babies and had a need to be with them that was so strong they would risk their very lives to hug them to their chests and . . . She stopped herself. Sloan Westin was a man.

Men didn't take to heart the responsibility for their children the way women did. That was why some women worked two jobs a day while their deadbeat husbands shrugged off the child support. That was why some girls were left high and dry and on their own to cope with a pregnancy that was as much or more the man's responsibility. . . . She stopped herself again.

She knew men.

She knew what they were capable of. And what they were incapable of. She did. She'd spent all her adult life painfully aware of it and learning from the lessons of her youth. She knew men. She just didn't know Sloan Westin. "And I don't want to," she muttered to the bush she squatted by.

It turned out he'd been right about the prickly pear. She stood on shaky legs, sore from riding, sore from squatting, sore from the sheer effort of holding her body away from Sloan's, and made her way back to where she thought she had left Sloan and the horse, but there was no sign of him. In the distance a small fire glowed, and she dragged her aching body toward it, hoping it was theirs, half-ready to surrender if it wasn't.

The fire was burning within a ring of rocks when she reached it, the familiar poncho stretched out beside it, Climber's saddle at one end like a pillow. Sloan and the baby were nowhere in sight.

The canteen hung from one of the odd-looking trees, and she shook it. Full! She fought the tree for possession, its spiky arms not willing to relinquish its prize without a fight. Too tired to wrestle, she finally allowed the strap to remain where it was, squatted some until she was low enough and treated herself to some fresh water. Hot, minerally, and a far cry from Evian, it was still the sweetest thing she had ever tasted.

She tipped her head back to indulge in one more small sip, not wanting to drink more than her share, when a shot rang out.

"No-o-o!" she screamed, running in the direction of the noise. She could hear the baby crying, and she pushed her skirt up into her waistband to give herself more freedom to run.

Her eyes down to make sure she was on firm ground, she nearly ran right into Sloan and the baby. "Whoa!" he said, stopping her in her tracks with two firm arms against her shoulders. "If the Tates don't get me, sweet lady, I'm afraid you will."

"Get down, you idiot," she hissed. "Didn't you hear that shot?"

She tried to pull at him, but he was immobile. In the

moonlight she thought she saw him smiling. What was the matter with him? Why was he letting the baby cry?

"Supper," he said, holding up a small brown animal she didn't recognize. "I got us a real supper."

"Supper?" She didn't think she even wanted to know. "The shot?"

"And a good thing, too, you little fool. What were you thinking to come running? You coulda got yourself killed."

The woman who faced him was more frightened than angry. Her breath was ragged, and she was trying to keep her emotions in check. She seemed unable to calm herself down, despite all his assurances, so he put one arm around her and pressed her to his side. One of her arms was wrapped around the baby nestled securely against his chest. The other clung to his back in a death grip. He waited for her to calm down, listening to her sharp intakes of air and the shuddering way she let each breath go.

If one little gunshot did this to her, he didn't want to think of her reaction should the Tate boys ever catch up to them. He moved his good leg, shifting his weight, hinting with his body that they should go back to the fire. She made no move, just held on all that much tighter for his having even suggested it.

So he just stood there, letting her burrow into his armpit with her shoulder, her hair tickling his neck, the outer curve of her breast rising and falling against his chest, and tried to think about other things. There were plenty of problems to occupy his mind: food, shelter, safety. But none seemed to be as pressing as how to stop Sweet Mary from rubbing her thigh against his privates and making his bones turn as limp as a dead snake.

He felt the sudden change in her. Her body stiffened.

Her weight returned to her own feet. She slipped the baby from the sack on his chest and turned toward the fire.

"Sweet Mary?" he said quietly, his concern for her masking his own sense of loss at her sudden distance. "You all right?"

She didn't answer him. She just started walking toward the fire, her body rigid, her steps flat and determined.

"Now where are you going?" he asked. Again, she didn't answer. "Look," he said to her back, "I shoulda told you where I was going. I shouldn'ta shot without you knowing it was coming. It was right of you to be scared."

She plopped down silently by the fire, the baby in her arms, the heat suffusing her face. She winced, and he guessed the sunburn hurt. Hell, nothing, probably not even her pride, hurt.

"I'm sorry I scared ya," he said. *But I ain't sorry about the way you was clinging to me, Sweet Mary,* he added silently. He bent his good knee so that he could somewhat squat in front of her and dropped one hand between his legs to hide any evidence of her effect on him. She looked up at him with glistening eyes.

"I don't understand anything. I thought we had to be really quiet so that the Tates wouldn't know where we are. Then you use your gun. I don't get it."

She was right, of course. He'd been careless. And with Mary Grace and the baby depending on him, he couldn't afford to be. "We're closer to home than to Oak Creek Canyon by now, Sweet Mary," he said. "And I figured we were all hungry. We ain't seen hide nor hair of 'em since the flood, and the boy's gotta eat. He ain't gonna grow on grass like a damn cow."

Somewhere in his explanation was an admission that he'd been reckless. She caught it despite his efforts to disguise it in concern for his son. If the child even was his son. If he wasn't, she and the baby were in for some rough times on their own.

"You don't think the Tates are still after us, do you?" she asked.

He shrugged. "Think they'da caught us by now, but you never can tell. Men like the Tates coulda been sidetracked by anything. Your mama ever tell you that story about the tortoise and the hare?"

"You think we're the tortoise?" she asked, wanting to believe that in the end they would beat the Tates to safety.

"We sure ain't the hare." He laughed. It was like a game to him suddenly, with his parents' ranch so near. Somehow, feeling as tired and beaten as she did, she just couldn't see it that way. He turned away from her and pulled his knife from his belt. It gleamed in the firelight, and her voice caught in her throat.

"I don't belong here," she told Sloan, realizing he was preparing the animal he had shot for roasting.

"No one belongs here, Sweet Mary. This is the desert. We'll be at my folks' before ya know it, eatin' the best food, sleepin' in the softest beds. Just wait till my mama sees this little cowboy." He chucked Ben under the chin. "She'll be willin' to forget everything when she sees him."

"It's a good thing Mason Tate doesn't know who your folks are," Mary Grace said, taking off Paddy's smelly garments and letting the fire warm his naked body.

"Sweet Mary, I'm not exactly a nobody. Mason Tate knows where my folks are, same as most people in the territory." He twisted around, turning his head to look at her. She hadn't realized until then that he had been shielding the dead animal from her sight.

"But then don't you think that's the first place the Tates will go looking for you and little Pad . . . Ben?"

He shrugged as if that didn't worry him.

"Is there something I don't know?" she asked him in exasperation. "Some reason that we, or you, and the baby will be safe there?"

"There'll be four, maybe five of us, against just three of them," he said, turning back to his work.

"That's it? That's the whole plan? You're kidding, right?"

"Hmm?" he answered, intent on threading the animal onto a stick and positioning him over the fire. The bile rose in Mary Grace's stomach. She'd been a vegetarian since she'd left home, when even the gray patty between the halves of a sesame seed bun made her stomach turn to mush. And that wasn't *animal* like this was animal. She kept her eyes on Sloan and her mind on the danger at hand.

"It never occurred to you that you were endangering your whole family, did it? That your mother could get killed? Your father? Ben?" She held the baby tightly and he squirmed.

Sloan's face was blank, as though he hadn't thought about the consequences to his family.

"Well, what would you do?" he asked finally.

She didn't know. She was tired, bone tired. She was hungry, and filthy, and sick of being scared. She missed her home and the comforts of her century. She wanted a cold drink, a hot meal, and a soft bed. And she didn't want to look down and check out what she felt crawling across her foot.

"Oh my God!" she whispered as the giant spider crawled over one foot and onto the other.

"What?" he said, turning around to stare at her.

Her eyes never left the hairy beast, bigger than the width of her foot, and now resting on it, two of its legs edging over the top of her moccasin.

"That?" Sloan asked, coming closer and pointing to

her leg. "It's just a tarantula." He reached down and put his hand where the spider would crawl onto it. She had never had a braver deed done for her, she thought. But he didn't drop it and step on it, or run his knife through it, or any such thing. Instead he let it crawl from one hand to the other, alternating his hands so the spider didn't run out of places to crawl.

"What are you doing?" she fairly shrieked, climbing atop the rock she had been sitting on.

"I told you. It's just a tarantula. He won't hurt you unless you scare him."

"Obviously," she said, trying to maintain her calm, "you've never seen *Arachnophobia*. Get rid of this spider. Now!"

He walked some distance from the fire and bent down, letting the spider loose. "Arachno . . . what?" he asked when he returned.

"Never mind." Her words were clipped, and her fear turned quickly to anger as he began to laugh at her. He made her feel silly and childish and like some spoiled rich girl who'd never had to deal with real life before.

A lot he knew. She'd dealt with the realities of life since she was a small child in a household where if her parents ever forgave even the smallest of transgressions, they assured her that God would not forget. And when she'd made her really big mistake, she'd grown up faster than anyone should have had to.

She didn't feel the least bit sorry for herself, but she resented terribly the fact that he seemed to think she was unable to cope with a little adversity. As if falling through time, being lost on the desert, and being chased by angry madmen were just some little inconveniences she should be able to take in stride.

"Come on," he said, standing in front of her, his hands out for the baby.

She handed Paddy up but refused the hand he offered to her.

"It'll cook a while," he said, gesturing toward the meat roasting over the fire and filling the air with a crisp smell that made her mouth water despite her mind's revulsion. "Come with me and take Ben's things."

He led her through the Joshua-tree forest, the flowers filling the air with an exotic scent that overpowered even the perspiration and the smell of the baby's clothing she held in her hands, toward a small outcropping of boulders. He turned sideways to slip between two rocks and then beckoned her to follow.

Moonlight glistened off a tiny pond. Surrounding the pool were tall rocks, jutting up toward the stars and providing complete privacy for the three of them. He handed her the baby and reached into his pocket.

"Soap," he said and handed her a small hard dirt-covered clump. "Of a sort."

She didn't care what sort. She crept toward the water as though it were a sacred altar and knelt before it as if in prayer. Her knees ached on the hard rock, but she ignored them as she reached in and tested the water. Warm! It was as warm as an inviting bathtub, and she let a sigh escape her lips.

"It's a natural pool," Sloan explained. "When the valley floods, water gets trapped in here, and then the sun warms it. It don't last long before it dries on up, but it's real clear 'cause there's a rock bottom, and with the yucca root, we can all clean up good."

She pushed up her sleeves. "Give me the baby." He took off the shirt he had draped around the child and handed him to Mary Grace. She leaned forward and eased him into the water, first his toes, then slowly his fat little legs until his raw bottom made contact with the soothing water, and finally his smooth chest. He squealed with delight, the first truly happy sounds they had heard him make. She heard Sloan's laughter behind her, mixing with her own.

Sloan moved closer, his body nearly touching hers, and tickled the baby's tummy. Ben laughed and kicked his legs, spraying them both with water.

"If he ain't the cutest," Sloan said, chucking him under his chin. "All babies got that little dent in their chins, Sweet Mary?"

"Uh-uh," she said, swaying slightly with all the baby's jumping around. Sloan reached out a hand and steadied her at the elbow. She recovered her balance, but he left his hand there, anyway. "Some babies have dimples," she said, dunking the child and bringing him up. "Some babies have clefts in their chins," she said and dunked again. "Some babies have blue eyes." Dunk. "Some babies have brown." Dunk. "Some babies look like their mamas." Dunk.

And then her hands seemed to freeze where they were, and the spell was broken. She wasn't his mama. She wasn't even sure Sloan was his dad. She did know that they weren't the happy little family they seemed to be.

She lifted the baby, his chubby legs kicking the water and soaking her, his arms flailing and splashing and finally clapping with the sheer joy of it. She smiled despite the lump that had grown in her chest. For right now, for this moment, the baby was hers.

Sloan suggested that they wash the clothes later, reminding her of the supper that awaited them. She made a face at the thought of eating the animal but said nothing, afraid that Sloan might make fun of her for being so prissy.

"It's already dead," he said as they walked back, his arm around her for warmth. "We might as well eat it."

Surprised, Mary Grace nodded. Of course, she

would feed it to the baby, but it wouldn't pass her lips. She tried to remember if she'd mentioned to Sloan about not eating animals. She must have. How else would he have known it bothered her?

He settled her and the baby on the horse's saddle, sitting sideways, and pulled the poncho up around them before checking on their meal. She winced when he wiggled a leg, testing for doneness.

He removed the animal from the fire and cut it into pieces with his knife. He gave her a small piece to tear up for the baby. Then he handed her a larger piece meant for herself. She looked first at it, then at him. Shaking her head, she held it back out to Sloan.

"I can't eat it. I'll just wait until we're at your parents' place and have something there. In the meantime the grass and stuff is just fine for me. But I agree that the baby should have some protein. I wish we had some milk for him." She looked down at her chest. Damn useless apparatus at the moment. "Well, when do you figure we'll be there? The day after tomorrow?"

He shook his head and held out the meat to her again. "Eat it, Sweet Mary. Tomorrow we change direction and head north."

"North?" She examined the meat, the traitorous acids in her stomach rumbling and calling for her to put the food in her mouth.

"I got to thinking about what you said. Truth is, I wouldn't want to come running home to my folks with my tail between my legs, expecting them to bail me out of another scrape. We been lucky so far, and there ought to be a marshall in Prescott or Jerome that would be pretty interested in where the Tates' hideout is, don't you think? Once I get rid of the Tates, then I can go home." He raised her chin with his finger and looked into her eyes. "So eat."

"You're gonna want them to follow us away from

your parents' ranch, aren't you?" she asked. She'd played the decoy before, once or twice, in her work. But never for such high stakes. And never without some kind of fail-safe system to ensure her safety as well as that of the child she sought.

"I won't let anything happen to you," he promised. "Think you can be brave a little longer?"

Brave? Did he really think she was being brave? She stored the compliment away in her heart and tried to stay with the matter at hand. Later, when they went to sleep, and she heard the howls of the coyotes and the screeches of other wild things, she might just pull out his compliment to keep her warm.

"And after the Tates aren't a threat to you anymore," she asked, "then what?"

Sloan leaned back, his hands behind his head, a wide grin of white teeth separating the dirty blond mustache from the dirty blond beard.

"Ah," he sighed. "Then my life starts again. Can't break horses anymore, I'll admit that, but I can still rope and ride worth a damn and drive cattle better than any two men my size."

"And Ben? You've got someone to watch Ben?" The thought was harder to swallow than the meat. It was getting harder and harder to imagine turning this child over to someone else's arms. She'd done it enough times before, but this wasn't her professional life, and this time she knew it was going to hurt as almost nothing had hurt her before.

He nodded. How many times was she gonna ask him the same damn thing? Hadn't he told her his ma would take the kid? What did she think he was gonna do? Leave him by the road somewheres? What did she expect him to do? Keep him strapped to his damn back for the rest of his life?

"You ain't eating."

"I ain't . . . I'm not hungry."

"Prairie dog is kinda an acquired taste, at best," he conceded. "Once we get to town you won't need to stay with us anymore, you know." He watched her arms tighten around the baby. He was going to have one heck of a time separating those two, that was for sure.

She fed the child a few strips more and then sat with the bone in her hand as if she wasn't even aware it was there. Her eyes were off somewhere in the sky, and he wondered what she was thinking about.

"So where are you really from, Sweet Mary, and how'd you wind up at the Tates' place? Took me four months to find that little hole in the wall. You can't expect me to buy that you just got there by some accident."

Her eyes never left the sky. When she spoke, Sloan got the impression she spoke as much to herself as to him. As if she was trying to keep things straight in her own mind, or maybe she was just sticking to her story, he wasn't sure. She didn't seem to be saying it for him, that much he believed.

"My name is Mary Grace O'Reilly. I was born in New York in 1966. I grew up in a little town called Roscoe, whose one claim to fame is that they have a diner on the main road. My father and mother, good Irish Catholics, had two boys before I was born, and six more children after me. I spent the better part of my fifteenth year with my grandmother in Watertown. I left home when I was eighteen."

New York. Well that would account for a lot. No wonder things like spiders and snakes got the better of her. And the gunshot. She'd probably never even heard a gun go off till she traveled west.

"That when you came to Arizona?" Except for the year of her birth, he wasn't having any trouble with her story so far. Of course, the year was a problem, a big one.

She shook her head. "I traveled a lot for about a year, looking for answers I was sorry I found."

The baby fussed in her arms. Without even looking down, she managed to give him her knuckle to chew on. Why they were developing that habit eluded Sloan, but he didn't want to interrupt to ask. In the last five minutes he'd finally got the woman who was risking her life for his son to tell him something about herself. He wasn't going to stop her now when she was so close to the end of her story.

"And then?" he prompted.

She rose and stretched her back. Then she pivoted and held the baby pointed away from her, guessing right that he would be making one of his frequent yellow fountains. She'd mastered a way of getting him to drink from the canteen and the water came out about as fast as it went in.

"Then," she said tersely, her voice suddenly signaling the end of the intimate conversation, "I moved to L.A., took a job, and devoted myself to my work."

"L.A.?"

"Los Angeles. In California." She looked for him to acknowledge there was such a place. Hell, everyone knew about the City of Angels. Why, since they finished the railroad, there had to be upward of fifty thousand people living there between the oil derricks and the mines. He nodded at her to indicate even a cowboy like himself had heard of it.

"So how'd you come to be in the Arizona Territory on Mason Tate's front porch?" Damned if he'd give up now.

"I was looking for a child who was being kidnapped by his shitheel father. I fell into the dried-up riverbed, only it wasn't, and—" she raised one hand, palm up, "—here I am."

"I guess you found him."

"Who?"

"The child whose papa was kidnappin' him." He gestured toward Ben.

Mary Grace shook her head and smiled. "No," she said. "Actually, I didn't find him at all."

The fire was dying out, and he could see Mary Grace beginning to shiver. Her clothes were wet from bathing Ben, and she was hugging him to her body for warmth.

"I'll put some more wood on the fire," he said. "You think you can find your way back to the pool yourself?"

She nodded.

"Well, go ahead then. Leave Ben with me and take the blanket."

"But Ben. . ."

"Ben'll be fine. He's got the fire, he's got my shirt, and he's got my body if he needs more warmth than that." He'd taken to wearing the sling all the time, and when she handed him the naked infant he slipped him right in. Then he unbuttoned his shirt and closed it around the baby, encasing the child in both his father's shirt and his warmth.

"Don't forget the soap," he called after her, and she waved. He watched until she faded out of his vision and blended into the darkness before he remembered the fire needed more wood.

He wandered over to a crop of trees and found a few sticks that would burn. She sure was an odd one, his Sweet Mary. She was willing to put up with about the worst conditions he'd ever seen a white woman manage to cope with—sleeping on the ground, eating whatever he could forage, riding all day behind him on the horse, all of it with hardly a complaint.

He'd known only two kinds of women in his life. Those that would, and those that wouldn't. On the whole, he much preferred those that would. In addition, there were those that would for a few bucks if there wasn't one around who'd just settle for a smile. But there were plenty that gave it away, too, at least to him.

Of course, that was before Harlin Tate left his calling card all over Sloan's body. If Mary Grace's reaction to seeing just his chest was any indication, he'd better be prepared to shell out a pretty penny for any favors that might come his way. And then there was the awkwardness of it all. He didn't even want to contemplate that.

From all her shyness it was clear that his Sweet Mary didn't fall into the same category as most of the women he knew. She was what he called a forever woman. Make love to them once, and they expected you to love them forever. And before you got in their drawers, you had to promise them forever. And if you weren't really careful, you'd wind up stuck with them forever.

He thought again of the woman who was taking care of his son. Oh, she was a forever woman all right, but not in the way he'd always taken it to mean. She made him wonder what it would be like to come home at night to a family that belonged to him. She made him think about tomorrow, and the next day, and even next year. She made him long for the other children he might never father, and she made him ache to try.

Dear God, but it scared him! This wasn't the time in his life to be thinking about women, forever or otherwise. Maybe after he'd taken care of the Tates, got his revenge, and sowed a few more oats, then he might be ready to settle down with Ben and some woman. Sure would be nice to see that little fellow grow.

While he scrounged for wood, Ben fell asleep. When he'd found enough to get them through the night, Sloan made his way over to the pond to check on Mary Grace. He'd meant just to call out to her, but with Ben asleep he thought it better simply to slip though the rocks and see that she was all right.

For a moment he stood just inside the natural doorway, taking in the sight. She had washed her clothes first, and they hung from a small tree that had defied the odds and grown from a crevice between two boulders. Wet from head to toe, she had come out of the water to pick something off the ground. The soap, he supposed.

He watched soundlessly as the moon shone off her wet body and set her aglow in the darkness. She was magnificent, and he cautioned himself to go slowly with her. He supposed he was just confused, what with suddenly having a son to worry about and her on top of that. Sometimes he felt as protective about her as he did about the boy. And something told him she was more scared of him crawling on her than another tarantula.

Her skin was smooth, unlined even when she bent over to reach the soap. An ugly bruise marred her back, no doubt the result of his pulling her up onto the rocks when the flood threatened.

He thought of the other women he knew and imagined the haranguing he'd have received if he'd been so careless as to cause one of them any injury. As she slipped back into the water and swam gracefully toward the other side, he tucked his head against his chest and eased out of the baby's sling. Poor Ben was so tired he didn't even stir.

Sloan laid him carefully on the rocks, making sure he could keep an eye on the sleeping child while he allowed himself the luxury of a soak in their private tub. He slithered out of his pants and entered the water in his long johns. Once submerged to the waist, he pulled the underwear off and tried to wash it, aware that Mary Grace was watching him carefully from the other side of the small lake.

She kept herself hidden, the water up to her chin, and all he could see clearly was her wet hair shimmering in the moonlight. But he knew what treasures lay buried beneath the surface of the water, and it was enough to make him grow hard with longing.

He swam up near her, not close enough to frighten her, and asked for the soap. He held his underwear in front of himself in spite of the darkness and the deep water. Whether it was for her sake or his own that he kept himself covered, he wasn't sure.

She told him that the soap rested safely on the shore once again. She'd been afraid she'd lose it in the water, and she wanted the luxury of using it again in the morning. Would they have time? Her attempts at a normal conversation amused him. If he was nervous, she was twice so.

The harder she tried to seem at ease, the more her hands flew to her hair, wiped water out of her eyes, hugged her own arms. And with each movement his own feelings grew bolder. When she lifted her arms, her breasts nearly escaped their protective waters. When she hugged herself, the empty space between her breasts became brazen cleavage, all the more provoking because she had no idea what she was doing to him, no intention of doing it, and no escape from the results.

"I brought the soap," he said slyly. "It seems only fair that you share it with me."

"Of course," she said, not understanding. "I told you it's on the rock over there."

"Would you get it for me? It's hard with my leg."

"Oh!" She moved closer to the shore and realized the water was quickly getting shallower. She was too nervous to pay any attention to his movements.

"Have you got it?" he whispered by her ear. She jumped at his nearness, her slippery body crashing up against his, knocking his feet out from under him. He tried to right himself, grabbing for a handhold and coming in contact with her nakedness.

Thinking he was in danger of drowning, she reached out a hand to him and tried to steady him. Instead, he held her hand and swam backward, dragging her into the deeper water with him, pulling her closer against him.

"The soap," she wailed, having lost it in the struggle.

"I'll find you more tomorrow."

"Ben. Do you think he's all right over there? I think I'd better check him."

He didn't let her go. He pulled her closer to him, his manhood brushing first one leg and then the other.

"I'm not a very good swimmer," she said, backing away from him slightly.

"Just hold on to me," he said. "You don't need to swim, at all." He tried to pull her to him, to lift her legs until they encircled his waist, but she shied away. She reminded him of a wild horse that needed taming. He had told her he was the best at that. He intended to prove it. Maybe he couldn't break horses anymore, but one young woman ought to be able to be persuaded. . . .

"Shhh, now, Sweet Mary. Let me get that soap out of your hair. There's nothing to be afraid of. Have I hurt you yet?" he asked. She trod water a mere two feet from him. He could hear her breath, ragged and heavy.

"Turn around," he directed, spinning her in the water until her back was to him. "Now put your head back. I ain't gonna hurt you. Further. There's soap up by the top."

She leaned back, and as she did her body began to float. Her breasts rose from the surface of the water like twin peaks, the tops ablaze with deepened color. Her femininity lifted out of the pond for a moment, the hair glistening in the moonlight and then falling again below the surface. Rivulets of water made lines across her belly, shimmering like veins of silver in a darkened mine.

He played with her hair as though he was trying to remove the soap, and followed it to its ends, trailing them over her chest. He thought for a moment about which nipple Ben had brutalized, looked quickly over to make sure the child was still asleep and safe, and then gently took the unbruised breast in his hand.

She stiffened beneath him, but she didn't pull away. Maybe he'd read her wrong after all. Maybe she was more willing than he'd figured. The thought emboldened him. He hadn't been with a woman who hadn't been bought and paid for since he'd lain with Emily Tate. And for some reason he couldn't put his finger on, Sweet Mary wasn't just any woman.

He eased his way down from Mary Grace's head so that he was next to her, subtly moving her to where he was able to stand, but continuing to ripple the water so that it danced over her floating body.

He dipped his head and kissed the tip of her nipple, his lips barely brushing the skin. She hardened under his gaze, and this time when he leaned to kiss her breast, he took the nub within his mouth, running his tongue over the captured bud. The water rushed in and out of his mouth, wetting her over and over, making his mouth slide over her nipple, encouraging him to explore the whole mound with his tongue.

One hand supported the small of her back, keeping her afloat. The other began to trail its way down her midriff, creeping lower and lower until his fingers tangled in the web of her curly hair. Her own hand rested against his torso, tentatively tracing his ribs. She reached his scars, and her probing fingers examined them.

He tried to ignore the image of his own body that came into his mind. His fingers were searching on their own, looking for the entrance to her femininity, wishing she would spread herself and let him in. His lips moved up to her neck, and the hand beneath her back slackened to let her middle sink slightly. As she sank in the warm water, her hand trailed down his stomach, and his own breath pounded in his ears. One hand still rested under her back, massaging her gently, but it was the hand that gripped her femininity that kept her afloat. She pressed herself against him, arching toward the moonlit sky, her eyes closed and her face serene.

Her hand trailed lower and lower on his abdomen until it reached his manhood. "Touch me," he whispered by her ear.

"Oh my God!" she said, tears coming to her eyes unexpectedly. She pulled away from him, pushing against his chest with her arm, her knee, eventually her foot, then swimming rapidly across to the other side of the pond as if she had discovered a Gila monster in her hand.

His own hand reached down, and he felt himself, now limp, his finger seeking out the familiar scar. He had been fooling himself if he thought it didn't matter. He couldn't get over his own stupidity. He'd have been able to take her, right there in the water, without her ever knowing, if he hadn't said those two little words. What was it that circus fellow once said? There's a sucker born every minute. And he was this minute's boy.

Had it been some two-bit whore, he might have been able to shrug it off. The fact that it was Sweet Mary cut him to his bones, leaving his pride to bleed him dry as he stood alone in the water.

Mary Grace bounded up onto the rocks, scraping her shin, and threw the poncho around her shoulders. The baby looked fine. Sure that Sloan would see to him, she ran, slipping through the crack in the rocks, back to the campfire and sat down by the dwindling embers.

So many years had passed. Still, it was not enough. Was she never going to get over her mistakes? And what did she think she was doing back there in the pond, except maybe making yet another mistake? Why hadn't she stopped him sooner? Because, she admitted, she liked what he was doing. Liked how it made her feel, all liquid inside, warm and limp and so different than a man must feel.

That was it. The feel of him in her own hand. Hearing him tell her what to do. So much like before, so close to disaster. Just when she'd thought that her past was behind her and that she could see each man for himself and think maybe, someday, about a life that included a husband and children, she'd touched the past with her fingers and the future had slipped through them.

And even if she'd been able to go through with it, could she ever tell a man like Sloan, a man whose world was so different from hers, revolving around revenge and good and bad and right and wrong, what she had done?

She could hear his footsteps coming toward the fire, and she lay down on the ground, pretending to be asleep. He came and stood near her, his naked body dripping on her face. He laid the baby down next to her, and then he was gone.

Through tiny slits she saw him throw more wood on the fire. Then he returned to her side.

"You're gonna have to share that blanket, Mary Grace, like it or no. I been good to you, and patient. I don't deserve to freeze to death just for bein' the man I am."

8

He took his place on the other side of the baby and pulled the covers out of Mary Grace's hands until she lay stark naked before his eyes. It took every ounce of strength he had not to reach out and touch her. Her hip was a mottled brown and blue from her ride over his saddle, and her knee was drawn up, hiding her womanhood from his view. Her breasts were pressed together as she lay on her side, her arm thrown across them modestly.

She was shuddering visibly, and Sloan didn't know whether cold or fear or pure misery made her quake beneath his gaze. He tucked the three of them under the poncho and put his arm under his head, gazing up at the clear night, listening for the sounds of Ben and Mary Grace sleeping.

Ben's quiet breathing was an even whistle near his father's ear. But Mary Grace lay silent, as if she was holding her breath. He raised himself up on one elbow to look at her in the firelight and could see wet streaks on her cheek.

"It's all right, Sweet Mary," he said quietly. "I'm not gonna touch you. Go to sleep."

The ragged breath she drew in startled him. It was so broken, so sad, so devoid of hope. He wasn't sure what he was supposed to say. How could he apologize for what had been done to him, and how it had affected her?

"It don't matter none. The scars don't hurt, 'cept the leg, and I'm used to the ugliness. My clothes'll be dry in the morning, and you won't need to be seeing no part of me from here on out."

He hadn't expected her to speak. He'd been talking as much to the sky or himself as he had been to her, and so it surprised him when he heard her voice.

"What scars?"

He moved out of the way of the fire, trying to get as much light on her face as possible. She was looking at him questioningly, her eyebrows lowered in concentration.

"What scars?" he repeated. "What scars? If it wasn't the scars, why the hell did you run like it was the undertaker measuring your ass?" He was sitting up now, and she struggled to keep the covers over her chest.

"I'm sorry," she said quietly. "I wanted to stay. I thought I could stay. But I couldn't."

She was breathing that ragged way again, and there was nothing he could do but sigh.

"It's OK, I told you," he said. "Don't go thinking you hurt my feelings or nothing. I know what I look like. I know what it feels like to touch. . . ."

A look of wonder came over Mary Grace's face. She nearly smiled as the thought dawned on her.

"You think I ran away because of you?" she asked. "Because of your gunshot wounds? Is that it?"

The blanket was nearly at his waist already. He

pulled it slightly lower, exposing the scars on his side, and then threw his stiff leg over the covers so that it too was visible in the light from the fire. His knee was gone, shattered by a bullet and then operated on by more than one Indian shaman who was trying to keep Chief Navaho convinced that he had the power to keep him alive. They had treated it with herbs, chants, poultices, and prayers, and they'd pinned it closed with yucca needle tips. It glowed red and angry in the dim light.

"Look at 'em, Mary Grace. Get your fill. After tonight you won't never have to look at 'em again."

Her fingers reached out toward him, and he flinched. What the hell was she doing? One of her fingertips traced the circular scars on his chest, and then made its way tentatively down his leg.

"How did you get them all? Did Harlin shoot you so many times?"

He nodded. Her hand was freezing cold on his leg, and yet it burned him everywhere she touched. "Emptied two six-shooters." At her shocked look he amended his words. "He was a lousy shot."

"He could have killed you."

He laughed. "That was the general idea." Her hand was more than he could stand. He removed it and tucked them both back under the covers.

"Why?"

He hesitated. It had never really made all that much sense to him. Well, it was as good a time as any to make her realize just what kind of man he was. "Caught me between his sister's legs. S'pose if they'd known about Ben they'd a made me part of the family, so you'd have to say I was lucky, wouldn'tcha? Course, at the time, I didn't think so. Prayed I'd die for a long time. Just didn't. Damn Havasupai shamans wouldn't let me."

"Native American spiritualists saved your life?"

"Huh? Who?"

"The Native American spiritualists."

What on earth was she talking about now? Every time he thought they were having a normal discussion, she'd change horses midstream and wind up on a mule going in the other direction.

"The Havasupai ain't Americans. They're Indians. Don't know what tribes you got near you, but we got Apache, Yavapai, Navajo, Hopi, and my good friends the Havasupai. Live down in the canyon. My luck they were up on the mesa hunting and found me after Harlin left me for dead."

"Why didn't the Tates just make you marry Emily? Or wouldn't you?"

He thought about it. "Hell of a price to pay for a roll in the hay, don't you think?"

Her eyes flew to Ben, his dark curly hair sticking up around his face, his lips sucking the air.

"You're thinkin' Emily paid," he said. "Maybe I'd a married her, I don't know. I didn't have the luxury of the choice. Bet Harlin caught hell for feeding me to the coyotes, though. Last thing I heard Emily say before I passed out was something like 'I didn't think you'd kill him, Harlin!' Damned if I know how the hell he ever found us. . . ."

"And then he just left you for dead?"

It was the first time he'd ever told the story, and it surprised him how exciting it sounded. The truth was it was a quick hop in the sack; a blur of gunfire; and a long, slow, painful recovery. Sweet Mary's wide eyes helped make it seem better than it was.

"Guess so. I woke up once or twice on the way down to the floor of the canyon. The pain was so bad I kept passing out. That, and I musta run outta blood, the way it was pouring outta me."

"Why did the Native Americans help you instead of bringing you to a hospital?"

"Who?"

"The Havasupai," she corrected herself. Sloan wondereed why she seemed to have a problem with the term "Indian." Maybe she'd had some trouble from them somewhere along the way. He'd have to remember to ask.

"Well, they aren't supposed to come out of the canyon, and they sure couldn't just go waltzing into some town, even if there'd been one nearbys. But Navaho's son was the real reason, I think. He didn't like what his father was doing to the shamans, and I guess he thought I was as good a way as any to stop him."

"I don't understand."

The fire was dying down, and Sloan turned over, reached the pile of sticks he'd gathered and threw a few more onto the burning embers. Sparks shot up and for a moment the little campsite looked like a party. He turned back to Mary Grace. That hair of hers sure did dance in the light. Little sparks danced in her eyes and shadows played across her pretty face. It took him a minute before he remembered what she'd wanted explained.

"The old man was killing off all the shamans that couldn't save his people. Well, everyone knows the Indian is a dying breed, and a couple years ago I'da said amen to that, but anyway, shamans was being thrown off the cliffs with a certain regularity, and the chief's son, who spoke English better than me, which I guess ain't so hard, convinced his father to let the medicine men live as long as they could keep me alive."

"So they kept themselves alive by keeping you alive."

He nodded. "It's late now, Sweet Mary. Go to sleep."

"I'm sorry," she said as they tried to get comfortable. "About before."

"Nothing for you to apologize for," he said, wishing the poncho reached all the way around him so that his back wasn't exposed to the fire. She couldn't help the way she felt about his body, Sloan thought. He'd had over a year to get used to it, so by now it didn't look like the insides of a dead coyote to him anymore. But to her . . . well, he couldn't blame her.

"So long as you know it wasn't you, back there in the pond," she said.

"I didn't see no one else, Mary Grace. Now go to sleep."

He waited, but she didn't say anything more. Ten minutes went by. Then ten more. He tried to adjust the blanket, but it hadn't grown any longer.

"What's wrong?" her quiet voice asked in the darkness.

"Fire's hot on my back without the blanket there," he said. "But if I let it go out we're likely to be mistook for a cougar's dinner."

"Oh." Mary Grace paused. "Take more of the blanket. I don't need so much."

She lay too far from the fire to be feeling its warmth. Without the blanket she'd be freezing. He reached across Ben, searching for her arm. Whatever part of her it was he came in contact with felt ice cold, and she jumped higher than a bull frog at the touch of his hand.

"You sure are one cold woman," he said. "Don't think I'll be takin' a blanket offa you. Might be sleeping with a corpse, come morning."

"Maybe we should change places," she suggested. It was one thought, but he had another.

"If the baby wasn't between us, and we spooned, there'd be plenty of blanket for all of us."

"Spooned?"

He told her to stay where she was and worked his way around her. He rolled her on her side, facing the fire, and curled himself tightly against her back, pulling her into his chest. He tucked his good leg against the backs of her knees, forcing them to bend. She was stiff, cold, and silent. It was like holding an icicle.

"I ain't gonna do nothing, Mary Grace," he said, trying to keep the disappointment out of his voice. "You don't have to be afraid. You could always outrun me, you know."

"I'm sorry," she said.

"You say that a lot, but you never say what for."

"For before. If I was a tease, or anything."

"Why'd you run, Sweet Mary? You seemed to be liking what I was doing."

"I did. I know I shouldn't have, but I did."

Things were getting clearer. And her shoulders were easing some in his arms. Her skin was warming slightly at his closeness, and he couldn't get over the fact that it was every bit as soft as Ben's. He gently made little circles with his thumb near the base of her neck, easing the muscles that led to her shoulders. She was strung as tight as barbed wire. He was afraid to touch her, for fear of making a bad thing worse.

"Were you scared?" he asked. She nodded, her whole body shaking against him.

"Of me?"

A shrug was his answer.

He swallowed hard. He'd been with so many women who gave themselves so easily that he just hadn't thought that she wouldn't be like the rest of them.

"You ain't never been with a man, have you, Sweet Mary? Is that it?"

She shook her head. Did that mean she had? Or she

hadn't? He didn't know. He tipped her back slightly, trying to see her face. She was fighting tears, her lip quivering, her eyes all scrunched against the onslaught.

"So then you ain't?"

She nodded. He still wasn't sure.

"You have?" he tried again.

She nodded again, her shivering worse. It could only be one other thing.

"You married, and goin' against your vows?"

But she shook her head, thoroughly confusing him.

"Then what?" he asked in the voice he used for calming frightened stallions, stroking her hair, letting her lean against him without pushing his own body back against hers.

"A long time ago. Very long."

She was a young woman. He'd seen her whole body and there wasn't a wrinkle on it. He'd seen her climb mountains, carry Climber's saddle. "How long?"

"Thirteen years."

Dear God! Thirteen years! She'd have been a child. "Then it wasn't your choice," he said as delicately as he could.

"It wasn't rape," she said, and this time it was him shivering.

"Still, a horse oughta know better than to mate with a rabbit. . . ."

"I told you. I was willing."

"Just 'cause a rabbit's got her tail raised, ain't no reason for a horse to indulge himself, Mary Grace! You were a baby! No wonder you're scared to death of me."

"I wasn't a baby, not really. I was fifteen years old. Old enough to know what I was doing, and what could happen."

"Fifteen? Thirteen years ago? You sayin' you're twenty-eight years old?"

She nodded in answer to his question. If she was twenty-eight, then he was no lady's man. Getting her to say what was festering inside her was harder than trying to push a bear through a prairie-dog burrow.

"And what happened?" He wondered how much of what she said could be the truth. All this nonsense about traveling through time and being nearly thirty. How was it she could lie so blatantly and still he believed every word she said?

"I got what I deserved."

"That ain't tellin' me much."

"It's all I'm gonna tell you."

"Suit yourself," he said, taking his hand back from around her body and trying to find a place for it on his own. He rested it on his hip, flung it behind him, then stretched it out over his head, denying to himself that it belonged around the woman lying next to him, whether or not she wanted to tell him all her secrets.

It took a long time, during which he tried not to move a muscle, but finally Mary Grace managed to fall asleep. Sloan tried to sleep too, but he was still awake to see the rising of the sun. It was a peaceful moment, Mary Grace still in his arms, his son beginning to stir just beyond. He stretched the moment for as long as he could, and then he sneaked silently out from under the covers and made his way back to the pond.

It was still warm, despite the coolness of the night, and he checked on the diapers they had washed, found them dry, and gathered them to bring back to Sweet Mary and Ben, along with their clothes. Damn if they weren't beginning to feel like a family to him. The last thing he needed was feeling saddled with a wife and a kid. Bad enough he'd lost a year of his life because of the Tate boys. He wasn't gonna lose the rest of it, too. Three dead men, and he would be a free man again.

And he wasn't gonna be limited by anything more than his bum leg and a few scars.

He waded into the warm water, wishing it was deep enough to dive. A quick dip helped clear away the cobwebs, and then he donned his clean, dry clothes and headed back to the campfire.

Mary Grace and the baby were awake, she sitting like an old Indian with the blanket wrapped around her shoulders, the baby in her lap playfully grabbing at her breasts. She stood up, leaving the baby on the blanket and turned to look for more firewood.

Sloan stared at her naked body in the morning light. Her hands, sunburned at first, were now a deep tan, which went a good portion of the way up her arms. Her torso was stark white, interrupted by dusky nipples and abundant freckles. Deep red hair curled where her legs met, and her ankles and shins were almost as tan as her forearms. Beautiful as she was, Sloan found his eyes riveted on just one place—her stomach, where the morning sun revealed several silvery stretch marks across her belly.

9

She threw onto the fire whatever sticks were left, hoping to take the chill out of the morning. And yet, in a few hours she would surely be drenched with sweat again and wishing for a breeze. The desert was full of extremes, not the least of which was Sloan Westin.

He was nothing she expected him to be. He could talk easily about killing another man while wiping the dirty bottom of his little son. He'd been shot for messing with Emily Tate and given Mary Grace the definite impression that it was hardly the first time he'd been with a woman, and yet he was infinitely patient and gentle with her.

They'd lain under the blanket together naked all night, and he'd kept his hands and other parts to himself. And yet in the pool he'd . . . She shook her head, unwilling to think about it. And yet the thought of his hands on her breast made her nearly dizzy. It was nothing like the furtive grabs she had tried to put out of her mind for so long. The truth was she had liked everything he had done in the pond. That was what scared her more than anything else.

On her feet, she arched, twisted, and stretched, her fists pressed against the small of her back, her eyes shut tight. She was sore everywhere. Ben cooed, and she glanced over at him. His attention was riveted on something behind her.

Whirling around, she found Sloan staring at her, a pile of clothing in his arms. Her cheeks grew hot as she dashed to the blanket, scooped up the baby, and covered herself. He still stood, just where he was, staring as if she hadn't moved. The man had a way of looking without seeing, as if it wasn't her body but her soul he was trying to examine.

He seemed to be figuring something out, and Mary Grace was afraid to ask what it was. She held the baby more tightly to her, hoping to remind him they weren't alone. Paddy objected and squealed, bringing them both back from some precipice they couldn't name.

"Did you find any food?" Mary Grace asked awkwardly. Sloan nodded.

"Put these on," he said, handing her the clean clothing he had brought from the pool. "I'll be right back."

She waited until he was out of sight before dropping the blanket and donning Emily's clothes. As she dressed the baby, she thought about the tone in his voice. It said "We're not finished," and she braced herself for his attack.

By the time Sloan returned with some stringy-looking green stems, Mary Grace sat stiff as a rod, the baby freshly diapered and fussing in her lap. He put the greens into a small pan, added some water from their canteen, and set the concoction in the fire without saying a word. For a while, he didn't even look in her direction.

"Could you watch Paddy for a minute?" she asked, and was surprised to see him scowl at her. He'd never objected to taking care of the baby before. She supposed the baby could come with her, but she preferred to do her business alone.

"His name is Ben," Sloan corrected. "This one's *my* son."

She closed her eyes and wished the whole world would disappear before she opened them. This was not a pain she could go through again. Her stomach cramped. Without looking at Sloan, she snapped, "Then you shouldn't mind watching him for a while," and stalked away from the campsite.

When she returned, she found him feeding the baby the limp green stems, mashing them with his fingers and squeezing them between the baby's lips. Unknowingly, he played that old game of trying to land the airplane inside the hangar, hoping to distract Paddy from the taste of his breakfast with some fancy hand gestures. It was touching to see the big man sitting Indian style, his son in his lap, trying to entice the boy to eat. He heard her footsteps and looked up at her. Suddenly self-conscious, he gestured toward her plate, on which lay three or four stalks and some lifeless leaves. She supposed she made a face, because he laughed at her.

"It's pokeweed. It won't kill you."

She nodded and took a stem in her hand. She had to hold it above her mouth to reach the end, and she steeled herself as she opened her mouth to try it.

"Eat the damn thing," Sloan shouted at her. "Do you think we've got all day? The Tates are stupider than a herd of cattle fighting for their place in the slaughter line, but turning north means we're headed back into their arms. Now eat!"

Mary Grace quickly put the pokeweed in her mouth, surprised by its mild, sweet taste. She ate the rest of what was on her plate quickly, rose, and stood waiting for Sloan to finish so that she could rinse his plate along with her own down at the pond.

Without looking up, Sloan spoke. "So it was brand and strand without no band, huh?" he asked.

She mulled over what he said silently. Leave it to Sloan Westin to have a more colorful way of saying "wham, bam, thank you, ma'am."

She nodded and stooped for his plate, but he wouldn't release it.

"And the year at your granny's?" he asked. "That more like nine months?"

Her cheeks burned, and her eyes stung. It was hard to swallow around the knot in her throat. What right did he have asking her about any of this? What business was it of his?

"Six," she answered tightly. "I was chubby, and it didn't show for a while. And then after, I was shipped home while I was still bleeding. Would you like more details? How long I was in labor? What he looked like?" She had meant to embarrass him, to punish him for poking around where he didn't belong, but it wasn't working.

"Did he look like Ben?" Sloan asked softly, his hand still on one side of his plate, hers on the other.

"I never saw him."

"Sit down," he ordered, yanking the plate from her hand.

"Why?"

"Because it's damn hard for me to get up, Sweet Mary, and I don't like having this conversation with your knees."

"This conversation is over," she said, turning on her heel. "Wash your own damn plate!"

She was halfway to the pond when she heard him shout.

"Him and me, we ain't two coyotes from the same damn pack, Mary Grace O'Reilly."

She was running now, tears streaming, hands over her ears.

"I got my son with me, Sweet Mary, so don't you go acting holier than thou on me. I don't see your son nowheres, so before you go casting blame . . ."

Once she was through the rocks, she couldn't hear him. But she didn't need him to tell her what she had done, letting herself get pregnant, letting them ship her off to Watertown, letting them give her baby away. She stood with her arms wrapped around herself on the edge of the rocks, staring at her reflection in the pond. It danced as though she were swaying to some distant music. In the water she looked happy, contented, as though none of the things she had done had followed her into the magical little circle of rocks and water.

She picked up a rock and threw it at her reflection, watching the pieces of her break up and float away in a hundred directions. She picked up another pebble, and another, throwing them at herself again and again until Sloan's strong hands pinned her arms to her body.

"They don't stone women for havin' babies outta wedlock anymore, Sweet Mary."

He pried the pebbles lose from her clenched fists, and they rattled to the ground.

"They don't have to, Mr. Westin. We're perfectly capable now of doing it to ourselves."

She could see them in the water in front of her, looking like a couple. Her red hair covered his beard, but his blond mustache, his eyes, and the deep blond hair that shone from last night's washing stood above her own head. His arms were around her, and his stiff right leg stood just beyond her billowing skirt. It could have been a photograph of a loving couple if she hadn't known better.

"You ever see his daddy again?"

She shook her head.

"You ever wonder about the boy anymore?"

She shook her head again. "No, not anymore."

"And you ain't been with a man since?" His arms crossed her chest, and as he ran his hands slowly up and down her arms, his forearms came in contact with her breasts. She felt her nipples stiffen and knew he must be aware of it, as well.

"No, never been with another man."

"That can't have been easy," he said. "A young woman like you must spend the better part of your days swattin' at flies with this pretty red tail." He ran his fingers through her hair, and she let her head tilt back against his chest.

"It was easier than the alternative," she answered, pushing away from him and dipping down to get the plates. He bent slightly and grabbed her arm, pulling her up and close in to his chest. She knew what was coming, and she knew, too, that she had only to run, or say no, or simply push against his pull. Even stiffening in his arms would have stopped a man like Sloan.

But every fiber in her body tingled. Instead of pulling away, she leaned forward, into him, and raised her lips. Before she closed her eyes, she saw Sloan's son, his head peeking over his father's back, watching their exchange with interest.

"I'd a married Emily," he said simply before placing a kiss on the end of her nose. "If I'd a known. Did he know?"

Her body felt heavy with disappointment. She'd left every remnant of her previous life behind her but one.

The only one she could never get away from. And it had followed her through time and space to a small little pool of rainwater in the middle of the Sonora Desert in 1894. And it would never, she knew, go away. Through her tears, she said, in a whisper, "He knew. They all knew."

If he wondered who all of them were, he didn't ask.

"And you never even saw the child? Never held him? You just . . ."

"I was fifteen years old, dammit! A sophomore in high school. I didn't have any rights, no means of support, no man who was gonna marry me and take care of us. No one asked me. They just took him and gave him away." She couldn't look at his face, so she concentrated on his boot. Within the well-worn black leather she could discern the outline of his foot. She didn't know how he managed to get it off his right foot at night nor back on in the morning. Since the start of their adventure together, he was the last to sleep and the first to get up.

"Who's they?" he asked.

"Mr. and Mrs. O'Reilly."

"Your family?" He couldn't hide the shock in his voice.

"Biologically," she conceded. "But it only takes sex to make a child. It takes love to make a family. I'd say we both know that pretty well, wouldn't you?"

"And you say that was thirteen years ago. I still don't see how you could be twenty-eight. You don't look nearly twenty. And fifteen ain't no baby. My ma was fifteen when she had me. And another thing—if you didn't have no means of support, how'd you get out to California?"

So there they were, all the things that were bothering him about her. All the things he'd probably never be able to accept. Mary Grace smiled. In 1994, no one would have had trouble understanding that she had been forced to give up her baby because she was only fifteen. Of course, no one knew, but they would have had a damn sight more understanding than some cowboy whose own mama probably married after her first period.

And her looks. That was funny, too. She hadn't even been carded in years. People were always saying she had old eyes, and no one disputed her age. Getting to L.A. was easier to explain.

"I took a job after school and in the summers, waiting tables at the diner. A year after I graduated I went as far as what was left of my money would take me. I never went home again."

"Never been with a man again. Never been back home. You got any more nevers?" he asked.

"Never been back to church."

"You ain't alone in that one, Sweet Mary." He played with her hair for a while, apparently digesting all she had told him.

"I just got one more question for you, Mary Grace O'Reilly," he said finally. "Now that you know I ain't gonna just leave you in the desert, and you're kinda calm, you want to tell me the real story behind how you wound up in that river in Oak Creek Canyon with all your clothes on? And wound up back there the next day on the back of Wilson Tate's horse?"

She couldn't help the look that must have crossed her face. He'd seen her! Seen her fall, seen her strip and lie in the sun, seen every inch of her, just like in the pond and again at the campfire just this morning.

"If you saw all that, then you know the answer as well as I do. I fell out of the sky. I'm from the future, Sloan. I don't know any better than you how I got here."

"Say that again," he said, a smile curling his lips and showing off those white teeth of his. "The middle part."

"I fell out of the sky?"

"After that. . . ."

"I'm from the future. I told you before, but if you saw me fall, you must have seen how I just . . ."

"Not that part," he interrupted. "The part with my name. Say my name again."

"Sloan?"

"I sure do like the sound of my name comin' outta your mouth, Sweet Mary." He wasn't two inches from her face, the breath from his words warming her cheek. One rough finger traced her upper lip and then tugged slightly on the lower one.

"Ah, Sweet Mary! How'm I ever gonna make it to Jerome?" His body rubbed against hers. She backed up, and he reached out, stopping her from plunging into the water behind her.

"What's in Jerome?" she asked, righting herself and shaking off his help.

"All the women a man can buy," he said, turning away, his limp more pronounced than usual. "Any man," he added as he walked away.

She ran after him, stumbled and fell, skinning her knee and crying out. He turned and shook his head, coming back to take a look at what she had done to herself. The knee looked raw, little bits of sand clinging to the bloodied skin. He stood over her, staring down at her exposed leg.

"Do you think I'll just stay in some hotel room while you find some, some . . ."

"They call 'em whores, Mary Grace. And I don't know what I expect. I only know it's gonna be hard enough with this." He pounded his right thigh so hard that she flinched. "I sure don't need a woman that's so scared of me that she can't stop shakin' long enough for me to take aim and hit my mark!"

"I suppose Emily just spread her legs for you at the batting of your eyes. I suppose she just welcomed you into her arms, and her bed, and . . ."

"She did better than that," he shouted at her. "She invited me. She started the whole damn thing, makin' eyes, makin' cozy, makin' a place to meet. I never saw a woman so eager."

"Well, you ought to have your eyes examined," she shouted back. "There's a hell of a lot you don't see clearly."

Like Emily set you up. Like I'm eager. She couldn't come out and say it in as many words, but he must know what she meant. Embarrassed, she turned away and quickly untied the moccasins and slipped them off her feet. It was now up to him, she thought, as she rose and stepped into the pond, raising her skirt to hip level so that the water could rinse her cut knee.

Sloan slipped the baby carrier over his head and kissed the dark down on the baby's head. He didn't even stir in his sleep. Mary Grace watched as he made a makeshift crib, rearranging the rocks around the baby so that he couldn't fall into the water. He peeled off his shirt and made a tent over the child to keep him from burning in the sun.

And then he started to struggle with his boots, wedging the heel into a crevice between two rocks and trying to pull his foot up. The pain etched lines across his forehead and down his cheeks. She'd sworn she was never going to let some man just take her. This was as good a time as any to reach out and grab her own destiny.

"Sit down," she said when she stood a foot or so in front of him. He opened his mouth and then closed it, apparently reconsidering arguing with her, and sank down onto a large rock. Bracing herself, she put one foot against the rock he rested on and tried to pull the boot from his foot. He slid rather ungracefully off the rock at her attempt.

"Don't you even know how to get a man's boots off?" he complained. "Turn around and straddle my leg, woman." She did as she was told, looking over her shoulder for approval. He nodded.

"Now pull."

His left foot settled on her behind, pressing her away from him. She held on to his boot with all her might and found herself reeling toward the water when it finally came off in her hand. She expected to hear his laughter when she pulled herself from the water, but he was too busy removing his other boot and shimmying out of his pants.

She wrung the bottom of her skirt, trying to keep busy and not look at Sloan's broad chest, fuzzy with pale curly hair that pointed unmistakably downward into the waistband of his long johns.

"You'd better take it off and hang it on the tree so it'll dry," he suggested, pointing at her skirt. His voice sounded different, huskier, even though he tried to keep it light.

She undid the button at the waist and stepped out of it, reaching up and putting it carefully on a few needles on the cactus tree.

"The blouse, too, Sweet Mary," he said, and this time there was no mistaking his tone.

"It's not wet," she said, ashamed of the tremor her own voice held.

"Then leave it."

She watched him trying to adjust his frame on the rocks, to find a place where he and she would both be comfortable enough. He eased himself down and held out his hand for her patiently. When she couldn't just stand there anymore, she came to where he was and stood within his reach. His thumb rubbed back and forth against her ankle forever, over and over until she found it hard to keep standing.

Propped up on one elbow, his head only as high as her knee, he drove her ankle crazy, then began to kiss the inside of her leg, just below the knee. First it was little kisses, almost pecks, and then he lengthened them, finally sucking her skin in between his lips. She didn't know when his hand moved from her foot, but now he rubbed her behind her knee, making her legs buckle and easing her down beside him.

The neckline of her blouse was tied with a small string that ran through the casing and ended in a bow beneath her collarbone. He pulled gently on the end of the cord, and the bow opened easily beneath his hands. He left the blouse where it was, trailing the ends of the ribbon against her neck, running his finger along the edge of the fabric. Then he dipped his head and put his mouth to the cloth, finding her nipple beneath it easily, and soaked it with his tongue. It was an exquisite sensation, at once covered and demure, and yet sensuous and wanton.

He wet the other breast, sucking on the gauze until both her nipples were no longer hidden beneath it.

"Now it's wet," he said. "Take it off."

She pulled it over her head and lay next to him with just her little twentieth-century panties on, hiding nearly nothing from his gaze.

He played with her hair, letting it tickle her breasts, running it between his lips, pulling it off her neck. He touched nothing except her hair until she went nearly wild with wanting to feel his arms surround her, his hands on her breasts, his mouth on her lips. Her uneven breathing made her breasts rise and fall, and though he stared at them, he didn't make a move to touch them.

She touched the whiskers on his face, the hair surprisingly soft. Her finger traced his lips, and he caught it with his mouth and held it gently with his teeth, letting his tongue run up and down its length. Her whole body was trembling, and she pushed herself against him, trying to nuzzle closer and closer to his chest.

"Are ya eager then, Sweet Mary?" he asked, his voice a whisper above her ear.

"I'm frightened," she admitted, her eyes searching his and finding compassion there.

"We don't have to do this, Mary Grace. We can stop now, put on our clothes, and move on. We got a lot of ground to cover," he said, but he made no move to rise. She rested her head against his chest, feeling the hard muscle beneath the coarse hairs that tickled her nose. She knew she could say no. Deny him. But it would be denying herself, and she was so very tired of running from her feelings.

"No," she whispered. "I'm eager."

"What?" he asked, unable to hear her muffled admission.

"I'm eager," she said, this time a little stronger.

"For what, Sweet Mary? What is it ya want from me?"

"I . . . I ache for you. I don't know what I want. I only know I need it. . . ."

He leaned over her and covered her mouth with his, cutting off her words. Her lips were even softer than he expected, especially when he sucked on the bottom one and then ran his tongue on its soft inside. Still, she didn't part her lips for him. He let his tongue dance across the seam of her smile, then try to press its way beyond. His hand wandered down her stomach and wriggled beneath the piece of fabric that hid her dark red curls from him.

When the "oh" he expected escaped her lips, his tongue shot into her mouth, taking her by surprise. Gently he probed the recesses of her mouth, the silky insides of her cheeks, the smooth surface of her teeth. Her mouth was warm, moist, inviting, an imitation of her womanhood that made it hard for him to breathe without gasping. His tongue invited her back with it into his mouth, but she didn't follow.

He stopped kissing her and raised up on one elbow to look at her face. She seemed divinely happy, but confused about what he could want from her.

"Haven't you ever kissed like this before?" he asked. She shook her head.

"Well, what have you done, then?" She shrugged and looked away as if she were still a schoolgirl. While he had been nearly panting, he thought she might have been holding her breath. Something was amiss. She'd had a baby, for Christ's sake.

"Look at me, Sweet Mary." Wide eyes stared trustingly at him. She was worse than a virgin. Virgins were just afraid of the unknown. For some reason, she was afraid of the known. "I ain't gonna hurt you, I promise."

She bit her lip slightly and nodded as if she believed him, trusted him.

"The other time," he tried to explain, "when you were with . . . him, it hurt because it was the first time. You understand that? It only hurts the first time."

Now she couldn't look at him. He reached across her and lifted her blouse from the ground, then handed it to her and sat up. Whatever need he had, whatever desires, they could wait. He wasn't about to make her do anything she wasn't of a mind to do. When she didn't move to put on her blouse, he looked down at her trembling form.

"Please don't stop," she said in a small voice, her eyes fixed on his chest. "I don't want to be afraid anymore. I don't want to think that what happened those times in a small dark room a lot of years ago is all I'm ever going to know about . . ."

Those times. He was going to need to know, but not now. Now all that mattered was her soft freckled skin and her tentative arms reaching out for him.

"You're sure then?" She'd said it wasn't rape, but he'd never seen a woman, even a virgin, more frightened than the woman whose twitching hands clung to his arm. And he felt that same protective surge that had troubled him before, that need to make sure she was safe and secure.

"Please," she said again.

"Ah, Sweet Mary mine," he said with an easiness he didn't feel. "Lie back and let me have my way with ya. I've been dyin' to touch and taste every inch of you from the moment I felt that fanny of yours under my rein hand." That much, at least, was true. He didn't know how he'd manage the actual coupling, but there was so much he could show her before they had to face that, so much he wanted to share with her, so much he wanted to feel himself, after all this time.

She was lying flat on her back, her eyes closed, her lips slightly parted, waiting for him to begin. When he did nothing, she opened one eye to see what was wrong. He smiled at her and just continued to take in the sight. Somewhere there were three brothers looking to stake him out for the buzzards, but he wasn't going to meet his maker without first tasting the angel he'd been sent.

He didn't know where they'd be the next time, if

there'd be a next time, if he'd be alive tomorrow. But right now she was there with her perfect body, made for loving, with high, firm breasts and a small waist. Her hips flared, and the silly little fabric that hid her feminine hair from him only made him want to see it more. And she wanted and needed him like no one else had ever needed him before. She needed his gentleness, not his strength, needed his honesty, not his bravado.

He put a finger under the band that rode across her belly. It stretched to make room for him, and he pulled at it until he could see the dark red curls of her womanhood. He put his hand over the mound, not invading, not exploring, just letting the warmth pass between them. She arched her back, thrusting her breasts in the air, and he grudgingly removed his hand and moved it upward, noting with satisfaction that she smiled when it made contact with her breast.

All right, he thought, *I'll start there. But you'll want me to touch you everywhere before I'm done. I promise you, Sweet Mary. You'll want me everywhere.*

He ran his finger in a circle just to the outside of the deepening pink until she squirmed her impatience. Then he moved his finger to just over her nipple, barely grazing it till it stood erect from her chest. Then he took it between his thumb and forefinger and rolled it, checking the expression on her face to make sure he wasn't pressing too hard.

Finally, he took that breast in his mouth, catching the nipple between his teeth and biting gently while his hand toyed with her other. She was moaning beneath him, not even aware of what she wanted until his hand began to trail down toward the juncture of her legs. He kneaded her soft inner thighs gently, feeling the tension rise within her. Her hands sought out his shoulders, and she squeezed him until her nails bit into his flesh.

Slowly his hand moved up from her thigh until he caught the crotch of the undergarment with his forefinger. He pulled on it until it slid down to her knees. He eased her leg up, and she slipped it through the hole and freed herself.

"Good girl," he encouraged her. "You know I won't hurt ya."

Then his hand returned to her dark curls and eased itself between her legs. They shut tight around him like a vise, and he reluctantly took his mouth from her breast to ask, "Does that mean you don't want me leaving, or don't want me staying?"

She didn't answer with words, but she didn't have to. Her legs opened and she undulated beneath him, offering all she had at what he knew was a steep price. He pulled himself up a little and kissed her soundly, pleased when her lips parted and she welcomed his tongue into her mouth. Back and forth his tongue went, imitating what was to come between them, until finally her tongue began to chase his back into his mouth, and he rolled onto his back, taking her with him so that she lay against the length of his body.

One hand held her head to his, encouraging her kiss, telling her how much he welcomed her boldness. The other arm settled her against him, nestling his manhood between her thighs. She pushed herself against him, and responded to his rhythm with hip movements of her own.

Her breathing was coming in short bursts, and he could feel the moistness of her against the length of his shaft. Her hands clutched his arms, the nails digging into his biceps. Her breasts rubbed his chest as his hands kneaded her soft bottom and rocked her against his hardness.

When kissing and breathing were no longer possible

together, she raised her head and looked down at him expectantly. In her eyes was the same trust a wounded animal might show when he knows you're going to take away his pain. It was a look of relief. Her weight lightened slightly as she began to roll off him, but his hands kept her hips in place.

"It looks like you'll be ridin' upright again, Sweet Mary, 'less you have some objection."

She blushed slightly, but she was too lost to object, too needy to care who was on top, what way was the right one.

"Bend your knees, then," he directed, controlling her hips with his hands. He pitched her slightly forward, and she held her weight on her hands, her breasts dangling over his face. He caught the end of one with his teeth and gently played over it with his tongue while he rocked beneath her, reminding her that he was knocking at her door.

He could feel the heat building within her, the tension moving her faster and faster against him until he knew she was ready. He held her steady and raised his hips, then lowered her until her eyes widened and she stretched around him to make a perfect fit.

"Oh, Sloan!" she said in wonder. "Oh, Sloan!" she repeated as his hands guided her hips up and down the length of him. And then his hands were merely along for the ride, her body rising and falling by its own accord, beating some ancient rhythm that she punctuated with grunts and sighs that echoed around them.

Her hands clenched and opened, clenched and opened, and he sensed the change in her as she slowed and savored the moments before her jaw went slack and she collapsed against him.

Every muscle in his body begged for release as he eased himself out of her and rolled her softly off him.

"I'll be right back," he whispered, rolling onto his belly and awkwardly getting up, shielding himself from her view. He dove into the water headfirst, his heart still hammering, and swam until his muscles relaxed and his manhood grew slack. He'd lost his sense of timing, but could that be all?

She was asleep in the sun when he returned to her. Twisted around her ankle was the strange undergarment he had seen that first day from up on the ridge. He eased it off her and examined it. Never, despite all his experience with women, even city women, had he seen anything like it. He didn't recognize the fabric, which had a slight stretch to it and a deep green color. It wasn't cotton or silk, and it was edged with lace too perfect to be made by hand. Stitched to the waistband, which stretched and snapped back into place, was a little white piece of cotton with writing on it. SIZE 5, it said, 88% COTTON, 12% SPANDEX, MACHINE WASH AND TUMBLE DRY. MADE IN EL SALVADOR.

Fussing from a wet diaper, Ben awoke and managed to disturb Mary Grace at the same time. Her body glowed with a thin sheen of sweat, and as she sat up, the sun danced off her breasts and her hair.

"Take a quick dip," Sloan said when she reached for the crying baby. "I'll see to Ben."

She slid into the water, and he looked again at the little green garment crushed in his hand. He tossed it into his own pile of clothes and then turned to Ben.

"Well, what do you make of that?" he asked the baby as he undid his diaper and lifted him out of the makeshift cradle. The baby grabbed a handful of his hair in answer and yanked it hard.

"Hey," Sloan chided the boy on their way to the water. "You know what we do to bad little boys? We give them a good soaking, that's what we do. Water 'em till they grow."

He slid into the water, the baby held in one arm, and made his way over to Mary Grace. She was nervously rinsing her hair, her trembling bottom lip giving her away.

"There's nothin' to fret over," he told her. "I didn't leave my seed, if that's what's got you doing your eye-water dance."

"I'm not gonna cry," Mary Grace corrected, wiping a stray tear and trying to smile.

"Course not," Sloan replied, handing the baby to her and diving into the water. He touched her ankles, then her knees, and let his hand run up her buttocks as he came to stand behind her and the baby. She looked properly shocked, despite the pleasure she couldn't hide.

"Sloan? Whatever else happens," she said, her voice low and tears glistening in her eyes, "I want to thank you. I . . ."

He put his finger to her lips to silence her. He was a man again. He'd satisfied a woman, a frightened, timid woman at that. It wasn't the way it used to be, but he felt damn good. "Thank you."

There was that shy smile again, the high color on her cheeks. Damned if she wasn't the shiest of women. It was hard to believe she was the same woman who had just been panting and squealing with pleasure on his bucking bronco.

"That thing you were wearin' underneath every-thing?" he asked, trying to ease her shame. "That got a name?"

"My panties? Is that what you mean?"

He nodded, taking the baby back from her, letting his arm brush against the wet, slick skin of her breast.

He couldn't help but smile when her cheeks turned pink at his touch. Hell, she'd just rode him and now a little touch had her coloring with embarrassment.

She submerged and came back up, her hair glistening, her eyes shining brightly like a woman who'd been made love to good and proper.

"What's El Salvador?" he asked her.

"The country? What are you talking about?"

Her breasts floated on the surface of the pond, and she kept bending her knees to hide them. Each time she did, he took another small step toward the shallow end, and as she neared him and the baby her breasts would come to the surface once again.

"Where'd you get them . . . panties?" he asked, uncomfortable with the word. It was almost like talking about a woman's time, or something.

She shrugged. "I don't know, probably some discount store—Ross's, Marshall's. . . . What is this all about? How come you're so interested in my panties all of a sudden?"

"I'm not just interested in your . . ." He reached through the water and touched her intimately. "I like what you keep in them panties, Sweet Mary. Now how could they get them . . . you knows . . . to Arizona from El Salvador? And how could El Salvador know how to make something we can't make here in the greatest country in the world? They ain't making 'em here, they ain't wearing 'em here, 'cept you, of course. I think they don't really exist here, do they?"

She shook her head. "Not yet, anyway."

"Well, I'll be matin' jackalopes and sellin' their skins! Did you do it on purpose? Are there more of you? Can you prove it?"

She smiled, that smile that made the day brighter, lit up the night, lightened his heart.

"I fell. That's all I did to get here. I don't know if there are other people who did it. People disappear everyday. We guess they're lost, or murdered, or kidnapped. Sometimes they're found."

"And that's what you do? Back there in 1990 something? You go searching for all them missing folks? Kinda like a bounty hunter?"

"No," she said. Her eyes clouded over with a sadness that made him sorry he'd asked. "Only children. I go looking for children."

Her fingers were shriveling from the water. She suggested they get out and dry off, and Sloan agreed. Since the previous night Ben had dirtied a few diapers, and Sloan set the sleeping baby down and went up to get them, knowing her eyes were following his naked body. Damn the scars, he thought, reaching for his long underwear. Returning, he leaned against a boulder to dress, but her hands stopped him.

"I'd rather we dried off before we put on our clothes, wouldn't you?" she asked. In her voice was a coyness he'd never heard before.

And then, while he simply stared, she knelt before him and kissed the two scars on his rib cage, then sank to her knees. She looked up at him, and he touched her chin. Dipping her head, she kissed his palm and then went back to examining his scars, first with her fingers and then with her lips.

She followed the trail lower and lower until only one raw scar remained between his abdomen and his mangled knee. Why he wasn't aroused, he'd never understand, except maybe he was just too scared of what she might do, too embarrassed about what she was seeing.

Gently she touched the soft sack that hung behind his manhood, her finger tracing the scar line where the best of the Havasupai shamans, A'mal, had cut him open and removed the bullet meant to end his life as a man. A'mal had sucked out the bad spirit from within the wound, and when Sloan had recovered sufficiently, A'mal had suggested testing his work.

Sloan flinched, remembering the shame of being watched by others who shared the wickiup while A'mal instructed and encouraged him.

"Does it hurt?" came the small voice beneath him.

He sucked in his breath. "Only the memories," he admitted.

"I should stop," she said quietly, but she didn't stand.

He couldn't imagine the courage it had to be taking for her to be so forward with him. She was trembling so much that he thought she might fall over if he even moved. He wanted to tell her not to stop, but that was for his sake, and he couldn't bring himself to make her suffer further humiliation for him. Silently he stood stock-still while she lowered her lips to his scar and kissed it so gently that had he not been watching, he might not have been sure of what she had done.

"We'd better get going," she said, looking up at him from her knees. "The Tates won't settle for just wounding you next time, will they?"

He thought of what would happen to Mary Grace if Wilson or Mason Tate ever got his hands on her. For the first time since he had woken up with the Havasupai and seen his wounds festering, he felt overwhelmingly nauseous.

10

"*You're one wanton woman,* Mary Grace O'Reilly," Sloan said as he kicked the horse and they moved slowly forward, Sloan leaning to see around her hair, Mary Grace bending into the baby and calming him.

"Hey, you were the one who suggested I ride up front," she said.

"I thought that poor little excuse for a fanny needed a little cushioning," he said, rubbing her bottom gently with his left hand while guiding the horse with his right. Beneath her soft bottom, Sloan had already begun to grow hard. It was difficult to keep his mind on his plan. And his plan depended on perfect timing and constant alertness. There would be no outrunning the Tates should the boys ever catch sight of them. He had to leave enough of a trail for three morons to follow, and still get Mary Grace and Ben to Jerome before they caught up to him.

"That looks easy," Mary Grace said, taking the reins

from Sloan's hand. Climber, sensing the change, immediately strayed from the path and began nibbling at some greenery that had the fortitude to poke through the sandy soil.

"Like this," Sloan instructed, putting his hand over hers and showing the horse who was boss. Climber responded at once and returned to his slow pace, always seeking higher and higher ground.

"He's a nice horse," Mary Grace admitted. "But he doesn't seem to think much of me as a rider. Lucky thing I don't have to depend on him myself."

"Don't knock 'em, Sweet Mary. Never forget—a man's horse is his lifeline in the desert. Take his horse, might as well just kill him on the spot, instead of lettin' him die slow."

He was merely thinking aloud, but her breathing changed, and he could have cursed himself for scaring her. There'd been no sign of the Tates, or anyone else, since the flood. So what if the hackles on the back of his neck were beginning to twitch. That didn't mean anything.

After all, they weren't all that far from Jerome anymore. Another day or two of hard riding, and Mary Grace and the baby would be safe. There was no reason for him to be getting those damn centipedes up the spine, and no excuse for scaring Sweet Mary.

"Why are you stopping?" Mary Grace asked when he brought Climber to a halt and turned to look behind them. Why *was* he stopping? For as far as he could see, across the flatlands, up into the mountains, nothing seemed amiss. Wary eyes looked into his, and he searched for words that would calm the woman in his arms.

"Leg's fallin' asleep," he lied. "Could do with a little stretch."

Her eyebrows came down as if she didn't quite believe what he said, but she nodded and let him help her off Climber's back without argument.

Once Mary Grace had been lowered to the ground, he handed her the baby and swung off the horse, as well. As long as they were tempting fate with a stopover, they might as well make use of the time and fill their bellies. He was riffling through his saddlebags, looking for something that didn't require cooking, when he heard Mary Grace singing to Ben.

She'd sung to the boy before. Sometimes the songs were ones Sloan remembered his own mother singing to him as a small child. Sometimes they were just pretty melodies he was sure he'd never heard. This time it was a song full of strange words and sounds, all about something called a bus. It was a city song, all about the noises a bus would make.

When she began a new stanza with "The wipers on the bus go swish, swish, swish," he stopped her. He'd never seen a bus, never seen a wiper, whatever that was.

"What's it like, where you're from?" he asked, handing her a slice of prickly pear and fixing one for Ben.

He was keeping one eye on the horizon at all times, but he stole a glance at Mary Grace, only to see her smile wistfully.

"You mean *when* I'm from? It's so different I can't begin to tell you. There are cars that can go a hundred miles an hour—more, even. There are airplanes that can fly you around the world in less than a day. Telephones—you have telephones now, don't you?" she asked, pausing.

He nodded. "They got 'em in the bigger cities. Once I was gonna try one in Denver, but there was no one there to call."

"Why didn't you call some other city?" she asked.

"Don't know no one in another city. Denver's as far as I've ever gone. It's always been far enough."

"Well, telephones are everywhere, and there are machines that you can leave messages on, and you can send letters through them—"

"Like telegraphs?"

"No. You put the paper in where you are and an exact copy comes out where you want to send it."

He smiled at her. Just how much of this did she think he'd believe?

"And there's television! When we have time, I want to tell you all about that. And computers, and—"

"Is anything the same?" he asked.

A grin split her face, and she patted Ben's head while he happily devoured another piece of the cactus fruit. "Men and women still fall in love, although, to be honest, so do men and men and women and women. . . ."

"Then nothing's changed," he laughed, "unless you mean that it ain't a secret anymore."

"They've come out of the closet," she answered, confusing him. "Anyway, men and women still get married and have babies, although not always in that order, and some are single parents. . . ."

He looked at her dubiously, and she amended her statement.

"Single in that they don't marry the child's other parent. It still takes two—of different sexes—" She paused and her eyebrows knit together. "Do you believe me?"

"I don't rightly know," he admitted. Maybe some little corner of his mind was considering the possibility. There was the remote chance. . . .

"The Havasupai have stories about their ancestors. Men and women who a long time ago just disappeared. Where you fell from—what did it look like?"

"It was a bridge, sort of. A red stone archway." He couldn't believe it. How could she know about the legends? He'd only just learned about them when he stayed with the Pai.

He shook his head at her.

"What?" she said. "You don't believe me?"

Her eyes were clear and steady, their soft green depths focused on his face as if she were trying to read his thoughts. "And you just jumped?" he asked.

"Are you crazy?" The green eyes widened and turned to two pools he thought he could drown in. "There were only rocks beneath me, I swear. I lost my balance, and I started to fall."

He had thought they were just stories. Like how the coyote brought corn to the desert, or how the eagle made the first woman, or some such nonsense. He'd paid very little attention when Navaho's son had tried to translate for him. "In the legends . . ." he began.

"There was something about falling off the rocks?"

He nodded. What else explained it? He had been up on the ridge from which she had fallen. But *she* hadn't been there. She hadn't appeared until she hit the water.

"They call it the Bridge to Somewhere Else. Their name for the river you fell in is, roughly translated, the River of Time."

She was very quiet, taking in what he had said. Finally, she asked, "Do the people that vanish off that bridge ever show up again? Do they ever come back?"

Truthfully, he had never asked. He'd never believed the old legends, so why bother? And he didn't know which answer she was hoping to hear. Since she'd come to him, she'd been cold, hungry, hot, frightened for her life, bruised, battered, and dragged around in dirty clothes while she took care of a baby that wasn't hers and satisfied his own needs.

And even though he'd taken time and care and seen the look of wonder on her face when he'd brought her to that place a woman hopes to find, it couldn't make up for what he'd already put her through, nor what might lie ahead.

"We better get going," he said, rising and lending her a hand.

She nodded and let him pull her up behind him, but the rest of their afternoon was spent in quiet thought. They waited until after dark to dismount, an outcropping of rocks serving as cover. He reminded Mary Grace of how far the smoke had carried that first night in the canyon when she'd followed it to the Tates' hideaway, and so she understood when he suggested they do without a fire.

Mary Grace accepted his reluctance to light a fire and call attention to themselves. All day she'd had the feeling that he was nervous, expectant. Now, as they lay together on the ground, she found that it was not just the temperature that made her feel so cold, but fear, as well. Sloan Westin was worried. And that scared her half to death. Even the warmth of his body snuggled up behind hers couldn't take away the chill.

Thankfully, Ben slept comfortably enough at her side beneath the poncho. But for her it was too cold to sleep. She lay in the dark, shuddering, until Sloan's hand slid beneath her blouse and found her breast.

"I like that little sorta jerk you do when I touch you, Sweet Mary," he whispered in the dark.

"It's called shivering."

"Then turn over," he said, spinning her in his arms until she was flat on her back, "and give me a try at warmin' ya."

His head disappeared beneath the blanket, and his breath burned her chest. Each place his mouth paused blazed with his warmth. And each place it paused was lower than the one before. Dear God, where was he going!

One hand pulled her skirt up, while the other was splayed across her chest. When her legs were bare beneath the blanket, he rubbed them hard, trying to warm them for her. Each swipe moved closer to where she was sure he was headed. But his hand moved further down her leg, and it was his lips that caressed her soft inner thigh.

"Oh my God," she gasped, and felt the laughter as he exhaled against her thigh.

He said something that sounded like "It's only me," but between the blanket, her breathing, and the other things his lips were doing at the same time, she wasn't sure.

The warmth radiated out from some inner core, her legs, her chest, her arms, her hands, all thawing and her face suffused with heat. She'd read about what he was doing, even seen it in movies. They had dirty names for it on the sides of dusty trucks and in bathroom stalls. She had been sure that it was something she could never allow done to her. Something she *knew* she would never enjoy.

And here she was, in the middle of the desert with some man she hardly knew, a baby asleep beside her, with her hips undulating and her breathing out of control. His tongue was doing wild things to her, and her hands were in his hair, grabbing handfuls, her gasps coming one upon the other. His tongue caressed her most private parts as it had her lips, exploring, teasing, darting. She forgot to be embarrassed. She forgot to try to stop him. She forgot to forbid herself the pleasure he was giving her.

She clamped her mouth shut to stop herself from crying out, but still the scream came. A piercing wail that brought Sloan's head up, taking the blanket with it. The cold night air on her nearly naked body sobered her. It wasn't her cry filling the night. It was Ben's.

It was an anguished cry, full of pain, and it scared her into crying out herself. Sloan grabbed for the matches he had left by their side and lit one. Something was coiled around Ben's leg. It looked like a twisted necklace with beads of shiny black and orange. Until she followed it up his leg and saw its head, its eye glistening in the match light, its jaw clamped firmly on the baby's thigh, she didn't even realize it was a snake. It was like the one she'd seen last night, but alive it was much more brilliant, and much more frightening.

"Shit!" Sloan shouted, grabbing the snake at the point where his upper and lower jaws met and squeezing until he could pull the fangs from the baby's tender skin. Then he held the snake at arms length, yelling impatiently at Mary Grace to give him his gun. He rammed the barrel into the snake's mouth. When most of the barrel had disappeared and the snake was sufficiently impaled, Sloan held the gun away from them and pulled the trigger. Pieces of the animal splattered into the darkness around them.

Mary Grace picked up the baby and jostled him in her arms, trying to calm him down.

"It was just a coral snake," she said. "Nothing to worry about."

"Don't shake him. Put him down as gently as you can and get my knife and another match." Sloan used that horrible voice she had come to recognize as a signal of danger or disaster. He had settled himself on the ground and was waiting for Mary Grace to put the baby carefully into his arms.

"But it was just a coral snake," she said feebly. "You told me . . ."

He looked up at her, and she could see his eyes glisten despite the dark night.

"A coral snake is just as deadly as a rattler, Mary girl. Now hurry!"

"But you said—"

"You were scared enough," he said quickly, dismissing her. "Hurry!"

Sloan held the baby nearly upright, hoping to keep the venom lower than Ben's little heart, while Mary Grace held a match beneath the hunting knife Sloan carried in his saddlebag, in a feeble attempt to sterilize it.

"I'll need some light," he told her, trying to keep his voice steady and calm in the cold night air. No point making her any more frantic than she already was. The baby had stopped crying. Now Ben busied himself trying to put his fingers into Sloan's mouth. "Shhh, Ben. Stay still now, boy."

Mary Grace followed Sloan's instructions to the letter, grabbing about for anything that might burn and quickly making a pile as close as she could to the tree where Sloan waited with the baby. After several feeble attempts, during which he promised himself he would teach Sweet Mary how to build a fire along with a million other things that refused to come to his mind, the bundle caught fire and he was able to get his first look at the bite on the baby's leg.

He examined the wound carefully, his intake of breath the only sound he made. Beyond the U-shaped mark of the snake's teeth were the two puncture wounds Sloan had dreaded. Examining the baby's pudgy thigh left him unsure about any swelling, but at least Ben didn't seem terribly uncomfortable. Of course, it wasn't the bite of the snake that did the damage. And only time would tell how much of his venom the snake had injected, and whether it would be fatal to the boy in his arms.

"Get your panties, quick." He was grateful she didn't ask why, didn't argue or make suggestions. For a change she seemed to defer to his experience. He forgave her all the other times she'd questioned him.

She scurried back to where they had been sleeping, then groped around on the ground until she found her underpants. As she ran back to him, she shook off the dirt that clung to them.

"Now get the blanket. Quick, darlin', quick!" While she ran back to the blanket, he wrapped the band to her panties around Ben's thigh, restricting the flow of blood up his leg. He felt around on the ground without jostling Ben and found a stick that he twisted into the panties to tighten and loosen the band easily.

Mary Grace stood with the blanket in her hand waiting for his instructions. He took the blanket and put it behind her, then leaned her against the tree, placing the baby upright in her arms. If there were thorns or bristles, she didn't complain.

"You know what I have to do, Sweet Mary, don'tcha?" he asked as he poised the knife over Ben's leg. At her nod, he pressed her back against the tree and then pushed Ben against her so that he was steady.

"Keep his leg as still as you can," he said, his hand shaking slightly as the knife came in contact with Ben's leg. He'd skinned a thousand rabbits, hacked the heads off a hundred birds, even buried his knife in one man's gut when the need had arisen, but making the half-inch cut in his son's leg was the hardest thing he'd ever done with that old hunting knife his pa had given him. The baby's scream pierced the night like a coyote in heat and pierced his heart like one of the Havasupai's poisoned arrows.

"Not an *X?*" Mary Grace asked, as he cut two straight lines in the same direction as the boy's thigh swelled. He ignored her as he tried to lower his mouth to the wound, his stiff leg making the exact angle difficult. Mary Grace could see him struggle and raised the baby higher until Ben's thigh was nearly at her shoulder. Sloan placed his lips around the tiny cut and sucked as hard as he could.

Ben didn't like the sensation and kicked at him. Both Mary Grace's hands were full holding Ben up. Sloan used one hand to steady her and the other to hold Ben's leg still. The baby's free leg smacked Sloan's head over and over, not hurting him but making it hard to stay fixed on the two incisions he had made in the boy's leg. Still, he sucked and spat, sucked and spat, and then bent again to clean the other wound, repeating the process over and over for what felt like hours.

When he finally stopped and released the pressure of the band slightly, he found the contents of his own stomach rising. He took a few steps away from Mary Grace and the child before pitching onto the ground between his boots what little dinner he had eaten.

"Get some water," Mary Grace suggested, lowering her arms slightly. They must have ached from holding his son in the air for so long.

He nodded and hurried to his canteen, ordering her to tighten the band once again. After he rinsed his mouth he went back to sucking out the snake's venom until he had to admit that they had done all they could and it was in God's hands.

He settled them onto the blanket, the baby's torso up against Mary Grace's side so that he was sitting upright despite the fact that he was very nearly asleep. She slumped against Sloan, and he bore her weight, encouraging her to relax and get some rest.

Her voice was thin and small in the night air. "Will he be all right? He isn't going to die, Sloan, is he?"

He rested his hand on her shoulder and felt her icy hand cover his. "Put those hands over the wound, Sweet Mary," he said. "Long as they're cold they'll help stop any swelling."

He hoped keeping her busy, giving her a distraction, might keep her focused on the present, instead of what might happen tomorrow. It was obvious she was glad to have something to do, something that would help the baby, but it didn't make her forget her question.

"Sloan?" she asked again.

"It's hard to know," he admitted. He steadied Mary Grace and then got up to feed the fire. Had he made one to begin with, would the snake have ventured so close to them? Had he killed his son trying to protect him?

"The boy's so small," he said softly. "Even a little poison could probably kill him. Course I sucked half his insides out. Still . . ."

On the ground again beside Mary Grace, Sloan felt the boy's forehead. He took solace in the cool absence of fever.

"He doesn't seem to be in any pain," Mary Grace said. "Tell me that's good."

"That's good," he granted. It would be hard to tell how much venom had gotten into Ben's bloodstream because the child was too young to talk. How could he know if the boy's vision was getting blurry or his speech was slurred? No, the only signs they'd recognize would be the ones signaling that death was imminent—heavy perspiration, foaming at the mouth, and an inability to breathe.

"His leg is very hot," Mary Grace said. Sloan reached over to feel it.

"Naw," he said, squeezing her hand. "You just got

icicles hangin' from your wrists there, girl. Surprised he can stand having them hands of yours on his thigh."

"Guess he is like his dad," Mary Grace said in a subdued voice, pushing the baby's dark hair off his forehead.

His dad. The words echoed in his head. He loosened the tourniquet again and rose, stretching out his back. "I'll be back in a few minutes," he said to the top of her head and walked away into the darkness with his thoughts.

It didn't take him long to say his prayers. Without much formal religious training, he'd developed a pretty loose relationship with God. He'd been a good boy growing up, going to church and obeying his folks. As a grown man he'd strayed a bit from the path, enjoying too many women, too much booze, and a bit of the wild life. And while it had always been in self-defense, there were four men who were pushing daisies on his account. All of that was before the Tates had entered his life. Then everything had changed.

In the year he'd spent with the Havasupai, he'd found them to be a deeply religious people, despite the fact that everyone thought Indians were heathens at heart. And while he couldn't follow their ways, they'd allowed him to join them in their Toholwa, where the men sweated together and chanted to their gods. He'd used the opportunity to commune with his own God. He wasn't sure quite whom to thank, but he knew that the fact that he was still riding a horse, and once again riding a woman, was nothing short of a miracle.

And now he had the boy. The doctor, a real one, white and schooled in the East, had taken one look at his privates and told him it was a wonder he could still enjoy a woman, but it would be a miracle if he could still father a child. Seems there were lots of men that could do the deed without planting the seed.

So maybe Ben was all there'd ever be. The boy was what was going to make it all up to his parents for their gimpy son. Ben was going to soften the blow when Sloan limped into the house and his mother saw her handsome son all full of scars and his father saw his broncobuster busted up himself.

He could just imagine his mama, her hair a mite grayer than when he left her that fine day over a year ago to deliver some horses and spend some well-earned pay. Wouldn't her eyes just sparkle to see a baby in the house! How she did love the little ones. He'd been old enough to remember the twins dying, and she'd told him often about the others.

"Now you're my only one," she'd tell him. "So be extra careful for me."

"Don't go making the boy a sissy with all your careful talk," his father used to say, and to get her crazy, he liked to suggest that young Sloan do something especially dangerous. At first, the things Sloan tried were brave, like breaking a feral horse and winding up eating gravel. Then he graduated to reckless, fooling around with a man's wife or his daughter and seeing if he could get away with it.

His mama didn't like it, but it sure seemed to please his pa to have a lady-killer in the family. He wondered how they'd feel about Mary Grace. Not that it mattered. Once he and Ben were safe, she probably wouldn't want anything to do with him anyway.

Hell, she'd never have wanted anything to do with him in the first place if it hadn't been for Ben. What a smile she had! When she and the boy both smiled, a man needed a bigger Stetson to shade his eyes from all that brightness.

Well, God, I ain't much. Maybe I never was. But them two sure are special, and I'm willing to give my life to

*keep 'em safe. So I'm putting it in Your hands. I done
what I know how for the boy. And I accept that it was
You what sent the woman. Ain't no other explanation I
can see. But Lord, I hope it was for Ben's sake that You
sent her, not mine. You know I got things to take care of,
and a woman like her . . . well, I just ain't looking for a
forever woman right now. You want my life, You can
take it. Hell, it ain't worth much. But them two . . . Lord,
them two are worth Your carin'. That's all I gotta say.*

He made his way silently back to the campfire. He
could hear Mary Grace murmuring to the baby, and he
stopped to listen. He wasn't surprised that she too, was
saying her prayers. And while he knew he should wait
until she was done and give her some privacy, he
stepped close enough to listen. Her voice was clear in
the night air and surprisingly steady, almost resigned.

". . . my fault. I know I should have learned from
before that no good can ever come from what I did, but
still . . . why punish this child? I promised You and the
church when my baby was born that I would keep
silent, and I kept that promise. And how did You pay
me back? But still, You brought me here, to this child.
And I thought maybe this was what it was all for. Then
You tempted me again. And again I failed Your test.
But I swear, if you let this child live, I will never . . ."

"Don't make that promise, Sweet Mary. God don't
want it, and I ain't gonna let you keep it." He gestured
toward the baby. "Is he feverish?"

She shrugged. Her icy hands touched his own as if to
gauge the temperature. "No more so than you," she
answered.

"Did you tighten that band again after I left?"

A slight nod was his answer.

"I'll watch him, if you got business to do," he said.
She didn't respond.

"Are you hungry, then? I got some supplies in my saddlebags." Again no response.

"Have you taken a vow of silence, along with the chastity one?" he demanded. "I can't take the quiet, woman. It ain't like you."

Her quiet resolve was unnerving. He'd never seen her so emotionless. It was like she'd just stopped pumping at the well. Nothing was coming forth. For a woman like her it didn't seem healthy. Oh, some women were made for holding it together, and he'd been proud to see Sweet Mary in a crisis. She'd been all the help he could ask for. But it was over and time for her to cry. And she wasn't crying. She was just sitting there dry-eyed, and he didn't even have to guess at what she was thinking.

"This was all my fault," she said. "All of it."

"How do you figure that?"

"Look, Sloan," she said with a big sigh as if he couldn't possibly understand and it was taking enormous patience to explain. "A woman ought to know better. Especially a woman like me. If I hadn't let you make love to me yesterday, none of this would ever have happened."

"What you really want to say is if I hadn'ta had my head buried between your thighs, I mighta heard the snake and killed it 'fore it got to Ben. And it seems if you're looking to place blame, it was my beard what sought out yours."

"That's disgusting!" Her voice shook slightly. A good sign. He pressed on.

"Didn't think that when I was down between your legs doing it to you, did you? I didn't hear you yelling stop. But then with your thighs squeezing my ears . . ."

Her arm shot out and caught him on the shin. It hurt like hell, but he didn't care because he could hear the tears in her voice when she yelled at him. Tears she needed to cry.

"Stop it!" She choked, coughed a little, and cried harder.

"That's it now, Mary girl," he said softly, lowering himself to take her in his arms. "You cry it out. Nothing left to do until the mornin'. You have yourself a good one."

Even while she cried in his arms, she kept one eye always on the baby, propped nearly upright against her. He slept no differently than he had any other night since Sloan had abducted him. The boy was really something to be proud of, making do, putting up with the rough life, smiling through it all with that grin of his. What a man he'd make someday if he could just weather this storm.

"My mama sure is gonna like having you around, little fella," Sloan said to the sleeping child. "And Pa won't mind the idea of a Little Ben none, neither."

Mary Grace had nearly been asleep in Sloan's arms, her weight heavy against his body. Now she stiffened and pulled away from him. After checking the baby's leg and putting her cold hands across the bite again, she turned to Sloan, trying to make out his features in the dark.

"Then you're still bringing him back to your parents?"

"Hey, I'm not gonna do that till after the Tates are all sleepin' under the grass. But then, what else did you expect, Mary Grace? I can't raise no baby by myself, can I? My folks'll be good to him, and I can get back to my life." *Don't ask me for forever, Sweet Mary. I can't promise it. Look what I've done so far. I ain't a man you can count on. Don't love me, Mary Grace. I ain't worth it.*

"How can you think of leaving him? After all of this,

could you just go on with your life as though he'd never been a part of it?" *As if I'd never been part of it?* She was shouting at him, and he really didn't want to, but he shouted back.

"Ain't it just what you did?" He hated what he was doing to her. It was low down. It was rotten. And it was the only way he could think of to make sure she would never fall in love with him. "Didn't you just leave your son and go on with your life? Ain't you doin' that now? Only I'd be giving Ben to my own folks, not strangers. Leastwise he'll know he's got a daddy."

He reached beyond her and ruffled the boy's hair. His head was hot, hotter than it should have been sleeping in the cool air.

"Get the blanket off him, Mary," he said brusquely. "And get them damn cold hands all over his body. I'll get the water."

Mary Grace peeled the blanket back and touched her hands to Ben's forehead. It was damp from sweat. She leaned over him, her face inches from the top of his head, and blew gently on his burning body, all the while touching him with her hands to help cool him down.

Sloan blocked out everything but taking care of his son. Whatever argument he had with Mary Grace could be settled later. There might not be any argument if they couldn't get Ben's fever down.

He hurried back with the canteen and slumped down beside Mary Grace and Ben, wetting the baby's lips with his fingers. In his sleep, Ben's mouth closed around one of Sloan's fingers and sucked on it.

"I ain't gonna let him die, Sweet Mary. Don't you worry."

Mary Grace was looking beyond him, eyes wide with fear, when Sloan looked up at her. He reached for his gun, but it was too late.

11

The rifle butt was pressed against his temple, and he tried to gauge from Mary Grace's face what he was up against. Now was a heck of a time for her to have to become a good poker player.

"Real easy, Westin," the man said.

The voice was familiar. Sloan rolled over slowly, his hands in plain sight and saw Daniel Jackson holding his own rifle on him. "Been a long time, Jackson," Sloan replied. "Thought we'd worked out our little differences."

"Still thinking I don't know shit," Jackson said, nudging Sloan onto his back so the two could get a good look at each other. "Still wrong. Heard you was dead."

"That what you got in mind?"

"Harlin Tate bragged to hell and back you was dead, Westin. And weren't a man around didn't breathe a little easier knowin' his wife was safe with you doin' your broncobustin' on Satan's own mares. No one but the Tates know you're alive. Wouldn't be no law to answer to if I did you in right here and now." He looked Mary Grace up and down, and Sloan felt her tense beside him.

"What makes you think the Tates know I'm alive?" he asked, trying to sound casual.

"Ran into your friends yesterday," Jackson said, gesturing with his head to one of the two men behind him, whose arm was bandaged against his side. "Wanted some fresh horses. We took exception to giving 'em ours. They had a lot to say about you. And Mason Tate's got some bug up his ass about some woman." His eyes raked Mary Grace, and one side of his mouth smiled.

Sloan searched the darkness for a sign of a third horse, but saw only two. That made two things to worry about. And that didn't include a baby with a snakebite and a beautiful woman. He had to at least save them. "So where are the Tates?" he asked. "How come they ain't caught up to us yet?"

"Cause they're stupider than we are, for one thing," one of Jackson's companions said, only to be cuffed by the other.

"They're about a half a day behind us," Jackson said, his eyes still dancing over Mary Grace's body. "Not that it'll matter to the two of you. They ran into a renegade Injun and thought they'd have some fun with his squaw. Leastwise Wilson and Harlin were gonna. It's like Mason's savin' himself for someone else. Didn't seem interested in planting his rod in no red soil."

Come on, Mary Grace, show how much that bothers you. Come on, Sloan urged her silently.

"What kind of fun?" she asked, as though she had read his mind.

"Fun, like we're gonna have with you," Jackson said, his meaning clear.

Sloan turned to look at Mary Grace. He gave her a lazy once over as if he hadn't really ever looked at her before, and then shrugged. "Suit yerself," he said to the three men who were beginning to drool at his companion. "If she's yer type. Course Mason Tate ain't gonna take too well to the idea."

"What's the woman to the Tates?" Jackson gestured in Mary Grace's direction with the rifle. Sloan thought about rolling out of the way and grabbing for his gun, but didn't dare risk it. There were three of them, two abler than he, one injured but still capable of pulling a trigger if need be. It was more important to ensure the safety of Sweet Mary and Ben in the event they killed him, than to chance a fight he could easily lose.

"She's Mason Tate's," he said, praying she wouldn't correct him and that Mason himself hadn't told them otherwise. "The kid belongs to Emily. Touching a hair on either of 'em is signing your own death warrant. Don't let me stop ya. I hear fear is one a them aphrodisiacs. That what you said, Miz O'Reilly?" He held his breath as he put one hand on her leg, patting her affectionately.

"Keep your hands off me," she said levelly. "Or Mason will cut them off one finger at a time before he tears you apart. I bet he's just counting the minutes until he gets his hands on you." Except that her voice rose to a full octave higher than he was used to, Sloan could hardly detect her terror.

"And I know you'd enjoy watchin'," he said with a smile. "But I'm afraid these men aim to do your man out of his pleasure." Her muscles tightened under his hand, and he massaged them gently, almost idly, in the way that used to drive women crazy. Jackson's eyes were on Sloan's hand, and his lips curled at the edges.

"You can say that twice, once for each of ya. Maybe a few times with her." Jackson gestured toward Mary Grace. "Westin, I can't make up my mind whether to shoot ya, plant my boots up your ass, or shake your hand. Ya got more nerve than brains, my friend. Always did."

The barrel of the rifle, Sloan's own rifle with the

silver dog embedded in the handle, which Jackson had obviously stolen while Sloan and Mary Grace had been busy with Ben, nuzzled against his side. Jackson pushed him farther and farther away from Sweet Mary and the baby. Calling over his shoulder, Jackson said, "What do you think, boys?" and the two men came fully into view.

Mary Grace didn't show an ounce of fear. He'd been proud of her before. He'd thought she was brave and strong. But she just kept getting braver and stronger as things got worse and worse. You'd have thought she really was Mason Tate's woman the way she sat there looking certain she was safe.

"So what's it gonna be, Jackson?" he asked, watching as Jackson's two traveling companions advanced toward them. "You lookin' to finish the job Tate started?"

At his words Mary Grace eased her body closer to his, and he prayed that her bravado wouldn't fail her now.

"Let's bring 'em both to Mason, like he told us to," one of the men said.

"The baby was bitten by a snake," she said, reaching for the canteen which was still in Sloan's hand. "He's running a fever."

Sloan's eyes returned to Jackson, but he could sense that she was getting the baby to take some water and tending to him as if nothing was happening.

"I think his fever's going up," she said. "You feel him," she ordered Sloan.

He turned around and looked at Ben, sleeping peacefully against Mary Grace's body. His chest rose and fell evenly, and Sloan reached out his hand and placed it on the baby's head. Cool skin, without a trace of the earlier sweat, greeted his palm. His body eased with relief.

"Shit!" he said, feigning annoyance. Then to Jackson he said, "Y'all can do what you like, but movin' this baby'll probably kill him. Not that I care, mind you, but

I got a feeling Wilson might. He was pretty fond of Emily, you know."

"What's the matter with the kid?" the man with the bandaged arm asked.

"Snakebite," Sloan said, gesturing toward the fire. "I shot it after it got him. You can see what's left of him."

"Coral snake," Mary Grace added. "That's why we've got him propped up. I love this child like he was my own." Her voice cracked, and Sloan ached to comfort her but didn't. "If anything happens to him, I'll watch Mason roast you alive and I'll eat you for lunch."

Sloan felt his eyebrows go up and fought to keep a straight face. He was glad Jackson didn't know the girl couldn't even swallow prairie dog.

"I ain't doin' anything what's gonna make them Tate boys any crazier than they already are," the injured man said. "Let's just tie him up, and leave the lady to take care of the kid. Harlin wants to do the deed right this time, and Wilson wants to be there to see it done."

It sounded like a good solution to Sloan, so he kept his mouth shut and prayed that Mary Grace would, too.

"Wouldn't think of deprivin' Mason Tate outta nothin' he might want," Jackson agreed. "'Specially since we both have the same end in mind. Don't make no difference to me whose gun is smokin', long as it's yer guts what's feedin' the buzzards." He turned to Mary Grace and smiled. "Now Miz O'Reilly, when your man catches up to y'all, you tell him to slice this here man's privates in real small pieces for all the men what shared their wives with the son of a bitch."

Mary Grace shifted her legs, moving them out of Sloan's reach. "And your wife, Mr. Jackson? Was she . . . ?"

Jackson stared at Sloan. "Some men ain't got no respect for another man's property. They think any woman's pussy is theirs for the pettin'."

"Think Mason would mind if we sampled his woman?" Williams asked, sauntering in her direction and rubbing his crotch with his free hand.

"Mind?" Sloan drawled as if he were giving it careful consideration. "All depends on what you mean by mind. The Tates are mighty fond of any excuse to empty a man of blood. Still, much as Harlin would enjoy seein' how many bullets he could put in ya before ya up and die on 'em, I don't think it would make it up to Mason for touchin' a hair on her head." His hand hovered at the top of her leg, but never came in contact with her body.

The men seemed to be considering whether it was worth the risk. Having lain with Mary Grace himself, Sloan thought it just might be and was glad that if his time had come, at least he'd tasted heaven before he got sent off to hell. But he wasn't about to let them hurt Mary Grace and the baby, not even if he had to die to stop them.

He wasn't convinced that they had the sense to keep their hands off Mason's woman. The three could easily overpower Mary Grace and himself even without his rifle. He could put up a fight, but they would surely kill him. And if he didn't, they would probably rape Sweet Mary. How many could he take out before he was dead? His gun rested on the dirt just out of his reach, just a lunge away.

He telegraphed a message with his eyes to Sweet Mary, who shook her head almost imperceptibly. His face grew sterner, and still she resisted. Then, on his way toward Mary Grace, Williams crossed in front of Jackson. It took only a second, but Sloan used it to roll onto his stomach and reach out for his gun.

His fingers had closed around the handle, one curling around the trigger, when suddenly he felt a pain split the side of his head. After that, he felt nothing.

They tied Sloan's hands behind his back and then tied
his left ankle with the same rope, yanking his leg up.
They tried to do the same with his right, despite Mary
Grace's warning that his leg no longer bent. It had to be
sheer agony for him, and she was grateful he was already
unconscious from the rifle blow and felt nothing. They
staked the rope into the ground with a branch, and then
they turned their attention to Mary Grace and the baby.

"Sloan Westin had quite the reputation, Miz Tate.
He hurt you any?" Jackson asked, raising Mary Grace's
skirt slightly with the barrel of Sloan's rifle.

"No," she answered, pushing at her skirt and pulling
the baby closer to her. Trying to pretend that Sloan
meant nothing to her was nearly impossible, but for
Ben's sake she had no choice.

"Well, I ain't gonna hurt you, either. We're just
gonna have a little fun, you and me. Kinda pay Westin
back for measuring my wife from the inside out."

"Well, you better enjoy it, because it'll be your last
hurrah. Mason Tate will do to you just what Harlin did
to that man," she said, gesturing toward Sloan with her
head.

"And what's that?" he asked, moving her skirt with
the rifle barrel until her thighs were exposed, more
interested in what he intended than in her response.

It felt like a betrayal to bring up Sloan's injuries.
Clearly, he wouldn't want the truth known, especially
since she was about to make it seem even more embar-
rassing than it already was. She wished she could have
thought faster, wished she could have come up with
some other threat, but she couldn't. So she said simply,
"Harlin Tate shot Sloan Westin in his privates, and I
think he was incapable of hurting me. It's also why he

kidnapped Emily's baby. It doesn't appear he'll be fathering any more children of his own."

It was as close to the truth as she could afford to come.

Finished with tying up Sloan, Williams shook his head. "Maybe this ain't such a great idea, Jackson. Maybe we should just get goin' before Tate and his brothers show up."

"This won't take long."

Beyond Jackson, Williams raised the gun he had taken away from Sloan. "I ain't losin' my short arm just to get some sand up my ass in the middle of nowheres."

"No one's invitin' you to this party," Jackson said, the barrel of the rifle now between Mary Grace's breasts, pushing just hard enough to make her lean back until she was fully prone on the ground, the baby slipping off her hip.

"I've got to keep Be . . . Horace upright," she warned. "Move the rifle and let me sit up."

The hammer of Sloan's own gun clicked as Williams pulled back on it. Jackson rose slightly, straightening, but remained crouched over Mary Grace's body.

"Mason Tate ain't gonna care who did and who didn't grind her bottom into the ground, Jackson. Don't make me pull this trigger. I got no desire to kill ya. Hell, I'll treat you to the prettiest whore in Jerome."

The injured man, Kyle, reappeared before Mary Grace had even noticed he was gone. Riding one of their horses, he held the reins to Climber, who followed behind. Mary Grace must have gasped, because Jackson's attention returned to her.

"Well, the little lady's got a fine sense of priorities. She's more afraid of losing her horse than her pussy! Such a big horse. Such a little pussy. Maybe you'd like to reconsider?"

"Come on, Jackson. She ain't Westin's woman, she's Tate's. You remember what Mason Tate said? Westin'll get what he deserves from them, and we'll be out of it. Get on the horse, now." Kyle held out the reins.

Jackson stood at last, glaring down at Mary Grace ominously, his features lit by what remained of the fire. "You tell Mason we didn't hurt you none," he ordered her. "You tell him we saved you from Westin and left him tied up like a Christmas present."

"You can't take our horse," Mary Grace pleaded. "And all the guns. We'll die out here." She thought of the snakes, the lack of food and water, the Tates. She remembered Sloan's words: "Take a man's horse in the desert, might as well kill him on the spot." She began to cry as she looked down at Ben, who was beginning to fuss. "Leave us a horse and a gun, and I'll tell Mason anything you want."

There was only silence for a moment while her offer hung in the air. Then Jackson began unbuckling his belt.

"I didn't mean . . ." Mary Grace said, her voice barely above a whisper.

He pulled out his manhood, thick and hard in his own hand, and began to come toward her. Her legs locked together, and her breath stopped in her chest.

"Jackson!" one of his companions yelled. Mary Grace scurried backward, the baby clutched to her, now awake and screaming in her ear, his screams mixing with her own.

"Asshole!" Kyle shouted angrily from atop the horse. His arm came up, and he smashed the butt of Sloan's gun into Jackson's skull. The surprised man crumbled beneath the crashing blow, falling first to his knees, teetering on them for a moment. Then, his hand still clutching himself, he pitched forward on his face, inches from Mary Grace.

Williams picked up the inert form and threw him over Climber's saddle. "I'd watch the offers I made, ma'am, if I was you," he warned, tipping his hat and turning away. "And if Westin wakes up before your man gets here, I'd hit him over the head with the biggest rock I could find if I was you. And do it before he talks your skirts up."

"But he can't . . ." the injured man interrupted.

"Harlin didn't cut out his tongue, too," he replied. "Man only did half the job."

If they said anything else, Mary Grace didn't hear them. Her hands were held crushingly over her ears.

She didn't dare move until the men were out of sight. Then she scrambled to her knees and untied Sloan with fumbling fingers. He was still unconscious. The baby began to fuss, and she quieted him down with a wet rag to suck. Then she sat with her knees hugged up against her chest, rocking herself numbly, unaware that the fire was going out, that the sun was beginning to rise, and that Sloan Westin was beginning to come around.

Pain shot through his right leg, bolted up his thigh, and clutched at his heart. He moaned and opened his eyes to dawn. Every part of him ached. Turning his head was agony. In front of him he saw nothing put sagebrush, cactus, and rock. There was no sign of Mary Grace or the baby.

"No!" he screamed, his voice carrying out over the desert, hollow and without hope. He flipped over and saw Mary Grace, her expression bleak and lifeless.

"Thank God! Are you all right?"

She looked over at him blankly and then looked away.

"The men?" he asked. "Are they gone?"

"Yes," she said softly. "They're gone."

He scrambled over to her on his stomach, not willing to take the time to get to his feet before touching her and reassuring himself that she was there, whole and safe. He took her face in his hands and dragged her to him.

"You're all right," he sighed, his fingers tangled in her hair. "Ben! Is Ben . . . ?"

She was stiff in his arms, and he released her. Ben lay just a few feet beyond her, and again he crawled on his belly, oblivious to the cactus needles that pricked at his palms, until he was beside his son.

"Ben!" he shouted, and the baby started at the sound of his name, his little arms and legs twitching in response. Sloan leaned over him and looked into his bright blue eyes, caught his wide grin, and watched the familiar drool trickle across his cheek.

"He's all right," he said, as much to himself as to Mary Grace. "He's all right and you're all right. . . ."

He looked up at Mary Grace, who still sat where he had left her, and his joy evaporated. They'd hurt her, he was sure, and he eased his way over to her, taking the baby with him.

"They took Climber," she said simply, without emotion.

He reached out to comfort her, and she pulled away from his touch.

"And the guns. Your rifle, the other, the regular ones, you know," she said in her monotone.

"The six-shooters?"

She nodded.

"Well, we're not that far from Jerome. We can walk it." There was no point in telling her how hopeless any escape was now. A gimp, a woman, and a baby, all hoping to outrun the Tate boys with no horse, no guns, and no food. And he still wasn't sure if it was all right to move Ben. And Mary Grace was sitting on the ground in some kind of

trance, staring off into the distance like she was watching
for the U.S. Cavalry. What in hell had they done to her?

"Did they stay all night with you?" he asked. *Did
they take turns with you, passing you around and
laughing?* He'd kill them all. Jackson, the others, if he
lived. They'd all die for hurting Sweet Mary.

She shook her head. It was as much of a response as
he was likely to get.

"Did they hurt you much?" he asked, so quietly he
wasn't even sure she heard.

"Mary?" There had been three of them, and he'd
been out for hours. Now here she sat, and he might as
well be asking Ben what happened, for all the answers
Sweet Mary was giving him.

She mumbled something he couldn't hear and sat
rubbing her arms as if she couldn't get warm.

"How long they been gone?" he tried, and leaned
toward her so that he would be able to hear her answer.
She jumped away at his touch.

"Hours. It was dark when they left."

"What did they do to you? Tell me what they did."
He tried to touch her again, but she jerked back. "What
did they do?"

She shrugged. What the hell kind of answer was
that? And the look she was giving him. . . . The hollow-
ness was quickly being replaced by something more
ominous. Damned if she didn't seem mad at him!

"Did they touch you?" he demanded.

She shook her head. "How could you?"

"Now look, Sweet Mary," he began.

"My name is Mary Grace. Or Miss O'Reilly. I'd
appreciate it if in the future you addressed me by either
of those names." Her words were clipped, and despite
her anger he felt an overwhelming relief to see her acting more like herself again.

"All right, Miss O'Reilly. You know I couldn't help what happened to you. I tried. You saw that. I was willing to let 'em shoot me before letting 'em touch you, but . . . I'm sorry if they hurt you. I'd do anything to change it, but I can't, and there ain't no use being mad at me. I'd never force myself on you or any other woman, and I don't see as why I should take the blame for Daniel Jackson and his bunch."

"Are you through?" She waited until he nodded curtly, and then she turned on him. Her eyes were sparkling with tears trying to escape down her face. Her hair was a mess of red curls, the early morning sun setting them on fire. And her freckles were so dark they stood out like punctuation marks from her sunburned cheeks. It took a great deal of concentration to listen to what she was saying.

"Those men treated me better than you have, especially considering your little transgressions with Mr. Jackson's wife, along with every other woman in the state of Arizona. They didn't lay a hand on me, Sloan Westin. . . ."

"Territory," he said, checking the angle of the sun and listening for any signs of the Tates. They really didn't have time for this argument.

"What?"

"Territory. Arizona ain't a state yet. It's a territory."

"Who gives a flying fig whether it's a state or a territory? You seduced me. You made me think you loved me and what we were doing was special. . . ."

"Wasn't it?" he asked, this time rising slowly and painfully to his feet. His leg hurt like hell, but he didn't want to scare Mary Grace into thinking he wouldn't be able to manage to get them all to safety. How the hell he'd do it, he wasn't sure, but there was no sense troubling her more than she already was.

"I thought I meant something to you. All these years

I've been so careful to not let it happen again, and then what happens? What do I go and do? I let you do it to me, just like I let him, and it didn't mean anything to either of you, and now I've slept with two men who weren't my husband and never will be and . . ."

"Maybe you just ain't too good at pickin' your men," Sloan said with a shrug. "You never heard me say nothin' about love, did you?" The thought of her letting some other man touch her wound around his neck like a rope. That she was lumping them both in the same saddlebag tightened the noose till he could hardly breathe. And then he heard what she had said. They hadn't touched her, Jackson and his men.

"You sure they didn't touch you?" he asked, searching her face.

"You're a pig," she said, and her nose wrinkled in disgust. "You think that all women are fair game whether or not they're married, or whether or not they're willing . . ."

"You was willing," he said, trying to give her a hand getting up. She batted it away.

"Damn you," she said, biting her lip to stop the tears. "Damn you to hell for making me break those vows."

"Listen, Sweet Mary, we ain't got time for this fight. The Tates can't be more than a couple hours behind us. I'll tell you now . . ."

"Miss O'Reilly. I don't want you to call me Sweet Mary or Mary Love or M.G. or any other endearment ever again." He studied her face. She was mad all right, but she seemed OK other than that. Mad he could handle. It was that sad, empty look that scared the bejeesus out of him.

"M.G.? That what *he* called you?"

"Who?" She wouldn't look him in the eye. *Fine.*

"You must be hungry. I'll find us something to eat."

She shrugged in response, and he sighed. They didn't have time for this. They didn't have time for anything he wanted to say, or do, to make her know in her heart what she did to him. Even when she was angry at him, his muscles twitched with longing to press her up against the length of him and hold her until he could feel his own heart seek out her rhythm and match her, beat for beat, as if they were only one being.

He limped past her, stopping to put his hand on her shoulder and give it a squeeze despite the unyielding body beneath his palm. He scanned the horizon, searching for something to feed his little family. A mesquite tree, fairly dripping with pods, stood within walking distance, even for a crippled man, and he started out for it.

Before he reached the tree, he found a dead coyote lying in his path. He kicked it over and let loose a whoop that brought Mary Grace running to his side, his knife clutched in her hand, the baby bouncing on her hip. So much for not caring, he thought as he smiled at his avenging angel.

"Dead coyote," he explained. His boot toe pointed out the arched row of teeth marks, complete with the two fang bites that floated above it. "Coral snake used up its venom on the coyote. Ben's gonna be just fine."

He ruffled the dark hair on Ben's head, the back of his hand brushing against Mary Grace's breast. The smile on her face melted, and he took his hand away. So that was how it was to be. Well, they didn't have time to celebrate, anyway. By now the Tates were surely up and back on their trail. The only question was whether Sloan could find them a hiding place before it was too late. It seemed to him Mason Tate had a personal interest in finding Mary Grace, and he didn't like the feel of that way down low in his gut.

12

Mary Grace focused all her energy and attention on Ben. He was going to be all right, and that was all that mattered. And if she was the kind of person who believed in signs from heaven and the like, she'd have allowed herself to imagine that finding the coyote and being assured Ben would live surely meant that what she had done was forgiven. After all, surely these circumstances were extraordinary.

Still, as she followed Sloan up higher and higher into the mountains, her breath coming in shorter and shorter gasps, she kept a safe distance between the two of them. She had no intention of making another mistake, nor was she going to relive her sordid past just to satisfy his idle curiosity. She let him touch her only when he was helping her to climb, and she kept her conversation confined to Ben, who now slept against her back.

Above her, Sloan sought a handhold from which to hoist himself higher still. His leg was a hindrance, her help an embarrassment. The muscles in his arms bulged against his sleeves, the back of his shirt strained at the seams, as he used all his upper-body strength to heave himself onto the rocky ledge above them and then lean over and put his hand down to pull Mary Grace and the baby up.

"We'll rest," he said between breaths once he had them both beside him. "We can see good from here, and it won't be long before we know where we stand."

To Mary Grace it was clear where they stood: on a precipice over a nameless desert in the middle of nowhere, where, if the Tates didn't finish them off, the elements would. She had bristled at him as though it was all his fault. If she'd uttered a single pleasant word to him all morning, she couldn't recall it now. She felt his eyes studying her and kept her own averted. The last thing she wanted in this world was to connect with him again. Open herself up for another round of pain and heartache.

"Why are you so damn mad at me, anyways?" he asked. "If Jackson didn't hurt you none, and you said he didn't, how come suddenly there's this wall you keep addin' bricks to?"

Why was she mad at him, anyway? He'd told her about being a ladies' man in his bronco days. He hadn't lied to her about anything, hadn't promised her anything, hadn't done anything to her that she hadn't encouraged him to do. And there she had it. He'd gotten her defenses down, but not without plenty of help on her part.

"I guess I'm mad at me," she admitted. "And you're handy."

He took her chin in his hand and raised her head until it was impossible not to look him in those cool gray eyes. The late morning sun glinted off his dark blond hair, reminding her of their bath in the warm water hole.

"Don't you never be mad at yourself, Mary Grace O'Reilly. I can't believe in your whole life you ever did nothin' that you couldn't be proud of. Givin' away your baby wasn't your doin', and lovin' a man ain't no sin."

She pulled her eyes away from his. "Loving that one was," she said quietly.

He was silent for a minute and then, just as softly as she had spoken, he told her, "I can't guess at what you mean. You're gonna have to tell me, Miss O'Reilly."

She missed the sound of Sweet Mary on his lips. It was her own fault, just like everything else in her life. She just kept getting what she deserved. From the first day she'd rolled up the waistband of her plaid uniform and her father had caught sight of her knees, she'd been learning about the price of sin. She'd had trouble sitting down for three full days after he'd taken his strap to her bottom.

And every misstep since, great or small, had cost her. And now Sloan was asking her about the most costly mistake of all.

"It isn't easy," she started. "There isn't a soul on the face of this earth who knows this story except my baby's father and my parish priest."

His hand touched her shoulder so gently she had to look down to see that it was him and not the baby. "If you're telling the truth about your fall, and I believe you are, there ain't a soul in this world who knows anything about you, and if you want, you can leave it that way."

It was true. If she pretended it never happened, no one would be any the wiser. If she pretended. But then there would have been no baby. And to deny the child would hurt infinitely more than the humiliation.

"I had a baby," she said, feeling the warm little body

she carried behind her and finding courage there. "I was unmarried, and the father of the baby wouldn't marry me."

"Wouldn't your father force him? What about all those brothers?"

"No one knew who the father was. Except me. And Father Kenney. He was the one who convinced me that it was my sin to bear and to bear it alone if I really loved the father and the church."

"But why? Why didn't he go to the man and force him to give the child his name? And the father himself? Why would he let his flesh and blood be given away?"

"He'd have had to give up everything he believed in, everything he'd worked for, bring dishonor and disgrace on his family, his church. And what would it have helped?"

"What would it have helped?" Sloan said, barely controlling his voice. "You. It woulda helped you."

"I thought I was doing the right thing, the pious thing, the holy thing. . . ."

His eyes were searching her face, trying to read what she wasn't saying. Behind his questioning gaze was a tenderness she felt she didn't deserve. Not after all the mistakes she'd made.

"How could you have thought it was the right thing? Givin' a child no dad?" There was no accusation in his voice, only confusion and a genuine desire to understand.

"Because it could have hurt so many other people, and the baby wasn't born yet, and he was just something growing inside me that I couldn't even feel yet, and . . ."

"And when you could?"

It was the question she'd asked herself a hundred times, a million times, in the last thirteen years. When the baby was real, why hadn't she been brave enough to shout the truth from the rooftops?

"By then it was too late."

"How old did you say you were?" he asked.

"Fifteen when he was born. Almost fifteen and a half." She remembered a time when she was so young that ages were measured in half years, quarter years, almost years. Seven and a half. Nine and three quarters. Almost fourteen. That was when it had ended. After she'd turned fifteen.

"There's something you ain't telling me, Sweet Mary, and that's all right. Now ain't the time." He swept his hand across the landscape. "And this ain't the place."

"Sloan," she said, putting her hand on his forearm and taking a deep breath, "I'm sorry. I wish things had been different."

"Don't see as how they could be any more changed for you than they already are, Mary Grace. Maybe you'd be best off just puttin' your lessons behind you and moving on."

"Until you, I hadn't been with a man since that time. I haven't been to church, nor back home. I meant to keep it that way for the rest of my life."

"And now?"

"Now everything is mixed up. Even the ground I walk on has shifted. I don't know anymore where the mines are hidden."

"The mines?"

"Landmines. I don't know where it's safe. I had my future mapped out to avoid any more pain or hurt. I knew what I was supposed to do, and I was reconciled to following the rules."

"Reconciled ain't no way to live, Sweet Mary. It's only how you mark time till you die."

"Maybe I have died. Did I? Is any of this real? The

Tates, Ben, you?" She reached out and touched him gently on the cheek as if checking to make sure he still existed. "It's like I've been in a dream since I landed in the river. . . ."

"Well," he said, looking past her. "It just turned into a nightmare."

"What?" she asked.

He took several steps to the right, dragging Mary Grace with him.

"Oh my God," she whispered. "They're here, aren't they?"

"Down below," he answered. "About an hour, I'd say. We've got about an hour."

They trod silently, Mary Grace following in Sloan's footsteps beneath the blessed shade of the tall trees that covered the mountains they now crawled over. The pines concealed them and kept them cool as they searched for a place to hide. Several times Sloan turned around and asked her with his eyes if she was all right. There was fear in his eyes as he looked at her and Ben, and she knew he wasn't afraid for himself.

After what seemed like hours, Sloan signaled for her to stop and wait, and she and Ben huddled against the trunk of a tree and prayed. She watched him limp cautiously toward a little cabin, his knife in his hand, ready for anything. The smell of smoke lingered in the air, and fresh wash hung on a line, almost horizontal in the strong breeze. The outhouse door stood ajar, fumes rising from it and fouling the air.

It was a miner's cabin. With any luck, Sloan had said, the occupant would be out somewhere hoping to strike it rich. He peered in the little window, so sooty that from where she stood Mary Grace couldn't see through it at all. Then he went around to the door and knocked.

Finally, he motioned to Mary Grace to come ahead, and she followed him into the dim cabin, the baby doing some sort of dance in his sling behind her.

A loaf of bread sat on the table. Her mouth watered. Sloan cut them each a chunk with his knife, and her hand trembled as she raised it to her mouth. Never had bread tasted so good.

With a heel of the bread in each hand, Ben was lifted out of the pouch behind Mary Grace and set on the floor. He happily stuffed his mouth with first one fist and then the other. Mary Grace worked her way around one side of the cabin, gathering food and delighting in the small niceties of life: a bar of soap, a straight razor, a shaving brush.

A part of her registered the crudeness of the shack, the sparce furnishings, and yet, amazingly, she looked around the cabin and only one word came to mind.

Civilization. Oh, they hadn't made it to a town yet, but here someone lived like a human being, not an animal. He drank water from a cup, not a canteen; he slept in a bed, not on the ground. He wasn't afraid to light a fire when he was cold, and he had a change of clothes and a door on his john, even if it was outdoors.

Around her, Sloan searched in drawers, under the bed, and in the corners of the little house. He cheered at finding some bullets, bemoaned the lack of weapons. Then he slumped down on the narrow cot dejectedly, refusing the bread Mary Grace offered him.

"I'm sorry," he said simply after a while. "I dragged you to hell and back, and you're no safer than when I found you."

"Of course we're safer," she said. "We're with you."

He shook his head and touched her nose, tracing

lines between her freckles. His hand wandered over her cheeks and rubbed her bottom lip. "We'll have to split up," he told her. "I'll divert them while you take Ben and try to get to town."

He was offering himself as bait. Not only couldn't she face the possibility that he would get hurt, she didn't believe for a minute it would work.

"I figure I can get 'em to follow me and keep 'em busy long enough for you to . . ."

It was insane. He didn't even have a goddamn weapon. And she wasn't going to let him get himself killed on her account. Regardless of how she felt about him—and she refused to even think about that, especially now—she was not about to willingly incur any more guilt. She had enough on her plate already.

"Well, figure again. You can't use yourself as bait for Mason Tate. He'll kill you. For God's sake, you stole his nephew."

"We got one thing to consider, Miss O'Reilly, and that's Ben's safety." They both looked at the child, rolling around on the floor, the bread still wadded in his mouth, one hand playing with his toes, a constant stream of gurgling coming from his lips.

"No," she argued. Even if he was doing it strictly for Ben, there had to be another way. A way with less dire consequences. A way that at least offered them some hope of getting all three of them out alive. She could only think of one. "There isn't just Ben's safety to consider. If I was to run, and Mason Tate found me, he and his brothers would rape and murder me." Sloan opened his mouth, but she continued. "They would. You know it. But if I stay here with Ben . . ."

"But your way they won't even have to go looking for you. You'll be waiting for them and once they get their hands on you and my son there's no telling what they'll do. And I'd rather be dead than let them touch you or take Ben and have him grow up to be just like them."

"Well, if we use your plan, they'll no doubt catch up to you and kill you. So, you're dead, which doesn't seem to worry you much, and Ben and I are back with the Tates. Only now, of course, he's Horace again, and if they let me live, I'm their moll, or whatever they call the bad guy's woman. I can't leave Ben—I mean Horace—so I am forced into a life of crime, as is the baby, who grows up to be the spitting image of his uncles, in looks and in deed."

"Don't you think he favors me, at all?" Sloan asked, picking up the baby and holding him beside his face. There was not a feature they had in common, except in their number—two eyes, one nose, one mouth. Sloan's blond hair contrasted with the baby's dark down, and even though they were both smiling at her expectantly, they couldn't have looked less alike.

But if she were to tell him, tell him she thought that not only didn't the baby look like him, but in her opinion, probably didn't have any relation to him, what good would it do? She didn't really believe that would convince him to abandon them and save his own life. And even if it did, at what cost? Being Ben's father seemed to mean so much to him. And if she were being totally honest with herself . . . Oh hell, this was no time for honesty.

"He favors you some," she hedged. "Although the eyes are definitely Emily's. Still, with you dead, Ben's future is forever linked to the Tates. He'll either be an outlaw or dead."

"You sure can paint a picture that's an undertaker's dream, Miss O'Reilly. I just know you've got a plan of your own. What're you waitin' for?" He busied himself checking what else the cabin had to offer, with more than an occasional look out the dirty window or through the open door.

It was a long shot, but what choice did they have? Here they were, holed up in a cabin with no weapons against three men, each with his own agenda and no conscience to appeal to. If only Sloan would agree, they had a chance, albeit a small one, to come out of this alive.

"OK," she said. "You tie up Ben and me and leave us in this cabin. Then you take off on foot for Jerome. When Ben's uncles get here, I say you left us and took off on a horse after Ben got bitten and you didn't want to hang around keeping him still. I keep them here as long as I can, and then I go back with them to their place."

"So far I don't see how this is any improvement over my plan. You jump in a puddle and crack yer skull, or you jump in the ocean and drown. Either way, you wind up wet and worse." He was rooting through a stack of cans in a corner of the cabin. "You just prefer they all have ya on the bed instead of the ground?"

"Mason won't hurt me," she said quietly. "And he won't let Wilson or Harlin touch me."

He studied her as though they had all the time in the world. "What makes ya think that?"

She shrugged and gave him a half-smile. "I think he likes me."

"Likes you? Likes you how?"

"How?"

"Yeah, how? Like you're a sweet young girl who don't deserve to get poked by the likes of him or like he'd like to poke ya?"

"He didn't touch me when I was at the cabin, Sloan," she said, picking up the baby and moving to the chair

with him. "I won't be with him long. I'll keep him at
arm's length until I escape again with the baby and meet
you in Jerome."

"How?"

"How?"

"Yeah, how?"

Again with the "hows." Did he think she had all the
answers? She hesitated.

Sloan warmed to the idea. "I'll get the sheriff and
we'll come after you. *You* don't try anything, understand?" He found a can of condensed milk and held it
up like a prize. He punctured it with his knife and let
the liquid spill into a cup. Then he added some water
from the pitcher on the table. As he handed it to her he
gestured toward Ben, as if she didn't know what he
expected her to do with milk. It didn't distract her,
despite what he might have hoped.

"Are you crazy? If you come after us, they'll shoot
you. The sheriff will shoot at them. What if Ben gets
caught in the crossfire? No, you'll wait for me." She
turned the baby on her lap and helped him with the
cup. He squealed loudly with delight, and when Sloan
laughed she thought maybe she'd convinced him. At
least he seemed to be considering it.

"No."

"No?"

"Absolutely no."

"Just a few days."

He sighed. "You don't seem to understand the men
you're dealing with, Mary Grace. While you're waitin'
to make your break, Mason could decide you ain't
telling the truth. He could kill you. He could bury his
sausage in your smokehouse."

"Bury his . . ." Her cheeks warmed, but she brushed
off the idea. "Mason's not going to hurt me. Just give

me a week. If I'm not in Jerome with the baby, you can come after us."

He was looking at her strangely, and she dropped her eyes from his gaze. It made her uncomfortable to be stared at so unrelentingly. And Sloan had a way of staring that gave away none of what he was thinking.

"How do I know you'll show up?"

He might as well have slapped her. "I guess you don't."

He kept staring at her, taking her measure, as if he had any choices left to him. Her patience ran out. Did he really think that now she'd run out on him?

"Look, you can go get shot and leave the baby and me with no chance, or you can run and let us come to you later. It's up to you." She wished she could honestly say she didn't care which option he chose. She wasn't that good a liar, so she didn't try.

"I'll get a rope," he said dully, leaving the cabin door open behind him. The sunlight streamed in and caught all the dust that rose in his wake. Mary Grace looked down at the baby, contentedly chasing the air with his little fists, trails of milk running down his chin.

"Nothing's going to happen to you," she promised the baby. And then Sloan was back, his mouth a tight line across his face, the rope dangling limply in his hand.

"It kills me to do this," he told her as he led her to the table and sat her down in one of the chairs. "I feel like some sissy, slinkin' away and leavin' a woman to face danger alone. I'd rather stand in front of that door and guard you both with my life."

"And get shot for your trouble. That would be real useful. Didn't anyone ever teach you the difference between bravery and recklessness, Sloan Westin? Haven't you ever heard that little poem: 'He who fights and runs away, lives to fight another day'?"

"It ain't me I'm worried about, dammit! Don't you

know yet that I'd be willin' to do whatever it takes to make sure you and Ben are safe?"

A shiver went through her, and she bit her lip. She would never let him risk his own life for hers. Her mind raced for another solution, but nothing came to her. And so she put her hands out in front of her, offering them up to him. He turned them palms up and kissed each one. There were tears in his eyes when he looked up at her, but there was nothing left for either of them to say.

Slowly, reluctantly, he tied her hands in her lap, making sure she could reach the baby if necessary, then tied her torso to the chair. To protect the baby from hurting himself or getting into trouble, he tied him to the chair leg. Then his head snapped up, and he went perfectly still.

In the far distance they could hear the sound of horses. He bent down over her and brushed her lips with his own.

"You taste so good, Sweet Mary," he said, pressing his lips more earnestly against hers. "Even with the fear in your mouth, you taste so good. You recall tellin' me you were eager? Remember?"

"You'd better go," she said, the tears scratching at her eyes, making her voice sound funny and her lip quiver. He caught the shaking lip between his own and bit it lightly.

"Tell me you remember the feelin', and I'll go," he insisted, waiting as if he had all the time in the world while the horses' hooves became louder and louder.

"I remember," she said, feeling her cheeks color at the memory.

"I can see you do." He laughed. And then his face went serious. "I won't be far. Scream your bloody head off so they don't try to shoot into the cabin. If they try to hurt you, scream my name and I'll be back. You understand?"

"They aren't going to hurt me. You've got to get as far away as you can. Don't hang around here!"

"Are you eager now, Sweet Mary? Was I right about fear bein' an aphrodisiac?" His hand trailed down her neck and brushed her nipple underneath her thin blouse. It stiffened at his touch.

"One week," he warned. "One week, or I'm comin' after you both. And I promise you, Sweet, Sweet Mary, we are all gonna be together and safe before Ben cuts that new tooth of his."

He kissed her soundly on the lips, his tongue invading the warmth of her mouth, and then straightened.

"Count to five, Sweet Mary, and then scream like hell."

When he opened the front door, the horses' hoofbeats were filling the canyon, bouncing off the mountains. She could feel the vibrations within her, her heart beating as fast and hard as the horses' steps, thundering in her ears, racing in her blood.

She screamed and screamed, yelling for Mason. The baby caught her fever and began to wail as loudly as she, and it was a comfort to hear herself and the child and not the horses nor any gunshots that might have echoed in the canyon. By the time the door burst open, she was hoarse and exhausted and hardly coherent.

13

Even Mary Grace herself couldn't tell how much of her confusion was acting and how much was pure fear and fatigue. Wilson had slit her ropes easily, Harlin had grabbed up the baby, and Mason was trying to get her to take some water from the canteen he offered.

"I went to the creek," she kept repeating, trying to convince them that she hadn't been running away and trying to steal Emily's baby herself. "And he was there. He grabbed the baby and I shouted for you, but he put his hand over my mouth and then there was this thing in my mouth. . . ."

Mason nodded, the deep scar on his cheek pulsing just inches from her face. "We found the handkerchief a ways back. How long has he been gone?"

They hadn't gone over that. How long would be believable? How long would be too long to go after him with her and the baby?

"I don't know," she hedged. "I'm so confused. I

don't know how long I've been gone. One day ran into the next. He hardly let me sleep."

Mason had risen to look around the room, and now he turned sharply away from whatever it was he was looking for and stared at her. Harlin giggled, and Wilson smacked him on the side of his head.

"What do you mean—he wouldn't let you sleep?" Mason was staring at her chest and she looked down. The fabric was wearing away from being worn day and night through storm and sand. She thought he might be able to see right through it, and crossed her arms over her breasts.

"We walked. That is, he rode and I walked. If I angered him, he made me walk behind the horse." She wasn't sure she was convincing them. She lifted her skirt to reveal the scrape on her knee from that day by the pool. "Once I fell, but he made me get up and keep going."

"I'm goin' after him," Harlin announced, heading for the door.

"You can't," Mary Grace said. "Because of Horace. That's why he left us. Horace got bitten by a coral snake. See there on his thigh? That was last night. For some reason the man didn't want to kill him by moving him and he didn't want to stay still and let you catch up to him, so he left."

"Westin!" Wilson said. "Why else would he take the kid, and then care whether he lived or died?"

Mason shrugged. "This man—can you describe him?"

Mary Grace nodded. "He was tall. Very tall. Of course, I'm pretty tall, but he was taller. Much taller."

"Yeah, yeah," Harlin said impatiently. "He was tall. He got blondish hair? All short and fancy lookin' like he just came from some barber shop?"

She thought of the mess that grew from Sloan

Westin's head. His hair flowed past his shoulders and he had a full beard and a mustache. She told them so.

Wilson suggested that he might have let it grow, and this was greeted with serious consideration.

"Did he say his name?" Mason asked.

They certainly hadn't planned out her answers very well. "Is Horace all right?" she said, changing the subject. "I tried to keep him upright so that the poison wouldn't get to his heart, and the man made those cuts and sucked on his leg, but then he started to run a fever. . . ."

Horace handed the boy to Mason, who looked him over. He pressed on the incision and the baby cried out. "Looks a little swollen," he said. "Might be infected."

"Let me see," Mary Grace said when she realized she hadn't checked the wounds in hours. They'd been living in the dirt, sleeping in it, resting in it, rolling in it. She'd been so concerned with the snake's venom, she hadn't even thought about the cuts themselves. How she had failed to consider the possibility of infection, she didn't know. The two straight lines were surrounded by very reddened skin that puffed around the cuts, making them appear indented.

"We're going to have to clean it," she told Mason, who nodded and looked around the miner's cabin. The two bottles of whiskey he found were empty, and he cursed under his breath and went outside to his saddlebags.

While he was gone, Mary Grace looked around for some clean cloth to wrap the baby's leg in. Her own clothing was beyond use, and the Tate boys' didn't look a lot better. Then she remembered the miner's wash hanging on the line. Harlin went to get it while she gently rocked the baby in her arms, crooning to him that everything would be all right.

They poured the whiskey onto the two cuts, and when Ben didn't cry, Mary Grace knew they would have to pick open the scabs to drain the pus and let the alcohol get at the infection. She gagged at the thought, and Mason sat her down on the bed and poured her a shot of the whiskey.

"Drink it," he ordered, handing her the dirty cup.

"I don't drink," she said.

"You do now," Mason replied. "I got enough on my hands without you fainting. If you'd taken proper care of the kid to begin with . . ."

Through the open door of the cabin, she heard the sounds of Harlin's raised voice. Clearly, he was arguing with someone not very far away. There was only one person Mary Grace thought that could be. Without even realizing it, she gulped the liquor she was holding. It burned the roof of her mouth, her tongue, and all the way down her throat to her stomach. It was like swallowing a burning match that ignited her insides until she thought she would explode.

Wilson drew his gun and smashed the window with it, peering outside and yelling, "What's your damn problem, Harlin?"

"Man doesn't like sharin' his things," Harlin answered back.

"We ain't sharin' 'em," Wilson said, smiling and baring his two gold teeth. "We're takin' 'em."

"Oh, that should clear it up," Mason said. "Bring 'im in here."

An old man nearly fell into the small cabin, now grossly overcrowded with Mary Grace, the baby, the Tates, and the cabin's owner. Behind him strode Harlin, looking incongruous, his little-boy face ringed with blond curls, his gun trained on the old man.

"Take whatever you want," the man said. "I ain't got much, but seein' as how you got a woman and a child with you, I don't want to be unfriendly."

Wilson laughed. "Thanks, old man. We was waitin' for your permission."

"Can I shoot him, Mason?" Harlin asked. Mason was running a flame beneath his knife in preparation for opening the baby's wounds. If he heard Harlin, he made no move to answer him.

"No," Mary Grace said in his stead. "The man offered you whatever you want, Harlin. Just take what you need and leave him alone. Did you get a clean cloth?"

"You spend last night in your cabin, old man?" Mason asked, ignoring the others and their talk.

"Course I did. Only a damn fool stays out in the desert."

Harlin put the barrel of his pistol against the man's nose, pushing until he could see clear up to his sinuses. "We all stayed out in the desert last night, pisshead. You callin' Mason Tate a damn fool?"

"Mason Tate?" the man repeated, leaning against the wall for support. "You the Tate boys?"

Mason Tate crossed the room swiftly and put his hand against the old man's neck, raising him until the man stood tottering on his tiptoes. "I asked you if you stayed in your cabin last night."

"I did, I did. I said I did," the man sputtered. "You were welcome, but I didn't know you were out there, though I did hear some noises in the night."

"This woman here last night?" Mason asked.

"No, oh no," he said, shaking his head vehemently. "I didn't touch your woman. Never saw your woman. Wasn't she with you?"

"Let me shoot him, Mason," Harlin begged. "I ain't shot no one in a long time. A week, maybe."

Mary Grace felt dizzy. The alcohol had gone to her head. She groped for the bed, stumbling over her feet, swaying back and forth, flailing her arms, falling against Wilson. He steadied her and pushed her toward the cot. She grabbed his arm and fought her thickening tongue. "He can't sloot sim," she said. "I mean, he can't hoot slim."

Mason lifted the man higher still off the floor. "What kind of noises did you hear last night?"

"Well, first I heard a shot. Leastwise, I thought that was what woke me up. Then I heard a scream way off in the distance. Miles maybe. Can't tell around here, what with the mountains and the desert and all the damn rocks. If I'd a known what direction it came from I'd a gone to help, but I'm tellin' ya around here there's just no telling . . ."

Mason turned and looked at Mary Grace, who was rocking slightly on the bed, her jaw feeling slack, her eyelids heavy.

"What was the gunshot?" he asked.

"Shake," she muttered. Wilson put one hand on her arm and shook her gently. "No, no. Corkle shake. Coral snake. That's it. Corkle snake."

Mason tried to keep a straight face as Mary Grace fought for her dignity. "And the scream?" he asked.

She sobered slightly, remembering Jackson coming toward her, his intentions hard and thick in his hand, coming closer and closer. Overwhelmed by nausea, she leaped toward the door and heaved onto the ground that surrounded the one rickety wooden step to the cabin. She leaned against the door frame weakly.

Behind her she could hear Harlin pleading with Mason to let him go after Sloan.

"Damn it, Harlin, stop pesterin' me. We're gonna stay here till tomorrow to make sure Horace is OK. If you gotta send someone hoppin' over coals in hell, you can have this guy. He don't have anythin' more to look forward to anyway, do you, old man?"

"Now look, I can make y'all a nice supper, maybe give your clothes a good washin'. I'm a useful man. I don't mean you no harm and I . . ."

A shot rang out. Mary Grace crumpled very ungracefully down the edge of the doorway and sprawled out, her face smacking into the step on its way toward the dirt.

He hid only a hundred yards or so from the house, far enough to be safely out of view, but not so far that he couldn't hear men's voices filtering up to him through the trees. Whoever had built the tumbledown cabin was either an idiot or hadn't an enemy in the world, until now. There were blinds everywhere, up to within feet of the house, where a man could hide and watch without being seen.

Everything seemed calm, and he figured their plan was working. But he wasn't going anywhere until he saw Mary Grace come out of that cabin and mount up with the Tates. Bile rose in his throat, and he spit it out on the ground next to him. Waiting had always been the hardest thing for him to do.

Sloan froze where he was when the shot rang out. He'd heard the men arguing, but there had been no screams from Mary Grace, no warning that she was in danger. He told himself it couldn't be her, but his heart refused to come down from his throat. He circled silently to where he could see the front of the house without being seen.

Mary Grace lay motionless in the doorway, Mason Tate leaning over her. A shout died in Sloan's throat as Mason gently lifted her torso and cradled it against his body, brushing the hair out of her eyes, stroking her face. Stunned, Sloan took in the whole tender scene: Mason yelling for water, Wilson running with the canteen and then stepping back, just watching, while Mason put the water to her lips.

"Get that body the hell outta there, Harlin," Mason yelled over his shoulder. "I don't want Miss O'Reilly seeing it when she wakes up."

Harlin dragged the small old man out the door and around the side of the house, leaving blood behind him like a slug's trail. When he returned, Mason still held Mary Grace, who lay limply in his arms.

"Make up the bed for her, and then find us something to eat."

"I don't make beds," Harlin said. "That's women's work." He stood on the step behind Mason, peering over his shoulder at Mary Grace. "Let her do it. She's wakin' up."

In a flash, Mason Tate struck Harlin behind the knees. He landed on his butt with a crash that startled a shriek out of the barely conscious Mary Grace. Her body jerked, and her arms went around Mason's neck. Well, he'd be damned! What an actress she'd been. He leaned against the tree trunk for support, but he couldn't drag his eyes away.

Mary Grace pulled as suddenly away from Mason as she had rushed into his embrace. She grabbed at her head and covered her eyes with her hands.

Mason let her go, backing away slightly. "You all right now?" he asked her gruffly. She nodded and he stood, letting her roll off his lap and back down into the dirt.

After they went into the house, Mary Grace got to her knees, her hands crossed against her stomach in obvious pain. Spasm after spasm racked her body as waves of dry heaves washed over her. Twice Mason came to the doorway and looked out, shook his head, and disappeared. The third time he came out, he whisked her off the ground like a sack of potatoes, and carried her into the cabin.

It was the most confusing few minutes of Sloan Westin's life.

Hours of what appeared to be ordinary domestic life went by. The odor of baked beans tortured his stomach, the sight of Ben drinking from a cup held by Harlin Tate stung his eyes, and not seeing Mary Grace at all pricked all his nerve endings.

The Tates all made use of the outhouse, their guns drawn for the trip both there and back, as though they were expecting unwanted company. Harlin, the only one small enough to fit into the dead miner's clothes, had changed into one of his clean shirts.

Just before dusk, Mary Grace came out with Mason following her. She was pale and shaky on her feet, and Sloan's arm stretched out to steady her despite the distance. But it was Mason's hand that caught her elbow and steered her to the outhouse, and it was Mason who handed her a small pile of clothing to take in with her, and it was Mason, a few minutes later, who led her back to the cabin in freshly washed blue jeans and a plaid flannel shirt.

When the last trips to the outhouse were made and the lights in the cabin blown out, Sloan moved to higher ground for safety's sake. He walked silently, listening to the sounds emanating from the shack, Mary Grace's crisp clear voice singing lullabies to Ben, Mason's deep voice ordering Harlin to bed, Harlin's petulant reply. A door slammed, and he guessed it was Wilson, caught between his brothers as always.

When it came to women, each of the Tates had his own philosophy. Harlin's had to do with killing. Wilson's had to do with raping. And Mason's, Sloan now realized, had to do with Mary Grace O'Reilly. And for that, he had to be grateful.

It would be impossible to sleep. Still, Sloan settled himself on the ground, covering himself with some pine boughs for warmth. Mary Grace's voice wafted up to him in the smoke that rose from the cabin where she was warm and, he hoped, safe. Seeing her in Mason's arms had rocked him. She didn't seem the kind of woman to double-cross him, but then she didn't exactly seem on a first-name basis with the truth.

Still, he couldn't believe that she could have been pretending with him, not back by the pool, not the night that Ben had gotten bitten. The woman hadn't even known how to kiss. And even that came more naturally to her than lying. He'd left her for Mason to find, and she was doing just what she was supposed to do. He just hadn't expected it to turn his insides out when he saw her do it.

His eyes drifted shut.

"Miss O'Reilly! Miss O'Reilly!"

Sloan came awake instantly, the sound of feet rushing by him. And then another set of footsteps, heavier, behind them.

"Leave me alone!"

If he reached out his hand, he could touch her ankle.

"Come back to the cabin. It's dark out here. You could twist a leg. Step on a snake. There's bear and cougar and . . ."

"And inside there are your brothers."

One hand searched furtively for his knife. A limb covering him rustled, and both Mary Grace and Mason stood stock still.

"Don't you worry none about Wilson and Harlin. They're harmless," Mason said after a while.

"Where's the man who owned the cabin?"

Sloan tried to reach his knife again. Mason fired two bullets into the ground inches from where he lay.

From the house Wilson called up to his brother asking if anything was wrong. Mason shouted back that it was probably just a rattler.

"We best head back," Mason said.

"The old man?"

"He knew it would be a mite crowded if he stayed. We paid 'im good. He'll probably be back in the morning," Mason lied. "I think I hear Horace crying." He reached out to take her by the hand. "They must be cleanin' his wounds again."

She backed up. He could feel her being torn between her fear and her love for Ben. He had no doubt how she would chose.

Mere inches separated them. One more step and she'd trip over him, scream, and Mason would start shooting again. He had four shots left in his gun. Again Sloan's options left him powerless. Even if he could manage to kill Mason, it wouldn't be without getting himself killed in the process, either by Mason himself or by his two brothers. And then Mary Grace would be left with Harlin and Wilson. And with them it was just a matter of which one went first. He wasn't even sure Wilson cared much about the order.

"Don't think I won't leave that child if I have to," Mary Grace said. "If Wilson so much as touches me accidently, I'm outta here."

Sloan inhaled silently, trying to take in at least her scent. He loved to hear her talk. It almost made him forget what she was saying, but not quite.

"He didn't mean nothing by what he said. There ain't no one gonna touch you, Miss O'Reilly, not as long as I'm alive." Mason put out his hand to guide her back to the house. Sloan could hear the baby crying in earnest and wondered if the boys had woken him up just to lure Mary Grace back to the house. He doubted they were that smart.

"I can find it myself," Mary Grace said, stumbling along in the dark.

"Suit yourself," Mason said. He cleared his throat and spat in Sloan's direction. "I can wait," he muttered.

14

Nothing, Mary Grace felt sure, smelled worse than an outhouse, so it was her plan to be the first one out there in the morning. At least, she thought, however incorrectly, after a night's rest the odor might have dissipated some. Mason accompanied her to the door, nothing except his ever-searching eyes giving away his nervousness.

Gallantly, Mason opened the door for her, checking inside to make sure no one lurked within. He handed her a wad of paper, which she took with some embarrassment, and then he shut the door and began whistling.

Inside, Mary Grace lowered her jeans and squatted over the hole in the ground. Of every modern convenience she missed, none came close to a real bathroom, with a porcelain toilet, soft toilet paper, and a sink to wash up at properly. Here, what was there, but a hole and a few twigs and scratches in the dirt. Scratches that resembled two letters. S.M. Sweet Mary!

She fell backward, losing her balance. Her hand broke her fall, pushing through a small pile of pine needles and discovering something silky.

"You all right in there?" Mason yelled.

"Mmm hmm," she said, holding up her panties and nearly laughing at Sloan's brazen attempt to let her know he was nearby and watching out for her. "I'm fine," she yelled at the top of her lungs. "Just fine," she said with a grunt as she struggled to get out of her jeans in the smelly little cubicle and slip her panties on beneath them.

For a second she had a brief flash of Sloan at the wheel of a convertible sports car, her by his side and Ben in a car seat behind them. She imagined herself reaching back to help Ben hold a bottle, and he seemed to be too far to touch. He started to cry, and Sloan took his eyes off the road. Mary Grace blinked furiously, trying to erase the images. Sloan and she and Ben all fit just perfectly on Climber, and she said the first prayer she had said since she was a teenager. It was to once again ride with her two men.

Instead, it was tacitly decided that Mary Grace would ride behind Mason Tate. Harlin would ride with his nephew strapped to his back, and Wilson, after a brief talk with his older brother that had left him sullen and quiet, would keep his distance from the others and ride on ahead. Little Ben's wounds looked less angry in the morning light. After what felt like a feast compared to what she'd eaten on the run, they mounted up in silence to begin the journey to the Tates' cabin.

Mason Tate was bigger than Sloan. Though his head seemed about the same distance above Mary Grace's, his buttocks took up much more of the saddle, his stockier legs pressed against hers, and his middle was too wide for Mary Grace's hands to find each other. With so little room left to her, Mary Grace's body was pressed up tightly against his. Because she couldn't seat herself properly the way Sloan had taught her, each step the horse took thrust her up against Mason. Her head was whipped back, her teeth smashed against each other, her breasts were pressed flat, and her breath rushed out of her.

"This ain't gonna work." Mason reached behind him as if she were some little rag doll and pulled her onto his lap.

"Mason, are ya thinkin' with yer short arm or what?" Harlin whined. "If ya ain't got room for her, give her over to Wilson."

Mary Grace stiffened and held her breath. They hadn't gone more than a hundred yards or so from the house. If the journey she and Sloan had made to the cabin was any indication, it was bound to be a long ride back to Oak Creek Canyon. She didn't relish the thought of sharing a saddle with Wilson Tate.

If it wasn't for Mary Grace and the baby, Sloan could have rigged some kind of snare to trip up the horses. Instead, he could only watch as they filed passed him, Mary Grace cuddled into Mason Tate's lap, his son nestled snugly behind Harlin.

"You want to ride like this, or with Wilson?" Mason asked her, whoaing his horse to a stop not more than twenty feet away from where Sloan hid.

"This is fine," she said quietly, adjusting herself in the lap of the man who had no doubt given Harlin the go-ahead to shoot Sloan so full of holes he should have been dead twice over and floated to heaven on a breeze.

Sloan's teeth hurt from how tightly he clenched his jaw. If he didn't know better, he'd think she was pretty damn comfortable up there on Mason's soft lap. He couldn't believe he'd agreed to this stupid plan, letting her walk right back into the Tates' clutches and take his baby with her. He'd be a lot more comfortable himself if she seemed a little more put out. Again he told himself it couldn't be that she had any interest in Mason Tate.

Mason clucked to the horse and they hit the trail. Mary

Grace bounced along in Mason's arms, her red hair flying behind her, and Ben gurgling as he practiced new sounds that carried back to Sloan on the wind, getting fainter and fainter as they rode away. The boy had changed so much in the short time he'd been with Sloan. Ben had begun to smile at the sight of Sloan, grabbing at his hair and laughing when Sloan made faces at his tugs. Mary Grace had shown him where Ben's first tooth was coming in, white under the surface of his gums. How changed would he be in a week? How changed would Mary Grace be?

It was something he didn't want to think about, so he turned on his heels and made his way back to the small cabin. A decent burial was something everyone was entitled to, and he aimed to give the miner one. He'd have liked to think someone would have done the same for him if Harlin Tate had accomplished what he'd set out to do. The miner and he had something in common after all, he thought, as he searched around the perimeter of the cabin for a shovel. Both of them had been shot to death by Harlin Tate. Only he'd been brought back to life by the Indians, with all their spiritual mumbo jumbo.

Without looking down at the old man's body, he stepped over it and reached for the shovel that rested against the old wooden siding. And what was it he was brought back for? To save Ben from the Tates? He knew that Mary Grace believed that was why she had fallen off that bridge and into the Tates' lives. Mary Grace. He didn't know what the hell to believe about her.

He didn't even know what to feel. There were new emotions that were coming over him left and right like a herd of cows stampeding through his heart. And he couldn't tell which feelings were reserved for Ben and which spilled over onto Sweet Mary. Protectiveness. Hell, he'd never had to look out for anyone but himself. Now he was responsible for Ben and Mary Grace both, not to mention making sure the Tates hadn't gone to his parents' ranch. Concern. He was worried about her right now, sitting in a hornet's nest, and he was worried about how Ben would turn out if everything went awry. Pride. What a big boy Ben was already, and handsome, too. And he hardly complained. And anything Mary Grace had tried to teach him, he'd learned fast. Mary Grace. He sure was proud of her. Proud and something else. He didn't want to think about the other thing.

He dug the miner's grave with a vengeance, slashing at the ground, hurling the dirt, slashing again, hurling. He didn't bother making the grave deep. He had places to go and promises to keep. Promises. Did they mean to Mary Grace what they meant to him? He'd made a million promises before. Just what did this one mean to him?

Gritting his teeth, he dragged the miner toward the yawning hole. Harlin had managed to kill him with one perfect shot to the chest. The same Harlin who had ridden off just over an hour ago with Ben strapped to his back. Nephew or not, blood or no, Sloan couldn't let that child be raised by the Tate boys. Even if it turned out they had Mary Grace on their side.

And there it was again, he thought, mounding the dirt over the miner's corpse. Mary Grace's slender body curved against Mason Tate's hulking form, her wild hair fluttering, her quiet voice acquiescing. He threw the last spadeful of dirt clear across the grave, and then the shovel after it.

If he could just look in her face, he'd know the answer in a minute. Even her ears blushed when she tried to hide anything from him. He was being foolish, stupid even, to think she could have had anything to do with the Tates. Plumb stupid. So why did it keep rankling him?

"Sorry, old man," he said over the grave. "But I'm gonna have to take whatever you got in the way of food, and be off. Rest in peace." He made the sign of the cross and turned to more pressing matters, entering the cabin and taking any food he could find.

"Too bad you ain't got a horse." He cocked his head and listened for any sound. "How the hell did you get here without a horse?" he said, rushing from the house and looking around. Somewhere, somewhere, there had to be a horse! He'd seen the miner coming, and he let his eyes run down the trail he'd followed. Nothing. He followed it for half a mile or so on foot until he could hear the braying. Using the sound to guide him, he found the mule. It was old, its bones sticking out of its swayed back, its belly hanging close to the ground. Its hide was worn thin in several places, and two sores festered on its rump. Half the nag's tail was missing, and one eye was swollen shut. Without a doubt he was the most beautiful creature Sloan Westin had ever laid eyes on.

And he only got more enchanting as Sloan went through his saddlebags and found nearly a hundred dollars' worth of silver, a piece of turquoise as big as Ben's fist, and a week's supply of provisions.

"I can see there's a God," he said, opening a bottle of whiskey and taking a long, satisfying swig. "And I can see there's a plan."

He looked up through the tall pine trees, their tips swaying against the deep blue sky as if pointing the very way to heaven.

"I just wish You'd tell me what the hell it is."

The sight of what had come to be his little family being toted away by the Tates haunted Sloan Westin all the way up Mingus Mountain as he rode to Jerome. What an unlikely place to put a town, he thought. Of course, where there was silver, or copper, there was reason enough. And where there were men and money . . .

Well, wine, women, and song, as the saying went, always followed.

Riding into Jerome on the back of a mule was humiliating. Especially on a mule like Providence, who looked like he'd been through the same ordeal as Sloan and not fared as well. But Sloan couldn't afford to be concerned with his dignity. And the truth was, no one was likely to even notice him. Life was too fast and frantic in the town to bother with some no-account drifter on some old mule. At the moment, that suited Sloan just fine.

Music poured out of the open doorways as he passed the Prestige Saloon on Hull Street. It was still daylight, yet the bar was in full swing, with the patrons overflowing the tavern and standing on the wooden sidewalks, their beers or whiskeys in hand. They looked right through Sloan and Providence, tipping their hats at passing ladies and jostling for positions against a leaning post. Sloan guessed the smelter had broken down again and wasn't sorry. It was a rare thing to breathe fresh air in Jerome. He kicked the mule, who ignored him, and together they sauntered slowly northward through town.

All of the action was still in the southern part of town, it being too early for the red lights to be on uptown. It all came back to Sloan in a rush—the noise, the excitement, the women. Especially the women. He'd spent enough money in Jennie Banter's place to be personally responsible for her being the richest woman in northern Arizona. Blonds, brunettes, little Chinese dolls. He tried to remember any one of them, but only a redhead came to mind, and she'd never been in Jerome, never been bought and paid for, never actually been beneath him, here or anywhere else.

He dismounted in front of the Connor Hotel, pulling the dead miner's saddlebags from his mule and throwing them over his shoulder. Once in the lobby, he was

stunned by the sight of his disheveled self peering back
at him from the mirror in the entryway.

"Can I help you, sir?" A man materialized behind the
counter, eyeing him suspiciously. Sloan didn't blame him.

"You sure can. I need a room, a bath, and a barber,
in that order." And a dry-goods store, a gun shop, a
good meal, an assayer's office, and who knew what else.

The hotel's register swung around and the clerk
handed him a pen. "Certainly sir. Room number fifteen,
bath at the end of the hall. Water's warmest in the
morning, but then the line is longest, as well. There's a
barber three blocks down on your left, next to the
Central Hotel, cross from Otto's Place."

Sloan stood with the pen poised over the hotel register. It had been over a year since he'd signed his own
name to anything.

"Sir?" The clerk held out the room key, waiting to
take the pen in exchange.

Sloan signed his name and turned the register
around so that the man could read it.

"Room fifteen, Mr. Westin," the clerk said, giving
him a thorough stare as if trying to place him. "Top of
the stairs, to your left."

Sloan nodded and headed for the stairs. Except for
the steps from the street up to the occasional sidewalk,
he hadn't attempted stairs since his injuries. The stair-
case stretched forever as he stood at the bottom and
craned his neck.

"I didn't notice your leg," the clerk said in a voice
barely above a whisper as he rushed to Sloan's side.
"Would you prefer something on the ground floor?"

He would have preferred nothing more. "Thank you,
no. I can manage just fine," he said, his voice ringing
out through the hotel lobby as he put his left hand on
the bannister and took the first step with his good leg,

followed it with his bad, and then moved up a tread only to do the same thing again. It was a slow, tedious process that proved nothing when he got to the top of the stairs except that he was stubborn. Maybe too stubborn for his own good, he thought, looking back down.

At twenty to six, Sloan Westin, his clothes brand-new, a gun strapped to his hip, and money jingling in his pocket, slipped into the first chair in J.H. Brown's Barber Shop. It was not his first visit to Joe's, nor his fifth or his tenth. He always took a shave before he visited the women up in the tenderloin district. He'd met a few women there who had done the same, he remembered with a smile that exposed his teeth in the mirror. God, he looked like shit.

Joe came over with a dirty bib and a clean, hot towel. He never wasted money, time, or effort on what didn't count. If the smock was going to get dirty anyway, why bother with a clean one?

"A trim or a shave?"

Sloan didn't hesitate. "Take the whole thing off. Leave the mustache, though."

"And the hair?"

Sloan described the style he wanted. It was the way he always wore it. Before.

Joe nodded and put the hot towel over Sloan's face to soften his beard. Sloan could feel his face relaxing, all the little lines and crevices opening up and spitting forth a year of filthy living and death and fear.

"You don't look like a miner," Joe said, sharpening his razor blade against the leather strap. Slap, slap. Slap, slap.

"Not." Sloan's voice was muffled by the towel.

"Cowboy? I didn't know they were running cattle already."

"Hunter," Sloan said, the edge of the towel dropping with his motion.

"Bear? Bobcat? Cougar? We got a lot of good game

in these parts." Joe removed the towel and began to lather his customer's face.

"Leave the mustache, Joe," Sloan reminded him, staying the barber's hand.

"Yes, sir," he agreed, looking more closely at the man in his chair. "Well, I'll be damned!" A smile broke out on the barber's round face, and he leaned back to take in the whole man. "It is you, Mr. Westin, ain't it?"

Sloan nodded. "It is."

"But I heard you was left to feed the buzzards by Harlin Tate hisself."

"You heard right."

"You know, I was thinking about you just this morning. Man came in here and put me in a mind to you, I swear it."

He had stopped shaving Sloan and was staring at him, his head cocked slightly, trying to remember what it was that made him think of him earlier.

"I know what it was! Had a rifle like you used to carry. You know, with that silver hunting dog in the lock plate." He went back to shaving, pleased that he had remembered.

The steel razor pulled at Sloan's jaw. He'd always been mighty fond of that rifle and was damn sorry when Mary Grace told him it was gone again, this time with his six-shooters and Climber. So Jackson was in Jerome. Wasn't it a small world?

He stared at the image in the mirror when Joe was done. From the chest up, he was nearly the same old Sloan. Leaner, a few more creases near the eyes, but on the whole, he looked like he used to after a night or two of carousing.

"Sure did think you was dead." Joe shook his head as he brushed off stray clippings from Sloan's neck. "Someone came looking for you, after. Your pa, I think it was. He sure musta been glad to find out you was alive, all right."

Sloan put his hat on over the freshly cut hair. He ought to wire his family, let them know.

Ben Westin, with the reluctant help of Sunny and a few extra hands, loaded up the second wagon bound for St. Louis. It was ridiculous to cart things so easily replaced to a city the size of St. Louis, but the more things he permitted Anna to bring, the longer the packing would take, and Ben was willing to take every extra minute he could wangle.

Twice he claimed that he could hear the dishes rattling, and since Anna would be upset were they to get broken, they had to be repacked. He refused to bring dirty linens and insisted several cloths be washed again before they could be set into trunks for the journey. Having always been fussy about his food, it was easy for him to insist that the cook make meals for the trip.

Anna stood on the porch, watching the loading, apparently unamused by Ben's tactics. "Enough already, Ben," she finally protested. "You've pushed me as far as I'll go."

"I've sent more wires," he said, still attending to the crates and not daring to look at his wife. "When I get my answers, we'll go, and not before."

Sunny fumbled with the rope and then stopped.

"What the hell are you doing, man?" Ben asked. When he looked at Sunny, the foreman nodded toward the porch.

Ben's eyes followed his. His wife was leaning against one of the wooden columns that supported the roof. In her hands, with great difficultly, she held his old hunting rifle. It weighed more than she did, especially since she'd taken to skipping meals with Sloan away, and she had to rest the end on her shoulder, rather than against it. Nonetheless, she was holding it, and it was trained on him as he kneeled in the wagon.

"Now, Anna," he began.

She cocked her head slightly to look down the sight.

"For God's sake, Anna," he said, pulling off his gloves as he got up off his knees and moved toward the back of the wagon. When was the last time he had used that rifle, anyway? When he'd taken Sloan hunting as a boy? And Sloan had been so impressed by the big gun, too heavy for him to even carry, let alone aim. Now Ben knew why he'd been saving it all these years. Someday he'd expected to take his grandson . . . Well, what difference did it make what he expected?

"Careful there, Miss Anna," Sunny warned, backing slowly out of the wagon himself. "Somebody might get hurt with that thing."

"It ain't loaded," Ben said, jumping down from the wagon. Just as he turned, a shot rang out above his head. "Jeez!" he shouted as he hit the ground.

The rebound had thrown his wife back against the outer wall of their house, and she slithered down the wooden siding slowly, the rifle slipping from her hands and hitting the porch with a thud.

By the time he got to her, Anna had dissolved in tears, and his anger had mellowed to pity.

"I can't stay here," she told him as he tried to help her up, a little bit of a woman who seemed to be getting smaller by the day. "Everywhere I look, he's missing from. His room, his chair, that rail by the corral. He's missing from all of them. Please, Ben. Please."

She hadn't said that word to him since Sloan had disappeared. She'd ordered him, bossed him, cold-shouldered him. She'd made him eat alone, sleep alone, and worry alone. Of course, he hadn't exactly been a saint. He'd flaunted his trips to the whorehouses, making more of them than they'd ever meant, taken his meals in town, and praised the cooking over hers. He was embarrassed to admit that more than once he'd come to her drunk, and in his hunger for her left her, with bruises he couldn't remember inflicting.

He lifted her gently from the floor and carried her to their bed. He laid her down on the fancy spread and kneeled beside her, stroking her graying hair and wiping her tears with his clean hanky.

"I know you think I can't miss him like you do," he said softly. "But I do. And I miss you, too."

She reached out and stroked his cheek with the back of her hand. She was still the softest woman he had ever known.

"I know."

"Tomorrow," he said, taking her hand and laying a kiss in her palm. "We'll leave tomorrow."

"Should be home before supper tomorrow," Mason said to Harlin once he caught up with him. Mary Grace stretched in his arms and tried to adjust herself to some more comfortable position. There was none.

"Aren't we going to stop for the night?" she asked sleepily as darkness fell over the mountains.

He looked surprised, but Mary Grace wasn't sure if he was surprised by her suggestion or by her mere presence. He seemed to have forgotten she was there, picking at his nose, farting, scratching itches as though she weren't sitting in his lap or even in the same county.

"Didn't think you'd wanna. With the kid's snake bite and all."

She hadn't thought about that. The last time she had slept out of doors, Ben had been bitten. And then they'd been set upon by those horrible men.

"You don't ordinarily stop and, you know, make camp for the night?"

"Ordinarily? You got a nice way of talkin', Miss O'Reilly," Mason said. He bit at the skin around the thumbnail of his right hand. His left hand supported her back and held the horse's reins.

Maybe it would be just as well to ride straight through. The thought of sleeping in her own room, with a door, on a bed, had great appeal.

"Gotta water some cactus." Harlin guided his horse until it was shoulder to shoulder with Mason's. He reeked from the baby's urine, baked by the sun until the odor stung Mary Grace's eyes. The baby's rash would no doubt be back with a vengeance by morning.

"Both of those boys need a bath," she told Mason.

"Take yer leak," Mason told Harlin. "We'll wait."

Harlin rode a few yards away, slipped off his horse, and did his business. He was within hearing distance, and had Mary Grace been facing the other direction, he would have been within her sight, as well.

Ben, who had apparently been asleep for some time, awakened at Harlin's sudden movements and began to cry.

"Wilson," Mason shouted ahead. Wilson had been riding ahead almost out of earshot all day, and Harlin had ridden for a while with one brother, and then with the other. Wilson reined his horse in and waited for Mason and Mary Grace to catch up. Mary Grace felt his eyes rake her body and she looked down to make sure she was fully covered. She was, she just felt naked. "Head for the East Verde River. We gotta baptize Harlin and the kid."

"What about *her*?" Wilson asked, gesturing at Mary Grace. "You gonna baptize her, too?"

Mary Grace felt a nudge beneath her leg and knew that just the idea had excited Mason.

"Ain't none of your concern," he said.

"I just wanna help ya," Wilson said with a laugh. "'Member that time down near Tombstone? With that whore with the tattoo? You was knockin' on her front door while I was coming in the rear?"

"That's a good one, Wilson." Harlin laughed. "*Coming in the rear!*"

Mary Grace was not so naive that she didn't realize what the men meant. She tried to sit up straighter, but her position was hopeless.

"Watch your mouth," Mason warned. "Or I'll keep it in the river till it's clean."

"She just spent a week with Westin," Wilson said. "If she ever was pure as the driven snow, she ain't no more."

Mason bent his head forward and whispered near her face. His breath was foul enough to turn her stomach. "Westin touch you, Mary Grace?"

So now it was Mary Grace. She shook her head. "I don't think he could." Hey, she was sorry, but it wouldn't have done her too much good, sitting on Mason Tate's lap, to sing the praises of Sloan's prowess at lovemaking.

"Did he touch you at all?" he asked. Beneath her, his manhood poked again.

"Well," she said, trying her best to appear naive, "he helped me up into the saddle, when he let me ride. And he helped me down, too."

Mason looked at her, his eyes narrowed, and she returned the stare with what she hoped were wide, innocent eyes.

"He didn't try to touch you nowhere private?"

She surely didn't want to say anything that was going to get him any more excited than he felt already.

"Once he was going to, I think," she said, lowering her eyes. "But I threw up."

With some satisfaction, she felt the bulge beneath her subside.

15

Sloan had no trouble spotting Climber tied in front of one of the cribs on Hull Street. The horse appeared to be as happy to see him as he was to see the horse. After some rubbing of noses, Sloan slipped quietly between two small buildings and peered through the glass.

A man's bare ass was raised toward the ceiling, the fat jiggling with every thrust as he drove himself home between a fine pair of legs, which still wore black kid booties. The man's head was obscured by his overly large bottom, but Sloan didn't need to see his face to rule out his being Daniel Jackson. He didn't credit Jackson with that much ass or that much energy.

The woman beneath the heavy man glanced his way, and he tipped his hat to her before disappearing from the window and moving on. Jackson had to be around there somewhere.

Grunts and laughter came from an opening farther back from the street, and Sloan followed the noise. It was quite a party going on in the back crib, and Sloan pulled his new Smith and Wesson revolvers out from their holsters and stood with his back pressed against the side of the building, just inches from the window. The curtain tickled his face, and he used it to hide behind as he stole a look into the crowded room.

"You come on back here now, honey," a man's voice called. "You know I ain't got but one arm to hold onto you with."

The tinkle of a woman's laughter floated out on the breeze. "Catch me, Kyle. Catch me and you can have me!"

"I got her for ya," another man said. "And she's more'n a handful!"

"Kyle, you just lie back and we'll get ya set up proper," Sloan heard. A smile cracked his face in two. Three men's voices. All in one little room. Tidy. It was right tidy.

The rest was just a matter of timing. Sloan paid close attention to the grunts and groans, waiting to hear all three men pumping away in earnest. It wasn't a very long wait. He only wished that he were more agile and could slip through the window on two good legs. Well, if life wasn't perfect, it was getting damn close. Besides, the windowsill would hide his own arousal. All that bumping and grinding had put him in a mood of his own, and he promised himself a return trip as soon as Jackson and his friends had been dispatched.

He moved until he was centered in the window, a gun in each hand. All three men were buried to their thighs in their women, and a fourth woman sat smack on Kyle's face.

"Howdy there, gentlemen," he said in a carrying voice. "Seems I've caught you at a rather inconvenient time."

Jackson and Williams looked up, and Sloan smiled.

"Ladies," he said politely, "I'd sure appreciate it if none of you moved."

"What the hell? . . ." the woman sitting on Kyle's

face said. Without taking his eyes or his guns off Jackson and Williams, Sloan addressed her.

"Especially you, ma'am. See, I got my hands full with these two, and I'd consider it a real favor if you just kept old Kyle there in the dark a while longer."

The woman laughed and rocked her body a little. Loud sucking sounds came from beneath her.

"Now, you gentlemen," he said to the two men. "I want you two to come over right by the window. Easy now."

"Whadaya have in mind, Westin?" Jackson asked, unmoving.

"It *is* you! I thought I recognized those dimples," one of the women squealed. "I heard you were dead."

"Yeah, twice now," Sloan agreed. "Guess I'm one of them cats with nine lives, sweetheart."

"What did these guys do?" another woman asked.

"Stole my horse and left me and my lady friend and my baby to die in the desert, that's all."

The woman who had recognized Sloan punched Jackson. "You ain't never plantin' your root in my garden again!"

"Mine neither!" the other one said. "Imagine! Sloan Westin's got a baby. . . ."

"How long do I gotta do this?" the woman on Kyle's face asked.

"What the heck is this?" Williams demanded finally. "Your horse is out front. You want him? Take him and get the heck outta here."

"Darlin', you got any rope in there?" Sloan asked, ignoring the man's questions.

"Course we do," a blond said with a giggle.

"Tie their hands behind their backs, will ya?" He leaned against the windowframe, still smiling.

"What about our pants?" Jackson said, moving toward a pile of clothes.

"Another step and you're a dead man," Sloan said, the smile finally gone from his face. "Just tie 'em up, ladies. They were anxious to get their pants down around my lady friend, now they can just keep 'em down."

The girls hurried to do Sloan's bidding, tying the men's hands with silken cords.

"Can I put a little bow on this one's pecker?" the blond asked.

"Touch it and I'll kill you," Jackson warned.

"Sure," Sloan said and then looked over toward Kyle. "He still breathing?"

"Yes! Yes! Yes!" the woman answered, fairly bouncing over his face more and more quickly until she screamed out and stopped, her hands supporting her on the bedpost as she gasped for air.

"Someone tied me up real good out there on the desert. Tried to restore the capacity to bend my bad leg. I'm obliged for the effort, gentlemen, and I'll be glad to do the same with old Kyle's arm."

Kyle was wiping his mouth and trying to get his bearings. One moment he'd been in heaven with two women, and now the ghost of Sloan Westin was standing in the window like some pirate with two guns drawn, and Jackson and Williams were standing in the middle of the room, their hands tied behind them and little red ribbons around their shafts.

"Confusin', ain't it?" Sloan sympathized. "Now get the hell outta that bed. Here, girls, you tie him up."

"Westin, I think you've had your fun. You want your rifle? Jennie's got it at her place. She kinda took it in trade, if you know what I mean."

"Thanks, Jackson. I can wait on the rifle till after I've delivered you boys over to the sheriff."

"Now how the heck you gonna do that without our pants on?" Williams asked. There was a great deal of scuffling between the women and Kyle, punctuated with howls and nasty words.

"It don't bother me none," Sloan shrugged. "You girls got old Kyle tied up yet?"

The women giggled and stood back. Kyle was tied like the others, with a third red bow decorating his manhood.

"All three of you stand against that far wall, with your tongues on the paper."

"What! Westin I'm gonna plant you so deep in the desert even the coyotes won't smell you."

Sloan cocked the revolver in his right hand and aimed it straight at Daniel Jackson's most vulnerable spot. The three men turned and walked slowly toward the wall, grumbling and cursing as they went.

Once their backs were turned, Sloan sat on the windowsill, swung his good leg in and then maneuvered his stiff one.

"Harlin Tate do that?" one of the women asked.

"That ain't all he did," Williams said, backing up slightly from the wall. "According to Mason Tate's woman, he ain't no man no more, neither."

The women stared at Sloan, and his finger itched to pull the trigger. *Mary Grace O'Reilly. How could you have done that to me?*

"Don't you worry none, darlin'," he said to the woman closest to him. "I'll be back later."

"They hang horse thieves," she shouted at Williams as Sloan herded them out the door in their long johns with their private parts tied up like early Christmas presents for all to see.

Out on the street he steered them down the hill to the jail, people gawking and pointing, the men laughing, the decent women turning their heads and hiding their smiles behind their hands.

Sheriff Roberts found it hard to keep a straight face in light of the cute little red bows tied to the three men's privates, but he sobered quickly as Sloan related his story of being set upon by the three in the desert. He told of how they had frightened his female companion and that he was still unsure what had actually occurred because they had knocked him out, tied him up, stolen all his weapons and his horse, and left him, Mary Grace, and his infant son out in the desert to die.

"Untie each other," the sheriff suggested after tossing the three into a cell without freeing their hands. Then he turned to Sloan and asked, "And where are the woman and the baby now?"

"Mason?" Mary Grace called quietly after opening her door just a crack. "Is anybody out there?"

"Just me," Wilson said with a wide smile as he stuck his head around the corner just inches from her door.

"Oh." *Oh, shit.* "Good morning, Wilson. Where's Mason?"

"Why I believe he's taking another bath, Mary Grace," he drawled, leaning against the wall and inching his way toward her room. "He's keepin' a whole lot cleaner since you came our way. Why do you suppose that is?"

"Maybe smelling like goat shit has lost its appeal."

He was close enough to reach out and grab her, and she was grateful when Ben began to cry.

"Oops. Gotta see to the baby." She slipped back into her room and slammed the door. She'd let her bladder burst before she'd make the trip to the outhouse with only Wilson Tate around. What a stupid plan she and Sloan had made. She'd been so panicked, so afraid he'd do something foolish, that she hadn't thought anything through. She'd promised to meet Sloan in Jerome, but she hadn't the faintest idea where Jerome even was, let alone how to get there.

She picked up the baby and tried to soothe him. She had no more diapers in the room with her, and she went to the window to look on the line. Instead of diapers she saw Harlin's face, a stupid grin on it, staring back at her. Her scream only made him howl with laughter and gave Wilson an excuse to burst into her room uninvited.

She was shaking like a leaf as he approached her. "Harlin," she said, gesturing toward the window. "He was, he was staring in and . . ."

Wilson reached out and put a hand on her neck. "You're almost pretty when you're scared. I can feel the blood pumpin' through your veins. I can feel you swallowin' real hard. You scared of me, Mary Grace?"

"She got a reason to be?" Mason Tate asked. He gestured at Wilson. "He the reason you screamed?"

She shook her head and tried to calm herself. Mason stood with his hair dripping on her floor, seething at his brother. Everything was out of control. "Harlin," she said. "He was just looking in the window and it startled me."

Ben was howling. Mason took him, noticed he was wet, and handed him over to Wilson.

"He needs changin'," Mason told him.

"So change him," Wilson answered, holding the baby out for someone to take.

Mason looked at him like some prairie dog that managed to steal a bear's honeycomb. "Who you askin' to do that, Willie?" he said smugly.

Wilson wouldn't bite. He put the baby on the braided floor mat and turned on his heel. "He can sit in his shit for all I care."

Mason stormed out the door after him, and Mary Grace was left with the now hysterical baby and her own racing heart. She looked around for something to put the baby in and remembered all of Emily's things. When everything was quiet in the hall, she took Ben, as much for her protection as his, and tiptoed across to Emily's room.

She opened the door only to find Mason standing there, his shirt off, shaving cream on his face and a razor in his hand.

"Oh," she stuttered. "I'm sorry. I thought this was Emily's room, and I was just looking for something to put Be . . . the baby in." She'd better stop thinking of him as Ben for the time being. The name *Horace* refused to come to her lips.

Mason turned to her slowly, the hair on his chest still glistening from his bath. He was the opposite of Sloan, his skin a deep yellow compared with Sloan's bronze, his hair nearly black, while Sloan's was dark blond. His weight puddled at his waist and spilled over his pants.

She turned to leave, but his voice stopped her. "You can come in, Mary Grace. I ain't gonna hurt ya. I gave you my room when Emily was still alive. I didn't know how to ask ya to leave. The room, I mean."

Sometimes, like when the shaving cream covered his scar and he tripped over his words, Mary Grace had to remind herself that he was a killer and the enemy. Right now he was also her protector and the only thing between her and rape at best. She didn't want to think of what Harlin might have in mind. The youngest of the brothers seemed to get bored easily, and she might be their only diversion for a while.

"I'd be happy to switch with you," she said. "This room is better for me anyway. If it's all right for me to use some of Emily's things."

"No point savin' 'em for her," he said. His eyes were fixed on the neckline of Emily's nightgown, which Mary Grace still wore. She clutched at it and mumbled about having no clothes.

"I'd like to get you some new things," Mason said. "But going into town ain't such a good idea for us, if you know what I mean."

She nodded. *Because you're all wanted killers and thieves.* "I guess," she said. "Where is town, anyway?"

"Southwest of here, maybe twelve miles or so. I never was much good with measurin'." He returned to his shaving.

She put the baby on the bed and opened what she suspected were the baby's drawers. Diapers filled the top one, and she took one out triumphantly. "OK, B . . . little fellow, let's get you changed."

"You got any children?" Mason asked, his eyes on her behind as she leaned over the bed and worked on the child.

"No, why?"

"You keep going to call Horace somethin' else, don't ya?"

"My little brother," she explained quickly. "Ben. He was just a baby when I left home. Guess I miss him more than I thought."

"You're a right handsome woman," Mason said. He had finished shaving and had put on his shirt, and was just leaning against the dresser looking at her.

Nervously she looked around the room. "I need a clean washcloth for this little one's bottom."

He nodded and turned to the door. Before he left the room he said, "I guess we'll have to get married."

16

Several sheets of crumpled paper lay on the writing desk at the Western Union office. Sloan added yet another to the growing mound and cursed softly under his breath. He'd come directly from the sheriff's office, thinking he would be just a moment and then could return to the cribs. But this was proving a lot harder than he'd anticipated. *Dear Pa, I'm alive?* He didn't think that quite covered the situation.

He started over again. Finally, he approached the counter with the scrawled note and his pile of scraps.

"I'd like to send a wire."

The man spoke without looking up. "You done now?"

"You got some kinda time limit?" He must have sounded annoyed, because the clerk's eyes widened as he shook his head.

"No, sir. You take all the time you need, all the time." He was fairly quaking in his boots, and Sloan turned around to see if some desperate hombre had shown up without him noticing.

"This the wire, sir?" The man's hand trembled so much Sloan was afraid he'd never be able to read the message.

"How much?"

"Be fifteen cents, sir, if that's all right."

Sloan put his new rifle on the counter so that he could reach into his pocket. The clerk jumped back, his hands in the air.

"What the? . . ." Sloan began and then looked down. In addition to the two guns strapped to his hips, he had the holster and six-shooters Jackson had taken from him thrown over one shoulder, his band of shotgun shells for the rifle over the other, and his new rifle lay between him and the trembling clerk. All in all, he looked ready for a small war.

"I ain't gonna hurt you," he told the clerk with a sigh. The man nodded, but left his hands in the air. "You gonna send that message with your toes?"

Slowly the man's hands came down and he looked at the wire. He read it aloud for Sloan to verify.

"Ben Westin, Bar W Ranch, Tombstone, Arizona. Not dead yet. Stop. In Jerome awaiting arrival of baby. Stop. Woman to consider. Stop. Signed, Sloan. That it, sir?"

Sloan reached his hand across the counter and took the paper from the clerk's hand, crushing it like all the rest. "Sounds pretty dumb, don't it?" *Woman to consider.* Jeez.

"No, sir. Must have been the way I read it, sir."

Sloan shook his head disgustedly and picked up his rifle. The clerk ducked behind the counter with a squeal.

"Forget it," Sloan said. "The news'll keep." Then he sauntered out of the telegraph office and enjoyed a wide berth all the way to the tenderloin district.

The way was familiar to him, though harder than it used to be. The stairs that connected several of the streets on the side of Mingus Mountain were a challenge for a man with only one good knee, and he found himself going more and more slowly, nearly dragging by the time he stood in front of Jennie Banter's door.

The girls had been watching through the window, and the door flew open before he raised his hand to knock. Jennie stood decked out in all her glory with several of his favorite girls flanking her, ready to welcome him back to the world of the living.

"Sloan Westin! As I live and breathe!" she gushed. "You know, I heard . . ."

" . . . I was dead." He limped over the threshold, and her eyes darted to his leg.

"Girls! Help him to the divan!" She backed out of their way, her red gown swishing as she moved, the feathers at the low neckline dancing at the edge of her breasts. She had more jewelry on her than Sloan had seen in a jeweler's window, the stones glistening in the lamplight of the room.

He handed one of the girls his new rifle; another, the holster over his arm. He unbuckled his new cartridge belt that held the Smith and Wessons and gave it to a third. That left only Mindy, a willowy brunette whose bed he had shared more times than he could count, waiting to assist him.

Slipping under his shoulder, she put one arm around him, encouraging him to lean on her. His hand hung limply in front of her chest, and he feigned weakness as he waited for one of the others to take up his other side. Jennie herself stepped in. His hands closed around one breast on each woman, squeezing tight and sighing with delight.

"Why don't you just help him right up to your

room," Jennie suggested to Mindy and then turned her head toward Sloan. "Or would you prefer someone else?" She reached for his crotch and got a nip on the ear for her efforts.

"Are you offerin', Jennie girl?" Sloan asked, surprised. Jennie rarely slept with the customers, unless things had changed since he'd been gone.

"Ain't never been with a ghost," she said.

"It ain't like raisin' the dead," he countered, and she stroked his crotch as if checking the truth of what he said.

"I can see that," she said. Several of the girls laughed.

"Why don't I just let you fight over me," Sloan said, his hands now working magic on both of the women in his arms.

"I don't know about you," Mindy said, her voice the whisper he remembered, "but I'm eager."

Someone might as well have pushed him in a pig's trough. To his senses, her words were a long dip in a cold pond. *I'm eager.* Two little words that punched him in the crotch. Mindy was always eager. She was paid to be eager, unlike Mary Grace.

I'm eager. Said with so much fear, so much trust. What the hell was he doing in Jennie Banter's place, anyways?

"That's nice, darlin'," he said, extricating himself, "but I've just come for my rifle. I understand you've got it, Jennie?"

"A souvenir," she said, shrugging. "I paid pretty handsomely for it."

"I'll be happy to pay whatever you like," he said. She snuggled up to him, then backed away when he didn't respond. "I just want the rifle for now, Jennie."

"You taking your business elsewheres, Sloan

Westin?" she asked, her eyes trailing up and down his body possessively.

He smiled and shrugged. Several painted faces read his silence. "Something like that," he said. "Something like that."

Mary Grace spent as much time as she could in Emily's room. She told Mason she wasn't feeling well, complaining of cramps, a headache, and other symptoms he might recognize as her monthly time in the hope that he would leave her alone. She only hoped he wasn't like some kind of dog who preferred his bitches in heat. He certainly was sniffing around her enough.

Ben was cranky all the time. His gums were paining him, and the wounds on his leg looked angry. Harlin had taken him down to the river to bathe him, and Wilson had gone hunting. Mason was around the house somewhere, but Mary Grace wasn't venturing out of her room to find out where.

Lying on the bed, she scanned the room for the hundredth time looking for a lantern to rub, a bottle to uncork, a wand to wave, anything to provide her with a way out of the stupid mess into which she'd gotten herself and Ben.

It wasn't a pretty room, not feminine, not even clean. The furniture was mismatched, scarred, of poor quality to begin with, and much the worse for wear. The drawers fought being opened, the bedside table wobbled, and the mirror was cracked and pitted. If all of it had fallen off a train somewhere and tumbled down to where it now rested, it wouldn't have surprised Mary Grace.

Footsteps in the hall stopped outside her door, and she prayed they would just keep going. They didn't.

Mason knocked gently and then let himself in without waiting for her reply.

"You didn't eat no breakfast," he said, carrying a battered tray with a tin mug from which steam rose and a chunk of bread with honey on it. There was also an old bottle with two black-eyed Susans limply standing in it.

"This is very nice of you," she said, pushing herself up on her elbows and backing up against the broken headboard. "So thoughtful. But I'm really not hungry."

"Somethin' you wanna tell me before we get hitched, Mary Grace?" he asked, standing there with the dishes in his hands.

"Mason, I haven't said yet that I would marry you." She checked herself to make sure she was well covered by Emily's nightgown and robe. When she looked at Mason, his knuckles were white and his mouth was a hard thin line.

"Just when I thought I could let that son of a bitch live, turns out I gotta kill him again."

"What?"

"Westin. He got ya in the family way, didn't he?" He put the tray down on the bed stand and kneeled by the side of her bed.

"No, Mason, of course not. I told you he never touched me. Besides, I'm not pregnant, I'm . . . definitely not pregnant." He reached out and opened the robe she wore over Emily's nightgown, laying his big hand on her stomach as if he expected to feel a baby that he thought was conceived just days ago. Despite everything, she wished it were so, and the wish surprised her.

Through her cotton gown his fingers traced the line of her panties across her stomach, and his brows came together.

"Mason," she said, almost pleading as she moved his hand. "I'm not pregnant. I'm definitely not pregnant."

"Oh," he said thoughtfully. Then a smile crossed his face. "Oh! That why we can't get married right away? It's your time and you wanna wait a few days?"

A few days was all she needed to buy. If she couldn't make it to town by then, she was sure Sloan would come looking for her. "At least a few days," she said. She tried to sound, if not eager, at least resigned. "Maybe more like a week."

He grimaced, but nodded his agreement, his hand once again seeking out the band of her panties through her nightgown as if to reassure himself that there were feminine wonders at work. At least he wasn't looking for soiled rags. She let his hand rest on her stomach for the time being.

"What did you mean about letting Sloan Westin live?" she asked.

He reached for the bread from the tray and handed it to her. "Eat this," he said. "You're gonna need your strength."

She didn't ask for what. She just took the bread, honey dripping down her hand, and bit into it. Mason took her hand and turned it so that the heel, covered with the sweet nectar, faced him. He dipped his head and licked it.

"You are the sweetest thing I ever tasted," he said. He was just inches from her face. The stench of his breath filled her nostrils. "I can't wait to taste more."

"Well, you're gonna have to," Mary Grace said, pulling her hand away. "No one's tasting any of my goodies until I'm married properly by a priest in a church!"

"Can you be ready by, say, a week from today?"

"I'd have to go to town," she said. "I can't be married in these old rags." She gestured at her nightgown, then at the meager contents of Emily's corner. She stuck her chin out as if she deserved better than someone else's scraps, hiding the smile of satisfaction that came with figuring out how not only to get to Jerome, but to be taken there.

"I'll get ya the fanciest dress in Prescott," he said, grabbing her hand back and sucking on it noisily.

"Prescott? Where the hell is Prescott?" She pulled her hand away and jumped back from him, wiping her hand on the bed covers.

"Don't you worry now, Mary Grace. I'll have that dress here for ya in just a few days." His hand ran up and down her leg and she pulled it away from him.

"I need to pick it out. I need a lot of things, Mason. I have to go to Jerome!" She swung her legs off the far side of the bed and sat with her back to the man who was now her intended.

"You just tell me what you need, you beautiful woman, and I'll see that you get it." He played idly with her hair.

"Women have to try things on, look at the whole selection, examine the quality. A woman's wedding should be the fulfillment of her fantasies."

His arms went around her as he flopped on the bed and pulled her to him. "I do love how you talk, girl. You gonna talk when we're . . ."

She tried to push herself up off his chest, but his arms held her fast. "We're not going to be . . ." she fished around for the right words " . . . celebrating our vows if I don't have everything I need, and if you don't let me go, this instant."

To her amazement, his arms loosened. She didn't understand the power she held over this man, but she was beginning to understand how to use it. She rose on straightened arms, but didn't roll off his chest.

"Will you take me to Jerome, or is the wedding off?"

"I can't do that, Mary Grace," he whined like a child. "But if you tell me what you need, I'll see to it that you have plenty of stuff to choose from."

"I want to go myself."

His eyes were searching her face, trailing down her neck and peeking into the gaping neckline of her gown as she hovered over him. His Adam's apple bobbed, and his fingers twitched as he held her forearms.

"Ya can't, and that's that. You go through Emily's things and take what ya need. I'll have the rest here before the weddin'."

"What wedding?"

Mary Grace jumped off Mason and spun around on the bed, clutching her robe tightly around her. Wilson stood in the doorway, his arms folded across his chest, his weight on one leg as if he had been watching them for a long time.

"I'm marryin' Mary Grace," Mason said to Wilson and then turned to her. "Get dressed now, girl, and start makin' that list." On his way out of the room, he tried to put his arm around Wilson, who shrugged it off, glaring at Mary Grace until Mason shut the door.

For a minute Mary Grace just stood there, her head in her hands, asking herself what she had done.

"There's a basin of water out here for ya, girl. You want I should bring it in?"

"Just leave it." She had already removed her robe, but Emily's cotton gown covered her sufficiently. She opened the door and brought the bowl of icy water into her room, placing it on the dresser.

Then she began searching through the drawers. Emily must have had some decent clothes somewhere; she'd attracted Sloan Westin after all. A sudden chill ran through her. Had Emily been wearing the same clothes she had when she and Sloan had lain together? Had he kissed Emily through her blouse, soaking it with his tongue as he had with her? Had he lifted that very same skirt before, only to find a different woman's thighs to lie between?

She put the thought aside. What Sloan had done before he met her didn't matter. Their pasts were behind them now. At least she hoped they were. She knew she could forget his, but a man like Sloan Westin—could he forgive her for hers?

She went through drawer after drawer of pitifully worn-out clothing, throwing things around the room, holding undergarments to her nose as if she could smell Sloan's presence on them still. In the bottom drawer she came to a pile of baby things, too small to fit Ben anymore.

A tiny cap, embroidered with little flowers lay atop the pile. Inside, the label was of a shop in France. Beneath it, preserved in thin paper, was a christening gown, the bodice carefully smocked and set with seed pearls. A tiny cotton sacque, so small she thought it could fit a doll, stopped her breath, and she hugged it to her chest.

It crackled, and she looked down at it, surprised. Buried inside the folds she found an envelope addressed in a primitive scrawl to Horace Tate.

"You dressed yet?" Mason's voice boomed through the door. The knob jiggled.

"No," she said quickly, putting the note under her pillow and rising to come to the doorway. Stopping the door with her foot so that it was only open a crack, she smiled at Mason. "Patience," she said sweetly. "I'll be out when I'm ready."

He frowned. "Don't be answerin' the door in your nightdress no more." Wilson banged around somewhere in the house, his heavy boots smacking the floor until the front door slammed behind him.

"All right," she agreed, and then remembered Harlin's Peeping-Tom performance from the previous day. "And I'll need a shade on my window, Mason."

He grunted and stalked away. A few moments later he was standing outside her window, his back to her, guarding her privacy from his brothers. Whether he would turn around or not, she wasn't sure. Erring on the side of caution, she slipped reluctantly into Emily's skirt while staying in her nightgown, and then made a tent of it, kept her back to the window, and hurried into a blouse. Looking down, she took a breast in each hand and squeezed them gently. Was this the blouse Emily was wearing when she'd lain with Sloan? Her hands fell to her sides. She fingered the fabric of the skirt and knew she was torturing herself. She just wasn't certain if it was out of guilt, or envy.

Wilson had found Mason, and the two argued outside her window, neither looking anywhere but straight out toward the hill where Emily lay buried. Mary Grace pulled the note out from under the pillow and quickly opened it.

> *To my darling son Horace—*
> *I wish I could be there to tell you this myself, my darling boy, but I guess I've gone to meet our Maker if you is reading this.*
> *I love you, son, just like I loved your pa. He was a good man. Don't let nobody tell you otherwise.*
> *He done loved me and I know he would have sent for us if he could of from San Francisco where he went to make some money.*
> *Your uncles ain't too bright nor too good, and*

some stuff they done been bad and wrong, but
they did it cause they love you and me so forgive
them and be a good boy.

                                    I love you.
                        Your mama, Emily Tate

Well, she couldn't say she was really surprised. She
told herself the note didn't really prove anything either
way. Even if Sloan had never been to San Francisco, he
still might have told Emily he was going, in which case
this letter just confirmed the fact that he was Ben's
father. She tried, but she didn't really believe that for a
minute. Ben wasn't Sloan's, Sloan wasn't hers. They
both had belonged to Emily Tate. But Emily was dead,
she reminded herself. And she, Sloan, and the baby
were all very much alive.

Outside, the men were shouting loud enough for her
to make out most of the words despite the closed window, even with Dukeboy barking his head off. Mason
threw the first punch, Wilson smacking up against the
outside of her bedroom wall with a thud. Then, like a
bull, Wilson went after Mason with his head bent, ram-
ming him in the stomach, the two of them traveling
several feet across the dirt before falling and tangling
with each other on the ground. The dog circled them
wildly, his teeth bared and his one ear bent back.

Groans rose from the brothers along with clouds of
dirt and handfuls of grass. Mason's head snapped back
at a punch to his jaw, and the look on his face ought to
have been enough to stop Wilson, but somehow it was
not. Instead, Wilson plowed into Mason's midsection,
one fist following the other until Mason's hand caught
Wilson's face and began to squeeze. Mary Grace
thought for sure that freeing himself could cost Wilson
an eye, at least. And it probably would have if Mason

hadn't just flung him away with a grunt that rattled her window and her nerves. Both men lay panting, inches from one another.

Wilson's mouth was bleeding; Mason's shirt was torn. He looked down at the sleeve, hanging by a thread, and yanked it off, trying to wipe Wilson's lip with it, but Wilson grabbed it with two hands and pulled it tightly across his brother's neck. Mason was not only older, but bigger, stronger, and fighting for the honor of the woman he loved. He put his hand under Wilson's chin and pushed up, raising Wilson's chest off his, easing the hands from his neck. He slipped his free hand into the waist of Wilson's pants, and grabbing enough of the waistband and belt buckle, lifted him into the air. He threw his brother several feet away, scaring Dukeboy, who ran off with a howl that would have made a coyote proud.

The sound of air rushing out of Wilson's lungs carried all the way to the house. If Mason lost this fight, Mary Grace knew her safety was as doubtful as a tortoise outrunning a cougar. God! She'd begun to think like Sloan.

Wilson was back on his feet, though somewhat unsteadily. He was making his way toward Mason, who was yelling about anyone ever touching Mary Grace. He surged toward Mason, but the big man shoved him aside, and he tumbled against the woodpile.

"Look out!" Mary Grace screamed, banging on the window as Wilson picked up the ax and wobbled toward Mason, his feet going in several directions at once. Mason looked up at her as she signaled and pointed, and then a gunshot rang out and Harlin's voice could be heard from the distance.

"What the fuck're you two doin'?" he yelled. "Drop it Wilson, or you'll only be grabbin' one tit at a time."

Wilson dropped the ax, went down on his knees, and then pitched forward in the dirt.

"Shit," Mason said. "And it was gonna be such a nice day, too."

Harlin slid off the horse, Horace strapped to his chest, and pushed Wilson's inert form with his foot, rolling him over. "What was that all about?"

"I'm gettin' married," Mason said. When Harlin said nothing, Mason spread his feet slightly and balled his hands into fists. "You wanna add your congratulations?" he asked belligerently.

"Oh, yeah." Harlin laughed, pointing to the baby. "Me and Horace wanna take you on together. But we figure two on one ain't fair odds."

By the window Mason called to her. "Open the window, Mary Grace, and give me your water basin."

Mary Grace did as she was told, and Mason tossed the dirty water at Wilson's face. When he sputtered, Mason seemed satisfied that he hadn't done too much damage. He placed one booted foot on Wilson's chest. "I don't just want yer hands off her, Wilson. I want your mind off her. I want your eyes off her. You even dream about her, I'll know."

Wilson slapped ineffectually at Mason's foot.

"You want some of my weight behind this, Wilson, or you wanna tell me I ain't got nothin' to worry about?" Mason asked.

Wilson spat out some blood.

"Boy, he sure got you good," Harlin said. "But it's over now, right? Right, boys?" He looked from one to the other. Mason's boot tip was pressed up against Wilson's throat.

"I don't rightly know. Is it over, Wilson?" he asked, rolling his weight forward toward his toes.

Wilson nodded as his eyes rolled back in his head.

"Pisshead," Mason muttered as he looked down at Wilson's battered body and spat just inches from his face. Harlin's wide eyes followed his oldest brother until Mason snapped at him. "What're you lookin' at?"

"Nothin', Mason. I wasn't lookin' at nothin'." He paused. Then, as if just remembering something, he asked, "You think Miss O'Reilly knows much about babies, Mason?"

Mason smiled with one side of his mouth. "Well, if she don't, she's gonna learn real quick. I plan to get started on havin' me some before the week's out. I been waiting a long time to be somebody's first and only. Can't wait much longer."

Harlin laughed the guffaw of a young boy being privy to a man's joke. Mary Grace was sure they had both forgotten she was at the open window.

"What do you want to know, Harlin?" she asked.

"Horace's leg don't look so good," he said. "It's real hot, and he don't seem to be movin' it too good, neither."

Mason, standing next to Horace, reached out and gently eased the baby's leg from the sling.

"Shit." He looked up at Mary Grace and shook his head.

17

"*I'll explain it to you one* more time," Wilson said out of the side of his mouth. He had a great deal of difficulty talking, and there was no question Wilson's mouth would only get worse as more time passed and the swelling increased. Mary Grace had done what she could for him, but her main concern was Ben, whose leg was red, tender, and oozing green pus.

"Just let me take him to the doctor," she begged. "What do you think I'm going to do? Run away with him? Look at him. He's sick. Do you think I'd risk his health?"

"Let's say you go into Jerome with the kid," Mason explained. "The doctor treats him and you turn around to come home. What's to stop the sheriff from following you?"

"What's to stop him your way?" She ran the cool washcloth over the baby's body as they spoke. This was a waste of time, all this arguing, when the baby needed a doctor so badly.

"We'll have the doc with us." Mason put a tiny bit of

whiskey on a clean piece of cloth, soaked it in water, and gave it to the baby to chew on. "Emily said it would ease the teethin'."

"Please," she begged. "It will get him to the doctor that much sooner if I bring him into town."

"You'd be a good part of the way there already, if you'd stop your damn arguing." Wilson groaned as Mason sunk his fingers into his brother's shoulder. "Sorry. Look, *Miss* O'Reilly, this is how it goes. Mason'll stay here with the kid, since he's the one what knows most about cuts and wounds and stuff. You'll go in the wagon with Harlin, since you ain't too fond of me. I'll ride separately to keep a watch till we ain't too far from town."

Mason took over. "Then you'll go into town, get the doc, and bring him back to where Harlin shows ya. Harlin'll blindfold the doc and bring him back here to take care of Horace."

"I don't know how to drive a wagon or buckboard or whatever it's called. This isn't going to work." The baby was fussing, and she could see she was getting nowhere. At least she would be in town alone, and maybe she could find Sloan or get a message to him. "All right. But Mason, can't you take me?"

Mason stood up and took Mary Grace's arm. "Wilson, you watch the baby, I gotta talk to Miss O'Reilly alone."

Wilson looked at Horace. Then he opened and closed his hand slowly, testing it for pain and wincing. "I got my own problems. You watch him, Harlin."

In her room, Mason held her by her arms and looked down at her face. "I didn't want to say this in front of Wilson, but this is the way I got it figured. I seen you with the kid. The way you love that boy is what made me want you for my wife. A mama ought to feel the way you do. So if I keep the kid here, you'll be back, no matter how you feel about me."

She opened her mouth, but he shook his head, silencing her.

"I ain't got no dumb hopes that you love me, or nothin', so don't go sayin' what ain't so. You're willin' to let me under your skirts and you'll carry my seed, and that's enough. I ain't no prize, so I'll take what I can get. You're better than I thought I'd wind up with, but that ain't here nor there."

"Mason, I . . ." she began.

"No. I don't deserve no love or affection from ya, and I ain't askin' for it. Now as to me takin' you myself, I wouldn't mind, but you can see how it is with the boys. Wilson don't give no mind if that kid joins his mama or not, and Harlin . . . Well, ya seen Harlin yourself. He ain't got the brains of a pissant. If ya want, I will, but leavin' him with Horace . . ."

She nodded. If one of them had to be in jeopardy, Mason was right that she'd choose herself instead of the baby.

"Ya gonna pick out your weddin' dress while you're in town?" he asked.

"I don't think so."

"Remember this, Mary Grace. If you're trickin' me, you're gonna get what you deserve." The scar on his cheek pulsed. "Maybe you'll learn to love me."

He was leaning down toward her, and she knew what he expected. He tipped up her chin and kissed her gently on the lips. His hands reached behind her, cradling her buttocks and lifting her against him so that she could feel his hardness pressing into her belly. His tongue pushed its way into her mouth, running across her clenched teeth.

He shifted her weight so that he could hold her to

him with just one hand, and with his other he pressed on her cheek until she opened her mouth. His tongue plunged in, nearly gagging her.

"Maybe you won't," he said huskily. "It don't much matter."

Waiting wasn't easy for a man like Sloan Westin, used to taking action and going after what he wanted. Now, suddenly, he was not going anywhere and not sure of what it was he wanted. He only knew what he didn't want, and that was any more of Jennie Banter's girls. And it didn't have anything to do with his leg, or not being any better than Daniel Jackson and his boys, or the memories he could never recapture.

It was one damn redheaded, small-waisted, little woman with more guts and brains than any ten men he knew, who had willingly walked into the Tates' lair to save a child who should have meant nothing to her. He had thought about little else since he'd taken care of recovering his horse, his guns, and his pride. He'd nearly managed to forget the sight of her in Mason Tate's arms, and the doubts he might have had about her bringing Ben back to him.

He'd almost forgotten what she felt like in his arms, what her voice sounded like when she sang to the baby, what her body looked like wet from the pool, glistening above him. Almost, but not quite. When he lay alone in his bed at night, the memory of her cold behind pressed up against him came crawling back. When he heard the raucous laughter of the saloon girls on Main Street, the strains of her high, clear voice singing a lullaby floated by. And when he bathed, oh, when he bathed, he could feel her hands on him and remember the slick wetness that was a woman.

"You gonna pass or bet, Westin?" Garner Thomas asked. "I ain't never seen someone so lucky at cards and so unawares he was playin' 'em."

Sloan looked at his hand. A pair of queens and a pair of deuces. He bet and took one card.

"So, Westin," a gambler with a fancy pipe full of tobacco said. "Heard from Fannie last night that you had quite a day. Seems you organized a parade down Main Street complete with ribbons. That right?"

Three queens. The stake the miner had left him was growing beyond his wildest expectations.

"Guess so," he said.

"Fannie said you got yourself a kid, too." The man with the pipe looked at his cards and tried to read Sloan's face.

"Could be."

"Everyone thought he was dead, you know," Garner Thomas told the gambler.

"Maybe that's why he's having so much luck," the gambler said, throwing another chip in the pot.

"How do you figure?" Thomas asked.

"Well, way I see it, we got the Father, the Son, and the Holy Ghost!"

The men at the table kicked back and roared with laughter, Sloan included. His full house was a low blow, which he softened with drinks for everyone. They sat cordially around the table for the better part of the afternoon, oblivious to the rumblings beneath them of the mining blasts, unmindful of the transactions that went on in the assayer's office, unaware of Mary Grace O'Reilly as she asked around town for a man in a full beard and long blond hair whom nobody had seen.

The pile of chips in front of Sloan grew steadily until the gambler pushed back from the table and pulled out a pocket watch from his vest. "Four-thirty." He sighed.

"Down a lot of money for only four-thirty in the afternoon."

Sloan eyed the watch. He really had to send a telegram to his father. And he had some thoughts on how to spend some of the money he'd just made, too. Promising the men a chance to win back some of their money another time, he bade them good day and headed out of the saloon. When he reached the door, he turned and pulled out a few silver dollars, tossing them to the bartender.

"Drinks on me," he said to a shout of approval. There were some things about his old life worth reclaiming.

This time, the wire to his father took but a moment, his thoughts clearer than they had been at his last attempt. Then he headed for the mercantile, visions of Mary Grace in something clean and pretty sashaying before his eyes. The shop was full of useful, sturdy goods that didn't interest Sloan at all. He wanted something frilly, and he stepped up to the counter and told the clerk so.

"I need something special, for a lady. She's about yea tall." His hand waved somewhere around his shoulder. "You got anything that don't look like my mama ought to be wearin' it?"

"Did. Sold it earlier this afternoon." The clerk stood smiling at Sloan, waiting to offer some other service.

"And you ain't got nothing else?"

"Oh, sure. Just that one really did fit your need, I think. Good for an occasion. Lady who bought it asked for a wedding dress. Pretty redheaded girl. Tried to convince her to get a hat to go with it to keep from frecklin' so, but she wasn't interested."

"Another dress? Have you got one?"

The man put up a finger and headed for the back of

the shop. He returned carrying two dresses Sloan thought appropriate for washday or maybe working the fields. "This the best you got?"

"I told you. Had just the one you wanted. Lady was in such a hurry she didn't even wait for her change. She sure was a strange one."

"Well, what about some pretty underthings? You got any of those?"

"Sure. Tried to sell her a corset straight from Paris, France, but she acted like she never saw anything like 'em." He opened a long box and pulled out something that looked like an instrument of torture. Sloan couldn't imagine Mary Grace in it, though he tried pretty hard.

"It doesn't look very comfortable," Sloan said fingering the practical cotton fabric. "Nor too pretty."

"You know what she said?" The clerk held up the corset to his own torso, trying to show Sloan how it might look on the body. "Said she was glad they didn't wear 'em no more where she came from."

Sloan felt the familiar prickles he'd begun to associate with Mary Grace. "Say where she was from?" he asked as nonchalantly as he could.

"Somewhere back east, I think."

"New York?" Redheaded, freckled. The right height.

"Coulda been. Don't rightly remember. You want this?"

Sloan shook his head. "She was buying a dress?"

"Said it was for a weddin'. Why you so interested in this woman?" The clerk pulled out another box and held up plain cotton bloomers. "You just like lookin' at women's underthings? We don't usually like to take these things out for the menfolk."

"Did she say anything else? Did she mention a baby, or the Tates, or . . ."

"Said she was waitin' on the doc. Seemed real nervous."

"The doctor? Why the hell did she want the doctor?" He ran his hands through his hair. It had to have been her. He could feel it, sense it. He just knew it. "Was she sick? Did she have a baby with her, maybe half a year old?"

"No, sir, no baby. That I'm sure of."

"Then Ben's all right. Thank God. Do you remember anything else she said?"

"Let me see," the man said. "While I think, maybe you want to see something else?" He stood waiting for Sloan to catch on.

"You got cigars?" The clerk nodded and pulled out several trays. "I'll take a box of these." They were narrow little cigarillos, just the kind he used to like so much.

"Yes, sir." He put the cigars near the register. "Anything else?"

Sloan reached over the counter and grabbed the man's shirt. He pulled him until they stood nose to nose, the wooden table between them. "What else did the woman say? Did she seem ill?"

The man stammered. "She seemed sorta nervous, lookin' over her shoulder and the like. Oh yes. She was lookin' for someone. A man. Long blond hair and a beard, I think. Scruffy lookin', she said."

His mouth opened, but no words came out. At least Ben wasn't worse or she'd have brought him. What the hell did Mary Grace O'Reilly need with a wedding dress? Or a doctor? Only one possibility came to mind. *I'd a married her if I knew,* he'd said to Mary Grace about Emily. And now Mary Grace was seeing a doctor and picking out a wedding dress. But where the hell was she? And where was Ben?

"Where's the doctor's office?" The man's feet were no longer touching the floor.

It wasn't easy for him to run, not with one bad leg and the town being on the side of a mountain, but run he did, only to find a note on the doctor's office door: "Back tonight."

The doctors had said he couldn't father a child. Well, probably not, anyway. But then they'd said he couldn't have fun trying, either, and look how wrong they'd been.

"I'm so very sorry about this," Mary Grace said after she and the doctor had ridden out of town. "I really wanted to bring the baby to you, but, well, that wasn't possible."

"Where did you say your place was?" The doctor had taken over the driving of the buckboard, much to Mary Grace's relief.

"A little bit farther down this road." She searched the horizon for any sign of Harlin or Wilson but saw none.

"Young lady," the doctor said, pulling the horses to a stop, "there are no houses out here. Now what is this all about?"

"Howdy, Doc," Wilson Tate said, materializing from thin air. His eye was swollen nearly closed, his jaw hung at an odd angle. He glared at Mary Grace for a moment and then returned his attention to the doctor. "Ain't seen you in quite a while."

"Well, well, well. What the hell happened to you, Wilson? Somebody finally give you yours? You've been askin' for it long enough."

Mary Grace didn't think Wilson wanted to tell the doctor that his own brother had beaten him to a bloody pulp. Besides, Wilson wasn't why the doctor was here. She hurried to explain. "It's the baby. He was bitten by a snake, and it seems to be infected."

Harlin came riding toward them, not very quickly, and they all turned and watched him take his time.

"Took you long enough," he scolded her. "Get your weddin' dress while you was there?" He eyed the box behind her in the buckboard.

"Mason told me to," she said very quietly, embarrassed. "I had to wait for Dr. Woods so I went to the whatchamacallit, the mercantile."

"Well, while you did, I went home and checked on Horace." He looked at Wilson and his eyes watered.

"He's worse!" Her heart beat wildly in her chest as if it wanted to escape its prison. *No!* it thundered over and over. *No! No!*

"He ain't just worse," Harlin said. He brought some phlegm up into his mouth and spit not inches from where Mary Grace sat. Quietly, almost without emotion, he studied her. "He's dead."

She gasped for air, unable to draw a breath, the landscape around her turning yellow like an old color photograph from the forties. There were two Harlins, two Wilsons, and the man next to her was shouting something she couldn't understand. The buzz in her head grew louder and louder, drowning him out, burning her brain, exploding her skull. A hand pushed at her back, forcing her head down until her cheekbone touched her knee.

"Take deep breaths." Oh, yes, he was the doctor. Mary Grace had brought him here to meet Harlin and bring him back for her baby. She tried to raise her head. It was held firmly in place.

"This here's the clothes what she came with," Harlin said. "She ain't to come back, ever."

"My baby!" She could hear the scream rip across the desert and fade. It took her a moment to realize it was her own.

"Don't come for me no more, boys," the doctor said. "With Emily and the baby gone now, I ain't making no more trips out your way. You understand me?"

"Now you don't mean that, do you, Doc?" Wilson fiddled with his rifle as he spoke. The implication, even to Mary Grace's muddled brain, was clear.

"Shoot *me*," she shouted, standing up in the wagon and flinging her hands away from her body. "Dear God, shoot *me*."

Harlin pulled the revolver he wore on his hip and aimed it straight at Mary Grace's heart.

"Dammit, Harlin, put that away," Wilson said. "We're gonna be in enough trouble with Mason. We don't need no more. She's gotta go back to town with the doc."

"Oh, yeah." He looked around, finally aiming his gun and shooting the flower off a cactus. "Just like my tool, huh, Wilson? Once I take it out and aim it, I just gotta shoot it off to feel good."

"For Christ's sake, Harlin! Emily's kid is dead and you're making jokes."

"But," Harlin began.

"No buts," Wilson said. "Now she ain't got no reason to come back and marry up with Mason." He rested his rifle across the saddle pommel and leaned on it, peering at Mary Grace, who still stood in the wagon, somewhat wobbly. "You all right, *Miss O'Reilly?*" He spat out her name.

"How could he be dead? I don't see how he could be dead." She jumped down from the buckboard, tripping on her skirt and falling hard on her knees. Dust rose up around her and she choked on it, the dry smell of the ground filling her nostrils and making her eyes feel gritty. She looked up at the clear blue sky and yelled. "How many times are you going to punish me?"

"We gotta go," Harlin said, guiding his horse so close to Mary Grace that she was forced off her knees. She fell against her elbow and groaned.

"Kill me, you son of a bitch," she yelled at Wilson, pushing herself to her feet and charging his horse. "You've wanted to, so do it. It's my fault he's dead. Kill me." She pulled on Wilson's leg, groping for the rifle barrel through half-closed eyes.

Wilson's boot caught her squarely on the chin, knocking her back several feet before she fell to the ground. When she looked up, the rifle was aimed at her. She got to her knees and begged.

"Shoot!" she screamed, crawling toward Wilson on her knees. She would take care of her child in heaven if she couldn't take care of him on earth. "Shoot!" Who would take care of Ben? Emily?

The horses' hooves pounded around her, raising dust and blotting out the sound of her cries. But she wouldn't go to heaven, not after all she'd done.

She stopped moving, and a deep stillness overtook her. She was already dead. That was it. She was condemned to loving and losing children forever. Like Sisyphus and his rock, this was her hell and her punishment.

"He's dead." The horses came in ever closer circles around her, the Tate brothers yelling at her. "Don't never come back. Horace is dead and you ain't marryin' Mason."

Something hit her back. A horse's hoof? A rifle butt? She didn't know. She fell forward and hugged herself. Another baby taken from her. Another baby gone.

*   *   *

Sloan saw the buckboard idling up Main Street and stood up to get a better look. He'd been waiting for the doctor to return since supper. A black suit, a string tie. It was either the doctor or the undertaker, Sloan figured. Probably the doctor, the way he kept looking over his shoulder as if he were checking on someone laid out in the back. After all, an undertaker wouldn't have to worry about a stiff going anywhere.

The wagon stopped in front of Sloan, and the doctor nodded at him.

"Need me, son?"

"You Doc Woods?" Again the doctor nodded, then looked over his shoulder once more, shaking his head.

Sloan threw an eye into the wagon to see what held the man's attention so, and felt his heart stop. Mary Grace lay there, her chin bruised to a deep blue in the dim light, the rest of her face a ghostly white. He reached out and touched her cheek with just his index finger. She didn't move.

Doc Woods watched without comment. He let Sloan touch her arms, her throat, run his fingers through her hair, all without a word. Finally, as Sloan's hands ran down her chest, he coughed loudly. "Take it you know this woman?" he asked.

Sloan continued checking her over, searching to find what was wrong. There was no blood, no broken bones that he could feel, nothing to explain her lifelessness.

"Mary Grace?" he whispered, his hand returning to her face and stroking her cheek. "Wake up, Sweet Mary. It's Sloan."

"Sloan Westin? That you? Well, I'll be damned," the doctor said. "Heard you was . . ."

Sloan finished the sentence for him. "Dead. Well, I

ain't. Why ain't she wakin' up, Doc? What's wrong with her?"

"Laudanum. That and the shock." The doctor put two fingers against Mary Grace's throat, then looked up at Sloan. "You ain't fooling around with another Tate woman, now, are you? You ain't a cat, you know."

"The shock? What shock?" From his gut, fear sent out gnarled feelers that wrapped themselves around his muscles and squeezed his heart. He raised his eyes from Mary Grace and connected with the doctor. "Where's the baby? Where's my son?"

"Yours?" The doctor closed his eyes and nodded. "The puzzle comes together. But where does she fit?" He gestured toward Mary Grace, who sighed pitifully in her sleep.

"Mine," Sloan confirmed of the baby. He realized that the doctor might think he meant Mary Grace, but let the comment stand. "Where's the boy?"

The doctor's eyes dropped. "You want to help me get her inside? I ain't as young as I used to be, and meetin' with the Tate boys always leaves me a little the worse for wear."

"Bein' evasive don't suit you. You ain't told me about my son, you ain't told me about her, and you ain't told me about the Tates. I got fear bugs crawlin' up and down my arms, and they're nippin' at my nerves and itchin' my patience. I'm askin' you again. What the hell is going on?"

Ignoring him, the doctor reached down for his medical bag. He descended from the buckboard carefully on thin, brittle legs that nearly buckled under him. Then he took a pile of clothing that lay near Mary Grace's head. They looked familiar, but Sloan couldn't place the pale blue shirt or the blue jeans.

"Let's bring her inside, Westin." The doctor

unlocked the door to his office and disappeared into the darkness within.

In the back of the wagon, Mary Grace moaned. Sloan reached in and lifted her in his arms. Her body tensed, her hands clenching into fists, but her eyes stayed shut.

"It's all right now, Sweet Mary," he said, hugging her against his body and turning toward the doctor's office. The lamps were lit and the doctor waited in the doorway, watching the exchange and shaking his head.

"Dead," she murmured, and at first Sloan wasn't sure what she said.

"What? Did you say something, honey?" She was incredibly light in his arms. He wondered how long it had been since she'd eaten a decent meal. Probably since before she'd fallen into his life.

"Dead," she repeated, this time quite clearly, her voice flat and lifeless.

"Who? Who's dead?" he asked. Before she could answer, a chill so strong ran through him that he felt his grip on her body loosen. He had to clutch her to him quickly to stop her from falling through his arms.

"Gone. All gone."

"Ben?" His voice cracked with the word. His son was dead. The baby who, in just a few short weeks, had become the center of his life, was dead.

In his arms, Mary Grace exhaled a ragged sigh against his chest, her warm breath soaking through his shirt and touching his skin. He looked down and found her eyes open, staring past him at nothing at all.

Inside the office, the doctor had prepared an examining table. He motioned to Sloan to place Mary Grace upon it. She rolled out of his arms limply, her eyes blank, her body spent. Sloan addressed himself to the doctor.

"What happened to her chin? Hell, what happened period? Were you there?" He touched the bruise on her face. She didn't flinch. In fact, she seemed not to notice.

Doc Woods told Sloan what he had witnessed. Sloan heard some of the words, missed others, as his brain raced around trying to escape from the truth just like a mouse trapped in a maze tries to evade the cat. Ben was dead. He had no son. Mary Grace had begged Wilson to shoot her. He looked down at the blank face on the table. What had he done?

"I'll take her home, if that's all right," he told the doctor, helping Mary Grace sit up and keeping a hand on her to make sure she didn't slip off the table.

"She'll sleep all right tonight. If you need me in the morning, I'll be here or out at the Little Daisy Mine." They eased her to her feet, a man on either side of her, and when it was clear she wouldn't make it on her own, Sloan lifted her in his arms. He nodded toward the doctor and carried her from the little office out into the street.

High notes from a piano tinkled somewhere, saloon noises drowning them out every now and then. Women's laughter peeled from open windows. But nothing seemed as loud to Sloan as the uneven thumping of his boots on the wooden sidewalk as he made his way up Hull Street with Sweet Mary limp in his arms.

Her eyes were half-closed, her breathing even. She didn't ask where he was taking her, didn't struggle to break free. He could probably walk to the top of Mingus Mountain and drop her off the edge and she wouldn't even scream as she went down. He could leap off with her in his arms, and neither one of them would even open their mouths to say good-bye.

At the entrance to his hotel he shifted her weight and

bent to turn the knob. With wide eyes the clerk hurried to assist him, flinging the door open and hovering a few feet away.

"I'm sorry, sir. We have rules about female visitors in this . . ." He looked hard at Mary Grace, then put his hand in front of her face. There was no reaction. "What's wrong with her?"

Sloan headed for the steps without answering. Climbing them with her in his arms wouldn't be easy.

"Mary Grace?" he asked. When there was no response, he tossed her over his shoulder like a sack of wheat and held tight to the bannister with his left hand. His right arm was wrapped around her thighs. If anyone took note of their undignified entrance, neither of them was aware of it. Mary Grace saw nothing through her haze, and Sloan saw only vague forms through his tears.

Was there anything worse than losing a child?

"All packed," Sunny said, pushing the last of the barrels into the wagon. "Guess there's no chance you'll change her mind."

Ben Westin shook his head. Three wagonloads of belongings were packed and ready to be driven to St. Louis. He and Anna were going by train. Sunny and some of the other hands would drive the wagons. Then Sunny would come back and run the Bar W. Probably right into the ground.

His watch said twelve-twenty. It was his coin silver work watch, heavy and dependable. Not like the fancy gold one he'd given Sloan. Each time he looked at the coin silver watch, it reminded him that Sloan was still missing. He put the watch back in his pocket and looked toward the barn.

"When're those fools supposed to be here?" Ben said. He'd had Sunny put the horses in their stalls, unable to watch them run in the corral while he was lassoed by Anna and taken to St. Louis. Anna. She still refused to understand, refused to believe that all of this was for Sloan, was always for Sloan.

"Another few minutes," Sunny said, his eyes surveying the horizon. "Anything can happen in a few minutes."

"If they're goin', they might as well go." Ben pointed to the wagons loaded with his wife's belongings. "Where the hell are they, anyway?"

"The boys?" Sunny looked away, scratched his chin, fiddled with the cheroot in his hand. He shrugged. "Town. They're in town."

Ben nodded. Hope didn't die as easily as everything else seemed to in the territory. But they needn't have made the trip. There was no way Ben Westin was leaving Tombstone without checking with Western Union. No matter what kind of fuss Anna might kick up.

He needed to know where his son was. Or his son's body.

18

Sloan had hardly slept all night. Finally, toward morning he'd nodded off, only to be awakened by Mary Grace's weak, disheartened voice.

"Gone."

"What?" He started at her words, shaking his head and trying to clear it. For a brief moment he'd forgotten everything except that Mary Grace was lying next to him, her hair teasing his nose.

She sat up on the edge of the bed, swaying slightly. He edged close enough to put a steadying hand around her waist.

"What did you say?" he asked. His throat was scratchy. The hours of crying silently as he lay next to her still form came back to him.

She tried to rise, but his arm was in her way.

"Where are you going?"

"Bathroom." It was the first answer he'd gotten since she'd shown up with Doc Woods the day before.

"Where?"

"The bathroom," she repeated.

"Out in the hall, turn left."

He let her go. She rose to her feet, wobbled badly, staggered, and reached for the bedpost to catch her balance.

"I'll take you." He rose, straightened the clothes he had slept in, and ran his fingers through his hair. He guided her toward the door as if she were blind or feeble. She didn't lean on him, nor pull away. She simply let him lead her out the door and down the hall.

"Will you be all right?" he asked her awkwardly at the door to the water closet. On the trail the one thing she had complained of, the only thing, was lack of privacy at times like this. Now he was sure that if he came into the room with her, she would hardly notice.

She didn't answer his question but walked in and shut the door behind her. He waited for what seemed like forever. How long *had* it been? He thought of his father's watch, resting in his bottom drawer at the Bar W. What his parents must have gone through, believing him dead.

He heard her pull on the chain and the rush of water that followed. A short time later she opened the door. In the light of day she was astonishing. Her skin, reddened by the sun just days before, was the blue-white of fresh milk. Her green eyes were bigger than he remembered, sunken in her face and dull, surrounded by dark purple circles. Her cheeks were bones beneath the flesh, hollows where a smile should end.

He took a bony arm and led her back to their room. Outside their door was a package wrapped in brown paper and some folded clothing. He bent his good knee and retrieved them, pushing Mary Grace into the room in front of him.

"When did you eat last?" he asked her, too angry to

keep the fury out of his voice. He touched her through
her thin muslin blouse and felt bone after bone down
her rib cage. "Dammit, couldn't you even take care of
yourself?"

Her eyes raised slowly to his, full of pain but dry, as
if she had no more tears to shed. "You look different,"
she said in the flat tone that had completely replaced
her lilting voice.

He ignored her, ripping open the package and finding a dress inside. "This your wedding dress?" He
threw it on the bed and limped to the armchair near the
window. "Put it on."

As though he had spoken to her in a foreign lan-
guage, she stood in the center of the room, confused
and unmoving.

"I said put it on. Now do it before I do it for you.
You are gonna dress, and then we're going down to
breakfast, which you're gonna eat. You understand
me?" How the hell was he supposed to leave her here
like this and go do what he had to do?

And still she stood there, like one of those store-
window dummies. Fine. She wanted to stand there like
a dummy, he'd treat her like one.

Pushing off on the arms of the chair, he rose and
came quickly toward her. He stood behind her, his leg
brushing against her skirt. From within the waistband
of the skirt she'd slept in, he pulled her blouse free, and
then bunched up the bottom in his hands. With a jerk
that rocked her, he whipped the cloth over her head,
catching her arm to steady her before searching for the
button which held her skirt in place.

The skirt puddled around her ankles and Sloan just
left it there, circling around to face her and work on her
underthings. He unbuttoned the top two buttons of her
camisole and reached within it. Her skin was as smooth

as ever, and he took her small breast in his hand and caressed it.

The thought that he might never again touch her body, see her face, or smell her hair twisted his insides into a knot, and his hand clenched and tightened around her softness. A small rush of air escaped her lips, and he realized he was hurting her.

Her hollow eyes stared at him as if seeing him for the first time.

"What is it that's different?" she asked.

He took his hand out from her underblouse and rebuttoned it. "Shaved. Now put on the wrapper." He reached for it and handed it to her. She held it by one sleeve. The rest of the dress hung to the floor beside her as if she wasn't even aware it was there. He balled it up and thrust it at her chest, picking up one of her arms and pressing it against the fabric. When she made no move to put the wrapper on, he grabbed her by the arms and shook her.

Her head wiggled back and forth as if she had no control over it and only stopped when he dragged her to him and pressed her tightly against his chest. She was limp in his arms. Inside him something fierce welled up until he couldn't contain it. His sob shattered the silence, and he let go of her and sank down on the bed, his head in his hands.

"Don't do this to me, Mary Grace. I've got a job to do, and you're the only thing gonna see me through it."

He didn't know how long she'd been pressed against him, her hands stroking his hair, her voice murmuring above his head that everything was going to be all right. He only knew she was warm and close and soft, and his hands went around her. Her drawers were wet against his face, soaked with his own tears, and he kissed her through them, kissed her on her belly, his hands slipping into the open seam and kneading her bottom, pressing her closer and closer.

His back hit the bed, taking her with him. His head was smothered beneath her chest, her hands still tangled in his hair, her voice still calming him.

"Let me love you, Sweet Mary. Let me love you before I go."

She rolled off him and scurried away to the edge of the bed, her eyes as wild as her hair. "Go? Go where?"

"He was my son, Sweet Mary. Before him I was no one. Nothing important."

"Don't do this," she begged, panic rising in her voice.

"I have no choice," he said simply. It was a matter of honor, and of love. "Now get dressed. I want to see you eat before I go."

The restaurant was the closest thing to civilization Mary Grace had seen since her fall off the bridge in Oak Creek Canyon. It should have made her happy to be handed a menu, helped into a chair, and poured a cup of real coffee. But none of it mattered. Nothing did.

She'd been without hope before. She'd searched for the child she'd borne with no real expectation of finding it. She'd made a career of searching for children, never knowing how tragic the results might be. She'd fought her way back from the brink of despair, only her work keeping her from ending it all with a bottle of pills or a razor blade.

She couldn't do it again. Wouldn't do it again.

"Eat," Sloan said, nudging her arm. "It's getting cold." In front of her sat a plate of eggs, a bloody steak beside it. There was toast, done to perfection and smothered with butter, and a small dish of some kind of jam. She lifted a wedge of toast, made it halfway to her lips, and then returned it to her plate.

Sloan's voice was more a hiss than a whisper. "Do you want it shoved down your throat in front of all these people, or are you gonna eat it yourself?"

He was a blur through her moist eyes, but she didn't need to see him to know that he was fed up with her. And why not? It was her stupid plan that had killed his child. The child he thought was his, anyway.

His hand cradled the back of her head, his fingers holding her hair tightly enough to prevent her head from moving. A forkful of food came toward her mouth.

"Not the meat—" she tried to say, but the fork was in her mouth before she was finished. She hadn't eaten meat by choice in at least ten years, but he couldn't know that. On the trail, with the exception of that awful thing he'd killed and she'd pretended to eat, there had been only fruits and grasses. She raised her napkin to her lips and felt him yank on her hair.

"Don't even think of it, Sweet Mary," he said between gritted teeth. "You ain't starving yourself to death as long as I'm around."

And how long would that be? No doubt he'd be gone soon enough and then she could eat or not eat, as she pleased. She could live or die, as she pleased. But for now she hadn't the strength to fight him.

She pushed the steak into her cheek so that she could talk. "I'll eat the eggs."

He let her hair go and she spit the meat out into her napkin and took a swig of coffee to get rid of the taste. Her whole mouth felt coated in fat. What were they doing eating and drinking and acting as though the world were normal when the baby they both loved was dead?

She pushed back her chair and ran from the room, tripping as usual on the hem of her dress. She stumbled and was caught once again by Sloan's strong arms.

There wasn't a pair of eyes in the dining room that wasn't focused on the two of them as he struggled to bring her back to her chair and sit her down in it. He smiled politely at the patrons around him and then took his own seat once again.

"Eat your goddamn breakfast so I can get the hell out of here and lay my son to rest proper." His jaw was clenched, and she noticed dimples in his cheeks for the first time.

"I can't." She must have sounded as hopeless as she felt, since his shoulders sagged and he touched her gently on the cheek.

"Please, Sweet Mary. Don't make it harder."

She took a bite of eggs. They were sweeter than she remembered eggs tasted. So was Sloan's smile of relief as he watched her swallow.

"There's a good girl. You'll need your strength for when I get back." He winked at her, a sad imitation of a lusty pass.

"You won't be back." She took a bite of toast and found it difficult to focus on his face. It seemed to be fading out in front of her.

"Don't you get all trancelike on me again," he said. "And eat that meat now."

She couldn't argue. It took too much will. When he put a small piece of steak in her mouth, she simply swallowed it. If it had been one of those poisonous desert plants he'd warned her about, she'd have eaten that, too.

"I'll be back. I promise." He went back to eating his breakfast, apparently satisfied that she was eating hers.

"I'll come with you." She said it quietly, as if it might

pass his notice and he would agree unwittingly to allow her to risk her life along with his.

"No."

"But . . ."

"No." There was no anger in his voice, just a finality that she understood. After all, she'd been there herself, and some things were meant to be borne alone.

But she was finished bearing them. Let him find his baby and bury him and see what solace he found in a stone marker with a name on it. She wasn't going to hang around and watch. "I won't be here when you return."

"Do what you have to," he said quietly.

She wiped at her cheeks with the back of her hand. They were quite a spectacle in the sedate dining hall. Sloan used his napkin to dry her tears. "I don't know what I have to do," she said. "I only know what I can't do. How does anyone know what to do?"

"The Havasupai say you gotta let reason guide your head, love guide your heart, and hope guide your feet," he answered.

"I have no hope."

He smiled a sad smile at her that crinkled his eyes and deepened the two dimples she hadn't yet gotten used to. "Then I guess you won't be goin' nowhere till I get back." He rose from the table and pulled out some money from his pocket. He counted out a few coins and left them next to his plate. "Come on," he said, extending his hand. "I'll see you to our room before I go."

Silently she followed him up the stairs, never more aware of his bad leg as he took the steps slowly: new step with the left, same with the right, new step with the left, same with the right. At the door he pulled out the room key and a pocketful of neatly folded money. He handed both to her.

"Stay in our room except for meals," he instructed her, closing her fingers over the money and allowing his hand to linger on hers. "This should last you until I come back."

"Aren't you coming in?" she asked, the key already in the lock.

"If I do, I might never leave." He pressed the hand he was still holding to his lips.

"And if you leave, you might never come back."

He didn't answer.

"I'll wait for you," she said, her cheeks coloring with the admission.

"I know." The dimples deepened and the money fluttered to the floor as he let go of her hand. He tried to bend to get it, but it was too hard for him. How was he going to fight the Tates if he couldn't even pick up a few lost dollars?

"I'll get them," she said and bent to the ground. A dollar or two blew down the hall a little and she reached to get them. When she looked up, Sloan was gone.

There were no tears left for her to cry. She sat stony faced by the window in a wrapper she'd bought with money Mason Tate had no doubt stolen in some train robbery. The sun baked her skin, and the dust from the street coated her throat and inflamed her eyes. He'd ridden out of town alone, as far as she could tell. There'd been no posse, no *Gunsmoke* let's-go-get-the-bad-guys gang of deputized men.

Lunchtime came and went without note. Around four o'clock she pulled back the ruffle at the end of her sleeve to glance at her hidden watch. As if time had any meaning anymore. A train whistle rang out, and Mary

Grace could just make out the glint of the sun on the metal wheels far in the distance. Tiny people ran around frantically to and fro, climbing into wagons drawn by mules. From where she sat, the mules appeared to sit down on their bottoms and slide down the mountain into town. Shrieks and screams carried in the wind as if the ride were the most fearsome thing that had ever happened in the travelers' lives.

Several of them made it wearily to the Connor Hotel, most nearly hysterical as they filed beneath her window. She'd missed her chance to dine alone, but by now she was hungry enough to brave the busy dining room. With more diners she was less likely to be noticed, anyway. After the scene at breakfast, a little anonymity would be a blessing.

A gentleman in a black suit with an apron tied around his middle hurried to seat her, obviously not pleased that she was dining alone.

"We prefer that females are escorted," he explained, searching the dining room for a free table. "One moment, please."

"Never saw anything like it," the man behind her said to his companion.

"It ought to be against the law," his lady friend replied, and then they both laughed. "But of course, it is!"

"Bringing a baby to rob a train . . ."

"At least it stopped them." She laughed again.

"But that Pinkerton couldn't bring himself to shoot after them. . . ."

"Well, he could have hit the child."

Mary Grace felt the room spinning around her. She reached out to steady herself and caught a waiter's arm, upsetting a tray of fancy desserts and decorating several customers with them. There was no graceful way out of it. And shouting "Shit!" didn't help matters. But she didn't care.

"Ben's alive," she said to the people standing behind her. "The baby—he was about six months old or so? Dark hair? Riding behind a young man with blond curls?"

They stared at her and then at each other. The woman nodded slowly.

"My baby!" She tried to calm herself, control her breathing, stifle the scream that was building inside her. "Sloan. Oh my God!" She grabbed the maitre d' by both arms. "The police. I mean the sheriff, or the marshall, or whatever the hell they call him—where can I find him?"

The man shrugged her off, distancing himself from her. She didn't care if he thought she was a maniac with a foul mouth. Ben was alive, and she had to get to Sloan before it was too late.

The waiter took her by the arm and led her to the front door, rather forcefully. He pointed out the sheriff's office just a few feet away. Mary Grace hugged him in thanks and left him with a smile of surprise on his lips.

Dodging the heavy traffic of early evening on Main Street, which included drunken men on mules, drunken men on horseback, and drunken men on foot, Mary Grace made her way across the street and into the sheriff's office.

Behind a desk with a placque that read James Franklin Roberts, Sheriff, sat a formidable man with a bristly mustache and close-cropped blond hair. He was in deep conversation with a gray-haired man whose back was to the door.

"I'm tellin' you I ain't seen him since he brought in those three men." He gestured toward the cells behind him. "Claimed they set on him and his woman. Sure as hell looked like the Sloan Westin I remember."

She couldn't make out the men in the cells, but the voice was familiar as a man shouted out that it sure was Westin, and if the Tates didn't get him, he'd see him buried himself.

The sheriff told the man to shut up and continued his conversation with the older man who sat across from him. "Heard now that he's got some woman and they're stayin' up at the Connor. Thought I'd mosey up there later myself. Damn fine supper they serve, you know."

The man slammed his fist on the sheriff's desk. "I been up and down this town three times over and ain't caught sight of him. And who's this Mary Grace O'Reilly I'm supposed to look after?"

Mary Grace tilted her head to try to get a look at the man's face. The resemblance was uncanny. "You're Sloan's father," she said. "I'd know you anywhere."

The men looked up, surprised at her presence. The sheriff rose and tipped his hat.

"Well if it ain't Mason Tate's woman," Jackson yelled from his cell.

"Mason Tate's?" the sheriff said, his hand going slowly toward his gun.

"Sheriff," Mary Grace said, trying to reassure him she meant no harm. "I'm Mary Grace O'Reilly. But that doesn't matter now. Sheriff, we have to go after Sloan. He's gone after the Tates thinking that Ben is dead, but Ben's not dead. There was this train robbery, and we have to go after them both." She looked expectantly from man to man.

"He thinks I'm dead?" Sloan's father said.

"No. Not you. His baby."

"I knew it," Jackson yelled. "Didn't I tell ya it was his?" he asked the other men in the cell.

"Just hold it," the sheriff said and waited for quiet. "Now, you wanna run that by me with a lasso on it, little lady?" Mary Grace smiled. Little lady! Unbelievable. And Ben Westin was here. He'd have to help.

"Sloan thought his son was dead. Well, that's because I told him he was. But I only told him that because that's what Harlin Tate told me. So he went off to kill the Tates for revenge, like Rambo or someone, but he doesn't know that the baby's alive and could get hurt, and so could Sloan. We have to go after him!" She stopped for a breath.

"Rambo?" the sheriff asked.

"Are you telling me my son is alive?" Ben asked.

"Your son is most definitely, most wonderfully alive. And so is your namesake." She was hopping from one foot to the other. "But I can't say for how long. We've got to get out there."

"Don't trust her, Sheriff," Jackson yelled. "She's Mason Tate's woman sure as Sloan Westin ain't no man no more."

Mary Grace's cheeks flushed. How could she have ever told them that? The sheriff stared at her. Ben Westin couldn't. He stared at the floor.

"Please," she begged. "We've got to hurry. Sloan and the baby are both in terrible danger."

"Now hold it a minute, young lady," the sheriff said slowly. "Just who are you in all of this?"

"I . . ." She hesitated for a second and then dove in. "I'm the baby's mother. The Tates kidnapped him and you have to help me get him back. Didn't you hear that they took him with them to rob a train? I think I can find the cabin. God, I hope I can."

"Come on, Sheriff," Ben said, placing his Stetson on his head. To Mary Grace he said, "How long ago did he leave?"

"Hold it," the sheriff said, refusing to be caught up in the frenzy. "How do I know this ain't some kind of a trap? She could be leadin' us right into the lion's den. Delivering us up to the Tate boys like lambs to the slaughter. If she's really Mason Tate's woman . . . and Tom down at the mercantile . . ."

"For God's sake! Do I look like I could be Mason Tate's woman? Why would I come here to you if I had Mason Tate on my side?"

The men just kept taking her measure.

"Fine," she said, "I'll go myself. Where can I rent a horse?"

"Rent a horse?" The sheriff said, his eyebrows coming together across his forehead like one big hairy caterpillar.

"Hire one. Lease one. Whatever you say to borrow one for money."

Ben Westin seemed suddenly to make up his mind about her. "I'll get you a horse," he said. "The livery's down at the south end of town." His hand was on the doorknob.

"And I'll need a gun," she said before he left.

"Now wait just a minute," Sheriff Roberts ordered. "I ain't havin' no woman goin' off half-cocked with a gun in her hand after the Tate boys. Specially when she might be Mason Tate's woman. Can you draw us a map?"

"It's a trap, Sheriff," Jackson warned. Mary Grace ignored him.

"Sheriff, I got told once today I wasn't going out to the Tates, and I'm not about to make that mistake again. Sloan left me with some money. I'm sure I can buy a gun."

"No," the sheriff said. "I can't take that risk."

"Look," she countered. "Those idiots left me in the

desert with Sloan Westin tied up. If I was on the Tates' side, would I have untied him? Wouldn't I have just left him to die the way they did?" Tears clogged her throat at the memory. "Sheriff, a baby's life is at stake. An infant who has no chance but us. He's counting on me. Can he count on you?"

Sheriff Roberts sighed. His shrug said it all. She had won. "Get her a horse. I'll find my deputy and anybody else with a grudge against the Tates."

She left the office on Ben Westin's heels. "I thought it might be some kind of trick," he said, "when I got the telegram."

"You didn't know he was alive?"

"Not until the day before yesterday," he said. "Don't know what got him to finally tell us he was alive. Guess he still had some growin' up to do. What's this about a son?"

Mary Grace smiled so widely she was sure Ben Westin could see the fillings in her molars. "You mean Ben? I guess we'd better call him Little Ben, now."

"We'd better hurry, little lady. I thought I lost Sloan once. I'm not about to lose him again. Let's go."

19

It looked different at night. She'd been so careful to memorize the landmarks, despite being deathly afraid of Wilson, concerned about Ben, and preoccupied with Mason's plans for her. Yet she'd still had the presence of mind to note the trees, the boulders, the turns in the road.

"Which way?" Sheriff Roberts asked, guiding his horse so close to Mary Grace's that it brushed her leg and caused her horse to shy sideways. She yanked on the reins, and the horse beneath her shook his head and jerked right back. Even in Girl Scout camp she'd been a lousy rider, and the intervening years hadn't helped any. While she could now ride behind Sloan with relative ease, handling her own horse was a challenge.

"There was a boulder with a rock that looked like an eagle," she said. Someone groaned, and she quickly apologized. "I made the trip once, and it was light. I know it better from the river. I went that way a few times."

"Why?" the sheriff asked.

"Why what?"

"I mean, what was you doin' at the Tate place more than once?" There was a murmur behind him that came toward her like a wall.

"Mason Tate wanted me to marry him. He kept me at the cabin, but I escaped."

"Without yer baby?" someone said.

"No. It wasn't like that, exactly. I took the baby the first time, and that's when I met Sloan. . . ."

"I thought he was your baby's pa," the sheriff said.

Oh, what a tangled web, Mary Grace. "He is. I mean, he found me, and we tried to get away together, with the baby. But Sloan's horse was stolen in the desert. . . ."

"Yeah, he told me about that when he brought in Jackson and his men."

"Then why didn't you believe me when I came to your office? Don't you believe what he said?"

"Oh, I ain't got no trouble believing Sloan. Know'd him before he disappeared off the face of the earth. But just 'cause he believed ya, ain't no reason for me to."

"But he told you the baby was his."

"Yeah," the sheriff allowed. "But he never told me nothin' about it bein' yours."

"I . . ." It was hard to blame the sheriff for doubting her. Even she was becoming confused by her story.

"Told me to keep an eye on ya till he got back. Didn't seem to trust that ya wouldn't leave town."

"What is this all about?" Ben Westin asked.

Oh, it was simple. Ben's grandson, who wasn't really his grandson, was stolen by Sloan, who wasn't really his father, from his uncles, the only ones who really did have some claim on him. And now she, who wasn't really his mother, was going after Sloan, who wasn't really anything to her, to get back what was not rightfully either of theirs. Somehow she didn't think her explanation would help.

"Moon's comin' out," one of the men said, and they all looked up. In front of the round, smiling face that glowed at them, somewhere around the Man in the Moon's chin, was the very rough outline of an eagle, its wings spread for flight.

"I'll be damned," the sheriff said.

"To the right," Mary Grace said, moving her horse into the lead. "The eagle should always be to our right."

Sloan had stationed himself near the outhouse, figuring that sooner or later, one at a time, the men he had come to kill would be showing their butts. In the four hours he'd been waiting, Harlin had taken two leaks by the front door, but no one had made the trip to the privy. Sloan had planned out every possible scenario for doing the boys in. More importantly, oh yes, much more importantly, he'd heard Ben cry.

Never, not in all his twenty-six years, not when the Havasupai found him, not ever, had anything sounded as wonderful as Ben's lusty wail. He'd even gotten a glimpse of the boy, sitting on Mason's lap on the front step for a few moments while Mason had a powerful-smelling cigar. Each time he inhaled, it glowed in the dark, and then the glow was lost in a cloud of white smoke. When he was done, he rose and returned to the house. From the way the door slammed behind him, Sloan could tell that Mason's mood was as foul as his smoke.

The waiting had been easy at first. Sloan just pictured the look on Sweet Mary's face when he came waltzing into the Connor Hotel with Little Ben on his arm. Later, a million thoughts taunted him as he thought of other endings to the bizarre drama they'd been taking part in. If he didn't succeed, Mary Grace would never know Ben had survived and the child would be brought up by Mason Tate. She might even think Sloan had willingly abandoned her. On the other hand, even if he succeeded, he could return to Jerome and find her gone. The sheriff had been wholly uninterested in keeping an eye on her, and he'd had to hint that she was not to be trusted in order to get him to agree to watch her at all. If she managed to leave Jerome, he couldn't guess at where to find her. Los Angeles? Back East? And what about the little matter of her claiming to be from another time?

A screech owl whistled in the distance, a weird trembling sound that set Sloan's teeth on edge and stirred up the night creatures around him. Wings fanned the air, rustling leaves and whooshing above him. Rodents scrambled for a safe hiding place, their sharp nails scratching on the rocks and dry ground beneath their paws. There was a sudden rush of wind not far from him, and then the scurry of activity quieted. The stillness of the night closed in around him. He stretched out on the ground behind the outhouse, the stench filling his nostrils, and tried to rest. It couldn't be long before nature called to one of the boys, and he'd have to get himself standing quickly without being seen.

There was no getting comfortable. His head was on his arm, his good leg poised to spring him to his feet. He shifted. There was a slight vibration beneath him. He slid his head off his arm and pressed his ear to the ground. Horses! Who the hell was coming this time of night? Three adversaries he had a chance of handling. More, he didn't think he could best.

He inched his way back into the woods to where

Climber stood silently waiting for him. The horse nickered softly, and Sloan rubbed his nose and muzzle. He mounted up and led the horse toward the trail as silently as he could, keeping to the trees for cover. Every now and then he stopped and listened. When he was confident that he'd be able to hear what he needed, he eased off Climber, grabbed his rifle, and moved into position.

The ridge banked Oak Creek on the Tates' side. Looking down, he would be able the see the riders when they filed in beneath him. What a site the boys had chosen. They might not be long on brains, but their instinct for survival worked from sunup to sunup.

There were five riders out there in the darkness, at least four of them packing rifles. This was no tea party. A hatless rider was gesturing, pointing, and the others were gathered close. Their voices were too low for Sloan to make out any words, and so he just watched, his body hugging the ground, his rifle trained on the rider leading the way.

He could pick off two with his twelve-gauge Barker, but then he'd have to reload and the other three would scatter. Even if he could get all five, the shots would bring the Tates running, and they'd be up here on the ridge with him. *Shit*. He watched in silence as the little group made its way down the creek and toward the hidden path that led to the Tates' cabin. And his son.

Of course, Ben changed everything. If necessary, Sloan would have to defend the Tates from the five men closing in on their hideaway so that he could ensure Ben's safety. He knew that the baby's physical well-being was in no danger from his uncles. These new men, this unknown quantity, could try to smoke the boys out. If they were Pinkertons, they might lob one of those bombs like they did at the James boys' house.

Jesse's mother had lost an arm, and another of her sons was killed.

If there was one thing to be grateful for in all of this, it was that at least Sweet Mary was back safe in the Connor Hotel in Jerome. He only wished there was some way he could be sure she would find out that Ben was still alive in the event that he couldn't make it back to her.

A strange calm came over him. If he didn't manage to get Ben, if he got killed in the attempt, he knew for a certainty that Mary Grace would find a way to get his son away from his uncles and raise him herself. He didn't know how. He didn't even know what made him so certain. He only knew, as his eyes followed the riders out of sight, that in some way she was with him, and between the two of them they would save his son.

Cautiously he went back for Climber. The area was becoming as familiar to him as the saddle beneath his legs, and he guided Climber through the brush to the point at which the lower trail turned steeply up. If the men were there, clearly they were coming to, or for, the Tates.

"Make camp?" Mary Grace hissed as quietly as she could at Sheriff Roberts. "What if Sloan is attacking now? What about the cover of darkness?"

The sheriff shook his head silently. He was not going to budge on this, either. Every step of the way he had fought her. When she'd come out of the hotel in her tight jeans, he had tried to order her either to change into decent clothes or to forget accompanying them. When she'd mounted the horse, he'd gone on and on about her sitting "clothespin fashion," until she'd nearly agreed to riding sidesaddle just to get the show on the road. And all the sheriff kept harping on was that he couldn't guarantee her safety if she insisted on displaying herself in such a manner.

She couldn't figure who it was she needed protection from. There was the sheriff himself, his deputy, an elderly gentleman whose wife had been injured during the train robbery, and Sloan's father. No one else had been brave enough to go looking for the Tates in their own nest, and in the end it was Ben Westin who had convinced the sheriff that he would take responsibility for Mary Grace. It was pointless trying to convince any of them that she was responsible for herself.

Sheriff Roberts refused to issue her a rifle and threatened to return to Jerome if Ben gave her one. When she complained that his condition made her the only one of them who had no weapon, the sheriff had simply nodded and said that was the whole idea.

He'd stopped to relieve his bladder more times than she could count but made no accommodation when Mary Grace had found it necessary to go herself. Clearly Sheriff Roberts did not trust Mary Grace O'Reilly, and the feeling was unquestionably mutual.

The men had all got off their horses and were waiting for her to dismount, Ben holding her reins and offering her a hand down. He nodded encouragingly, and she threw her leg over and slid down the horse's side. In the process she managed to jab her breast with the horn. Her wince brought a snort from the deputy. The sheriff shoved him toward a small clearing, and Sloan's father diplomatically pretended not to notice anything that had taken place.

Taking her hand, Ben pulled her slightly away from the other men and whispered, "You know how to use a weapon?" He was bending down, and she knelt beside him.

"No." She couldn't help it. The man was so much like his son, it was impossible to be less than honest with him.

"Didn't think so." He pressed a hard small object into her hand. "Still, you'd better take this. Find a place to hide it."

It was one of those small guns that women pulled out of their purses in old movies. A derringer, maybe. "How do I . . ." She wrapped her hand around it and felt for the trigger. A sense of power surged through her. Life and death sat in her hand, and all she had to do was aim and squeeze. No more Wilson, or Harlin, or Mason. She pulled her finger out from the trigger guard and opened her palm. "I couldn't . . ."

"Hide it. Use it if you need to defend yourself." Ben lacked Sloan's easy way of talking, but the sound of his voice was still comforting. Her shirttails, never tucked in during her hasty exit from the hotel, covered her pockets. She reached under her shirt and slipped the gun into her left front pocket. It was a tight fit, but she wedged it in.

"I'll take the first watch," the sheriff whispered. Then he nodded at Mary Grace. "And I want you where I can see you."

"She'll bed with me, Sheriff," Ben said. When the sheriff looked up, surprised, Ben asked, "You got a problem with that?"

"It's your neck," Roberts said, as much to himself as to Ben. "But it don't add up. Why'd the Tates take your baby, ma'am?"

"Because they're thieves and murderers," the elderly gentleman answered. He'd been quiet throughout the journey, following along slightly behind, lost in his thoughts, or so it seemed. "Why'd they bother my wife? Plenty of pretty young women on the train. Why'd that scarface slap my wife, rip her dress? All she said was we were on our way to our daughter's wedding."

"OK," the sheriff said, putting the man's comments aside. "You say this baby's yours and Westin's? I heard Emily Tate had a kid before she died. Rumor says it was Westin's. The way I figure it, that baby's his all right, but it ain't yours, unless . . . Where're you from, Miss O'Reilly?"

"What are you getting at?" Ben seemed annoyed at the implication and moved his body between hers and the sheriff's.

"I ain't never seen Emily Tate, myself," Roberts said. "Any of you seen her?" His eyes met with everyone's in turn, ending with Mary Grace.

"I saw her die," Mary Grace said. "And be buried. There's a grave near the cabin."

"How do we know that ain't some kind of trick and we ain't just sitting here with one Tate who's fixin' to take us to the rest of them?" The deputy pulled out his gun and aimed it at Mary Grace.

"Because I say so," a familiar voice drawled. Mary Grace spun around to see Sloan coming toward them out of the darkness, his rifle only waist high but aimed at the deputy.

"Sloan!" A choked whisper escaped Ben Westin's lips as if he couldn't let himself believe what he had hoped for so long.

"Pa?"

Mary Grace nodded wildly, assuring him it was indeed his father. With a quick glance at the sheriff, she jumped up and ran to Sloan's side, her body molding itself to his like the right piece of a jigsaw puzzle.

"Ben's alive. I don't know how he is, but Harlin took him to rob this man's train." She pointed at the old man.

"He's fine," Sloan said, hugging her to him. "I saw him on the porch with Mason. He don't care much for cigar smoke, though."

Ben Westin was standing where she had left him, watching their exchange. She could see Sloan's eyes on him and pushed him gently toward the older man.

"You're wounded," Ben said as Sloan limped toward him, hurrying to aid his son.

Sloan stopped and turned around to stare at her in utter disbelief. "You didn't tell him?" His fury was barely contained.

She shrugged. "I forgot." It was the truth.

"You forgot?" His voice was raised, and she had to quiet him down. "How the hell could you ever forget?"

"It's not the first thing I think of when I wake up in the morning. . . ."

The anger left his face, replaced by a look of wonder, as if he was just realizing that it was no longer the first thing he thought of, either.

"And what is?" he asked her, a slight tremor in his voice.

"You. Ben. You and me and Ben," she said, running into the arms he opened for her. He closed them around her and rubbed her back and kissed her hair. And then she felt one hand leave her and looked up to see him shaking hands with his father.

"I can't believe you're alive. For so long I refused to believe you were dead, and now here you are, and I can't believe my own eyes. Your mother! Wait until your mother sees you."

Sloan's face fell. "I'm not the man I was when I left," he started to explain.

"No, son, I can see that. Seems you're twice the man, now." He patted Mary Grace's back, still shaking his head in disbelief.

"This party's a mite premature," Sloan said. "Sweet Mary and I have a son back in that cabin we gotta get out."

"You saying that boy belongs to her?" Sheriff Roberts came forward. The deputy still had his gun drawn.

Ben wasn't hers. Hell, most likely he wasn't even Sloan's. Did she really have the right to keep that to herself and let him risk his life for a child who wasn't really his flesh and blood? And how did she tell him now, after all she and the baby had put him through? *Keep your mouth shut, Mary Grace, or who knows what he'll do.* She needed him to save Ben. She needed him for a lot more than that, but at least that seemed noble.

Still, it wasn't his child, wasn't his fight, and he had a right to know it. The sheriff stood waiting for his answer.

"Sloan, I have to talk to you," Mary Grace said, pulling him slightly away from the crowd. "There's something you should know, in case you want to change your mind about anything. . . ."

Still holding his rifle, he released her and nodded his head toward the trees. She preceded him, and he kept the gun casually trained on the sheriff and deputy while she spoke.

"I think, that is, I'm pretty sure that Ben is no more yours than he is mine. If you don't want to risk your . . ."

He shook his head, and his shoulders drooped slightly. "Sweet Mary," he said impatiently. "Do you think I'm stupid, or maybe blind?"

"What?" Did he know? Had he guessed? If he had, what was he doing here now, risking his life for Horace Tate?

"Well, he don't favor his mama, and he don't favor me. He's awful big for one so young, and . . ."

"But then why are you . . . ?" She didn't know what to say.

"Why'd you give him your tit?" he asked, smiling

when she blushed. "Why'd you ask Wilson to shoot you, dammit, when you thought he was dead?"

She thought it was different for her, because of her past, because she was a woman. She had underestimated him, maybe from the beginning.

"How long have you known?"

Sloan smiled and put one arm around her, leading her back toward the three men. "Oh, somewheres around the time you explained to me 'bout how bein' with a woman can make a child, but it's love what makes a family. Havin' a kid of your own, Sweet Mary, has more to do with love and maybe not so much to do with blood. Don'tcha think?"

He stood in front of the sheriff. "Ben is mine and this here lady's. Proof's on his leg. My kid was bitten by a snake one day when we was havin' a picnic. When we get him back, you'll see the scars where I sucked out the poison."

"How do we know it's hers? I ain't heard you call her your wife."

She'd been thinking biologically. The morality hadn't even occurred to her. Like her own child, Ben was a bastard, and she was no better than a common whore, sleeping around with any man who asked her. So she hadn't really been with Sloan and conceived Ben. It was only luck, good or bad, that she wasn't carrying his child now, yet another bastard. . . .

"Don't take a weddin' certificate to make a baby," Sloan said. "You thought it was Emily's kid, and I sure didn't marry her, neither."

Mary Grace's head snapped back like she'd been slapped. So she was just like Emily to him. He didn't claim that she was his wife, or that she was going to be.

"Then this man and you have . . . well, been intimate?" the sheriff asked.

She nodded, aware the sheriff was trying to embarrass her. Well, this was old territory. The terrain was all too familiar as she met the sheriff's eyes defiantly.

"And you and he . . . well, created this baby out of wedlock?"

"Now that's enough," Ben Westin said. "You're talking about my grandson, Sheriff Roberts, so you'd best watch what you say."

"I'm still not sure she ain't foolin' us," the sheriff began again.

"Doctor Woods knew Emily Tate," Mary Grace said, remembering that he hadn't been surprised to see Wilson and had mentioned Emily's illness. "He treated her. You can ask him when we get back to Jerome."

"That'll have to do," Sloan said. "We've only a few hours till daylight, and you sure have messed up my plans."

"They might come down here to bathe." Mary Grace remembered coming to wash Ben's diapers in the creek. Her cheeks reddened as she remembered that Sloan had been watching then, and before.

"See," the sheriff said. "That's what I mean. You ain't just guessin', are you? You know too much about the Tates for me." He looked at his deputy and at the elderly man, who was still sitting on the ground where they had left him, probably asleep.

"This whole thing smells like three-day-old fish to me. I ain't walkin' into a trap with the likes of you. If it turns out you're in with them, its gonna be five . . . no, six—" the sheriff pointed at Ben Westin, including him in the number "—against two. Can't count the old man."

Sloan shrugged. With his father and Mary Grace the odds had increased threefold. If the sheriff wanted to take his marbles and go home, Sloan wasn't gonna beg him to stay. Without trust he wouldn't be much help, anyway. With Ben, Sweet Mary, and himself, he knew everyone's first thoughts would be for the baby, not for the glory of bringing in the Tate boys, dead or alive.

"We need a plan," Mary Grace said, and the three of them turned their backs on the three others, not even acknowledging the sheriff and the deputy as they shook the old man awake, then took him with them as they left.

"We need a miracle," Sloan corrected.

Ben Westin looked at his son, reaching out and touching him as though he wanted to reassure himself that the man was real. "We already got one," he said with awe.

Gentle snoring filled the dark air around them, but neither Mary Grace nor Sloan could sleep as easily as Sloan's father. She could feel Sloan's heart beating beneath her palm as she snuggled against him in the coolness. His breath ruffled her hair. For a long time they didn't speak, or move, or even think. They just lay there breathing in each other's essence until Sloan's hand began to wander farther and farther down Mary Grace's back, and he cupped her behind and drew her closer to him.

"Sloan!" she hissed in the darkness. "Your father's not ten feet from us. What are you doing?"

He kissed her temple and breathed softly in her ear. One hand worked on the buttons of her shirt, his breaths coming faster against her face.

"Sloan," she said again, trying to still his hand with her own but giving his lips access to her neck. "We can't."

"Shhh." His mouth was doing incredible things to her neck, his tongue trailing lower and lower until she was as anxious to open her blouse as he was. "You'll wake my father."

His mouth clamped onto her breast, and she arched against him. This was madness. Still, she reached down and felt his hardness straining against his jeans. Five buttons were all that stood between her and heaven. Five buttons and Sloan's father. Her fingers stopped their work.

"Did you know that the Indians make love when they get the notion, no matter who's in their wickiup with 'em?" he asked, his hand insinuating itself into the waistband of her jeans. "Their kids can be there, their guests, and suddenly in the dark you can hear heavy breathing."

Their own breaths were becoming ragged as he spoke. She had to do something to put out the fire that was building in her belly. "And you? Did you make love in their wickiup?" His tongue danced around her breast, skimming her nipple, his warm breath teasing her wet skin.

"Get 'em off," he said huskily when his efforts failed to free her from her jeans. "No damn buttons," he murmured against her midriff, his hands everywhere at once, touching, probing, teasing.

It was light enough to see Ben, his back rising and falling evenly. He slept on his side, facing away from them. As she slid the zipper of her jeans down, the metallic hiss seemed to fill the air and her cheeks warmed with embarrassment. "I can't . . ." she started to say. Sloan nudged her and pulled the blanket they rested on out from under them, wrapping it around them until they were hidden from any prying eyes.

"Get 'em off," he said again, releasing his own buttons quickly and shimmying his jeans down toward his knees. When she reached down to get her moccasins off, he cursed softly. Mary Grace wondered if he thought he was the only one in a hurry. To hell with the moccasins. She reached for the waistband of her jeans and wrested them down over her hips.

"Oh, God!" he said, the air rushing out of his chest as his hands found her naked bottom. One strong hand lowered the pants to her knees. One adept foot pushed them further to her ankles. And then he pushed her prone onto the ground and let his hands roam over her skin until the goosebumps melted and the sweat began to coat her body.

He left no part of her unkissed as he twisted her this way and that, squeezing her behind, burying his head in her belly, tracing her ribs, suckling her breast. She bit her lip to keep from crying out as each fiber in her body reacted to his touch, her arms reaching for him of their own accord, her legs fighting her jeans for the freedom to wind around his waist, to do instinctively what seemed impossible with his stiff leg.

And then her knees were bent and he was inside her, filling her up, pounding rhythmically against her, each of them thrusting toward each other. His face hung over hers for a moment, the dawn light revealing the wonder he felt at his own prowess. When he lowered his lips to hers, she strained to touch each part of him with each inch of herself.

Her legs were imprisoned at the ankles by her clothing, and she bucked and fought to free herself. "Don't," he warned her, his breath ragged and irregular. "I . . . oh! Oh, God!"

Everything was on fire, hot and liquid and pulsing, and she didn't know which spasms were his and which were her own. She only knew when he collapsed above her that the day that was dawning was the most important one in her life, and the promise it had begun with was only the beginning.

"No," he said, stroking her hair with one hand and making sure they were covered with the blanket with the other. "I didn't make love in that wickiup, Sweet Mary."

She raised her head to look in his eyes. There was something new there. Something she had never seen before.

"I musta poked a hundred women, Mary Grace O'Reilly. But I never made love until you."

The horses were restless under the three silent riders as Little Ben's family waited behind some rocks to rescue him. Mary Grace felt strangely alone on Climber's back. But she had no doubt that when it came to horses, Sloan's judgment was unquestionable. If he thought they should switch mounts, it was the least of her concerns.

The three had agreed that the important thing was getting Ben out safely. The disposing of the Tates could be left to Sheriff Roberts. It had been hard for Sloan to give up his vendetta against Harlin, but in the end he had to agree with Sweet Mary and his father. If the four of them could come out of this alive, then they would declare it a success and be content.

Mary Grace checked her watch. After six. Any minute now the Tates should come down that steep hill, follow the narrow path, and wend their way to the water. Sloan had set everything up in advance, allowing for as many contingencies as he could think of, and now all that was left to do was wait and hope. Her heart was pounding so loudly in her ears that she missed the horses' hooves. But Little Ben's voice carried over the treetops, and her head went up at the sound of his gurgling. Sloan caught her eye and nodded. He had heard it too. They exchanged smiles, his wide and open, hers tentative and there for his sake only.

His eyebrows came down with a question. *What's wrong?*

She shook her head. *Nothing.*

He looked at her more closely, and she tore her eyes away. This wasn't the time to discuss what would become of her after Sloan recovered his son. He'd had every opportunity over the last several hours to let her know he wanted to marry her. He'd filled his father in on all their exploits, taking pleasure in reassuring him he was still a fully functional male, capable of upholding what was apparently a Westin tradition. But he hadn't mentioned anything beyond the morning, beyond grabbing what was his, and everything else be damned.

Harlin's horse emerged by the creek, Ben strapped to his back in a sling. They were alone, Harlin whistling, Ben cooing, the horse stepping high. Near the river's edge, Harlin halted the stallion and swung his leg over the saddle.

"How far you think you can piss, Horace?" he said, one foot holding all his weight in the stirrup while he fiddled with his buttons. "Think you can piss clear across the creek?"

Only Sloan was watching through a small crack in the rocks. His father and Mary Grace were a few feet away, their horses steady, thanks to Ben's hands on both mares' reins. Listening to Harlin, Mary Grace had to stifle a smile, while Ben looked decidedly uncomfortable.

Harlin slipped the baby's strap off his back, hung it from the saddle horn, and made ready to get down and demonstrate his great pissing ability. "Your Uncle Harlin can piss farther than both your other uncles. Maybe combined."

Sloan backed up slightly and leaned toward Mary Grace's ear. She nodded, passing the word on to Ben. Then Sloan peered through the crack again.

"Now!" He kicked the horse's flanks hard and the three took off at a gallop toward Harlin's horse and the baby. Before Mary Grace could even digest the new plan, Sloan had jumped from the horse he was riding. Despite his stiff leg, he landed in Harlin's saddle, the baby swinging dangerously by his knee. He steadied Little Ben with his left hand and rode toward Harlin. In his raised hand, Sloan held the horse's reins and his rifle. Mary Grace winced when it came crashing down on Harlin's skull. Sloan grabbed the baby up against his chest and took off at a full gallop.

She rode for her life behind him. Sloan's father slapped the horse Sloan had been on. It joined the pack of them, and four horses thundered down the creek bed leaving Harlin Tate unconscious, his manhood still in his hand.

There was precious little time before Mason and Wilson might show up, guns blazing, to reclaim their nephew. But a few moments were all they needed. Sloan's rope hung neatly in place, and Mary Grace leaped off her horse and ran to it. Sloan had managed during the dawn to get the rope up over the rocky ledge. Once they were up on top, they'd be almost impossible to reach. She would be the first one up, then Ben with his namesake, and finally Sloan.

"Give me Little Ben," she pleaded, but Sloan refused.

"We need someone up there to hand him to. You can't climb the rocks with him on you. It's too dangerous. For both of you." He knew how to handle her all right, even in a crisis. Just tell her it was better for Little Ben, and she did as she was told.

She slipped into the ring of rope and tightened it

around her waist. "OK," she shouted, and Sloan tied
the other end to Climber's saddle. As the horse moved
away, Mary Grace rose in the air. She held tight to the
rope with her hands, keeping herself upright. Falling
through the air was horrifying, but not as frightening as
being suspended there, moving farther and farther from
the ground.

"Keep going," she heard Sloan's father shout, and
the ledge was nearly in reach.

Her legs dangled beneath her and her fingers clawed
at the air, hoping to reach the rocky surface just inches
away.

"A little more," she yelled down. "Sloan?"

"Sweet Mary!" he screamed. "No-o-o!"

And then she heard nothing at all. Not Sloan, nor
Ben, nor Little Ben. Only silence. She hung there, her
eyes closed, waiting for the sound of guns. Nothing.
Stillness. One hand swung into the rock, brushed
against it, and was scraped.

"Sloan?" She looked down at the rocks beneath her,
dry in the afternoon sun. There was no sign of the river,
just a dried-up riverbed. "Sloan!" she screamed. Her
foot hooked into an indentation, and her empty hand
grabbed the stump of a small tree. There was no rope
to hold on to anymore.

A plane passed overhead, drowning out the sound of
her scream.

20

"Just hold on," a man *was* saying, his hand firmly wrapped around her wrist. "I won't let you fall."

"Sloan," she said, trying to make the man understand. "I have to help Sloan and Ben."

"Everyone's fine," the soothing voice told her. To someone else he said, "Get her right arm. OK, on three. One. Two. Three."

She was hauled onto the rocky surface like a dead fish, laid out flat on her stomach. She lifted her head. About twenty feet away from her stood her Ford Mustang. "Where am I?"

"Lady, the question is where have you been? We've been searching this canyon for days without a trace of you. How the hell did you wind up here?"

Mary Grace sat up and tried to figure out where she was. Tears welled up. Oak Creek Canyon. They were sitting on the Bridge to Somewhere Else.

"The year. What year is it?" She grabbed at the state trooper with a bloody hand.

"Jeez," he said looking at her hand. "Can you bend it?"

"The year," she screamed again. "What year is it?" How long had he said they'd looked for her? Days? But she'd been gone weeks. Weeks in the year 1894. "What day? What's the goddamn date?"

The troopers exchanged looks. The one holding on to her pulled the lower lids of her eyes down like a doctor would. She couldn't imagine what he was looking for.

"I think we better get her to the medical center, Harold. She's pretty cut up and . . ." He looked at her as if he didn't want to upset her with the fact that she was crazy.

Through gritted teeth she asked him again. "Today's date. What is it?"

"April the tenth, I think. The tenth, right Harold?"

Mary Grace looked up at Harold. He was just a silhouette against the sun. He didn't contradict his partner.

"But I left on the third," she said. Seven days. She shook her head in confusion. Was she looking for it to make sense? Well, what difference did it make? She was going right back. Wrenching her arm away from the trooper, she made a move for the edge, only to be hauled back.

"Whoa! Careful there," the trooper warned. "You want to fall down again? You might not be so lucky the next time." He inched them back toward the highway, Mary Grace's bottom skimming the rocks, the trooper crouching beside her.

What was she doing? Her stomach lurched and her head spun. Seven days? In another century? It must have been a dream. She must have been like Dorothy in Munchkinland. Certainly she could have banged her head, *must* have banged her head when she fell. She could have landed on a ledge and been unconscious. . . .

They were helping her to their jeep, and she went along limply. Every muscle in her body ached. She felt beaten and bruised. Her jeans were torn at the knees, her shirtsleeve was separating from the shoulder. The skin she could see peeking through was caked with dried blood.

With a trooper on either side of her, they half dragged, half carried her to their jeep and put her in the backseat. One of the troopers went around to the other side and climbed in next to her, encouraging her to lean against him. "You're safe now. That must have been some hell out there in the canyons. How did you miss all the people looking for you?"

She thought about the Tates. "I didn't want to be found. Not until I got Ben back."

"The Weaver kid? Hey, they found him in Sedona. Not ten miles from here. You'd a probably found him yourself if you hadn't taken that fall. It was all over the news. They used the map from your car to find him."

Benjamin Weaver. That was why she'd come to Sedona in the first place. Everything else must have been just a dream. It must have been. Because if it was the present, and of course it was, then Sloan and the baby were already dead. Long gone even if they lived to ripe old ages. And a hundred years away from her, in any event. "It's 1994, right?"

"Yeah," the trooper assured her. "Maybe you'd better just rest." He shifted his weight under her and patted her hand. "Step on it, Harold. She don't look so good to me."

They radioed ahead, and by the time they pulled into the hospital's emergency room, a crowd of photographers had gathered. Mary Grace had no statement to make, and several nurses whisked her quickly into a little curtained cubicle.

One began unbuttoning her blouse, another stood by with a chart asking her questions. Name, age, address, Blue Cross, Blue Shield? She wasn't sure how many she answered. The light in the little room was blinding, the noise beyond the curtain deafening.

When the nurse who had unbuttoned her blouse tried to remove it, Mary Grace grabbed at the edges and hugged it to her body.

"It's freezing in here," she said. "Isn't it?" she asked when the nurse seemed surprised by her complaint.

"Honey, after all that time in the desert I'd think seventy-five degrees would feel pretty damn good." She reached for a thermometer while she complained about energy-saving regulations. "Slip this under your tongue, honey. Maybe you got a fever."

Then she pulled once again at the ragged blouse, and Mary Grace felt herself let go of it and allowed the nurse to help her into a blue hospital gown. With a nurse on either side, she was half lifted, half assisted onto the high gurney and was assured a doctor would see her soon. Then she was left alone.

To shield her eyes from the light, she threw one arm across her face and tried to find a comfortable position in which to lie still. It felt as though she were still lying on a bed of rocks. Everything hurt—her back, her shoulders, her hand.

"Do you want to report any crime?" a voice asked, startling her. Mary Grace put her arm down and looked at the pretty young nurse by her side. Her badge said she was N. Rivera, R.N. A gentle hand rubbed Mary Grace's arm.

Kidnapping, attempted rape, murder, horse stealing—the list went on and on. You couldn't call a nightmare a crime. "No."

"The doctor will be in to see you in a minute," Miss Rivera said. "Let's just get you out of the rest of your things, if you're sure there isn't anything you need to tell me."

So they'd left her jeans on for evidence, if they needed any. Within her there might just be evidence all right, but what would it prove? Did DNA change in a hundred years? If it had happened, was the proof of Sloan's lovemaking still there?

"Miss O'Reilly?" The nurse was watching her closely. She could be a medical wonder, like that E.T. character of Steven Spielberg's. And like him she was beginning to feel like an alien, trapped in a time and place in which she didn't belong.

"Would you like to tell me what happened?" the nurse said. Her voice was soothing, almost conspiratorial. As if it could be their secret. "If you like, I can ask Dr. Leeman to wait."

"No," Mary Grace said, her voice barely audible. "There's nothing to tell. I'd like to use the bathroom, though."

"But . . ." the nurse began hesitantly.

"I wasn't raped," Mary Grace said. "I wasn't attacked. I just want to go to the bathroom and then go home. Please."

The nurse shrugged and then gestured toward the curtain. "But hurry. Dr. Leeman isn't going to like this."

The bathroom was a modern wonder, all stainless steel and automatic. There were no handles on the sink, no flusher on the toilet. What had she done for the past four days?

She lowered her jeans, and a small antique gun clattered on the ceramic floor. She picked it up as though she had never seen it before, turning it over and over in her hands before clutching it to her breast. *I was there.*

I was there, and Sloan Westin loved me. She'd forgotten all about the derringer. She stared at the hundred-year-old gun and wondered if anyone would believe her if she told them where she'd gotten it. She had trouble believing it herself. Giving up the dream was painful. Giving up the reality was unbearable. She slid down the wall to the cold tile floor and cried. She cried for Sloan, and Ben, and she cried for herself.

Eventually, she pried off her boots and slipped the gun into the left one, then emerged from the bathroom in the hospital gown Miss Rivera had given her, carrying her belongings. It seemed to her as if everyone was moving quickly around her and she was caught in some slow-motion mode. She dragged her feet back to her little curtained area and carefully placed her clothing on the chair beside her bed. A litany chanted over and over in her head. *I want my family. I want to go home.*

Miss Rivera held the sheet back for her, and she climbed up onto the gurney more tired than she had ever been. She was nearly asleep when she heard a man's voice not far from her bed.

"Why isn't she on I.V.?" he demanded. "Who the hell admitted this woman?"

She opened her eyes and watched him make his way quickly to her side, all efficiency and business. And yet, when he reached her, a gentle hand smoothed the hair back from her brow and two brown eyes searched her face as if reading all her secrets without any effort at all.

"Tired, huh?" he asked. He tilted her head slightly and touched her jawline. She winced, and he nodded understandingly, then glanced at her chart.

"I'd like to have a look at that shoulder," he said, as if asking her permission before easing the hospital gown down just enough to reveal her shoulder without uncovering anything more. He grimaced and shook his head. "Nasty looking," he told her. "But nothing serious."

He turned her on her side, gentle fingers poking here and there, asking about bruises and cuts she couldn't explain even if she had been willing.

"You must have been very frightened," he said, shining a light in her eyes while he spoke. "Did you think you might not be found?"

"I was found," she said like a little girl who'd been separated from her mother and then insisted it was her mother who had been missing. "Now I'm lost. Now I'm where I don't belong."

She sat up, pushing against the doctor's restraining arms, and tried to swing her legs over the side of the bed. There was no reason for her to be here in the hospital answering their questions. There was no reason for her to be.

The doctor replaced the hospital gown, which had slid from her shoulder. His eyes made her uncomfortable as they bored into her soul. "He isn't worth it," the doctor said.

"What?" She pulled at the covers, feeling naked in front of the man.

"The man you tried to kill yourself over. He isn't worth it." His eyes stayed on her face.

"I didn't try to kill myself," Mary Grace said indignantly. "I would never try to kill myself."

He nodded, as if accepting what she said, but she knew he didn't. "The ranger who brought you in said you tried to jump after he hauled you to safety."

"He was mistaken," she said, but she found it difficult to look at those penetrating eyes of his. She concentrated on her clothing on the chair. "I'd like to go home, now."

He smiled at her and shook his head. "Not just ye

Mary Grace. Is that what your friends call you? Or is it just Mary?" He waited, while Sloan's voice rang in her ears. *Sweet Mary. Sweet, Sweet Mary.*

"I'd like to go home," she said again. Much to her dismay, it sounded more like a wish than a demand.

"Four days in the canyons takes its toll on the body. I'd like you to stay for a few days. We'll keep that I.V. going, get some super nourishment into you, and send you out of here ready to take on anything. Or anyone."

"There isn't anyone," she mumbled. "Not anymore."

He smiled knowingly at her, and he seemed much older and wiser than she had at first thought. "There will be again," he said, patting her arm. To the nurse, who had quietly witnessed the whole exchange, he said, "Get Miss O'Reilly a room. And notify Dr. Ehrlich I'd like a consult, please."

Aside from the fact that she was unable to account for her time, the doctors thought she had held up remarkably well. They weren't distressed by her despondency, as Dr. Ehrlich labeled it later that day. This was a natural reaction to trauma. They prescribed an I.V. to rehydrate her, and plenty of rest. When Dr. Leeman failed to reappear, she was relieved that someone else had taken over her case.

She slept on and off all day. Her dreams were full of Sloan and the baby, and each awakening found her surprised to be in a hospital in the twentieth century. Cheery nurses bustled in and out of her room with flowers and words from the outside wishing her well.

"You're quite the celebrity, you know," Miss Rivera said as she pushed open the door with her fanny and set down a vase of flowers from Benjamin Weaver's grandfather. "You're on TV, and everything."

She picked the remote control off the bedside table and flicked the TV on for Mary Grace. A game show came on, and Mary Grace turned her face into the pillow and tried to go back to sleep. She didn't care what they were saying about her, anyway. She just wanted to sleep forever and dream about another life.

The TV channels flicked by until Miss Rivera squealed. "Look, look! That's your picture!"

Mary Grace rolled over. A photograph of her was at the top left side of the screen. In the center was a woman with a microphone climbing the steps to her family's house. Roscoe, New York, read the white letters at the bottom of the picture.

Her mother answered the door. She was grayer and heavier than Mary Grace remembered, but it had been thirteen years. Remarkably, there was yet another baby on her hip. There was always a baby on her hip. But not Mary Grace's baby. No.

"This about Mary Grace?" her mother asked. She opened the screen door only slightly, and poked her head out partway. "She in some kind of trouble?"

"Did you know your daughter was missing?" the interviewer asked.

"Who's out there?" a gruff voice asked behind her. Mary Grace's father. His hair was white, his nose red. His temper was up.

"Are you Mr. O'Reilly?" The microphone was shoved in his face.

"Who the hell are you?"

The microphone was covered for a minute and then her father grabbed it from the woman's hands.

"Yeah, I'll make a statement. Mary Grace O'Reilly ain't no daughter of mine. Spends all her time putting other people's families together, but don't pay no mind to her own. Don't give a damn about her mother or me. So much for flesh and blood. We done the best we could, and we wash our hands of her."

The door slammed, and the reporter stood stunned on the front steps. He'd taken her microphone with him.

"Family!" Miss Rivera said with a huff. "Nothing's supposed to be stronger, huh? Be nice if you got to choose. . . ." She flicked off the TV. "Sorry about that."

Mary Grace turned over and tried once again to sleep. Over and over in her head she played out every moment she'd spent with Sloan, the good ones, the bad ones, the last one, when suddenly he was gone and all she could hear was his anguished cry.

She ignored the knock on her door, hoping whoever it was would go away. When she heard it again, she burrowed deeper into her pillow. The metal latch made a clunk as the door opened, and she heard footsteps behind her back. Maybe if they thought she was asleep . . .

"M.G.?" No one had called her that in at least ten years. Not since she'd left St. Andrew's. A hand touched her shoulder, and she rolled on to her back.

If he had't been wearing the clerical collar, she would never have recognized him. Without it, she could have passed him on the street, sat across a lunch counter from him, bought his used car, and she would never have guessed who he was. But in his priestly garments he could not go unrecognized.

"Father Dougan." Her voice was a croak, as if she hadn't spoken in a long time. The truth was she hadn't spoken his name since they had sat in Father Kenney's office and been told what was to become of their future.

"I was very worried about you," he said. He dragged a chair toward her bed.

"Since 1981?" She looked down and made sure that she was fully covered by the bedsheets, pulling on them until they nearly went to her chin. As she looked at the black rabat covering his chest, the silver cross hanging boldly against it, every intimate moment in the darkened cubicle came back to her in which her life had taken an irreversible turn. And now, none of it seemed to matter the way it once did.

"I mean, I heard you were missing." He seemed very uncomfortable. She pulled her eyes from his neck and let them wander over his face. There were her son's eyes. There was his nose. From the picture her baby's family had let her keep, she could see it had already begun to sharpen despite the fact that he was barely two years old. Dennis's cheeks had none of the pudginess of their son's, but the family resemblance was there all the same.

"It seems I've been found." She looked around her room. Surely the trooper, or the police, had found her purse and brought it to the hospital. She tried to sit up, but the I.V. pulled at her arm.

"Can I get you something?" Dennis offered. "Anything?" He stood indecisively, as if he didn't know how to help.

"My purse. Do you see my purse anywhere?"

He looked around and shook his head.

"M.G., I've come because I . . ."

"Check the closet. Please." It had to be there somewhere. In it was her only picture of her son. Tattered and worn, it had traveled with her the three thousand miles she'd moved when she left home. It had accompanied her on every search, as if in finding someone else's child she could somehow reclaim her own.

"It's not there," he said after searching the top shelf and throwing an eye at the floor of the closet. "Unless it's small enough to fit in your boots."

"No," she said quickly, knowing what was snugly resting in her left boot. Damn. And damn again.

"I hoped . . ." Dennis began. "M.G., I don't even know where to begin. I'm so sorry. How feeble that sounds. I . . . I've come to fix everything. That is . . ."

"Oh, Dennis!" When she had indulged herself in the fantasy that he would come back to save her, she had always used his first name. Dennis would come to her grandmother's and offer to marry her. Dennis would be there for the birth of their child and stop them from giving the baby to someone she didn't even know. Even after she had given birth, her fantasies continued. Dennis would come back and together they would search for their son, reclaim him, and be a family. In the end, though, when he failed to materialize, she finally filed him away and labeled him Father Dougan, someone she once knew.

"I know it's been a long time and that I can't ever make up for the pain I've caused both you and . . . should I say our son, or our daughter?"

"Father, you shouldn't say any more. Think of your position. You can't do any good here. You should go, now, before somebody from the press gets wind of your visit. They come in and out. . . ."

"A son or a daughter, M.G.?" He stood at the foot of her bed, and when she tried to look at him, the sun blinded her. It was just as well. The tears she thought were over filled her eyes, and she squeezed them shut.

"A son. Eight pounds, four ounces. Twenty-one inches long. Born September 18, 1981." Had she ever in her life uttered those words aloud? She didn't remember if she had.

He came and sat by her side, his dark form blocking the sunlight so that she could see the wide smile on his face. "A son," he said. "Thank you, Mary Grace."

"You'd better go," she said, seeing in his eyes the same pride that lit Sloan's face when he stared in wonder at Ben's smallest achievement. Did either of them need to know the truth?

"I'm not going anywhere," Dennis said, taking her hand in his. His palm was clammy and soft, not toughened by reins and hard work like Sloan's. His fingernails were clean, and there was a smell about him of Irish Spring or some other soap that was more chemical than fresh. "I spent the last thirteen lousy years in Zimbabwe, doing the work of the Lord, and now I'm back, M.G., to do what I should have done thirteen years ago. I'll take care of you. Both of you. If you'll let me."

There was so much hope in his face that it was painful to deny him. "It's too late," she said quietly.

"No," he told her. "It doesn't have to be. We can explain things to him. Explain that it was all my fault. I mean I'm glad he was the result, but he shouldn't think that you . . . I could tell him it was all my doing. It *was* all my doing."

She smiled weakly at him. What did it matter now? "You couldn't have done it alone," she said quietly.

He raised his eyebrows. "You think you were at fault?" he asked. "Even a little? Mary Grace, you were a child. I swore you were pleasing God and helping me be sure of my calling. I've lived with the guilt so long. . . . It would be a relief to . . . "

Guilt. Fault. They made no difference to the outcome. "It's too late," she said again, this time more firmly. It was kind of him to try, and maybe what he said was even true. Still, it didn't matter anymore. The naked pain on his face reflected her own. *Go away. I can't help you. I can't even help myself.* The salty taste of tears found its way into her mouth.

"No," he said more adamantly. "I know I don't deserve a second chance, but the boy, M.G., think of the boy. A boy needs a father. She said . . . the woman at your office, she said you had no family. You never married, did you?"

She shook her head. "I have no family. Not even the boy."

"But . . ." His eyes darted around the room as if there would be some clue as to what she had done with him.

"They gave him away when he was born. My parents did. I never even held him in my arms."

He took the news quietly. *Of course,* his face said. He should have expected as much. "We could try to find him," he began.

She shook her head. "Leave it alone. Please, Father, just leave it be."

He sat beside her, silent, for a long time. When he finally spoke, his voice was hopeful, the end of each sentence rising in question. "We could find him somehow. You search for children. You could find him and we could be, I don't know, his guardian angels and watch over him and make sure nothing happened to him and . . ."

She bit her tongue, but she couldn't hold back the tears. For the first time in ten years the anger was gone, and all that was left was the sadness. "It's too late."

"I understand that you can't forgive me. I don't deserve another chance, but I swear, Mary Grace, I will make it up to you, to both of you. I'll marry you, if you'll have me. I'll give up my position." He unfastened the clerical collar along with his rabat and placed it softly on her stomach. "See me as a man. A man who wants to do what's right."

"Father Dougan," Mary Grace began, "you don't understand."

"Dennis. You should call me Dennis, since I'm going to be your husband."

"No," she shook her head at him, but he was so far

gone in his need to set things right that he didn't seem to hear or see her.

"First, we'll be married, and then we'll find our son and be a family. I'll hold you sacred and I will . . ."

"He's dead."

There was no reaction.

"He's dead, Dennis. I went after him. I searched for him for a year once I turned eighteen. No one would hear me before then. I was a nonperson."

His eyes were fixed on a spot behind her, and he said nothing, so she continued.

"He needed a liver transplant. His best hope was us, his biological parents. I don't know how, but somehow they managed to keep our names a secret. His parents tried to find out who we were, but they kept running into the same brick walls I did. By the time I found them, it was too late."

"But surely, I mean, there must have been . . . I would have . . . I . . ."

"I know." She touched his hand, but he pulled back from her as if he couldn't bear her touch. "They were wonderful people. Kind and loving. Maybe your God . . ."

He rose slowly, his movements strained and his shoulders low. His jacket, without the bulk of his vestments, seemed to hang on him the way an old man's clothes highlight the lack of vigor and robustness that time has stolen.

"Is there anything you need?" he asked her politely, his eyes vacant, his voice hollow.

"I'm sorry," she said.

"No, no. You never had anything to apologize for. You were never to blame." He reached for his collar and rabat that still lay across her. "There's nothing you need?"

"Nothing you can give me," she said.

"I wanted to be his guardian angel," he said as he dropped the vestments in the waste pail by the door.

"Maybe instead, he's ours," she said as the door slowly closed behind him and a thin beam of sunlight crossed the floor and climbed the closet door. Before the door was fully closed, she had ripped the I.V. from her arm and was out of the bed and slipping into her dirty clothes. Everything was suddenly so clear to her. But time was of the essence. Who knew how long a minute was when it was passing in another century? And a minute could change everything. How long had it taken her to become pregnant all those years ago? How long to fall into Oak Creek Canyon? How long to come back?

She looked at her watch. No matter how many time zones it might feature, it couldn't tell her what time it was in Oak Creek Canyon in 1894, nor whether everyone she had come to love was safe by now.

She knew she must look a mess in her tattered clothes as she slipped out of her room. A desperate woman, she kept the derringer in her hand as she checked up and down the corridor. Except for a woman with a walker at one end, the hall was empty. She hurried down it toward a door marked "Exit."

She had one foot out when a hand grabbed her arm. "That's an emergency exit only." The man who looked at the plastic bracelet on her right hand was in his early sixties, bulky, but not too formidable. "You been released?"

"Does an alarm go off if we leave this way?" she asked. She hadn't heard anything yet, and the door was already partially open, but she wasn't taking any chances.

"No, but—" the security guard started. He stopped when he saw the gun in her left hand.

"That a toy?"

She shook her head. "You have a car?"

"You don't want to do this, lady," he said. "This ain't a good idea. I'm twice as big as you are, and you ain't gonna win. I don't wanna hurt you, so let's just . . ."

"How long till retirement?" she asked.

"A couple of months. Jeez, don't make me do this." He reached for her gun, and struggled with her. She slipped behind him and managed to get his gun out of his holster while giving up her own.

"Look lady, this ain't a game. Give me my gun." He was more afraid of the big silver weapon she was holding than she was of the derringer in his hand, though she'd be sorry to have to leave it behind. "You got a gun, I got a gun. But I ain't afraid to use mine. That is . . . yours."

"This gun loaded?" she asked, feeling its weight. It was a hefty thing and the barrel kept pointing to the ground.

"No."

"Then you're right, we are even. Neither is mine." She put her finger around the trigger of his and aimed it at him, steadying it with two hands.

Sweat beaded on his upper lip and his arms shook. "Don't do nothing rash," he said.

"Then yours is loaded," she surmised. "Now. This is easy." She heard footsteps in the hall and motioned him to precede her out the door. "I want you to drive me up 89A. I'll tell you when to turn off, and then you'll leave me there. That's it. Piece of cake, no?"

"You're the one with the gun." He shrugged and pointed to the car marked "Security" a few feet away.

"Sorry. I've got a lot of western blood in me lately. And I'm in a big hurry. I don't know how time works, and I'm afraid I might be too late." They made their way to the car and got in. It seemed as though he believed she wouldn't hurt him.

"Too late for what?" he asked, starting the engine.

"Too late for something that happened a long time ago. Isn't that ridiculous?" She was giddy with her plan. It was hard to sit still in the car. "How far is Oak Creek Canyon?"

"Just leave you? I can't do that," the security guard said when Mary Grace instructed him to pull off the road.

"It's OK. That's my car." She pointed to the Mustang still parked where she had left it a lifetime ago.

"Lady, you know you could have just taken a cab." He shook his head, his mouth a thin line of disgust.

"I hadn't thought of that," she admitted, feeling stupid. "I just had to get here. Can you understand?" Of course he couldn't, and explaining would only make it harder for anyone to accept.

"Can I have my gun back now?" the security guard asked.

She began to hand it to him, but the eagerness in his eyes stopped her. What if he insisted on bringing her back to the hospital? She could miss her chance and maybe wind up in some padded cell telling everyone that she traveled through time and loved a man who died before she was even born.

"I'll give it back to you when I come back to the hospital, OK? There might be snakes here and I could need it." Feeble. Very feeble. Why did she have such trouble thinking on her feet?

"You expect me to believe you're planning on coming back to the hospital? Now why don't I think so?" He began to get out of the car.

"Of course. I just needed to see something down in the canyon." She started walking toward the precipice, the guard a few feet behind her.

"What?"

"I said, I just . . ."

"I heard you," he said. "What do you have to see?"

"I think I left something important down there." She was nearly at the edge, and he was close enough to reach her. Below her was the dried-up riverbed she had seen just a few days before. It was dull and lifeless, and nothing stirred around her. She tucked the gun into the back of her jeans and sidled closer and closer to the brink of the rocks, ready for destiny to sweep her over the edge. Nothing happened.

"Come away from there." He took her gently by the arm, and she let him lead her to a safer vantage point. "There's nothing down there for you," he said softly.

"Maybe not now," she said. There was no guarantee it would happen again. She could simply plunge to her death. Worse, she could live and be trapped in a crippled body for life. Worse still, she could make it back only to find Sloan and the baby dead. With heavy feet she accompanied the guard back toward his car.

He opened the car door for her. "You have to have hope."

But how will I know what to do? Let reason guide your head. Let love guide your heart. Let hope guide your feet. There was nothing for her here. It was all at the bottom of the canyon. If there was a chance . . .

She broke away from the guard at a run. She didn't even stop at the edge of the bridge. Her feet kept on pedaling like a cartoon character's even after there was no more land beneath her.

21

Water. It surrounded her, filling her lungs, choking her. Her arm hit something hard, and pain seared through her. Still more water rushed into her mouth and her chest as she gulped for air. She tried to swim for the surface but any movement of her arm was agonizing.

Two strong hands dug into her armpits and yanked her from the creek. Sputtering and coughing, she lay on her back on the bank of the creek, her head resting against muscular thighs.

"My arm!" she moaned, cradling it to her. She was soaked through to the skin, her arm was certainly broken, but what did it matter? The trees above her, the rushing water, all told her she'd managed to do it again.

"Well, if it ain't Mary Grace O'Reilly floatin' into my arms once more." With a great deal of pain she rolled over to stare at her rescuer.

Wilson Tate's angry eyes flashed back at her, his two gold teeth glistening in the sun as he smiled widely. His hand tangled in her hair and yanked her head.

"You're hurting me," Mary Grace said, her eyes overflowing with tears of pain and fear.

Wilson pulled her closer to him, unmindful of her arm. "This ain't pain, darlin'. That comes later. When this mess is settled and I take you to my bed. And that ain't nothin' compared to what Mason'll do to ya when I'm done."

"What mess?" What had happened since she'd been gone? Where was Sloan, Ben, the baby?

"Never you mind. You'll get what you deserve later." He shoved her away from him, her pain nearly unbearable, and ordered her to her feet. On the ground lay Harlin Tate, his mouth open, along with his fly. He was still unconscious. Then no time had passed at all.

Wilson grabbed her good arm and headed for the trees. "Mason?" he yelled. Only the sounds of nature answered him, the rustling leaves on the mesquite trees, the noisy chirping of the blue jays. "Damn. If Westin's got him, you're the one that's gonna pay."

"Westin? Sloan's here?" She had told so many lies she could hardly remember where she stood with the Tates anymore.

He gave a quick jerk of his hand, and the front of her shirt came open. Beneath it she was wearing nothing. Wilson roughly grabbed her breast and squeezed. His ragged fingernails bit into her skin as he pushed her back against a tree. Something hard pressed into the small of her back. For a moment she thought it was the tree itself, but then it came to her. "And he's gonna watch you get what you deserve."

"Get off me," she hissed at Wilson. "Or I'll kill you." Her left hand reached behind her and pulled the security guard's gun from her waistband. She pressed the barrel into Wilson's belly. His eyes widened and he took a step back. "Who are you to tell me what I deserve?" Mary Grace shouted. "All my life I've let people tell me about what I deserved, and I never deserved any of it."

"Put it down," Wilson said, close enough to reach out and take the gun away from her. "Before I break the other arm."

She sidled her way beside the tree and backed up a few feet until she was out of his reach. "I deserve to give my love to someone who wants to love me back. I deserve to be happy. I didn't come all this way to be raped by the likes of you."

Wilson took one step toward her, then another. For each step he took, she inched back. The gun was heavy in her hand. Her right arm was useless. She could hardly keep the barrel horizontal.

"You ain't gonna shoot me," Wilson said, coming closer and closer to her and to the truth.

"I don't want to," she said honestly. "But I will if I have to."

"Gimme the gun, Mary Grace, before I forget you've got other uses than just bein' a target." He bridged the gap between them, narrowing the distance to only a few feet.

"Wilson," she warned, pulling the hammer of the gun back. "I'll shoot if you take one more step."

"You ain't gonna shoot me," Wilson said again in his smug, self-assured way as he shifted his weight and raised one foot dramatically.

"Maybe not, but *I* will," Sloan said, coming out from the trees into the clearing, his rifle aimed at Wilson's heart.

"Sloan!" She ran to him, wincing with pain as each step jostled her arm.

"How many times am I gonna have to rescue you, woman?" he said. If his voice hadn't broken, she might have actually thought he was angry with her.

"Where's the baby? Where's Ben?" While she talked, Sloan motioned Wilson out into the open and eased himself and Mary Grace over to a boulder so that no one could come up behind them.

"You do have a problem keepin' your clothes on by this creek, don'tcha?"

She looked down at her open blouse. "Hold this," she said, handing Sloan the gun so that she could use her left hand to close her shirt.

Sloan looked at the gun as if he'd never seen one before. "What kind of gun is this?" he asked.

She shrugged. It hurt like hell, and she gasped.

"What's wrong?" he asked, throwing an eye at her. It was all Wilson needed. His gun was in his hand and smoking. At the crack of the gun, Sloan threw himself over Mary Grace, flinging them both to the ground while he sent both barrels of his rifle into Wilson Tate's chest.

Mary Grace was screaming in his ear. He rolled off her quickly and looked down. On her shirt was a fresh red stain covering her shoulder. "Oh, God!" he yelled, ripping the shirt open but finding no wound. "Where? Where are you hit?" He could feel the bone in her arm as it jutted nearly out of her skin, knew how much pain it must be causing, but where was all the blood coming from?

Her eyes were full of terror and pain, and he felt the panic rising inside him. His own shoulder burned like hell, but he would be glad to take the pain for her. "It's you," she said. "You're bleeding, not me. Oh my God, Sloan. Don't die!"

He threw back his head and laughed. Harlin Tate had plugged him eight times and it hadn't killed him.

And then he hadn't even had anything to live for. He looked at his shoulder. The bullet had only grazed him. "It's nothing," he said.

The sound of horses coming quickly sobered him, and he grabbed for Mary Grace in an attempt to hide them both on the far side of the boulder. He could see the pain nearly knock her out and realized he couldn't move her in time. He blocked her body with his own and aimed his rifle at the oncoming riders.

"You two all right?" He could hardly make out Sheriff Roberts. He put his hand up to block out the sun coming over the canyon wall. Now he could see the others with him, their rifles in hand.

"Where's the baby?" Sloan asked Ben.

"The old man's got him." He gestured with his head indicating that he wasn't far away.

"I see you got Wilson and Harlin," Roberts said. "Where's Mason?"

Sloan squinted. Beyond the sheriff up on the natural bridge something moved. The sun was nearly blinding, and until it glinted off Mason's rifle, Sloan wasn't sure he wasn't seeing things.

"There," he said, and raised his rifle, firing before anyone seemed to know what he meant.

Mason Tate's body tumbled off the rocks and turned over and over. To Sloan he seemed to be falling slowly, like a leaf or a snowflake, in no particular hurry to hit the water. Mary Grace, hidden by his body, shivered beneath him. There was a thud as Mason came down. It must have been the angle of his body, but damned if there wasn't any splash.

The deputy rode over to the water's edge. "No sign of him," he shouted back. "You want me to search?"

Sloan looked at Mary Grace, knowing what she must be thinking. On her wrist was some sort of paper bracelet which hadn't been there before he had hauled her up to the Bridge to Somewhere Else. He fingered it, rolling it around her wrist until he could find his voice.

"I thought you were gone," he said huskily. She was quiet. Obviously she was in pain, but it was more than that. "You *were* gone then, weren't you?"

She nodded.

"But you made it back. Is that how your arm . . . ?"

Again she nodded, her eyes watching the halfhearted search being carried out in the creek. When the sheriff finally told the deputy not to waste his time on the likes of Mason Tate, Sloan couldn't have been more in agreement.

"The baby," she said, trying to sit up. "Are you sure the baby is all right?"

The sheriff sent his deputy off after the old man and Little Ben, then focused his attention on Mary Grace.

"She all right?" He dismounted and came slowly toward Sloan and Mary Grace. Sloan closed her shirt for her and nodded at Roberts.

"Broken arm. She'll be fine."

"You look like you took one in the shoulder." The sheriff kneeled by the pair, touching Sloan's wound gingerly. "Just grazed you. Always the bleeders, those."

He offered a hand to Sloan, who rose awkwardly. Then the two helped Mary Grace to her feet.

"I owe you an apology, ma'am." The sheriff tipped his hat to her.

"What made you decide to come back?" she asked.

"I got to thinkin'. When Mr. Ben Westin came to my office lookin' for his son, he said he got a telegram saying his son was alive. He also said that his son told him to take care of one Mary Grace O'Reilly if he wasn't to come back from what he had to do."

Mary Grace looked up at Sloan with that awestruck

look she got every time she realized that he was in love with her. Hell, he thought, she ought to be used to the idea by now. He'd like to think she didn't go jumping off cliffs for men that could just take her or leave her.

"You'da been set for life if your man didn't come back, but you went off after 'im, anyway. Maybe it's your kid, maybe it's Emily Tate's. I don't rightly know. But I know if you're willin' to take him to your heart and call him your own, bearin' the shame of it, I ain't got no business stoppin' you."

Before they could actually see him, they could clearly hear Ben crying. Sloan's father, still mounted, rode off, and the crying ceased. A few moments later, with a big smile on his face, Ben Westin, Sr., rode into the clearing, carrying the baby in his arms.

"Whoever's son he is, there's no question he's my grandson," he said proudly.

Sloan looked down at Mary Grace, begging her not to say anything. He should have known it wasn't necessary. He saw her relief at the sight of the baby, and he reached up and took Ben in his arms. He held him close enough for Sweet Mary to touch him, but not that close so as not to jostle her injured arm. The first thing she did was inspect the wound on his leg, clearly healing well and not bothering the boy at all.

Her smile of relief was warmer than the Arizona sun as it shined on him.

"Well, Sweet Mary, as I recall, you got three nevers in yer life. That right?"

"Three nevers?" She was paying him no mind. With her good hand she was checking the cuts on Ben's chubby leg, touching his hair, trying to see if his new tooth had come in.

"You was never gonna be with a man, never go home, and never go to church. Wasn't that it?"

Now he had her full attention. He waited for her to show some sign of agreement, though he was certain he'd gotten it right. She nodded hesitantly, wary. Didn't she know just what he was getting at?

"Well, you already broke your first one, right?"

"You know I did." Her cheeks reddened, but she didn't look away.

He thought it was going to be easier than this. He swallowed before continuing. "Now I think we gotta break the other two."

"What?"

Hell, she could say no. Just like that. How come he hadn't thought of that before? He was so good at anticipating all possibilities. How could he have forgotten that one?

"The church. Home. You know."

A smile lit her eyes and he let go of the breath he hadn't realized he was holding. Like a flirt she asked him, "What church? What home?"

"It don't matter what church, just so long as we get married up proper." She was trying to keep the smile from her lips, but she wasn't having a lot of luck at it.

"And home is the Bar W," Ben said, taking his namesake from Sloan so that his son could kiss his bride. "It was always for you, anyway."

The baby's little arms went around his grandfather's neck and squeezed. Then he squirmed around and put his arms out for Mary Grace.

"Ma!" he squealed, trying to get to her. "Ma!"

She stared at their son, tears streaking down her cheeks, while Sloan held her.

"Come on, little mama," Sloan said quietly, leading her toward one of the horses. "It's time to take our son and go home."

Epilogue

Sloan Westin tore himself out of his new wife's arms and padded to the door of their room. From down the hall came the anguished cry of a little boy whose diapers were wet. He looked back at Mary Grace who slept with a contented smile on her face, her red hair splayed out around her like the halo she deserved.

In his long johns he crept silently down the corridor, stopping at the baby's door. Silence. He shrugged and turned to return to his warm bed when a voice filtered through the partially opened door. In the dim light of dawn he saw his mother, her back to him, lifting his son from his cradle.

"Now what's all this cryin'?" she asked the baby. "All over a little discomfort? Gramma's gonna get you clean and dry in a moment. Then you can come back into bed with me and Grandpa. Tired himself out like he was still a young man last night, yer Grandpa did."

Efficiently she disposed of the used diaper and reached for a clean one while Sloan slipped into the room behind her and watched her coo and aah at his little boy.

"I have somethin' for you," she said to Little Ben in a whisper. "I ain't supposed to be the one to give it to ya, but I don't see no harm in lettin' you look at it now."

From her pocket she pulled a gold watch on a long chain. Sloan's palm itched to grasp it, but he balled his fist and let her continue.

"Your Uncle Sunny brought it back from St. Louis last night. I never saw a man so happy to give somethin' away. When he got the wire that you and your daddy were all right, well . . . I do believe St. Louis will never be the same."

Ben was fascinated by the watch, reaching for it as Anna held it above him with one hand and closed up his little shirt with the other.

Sloan's hand closed over hers, and she spun around, surprised. He stood inches from her, his hand easing the watch chain out from hers.

"I believe I'll hold on to this for a while," he said as he kissed the top of her head gently. She was shorter than he remembered, her hair grayer, but the twinkle in her eyes made her look younger even than Mary Grace. "In trust."

"Oh, Sloan," she said, tears in her eyes. "Children, Sloan. They're everything." She turned back to Little Ben and picked him up. "Let's go visit Grandpa," she said. "And let your papa get back to your ma."

"Pa's sleepin' kinda late this morning," Sloan teased and saw the color come up in his mother's cheeks.

"Did I say children are everything?" she said, kissing the top of the baby's head. "I meant *almost* everything. Go on back to Mary Grace. I'll see to your son."

Sloan patted Ben's back, kissed his mother's cheek, and headed back to his bedroom and his wife. He carefully placed the watch on the dresser next to a large chunk of turquoise and stared at it for a moment.

"Your dad's watch?" a sleepy voice asked.

"Mm."

"What time is it?" Mary Grace sat up in bed and scratched her head, sending her hair flying in all directions.

"Time to tell you again how much I love you." He dove under the covers and pulled his wife's thin frame against him.

"And I love you," she said as she scrambled under the covers and snuggled against him.

"How much?" he asked, easing her nightgown up and seeking out her warmth.

"Enough to move time and space," she told him, the lightness gone from her voice.

"And I would move heaven and earth." After they made love again, after they slept, and when they finally rose, he would put away the watch for his son in the little box that held the paper bracelet from the future and the certificate that said that he and Mary Grace were man and wife.

Author's Note

Oak Creek Canyon, not far from Sedona, is still there today, for the most part untouched by civilization. Books report on its mystical properties; Indians from the area still revere it. To go there is to feel its power and understand the hold it can have over those who let it touch their spirits.

The Havasupai Indians still live at the bottom of the Grand Canyon. While the Bridge to Somewhere Else and the River of Time are my creations, as is the saying about love ruling your heart, reason ruling your head, and hope guiding your feet, most of the facts about them are accurate. There was a shaman named A'mal and a chief named Navaho. Many of the Havasupai, including the chief's own son, were very upset by Navaho's actions, which included taking a discredited medicine man up to a cliff and cutting out his heart before tossing his body over the rocks. Others were similarly killed, and while it is my invention that the remaining shamans made a contest of keeping Sloan alive in order to save themselves, it is true that they became so afraid of

Navaho that they refused to treat his son for fear that they would be killed if they failed to save him. The Havasupai also did barter food for the favors of women when other tribes visited and had different notions of privacy than Sloan might have expected.

As for Jerome, it too still stands, a town brought back from near oblivion in the 1960s. Its old hotels, businesses, and brothels now house upscale gift shops and restaurants, but the town has managed to retain its Old West flavor, and a stroll of its narrow streets can make a visitor feel a bit like a time traveler even in the 1990s. The sheriff in *Bridge to Yesterday,* James Franklin Roberts, lived and worked in Jerome from 1891 until his death in 1934 and was known as the Last of the Old Time Shootin' Sheriffs. He brought in many a desperado, often single-handedly, and therefore had good reason to distrust Mary Grace. Doc Woods, too, was a credit to Jerome, and I was glad he was there to help my heroine in her time of need.

Jennie Banter was indeed a madam in the "wickedest city in America." Some say she was also the richest woman in northern Arizona in the 1890s. Her establishments were burned down in three separate fires and were always the first to be rebuilt. The last time, her building was rebuilt in brick.

The Connor Hotel, too, was rebuilt in brick after the fire of 1898 and still stands on Main Street, having been renovated. A lovely restaurant known as Murphy's was originally the mercantile store.

The town jail, built over the fault area, has slid approximately 225 feet from where it was built as a result of the blasting of the United Verde Copper Company. It is in the process of being renovated. Unfortunately, I don't expect that any beribboned prisoners will be on view!

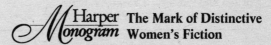

101 DAYS OF ROMANCE
BUY 3 BOOKS, GET 1 FREE!

CHOOSE A FREE BOOK FROM THIS OUTSTANDING
LIST OF AUTHORS AND TITLES:

HarperMonogram

____LORD OF THE NIGHT Susan Wiggs 0-06-108052-7
____ORCHIDS IN MOONLIGHT Patricia Hagan 0-06-108038-1
____TEARS OF JADE Leigh Riker 0-06-108047-0
____DIAMOND IN THE ROUGH Millie Criswell 0-06-108093-4
____HIGHLAND LOVE SONG Constance O'Banyon 0-06-108121-3
____CHEYENNE AMBER Catherine Anderson 0-06-108061-6
____OUTRAGEOUS Christina Dodd 0-06-108151-5
____THE COURT OF THREE SISTERS Marianne Willman 0-06-108053-5
____DIAMOND Sharon Sala 0-06-108196-5
____MOMENTS Georgia Bockoven 0-06-108164-7

HarperPaperbacks

____THE SECRET SISTERS Ann Maxwell 0-06-104236-6
____EVERYWHERE THAT MARY WENT Lisa Scottoline 0-06-104293-5
____NOTHING PERSONAL Eileen Dreyer 0-06-104275-7
____OTHER LOVERS Erin Pizzey 0-06-109032-8
____MAGIC HOUR Susan Isaacs 0-06-109948-1
____A WOMAN BETRAYED Barbara Delinsky 0-06-104034-7
____OUTER BANKS Anne Rivers Siddons 0-06-109973-2
____KEEPER OF THE LIGHT Diane Chamberlain 0-06-109040-9
____ALMONDS AND RAISINS Maisie Mosco 0-06-100142-2
____HERE I STAY Barbara Michaels 0-06-100726-9

To receive your free book, simply send in this coupon **and** your store receipt with the purchase prices circled. You may take part in this exclusive offer as many times as you wish, but all qualifying purchases must be made by September 4, 1995, and all requests must be postmarked by October 4, 1995. Please allow 6-8 weeks for delivery.

MAIL TO: HarperCollins Publishers
         P.O. Box 588 Dunmore, PA 18512-0588

Name_____

Address_____

City_____State_____Zip_____

Offer is subject to availability. HarperPaperbacks may make substitutions for requested titles.

H09511